MICHELLE BETHAM

I'm an ex-media technician turned rock-music-loving author of hot, sexy romance and chick lit with a kick! My love of books began the second I could read, and some of my happiest memories are of me curled up in bed as a child devouring every Malory Towers and Famous Five book I could get my hands on. As the years progressed I read everything from horror to Harry Potter, Jackie Collins to Jilly Cooper, but I always knew that I wanted to write romance. I love the idea of escapism – of creating a world in which readers can lose themselves, and characters they'll want to spend time with. And thanks to inspiration from the aforementioned Ms. Collins, I always knew that I wanted to write romance of the more racy variety, and to be able to do that every day is a dream come true for me.

After a spell living on the beautiful Canarian island of Tenerife, I'm now back in the UK and settled in County Durham with my wonderful husband and my gorgeous West Highland Terrier, Archie. A proud Geordie girl, I adore the north east of England, but I also love the odd glass of wine, Keanu Reeves, a decent TV drama, Peter Kay… and darts!

You can follow me on Twitter @michellebetham, find me on Facebook www.facebook.com/AuthorMichelleBetham or chat to me on my blog http://michellebethamwriter.blogspot.co.uk/.

Final Score

MICHELLE BETHAM

Harper*Impulse* an imprint of
HarperCollins*Publishers* Ltd
77–85 Fulham Palace Road
Hammersmith, London W6 8JB

www.harpercollins.co.uk

A Paperback Original 2014

First published in Great Britain in ebook format by Harper*Impulse* 2014

A catalogue record for this book is
available from the British Library

ISBN: 978-0-00-811354-4

Automatically produced by Atomik ePublisher from Easypress

To my family and friends - thank you.

Chapter One

'You gonna let me in or what?'

Amber folded her arms and leaned back against the doorpost, her eyes fixed upon Ryan – Ryan Fisher, famous footballer, local north-east hero; a man who'd crashed into her life just a couple of years ago. Even though she'd done everything in her power, at the time, to stop that from happening.

She had a slight smile on her face. She couldn't help it. Sometimes he just had the ability to make her smile, whether she felt like it or not.

'You don't have to bring him something *every* time you call round, you know.' She stood aside to let him through into the hall.

'I know. But I want to. Where is my beautiful boy anyway?'

'He's in the living room, and he's asleep. Which is how I'd like him to stay for the time being. And I'm sure *you'd* like him to stay that way, too, seeing as you're looking after him this afternoon.'

Ryan turned to look at her, his handsome face lit up by the widest smile, and Amber felt her heart dance around in her chest, followed by a succession of feelings she couldn't explain, and didn't really want. But sometimes, just the sound of his voice – that beautiful, soft Geordie accent of his – it could set off waves of confusion she didn't always welcome.

For months, she'd tried so hard to fight against everything

she was feeling for this man, because she'd never really been sure how much of it was real, and how much of it had to do with the fact she'd been pregnant, and therefore probably slightly more emotionally unstable than usual. But she'd given birth three months ago. And she still couldn't shake those feelings Ryan Fisher could stir up inside her. He'd been there for her after her split from Jim – the love of her life. Her ex-husband, Ryan's manager at top-flight football club Newcastle Red Star. He'd helped her deal with everything that came with that, in ways that probably hadn't been the most sensible course of action. Sex never had been the best form of therapy as far as Amber was concerned. It only led to more trouble. So why did she seem to turn to it so readily these days? But just having him around, well, she'd needed that. She'd needed to have him with her, and not just because she'd been carrying his baby. She'd needed him. Simple as that.

'You got a bit of time to spare?' Ryan grinned, placing the tiny t-shirt emblazoned with the words *'I Love my Daddy'* on the table behind him.

'Seriously?' Amber arched an eyebrow as Ryan pulled her towards him, circling her waist with his arm. 'Do you know how much sleep I've had lately? Or how much sleep I *haven't* had, that should be.'

'Well,' Ryan began, gently nuzzling her neck, his fingers playing with her long, dark-red hair, 'if we moved in together then I could help you, couldn't I? I could take some of the load off your shoulders.'

'Don't start, Ryan, please. We've been over this.'

'I'm serious, Amber.' He stroked a strand of hair from her pale-blue eyes, kissing her lightly on her slightly open mouth. 'It seems crazy, you and the baby living here and me all on my own in that huge new house of mine. I mean, I'm over here most of the time anyway, when you're not in London, that is, so surely it'd make more sense if we…'

Amber shook her head, but she still let him push her back

against the wall. She didn't put up much of a fight, despite the constant wave of tiredness that seemed to inhabit her body these days, as he sneakily ran a hand up her thigh before sliding it up and under her t-shirt.

'Jesus, Ryan, do you ever stop?'

'I'm dying here, babe. All I can think about is fucking you, which is hardly surprising, considering we haven't done much of that lately.'

Amber looked at him, shaking her head again. 'I don't believe you…'

'What?' Ryan shrugged as she pushed past him and walked into the living room. 'Come on! What have I done now?'

But she wasn't listening any more. She was looking down at their beautiful baby boy. Rico Alejandro Fisher had been born three months ago, just two days before the start of the new football season back in August. With Ryan by her side – although, only just – and a labour so short she figured she must have done something really good in a past life to have deserved that – she'd given birth just after 11am and been home by tea-time, back to a house full of people and all the help she'd so desperately needed in those early days. Days when she'd missed her mum so much, with a pain so physical it almost wore her down. So she'd had no hesitation in giving her son a Spanish name, as a nod to her Mediterranean heritage – Rico, because she liked it, and Alejandro after her Spanish grandfather.

He was the most beautiful baby, and she was all too aware that everybody said that about their own children, but he really was. She could spend hours just looking at him, and there were times when she did just that. When her busy schedule allowed. Because every second she spent with her son was precious.

'Amber?'

She turned around, folding her arms as she looked at Ryan. 'You think I don't want a little bit of relief, too, huh? A little bit of time to feel sexy again because, God knows, it's the last thing

I feel these days.'

She pushed a hand through her hair as Ryan came closer, reaching out to take her hand. 'You're always sexy to me. Even with baby sick down the front of your t-shirt and your hair all over the place.'

She couldn't help laughing, looking down at the floor as he gave her hand a quick squeeze before bringing it up to his lips and kissing it gently. 'Yeah. Thanks for that.'

'And I still don't understand why you haven't taken up the option of maternity leave. Cloud Sports are quite willing to let you have the time off, aren't they?'

'Yes,' Amber sighed, letting go of Ryan's hand, folding her arms against her once more. 'But it's just not for me, Ryan. And we've already been over this. In fact, I've been over this countless times – with you, my dad, Ronnie… I'm tired of explaining it. It's just the way I am, okay? Rico isn't suffering; he comes with me whenever he can, and between you, my dad, and my wonderful family we're managing just fine, aren't we?'

'Yeah. I suppose we are. But you've been working yourself into the ground for months now. I mean, come on, you were back at work two days after giving birth! Isn't it about time you gave yourself a break?'

'I don't want a break. Breaks give you far too much time to think about things.'

She walked over to the dining table at the back of the room and started folding a pile of baby clothes that was lying on it.

'Like what?' Ryan asked, sitting down on the arm of the chair next to Rico's carry-cot.

Amber said nothing for a few seconds. She wasn't in the mood for some deep conversation; she was way too tired for that. 'Nothing.'

'I hate it when you say that,' Ryan sighed, throwing himself down into the chair. 'There's quite obviously *something* wrong, I can tell. You're in one of those moods.'

'One of those…? Jesus, Ryan.'

'Okay, okay. I'm sorry.'

She couldn't help smiling, throwing a babygro at him.

He grinned, flinging his legs over the arm of the chair as he held the babygro up in the air. 'I can't believe how small he is.'

'Yeah, well, one day he'll be as big as his daddy. I'm just hoping that doesn't apply to his head, too.'

Ryan looked at her, still grinning. 'You got something to say there, Ms. Sullivan?'

She just smiled at him, nudging his legs down. 'Right, I've got to be somewhere.'

'What? Already?'

'Yes, Ryan. Unlike you, my working day is only just starting. You gonna be okay looking after him for the afternoon?'

'I'm his dad, Amber.'

She fixed him with a look. 'Alright. I'll be at Tynebridge if you need me.'

Ryan sat up straight. 'You're going to Tynebridge?'

She looked down into Rico's carrycot, smiling at her son as his eyes flickered open. 'Hey there, baby. You gonna be a good boy for daddy while I'm out earning us some pennies?'

'Amber. Why are you going to Tynebridge?'

She reached into the cot and carefully picked up Rico, cuddling him to her, kissing the top of his head as she gently ruffled his mass of dark hair. 'Because, unless it's slipped your notice, it's the derby weekend. And Cloud Sports are showing the game live, as you well know. Me and Ronnie are going over there to set things up. He's one of the pundits, and I'm presenting… Ryan, you know all of this.'

'Is Jim gonna be there?'

She nestled Rico in the crook of her arm as she fixed Ryan with another look. 'I have absolutely no idea. Would it be a problem if he was?'

Ryan shrugged, his manner verging on the petulant. 'I've got to be at the ground myself by six. The boss wants us ready to leave for the hotel by half past. You gonna be back by then?'

'I'll let you know. If I'm not gonna make it you can just bring Rico down there. He can stay with me. Ryan, will you quit acting like a sulky teenager? Please? Me and Jim, it's over. You know that. But I can't avoid him forever; it's impossible. So just grow up and deal with it. You know, sometimes it's like having two kids…' She kissed Rico again, reluctant to let him go. He was so warm and soft, and he smelt of baby talc, and all of a sudden Amber had an overwhelming urge to just stay there and cuddle him all afternoon. Just one mention of Jim's name had done what it usually did – change her mood entirely. 'Okay, poppet. Daddy's taking charge now, so, you keep an eye on him and make sure he behaves himself.'

'Yeah, you're funny,' Ryan said, standing up and carefully taking Rico from Amber, holding him up in the air and bringing him back down for a huge kiss. 'Hey there, little fella. We're gonna have some fun, me and you.'

'Wear him out, will you?' Amber half-smiled, grabbing her jacket from the back of the sofa. 'It's a busy weekend this weekend and I could do with a few more hours' sleep. I'll call you later, but you know where I am if you need me.'

She was about to run out of the door when Ryan stopped her. 'Amber?'

She turned around. 'Yeah?'

'Come here. Please.'

She walked back over to him, watching as he lay Rico back down in his cot. 'What do you want, Ryan?'

He moved closer to her, resting his hand lightly against her cheek. 'I want *you*, Amber. And you know that.'

'Ryan…' His mouth was on hers before she had a chance to say anything else, and she gave in to his kiss, she couldn't help it. Despite everything they'd been through in the past; despite the kind of man he'd used to be, he was giving her a sense of calm she really needed right now.

She pulled him closer by his t-shirt, slipping a hand around the back of his neck, and for a few, beautiful seconds she lost herself in that kiss; lost herself in something she could have, if she wanted it. A wonderful life with a man who'd finally grown up, and he loved her. Ryan Fisher truly did love her. So she could have this, all of it. If she wanted it.

He pulled away slightly, running his thumb lightly over her parted lips. 'Things are crazy right now, Amber, I know that, but…'

She backed away, grabbing her bag and jacket as she headed for the door. 'I'm gonna be late. Call me if you need me, okay?'

'Jesus… Amber!'

She turned around again, but she had no intention of going back this time. 'I've really got to go.'

He looked at her, his hands in his pockets, his eyes locked onto hers. 'Me and you… what's really happening here?'

She stared back at him, not really knowing what to say. 'You know what's happening, Ryan.'

She knew as well as he did that that was no kind of answer. But it was the only one she had.

*

'Well, if it isn't Superwoman herself.'

'Don't you start,' Amber sighed, throwing her bag down onto the couch in the Players' Lounge before going over to quickly kiss Ronnie's cheek.

'Trouble in paradise?' Ronnie grinned, leaning back against the wall and folding his arms.

Amber threw him a look out of the corner of her eye but said nothing in reply.

'Everything's okay, though, isn't it?' Ronnie asked, dropping the flippancy.

'Everything's fine, thank you. I'm just really busy.'

'Yeah, I'm aware of that, Amber. I work with you.'

She sat down, pushing her hands through her long, tousled hair. 'It's been good, you know? Having him around. And since we found out I was having Rico he's changed, he really has.'

'I take it we're talking about Ryan?'

She nodded, fiddling with the bracelet hanging on her left wrist.

'Am I waiting for a "but" here?' Ronnie asked, narrowing his eyes slightly.

Amber sat back, letting out a small sigh. 'No. Things just feel a bit weird, that's all.'

'Weird?' Ronnie frowned.

'I'm still getting used to being a mum, Ronnie. Something I never thought I'd be. I'm a mum. And every day I worry about whether I'm doing it right and if Rico's okay and… it's hard, sometimes. Especially when Ryan's going on at me constantly.'

'About what?'

'Sex.'

'Okay.'

She looked up at him. 'It's not that I don't want it, Ronnie… Are you uncomfortable talking about this?'

He shook his head. 'Too tired, huh?'

'You could say that.'

'You sure that's not just an excuse?'

It was her turn to narrow her eyes as she looked at her best friend. 'What's that supposed to mean?'

Ronnie looked down at the ground, his hands in his pockets. 'I don't know, Amber. It's just that, sometimes, I wonder whether you going back to Ryan… I wonder whether it was the right thing to do.'

'He's Rico's dad, Ronnie.'

'That doesn't mean you actually have to be *with* him. Not if you don't want to be.'

'Who said I don't want to be with him?'

'Well, that's the impression you're giving off here, kiddo.'

'Is it?'

'Yeah.'

Amber sat forward, pushing her hands through her hair again. 'I never said we were love's young dream or anything.'

'No. I know you didn't.'

'But, I needed him, you know? I was pregnant, going through a divorce.' She trailed off, absent-mindedly looking at her naked left hand. She still couldn't get used to not wearing her rings. Even though they'd only really been there for the shortest of times.

'And now Rico's here?'

'Hmm? Sorry?' She looked back at Ronnie.

'Now that Rico's here, do you still need him? Ryan, I mean.'

'Of course I do.'

'You paused for a second there.'

'I didn't.'

'You did.'

'Jesus. I'd forgotten how irritating you could be.'

'He's here, you know.'

She sighed again, throwing herself back against the couch. 'Who?' As if she didn't know.

'Manager of the Month, two months running.'

She eyed Ronnie with a look of something verging on suspicion. 'Shouldn't we be doing something other than sitting here?'

'Probably. But I quite like watching you squirm.'

'You're such a bastard.'

He smiled, walking over to her and holding out his hand, pulling her up off the couch. 'You need to sort out what you really want, Amber.'

'I just want to get on with my life, Ronnie. As simple as that.'

'There's nothing simple when it comes to you getting on with your life, kiddo.'

'Yeah. Thanks for reminding me. What about you, anyway? Any sign of a new romance on the cards?'

'You've got to be kidding me! No time for any of that.'

She couldn't help smiling as she looked at him, cocking her head slightly. 'Surely you've got women falling at your feet, Ronnie White. Good-looking bloke like you. You've still got it, even at your age.'

'Yeah, okay, enough with the smart remarks. Come on. We've got work to do.'

Work. The only thing that was keeping Amber's mind off the one thing she couldn't stop thinking about.

*

Jim Allen sat back in his chair, his eyes scanning the computer screen, but he was taking nothing in. His mind was on way too many other things, and for a man who was usually so focused and in control it was a feeling that didn't sit well with him. But these past few months had been nothing short of crazy. Unpredictable. Painful.

A knock on his office door broke into his thoughts and he looked up from his laptop. 'Come in.'

'Hey, Dad!'

Jim smiled at the sight of his son. Brandon Palmer. Twenty-one years old, tall and handsome, and a player with the region's rival top-flight team, Wearside Spartans.

'Hey back. What you doing here? Spartans sent you over enemy lines to spy on what we're up to before the big game?'

'Well, if I'd wanted to do that I could have sneaked over to the training ground this morning, couldn't I? No, I just came over to see how you're doing.'

Jim eyed Brandon warily, smiling slightly as his son perched himself on the edge of his desk. 'I'm doing just fine. Why wouldn't I be?'

Brandon shrugged. 'Dunno. You just seem to have been throwing yourself into your work a lot lately, that's all.'

'I'm the manager of a top-flight football club, Brandon. It isn't exactly a nine-to-five kinda thing.'

'You don't take any time off.'

'I don't want to take any time off. Manager of the Month awards aren't given out to just anybody, you know. You've got to put the work in.'

'Is that all that matters to you?'

Jim narrowed his eyes as he looked at his son. 'Have you come here for any particular reason, Brandon? Apart from to give me a headache I don't need.'

'I worry about you.'

'Why?'

'I mean, Ellen and me, we asked you over for dinner the other night and you refused to come. You won't even take a night off to spend a bit of quality time with your own son.'

'I'm fine, okay? I've just got a lot on.'

'Yeah. You seem to have had a lot on for a while now.'

Jim fixed Brandon with a hard stare, which Brandon returned.

'Ever since Amber became pregnant. Ever since she took up with Ryan Fisher. Again.'

'She hasn't "taken up" with Ryan Fisher, as you put it.' Jim got up and walked over to the sideboard, pouring himself a small measure of whiskey.

'So, you're not bothered, then?'

'About what?'

'About Amber and Ryan.'

'There *is* no Amber and Ryan.'

'Oh, really?'

Jim turned around, leaning back against the sideboard, his eyes once more locking with Brandon's. 'Really.'

Brandon gave another shrug, sliding down from the desk and heading back towards the door, his hands in his pockets. 'Okay. Whatever. Anyway, I just thought I'd drop by and say hi, see how you were. But you still look like the same old Jim Allen to me.'

Jim said nothing to that, he just took a sip of his drink and remained silent.

'Look, Dad...' Brandon turned around and faced his father. 'Have you thought about getting out more? Maybe meeting someone else, you know, to take your mind off...'

'I'll see you later, Brandon.'

Brandon held up his hands as he turned to go. 'I'm outta here.'

Jim waited until he'd closed the door behind him before he took the letter from his inside jacket pocket, opening it up and reading it through. One more piece of proof. Another piece of a jigsaw he'd been trying to put together. But he had all he needed now. The ball was very much in his court. And it was up to him whether he chose to hit out or not.

Chapter Two

'She's left you in charge?' Max asked, looking at Ryan with an element of surprise as he stood there in the doorway with Rico in one arm and a towel slung over his shoulder.

'Y'know, anyone would think I was incapable of looking after my own child. And I thought you were in London. What you doing up here?'

'It's derby weekend.'

'I'm really glad people keep reminding me of that because I'd almost forgotten.'

'Fatherhood hasn't dulled your wit, then. You going to let me in? It's freezing out here.'

Ryan stood aside to let Max through, kicking the door shut behind him. 'You need to see me about something?' Ryan asked, following him into the kitchen.

Max leaned back against the counter, digging his hands deep into the pockets of his expensive dark-grey suit. As one of football's most respected, not to mention most famous agents, he had a reputation to keep up, and, as far as Max Mandell was concerned, image was everything.

'Not really. I just thought I'd come up north and visit some of my favourite clients.'

Ryan looked at him out the corner of his eye as he rocked Rico gently in his arms. 'And that's it?'

'That's it. You have a really suspicious mind at times, Ryan Fisher. Anyway, let me have a look at my little future client here.' He walked over to Ryan, smiling down at Rico, whose eyes had begun to slowly close. 'Let's hope he's inherited some of his father's talent, huh? The on-the-pitch stuff, that is.'

Ryan held his son close, lowering his head to gently kiss his cheek.

'You know, I really think he's changed you,' Max said, switching the kettle on.

'It's hard not to let something like this change you.' Ryan smiled, stroking Rico's hair as he slept in his arms. 'I don't want to let him down. Or Amber. I've let her down enough.'

'So, how *are* things between you and my prettiest client?'

Ryan's eyes stayed focused on his baby boy. 'I wish I knew.'

'Oh, Jesus, we're not heading towards another relationship melt-down, are we?' Max sighed, rolling his eyes.

Ryan looked up. 'I'm not twelve.'

'Yeah, okay. I guess I should give you the benefit of the doubt. It certainly seems as though the little fella over there has given you a good kick up the backside.'

Ryan looked back down at his sleeping son's face. 'He's every-thing I needed, Max. He's my reason for getting up in the morning. My reason for doing everything now.'

'Christ, am I talking to the real Ryan Fisher here? Or has he been cloned and replaced with a grown-up version?'

Ryan couldn't help smiling as he looked up at his agent. 'The world is full of frigging comedians today. Is it so hard to believe that I might really have changed this time?'

'Well,' Max sighed, turning around to make himself a cup of tea. 'It's about time, that's all I can say. And you certainly look as though you've settled into fatherhood.'

'Things would be a hell of a lot better if Amber just realised how much more sensible it would be if we actually lived under the same roof.'

'She not keen, then?'

'She doesn't even want to talk about it.'

'But you really want to move things forward, I take it?'

'Of course I do.'

'You got any idea why Amber's reluctant to make things more permanent?'

Ryan just threw Max a look, sending out a message Max received loud and clear. A look that said of course he knew why she was reluctant to make things more permanent. Jim Allen. What other reason was there?

'Well, I'm not sure what I can do about that one, kiddo. Short of some miracle, you're just going to have to learn to deal with it.'

Ryan continued to gently rock Rico. 'I really thought this little guy would change things between me and Amber. I thought he'd bring us closer, make her need me more. Guess that just shows how naïve I still am.'

'You don't know she's still hankering after Jim. You're only assuming.'

Ryan's eyes met Max's. 'She doesn't want to have sex, she barely even comes near me now. What does that tell you, huh?'

'She's just had a baby, Ryan.'

'Three months ago.'

'Oh, so you think, what? A couple of weeks and she should have been dragging you back off to bed?'

'I didn't say that.'

'You're being paranoid.'

Ryan ignored that comment. 'And couldn't you try and get her to take more time off work?'

'Have you tried getting Amber Sullivan to do anything she doesn't want to?'

'Frequently,' Ryan sighed, absent-mindedly stroking Rico's dark hair as he slept. 'I just wish she'd take a step back sometimes. Look at the bigger picture.'

'And what bigger picture would that be?' Max asked, sipping his tea.

Ryan threw his head back, letting out another long sigh. 'Jesus, *I* don't know, do I?'

'You might want to start getting your head straight, kiddo. Big match tomorrow, and Wearside Spartans are no pushover. They've had a cracking start to this season, and Brandon Palmer is proving to be a force to be reckoned with. Just like his father used to be in his playing days. That kid's certainly inherited some of the Allen genes.'

Ryan threw Max another look.

'Deal with it, Ryan.' Max placed his half-drunk mug of tea down onto the counter. 'I'm off to Tynebridge. Want me to pass a message on to Amber?'

Ryan shook his head. 'Would there be any point?'

*

Amber walked briskly down the tunnel and up the stairs that led back into the ground itself. Her head was down as she reached the top, checking her emails on her phone, so she didn't see him coming towards her. He was equally as engrossed in something on his own phone, his head also down, so the resulting, inevitable clash couldn't really have been avoided.

'Oh, I'm sorry, I…' She stepped back slightly as her eyes met his, her heart immediately jarring, causing her to take a deep breath. 'I wasn't looking where I was going.'

'No, well, neither was I.' He smiled, just a small smile, but it reminded Amber of how devastating his smile could be – to her. How it always had been. How it probably always would be. 'Are you okay? I mean, in general. I haven't really spoken to you, properly, in a while, so… how are things, with the baby and… is Rico… is he alright?'

'Rico's doing just fine, thank you.' She couldn't help smiling herself, but this time it was because of the mention of her son's name. Her perfect boy. 'He… he's beautiful. And, yeah, I know every mother probably says that about their baby, but…'

'If he takes after you then I can only imagine how beautiful he really is.' Jim's eyes were still boring into hers, but then, almost as if someone had flicked a switch, he broke the stare and looked back down at his phone. 'I'd better be going. Got a lot to catch up with before we leave for the hotel tonight. Good to see you, Amber.'

She stood rooted to the spot, watching him as he walked away, back towards his office, her stomach turning involuntary somersaults. Even after everything that had happened.

'Shit!' she muttered under her breath, finding Ryan's number and pressing dial.

'Hey, beautiful. What's up?'

'I'm gonna be tied up here for a bit longer. Can you bring Rico with you when you come down to the stadium?'

'Yeah, okay. I'll get him ready and we'll be with you in about half an hour. Everything alright?'

'Yeah. Fine. Just a little behind with a few things, that's all. I'll see you soon.' She hung up before he could start anything resembling a conversation. She wasn't really in the mood, not now.

'You okay?'

'I'm fine, Ronnie.' Amber slid her phone back into her jeans pocket. 'Where did you spring from, anyway? I thought you were up in the studio.'

'I was. But they've sorted out that lighting problem now. You ready to get out of here?'

Amber fell into step beside him as they made their way through the ground and back up to the studio that had been set up for the live broadcast of tomorrow's match.

'Almost. I just want to check over a few things before I go.'

'What things?' Ronnie asked, frowning slightly. 'You're all but done; you should be heading home now.'

'Ryan's bringing Rico with him. He's got to come here to join the rest of the team before they head off for the hotel, so…'

'What's going on, Amber?' Ronnie stopped walking and leaned back against the wall, folding his arms, his eyes meeting hers, even though she was trying anything she could to avoid looking directly at him.

'Nothing's going on.'

'Cut the crap and talk to me. Come on, I'm your best friend and I know when you've got something on your mind. Or should that be some*one*? Actually, come to think of it, maybe it should be Ryan you're talking to. I'm no fan of his, as you well know, but that doesn't mean I agree with you stringing the guy along.'

'No one's stringing anyone along.'

Ronnie just arched an eyebrow.

'Jesus Christ…' Amber sighed, pushing a hand through her hair. 'I don't know.' She leaned back against the wall beside Ronnie. 'I can't stop thinking about him.'

'Then you need to do something about that.'

'Like what?'

'How the hell should *I* know?'

Amber turned her head to look at Ronnie. 'This is ridiculous. I'm a frigging mess.'

'Your *life* is a mess.'

'Thanks for that.'

'Do you want me to lie to you?'

'No.'

'Then deal with the truth.'

'I love you, too.'

He looked at her. 'I'm not doing this to be cruel, Amber. But you really need to get this sorted. You've got a child now. You've got someone other than yourself to think about.'

'I'm aware of that.' Her eyes locked with his. 'I thought I loved him, Ronnie. I really thought I did. Or that I could, again. I thought it would all come back, all those feelings, and I thought I'd just fall in love with him all over again.'

'I don't think you've ever loved Ryan Fisher. Not really.'

'Hang on. You don't know…'

'Amber, I do. I *do* know. And I don't think you ever really loved him.'

Amber looked down at the floor, scraping her heel against the skirting board. 'He's never going to go away, is he? Jim. He's never going to go away.'

'Not if you don't want him to.'

She looked back up at Ronnie. 'He doesn't want me any more.'

'And he's told you that, has he?'

'He divorced me, Ronnie. What more proof do I need?'

'That means nothing where you two are concerned.'

'He doesn't want me any more,' Amber repeated, staring back down at the floor. 'The way he's acting. I saw him just now and… He doesn't want me, Ronnie. It's over.' She threw her head back and let out a heavy sigh, one that wracked her entire body. 'Okay.' She took a long, deep breath, shaking her hair out before pushing both hands through it. 'It's time to grow up and do the only thing I *can* do right now.'

Ronnie frowned slightly. 'And what's that, exactly?'

Her eyes met his again, and this time there was a look of determination that he hadn't seen from her in a while. 'I'm moving to London.'

Chapter Three

'London.' Ryan looked at her as though she'd suddenly started talking in a foreign language. 'You're moving to London? And you're telling me this *now*? An hour before frigging kick-off?'

'I don't *want* to move to London...'

'Then why the hell are you going? Jesus, Amber...'

'Because I have to, Ryan. I have to.'

He stared at her, his dark eyes boring deep into hers. 'You have to.'

'I have to,' she repeated, her voice quiet but steady. Surprisingly so. 'I can't stay here, Ryan. I can't do it any more.'

Ryan took a couple of steps back, pushing a hand through his hair. 'I fucking hate it when I'm right.'

Amber frowned, folding her arms against herself. 'Sorry?'

His eyes were back on hers, wide and full of something Amber couldn't quite read. 'You and Jim. It isn't ever gonna be over, is it?'

What could she say to that? 'He doesn't want me, Ryan.'

Ryan laughed, turning away from her for a brief second or two. 'Jesus... you really believe that, do you? You really believe he doesn't want you?' He turned back to face her. '*I* want you, Amber. Me. I love you, do you know that? Do you know just how much I love you?'

'Ryan...'

'But it isn't ever gonna be enough. Not while *he's* still around. Nobody else stands a fucking chance.'

'It doesn't have to be this way, Ryan.'

'Oh, really? It doesn't, huh? You've just told me you're taking my son to the other end of the country, Amber. He's three months old and you're taking him away from me.'

'I'm not taking him away from you…'

'Yes. You are. If you're living down there I can't see him every day. I can't just pop round and hold him, or rock him to sleep or feed him. I can't do that if you're hundreds of miles away.'

'And you know as well as I do, Ryan, that I will be up here almost as much as I am now.'

'And that's good for Rico, is it? Being dragged up and down the country just because you can't get your fucking head straight.'

'I'm not listening to this…'

He reached out and grabbed her arm, swinging her around to face him. 'You won't even give us a chance, Amber.' His voice was softer now, almost pleading in tone. 'If you really believe he doesn't want you then why don't you just move on and give *us* a chance?'

She looked at him, her eyes staring deep into his even though meeting his gaze was the last thing she really wanted to do.

'We have a baby together, Amber. A baby. Our son. How incredible is that, huh?'

'And what if that isn't enough, Ryan?' She wasn't entirely sure she'd meant to say those words out loud, but they were out there now. She'd said them. She couldn't take them back.

Ryan laughed, one of those laughs that carried no humour. No real feeling. 'I can't believe you're laying this on me right before one of the biggest matches of the season.' He let go of her arm, turning away from her for a second. 'Jesus, Amber, your timing really sucks, sweetheart.'

'I couldn't agree more.'

Amber swung around, her heart shuddering to some kind of brief standstill in her chest as she saw Jim standing there, tall and handsome in a dark suit and white shirt, his face impassive as he stared at her.

'You should know better than to distract my players so close to kick-off, Amber.' He focused his attention on Ryan, who'd turned back around now, his eyes down on the ground. 'Back to the dressing room, Ryan, come on. Get your head back in the game and keep your private life off the pitch. You got that?'

Ryan nodded, throwing Amber a brief look before walking away. Amber leaned back against the wall, closing her eyes for a second or two as she willed her heart to slow down, to stop beating so wildly because it hurt. Everything that was happening now – Jim being so close to her, what she was doing to Ryan; her ridiculously messed-up feelings. It all hurt.

'We need to talk.'

She slowly opened her eyes, daring to meet his, this man who would never go away. She'd thought he had, once upon a time. She thought she'd safely put him and everything they'd shared to one side, learnt to live with the past and move on. But she hadn't done any of that. She'd never put him to one side or learnt to live without him. She'd only kidded herself that she had.

'Do we?' She swallowed hard, her eyes still on his. They were locked there, refusing to leave, and it was doing nothing for that irrational heartbeat of hers. 'Now? I mean, I'm supposed to be...'

'We need to talk,' he repeated. 'So, yes. Now.'

She blinked a couple of times, trying to work out whether she was actually in the middle of some kind of weird dream that had made her mess this day up so spectacularly. What the hell had she been thinking? Telling Ryan she was moving away from the north-east on the day of the derby! One of the biggest, most important matches of the entire season, and she'd just distracted Red Star's striker in the worst possible way. What was wrong with her? She would never have acted this way a couple of years ago, when her life was well-ordered and safe. When Jim had still been nothing but a distant memory and Ryan was just one of those names she talked about at work.

She watched as Jim walked away, in the direction of his office down the corridor, but it was as though her feet were glued to the spot. She couldn't move, couldn't follow him.

He turned around, digging his hands in his pockets. 'Amber?'

She bit down on her lip, confusion washing over her. What was going on here? With her feet finally allowing her to move, she followed him to his office, walking inside as he closed the door behind them – a door that still had no lock on it. A door that, on a day such as this, could have more traffic coming through it than the busiest of motorways. So why didn't she care when he reached out and took her hand, swinging her around and pushing her back against that door, his mouth hitting hers with a kiss so hard it literally took her breath away. Because she just hadn't been expecting that. She hadn't… had she?

It was crazy, the sudden rush of intense and painful feelings that engulfed her as she shrugged off her shirt, pulling at his jacket, almost ripping it away from him as fingers pulled at clothes and the inevitability of what was happening here became nothing but an action neither of them was willing to stop. Even though Amber didn't understand it, or know what the implications of this would be. She just wanted him, pure and simple. She needed him. She always had, and she always would. No matter what.

She closed her eyes as he yanked down her jeans, and she stepped out of them, kicking them away, keeping her eyes closed as he did the same with her knickers, almost tearing them away from her body with an indecent haste, but she didn't care. To be naked in his arms again was the only thing she'd wanted for so long, even if she hadn't been grown-up enough to admit that.

She heard him unzip his pants before his hands slipped underneath her bottom, lifting her up, and she finally opened her eyes as he backed her up against the door, pushing into her so hard it took all the strength she had not to cry out loud. Her legs were wrapped around his hips, her fingers buried in his hair as he thrust into her with an almost violent force that was both painful and beautiful, every inch of her body tingling as the pressure built, getting ready to explode, and she clung on tighter, waiting for him to give her everything she'd needed, everything she'd craved from this man since she'd been sixteen years old. And when he came, just minutes after he'd pushed inside her, she couldn't help but cry out his name, quickly burying her face in his hair to stifle the volume. And he held her as she shuddered in his arms, as those tingles and those shivers took over, making her feel more alive than she'd felt in months. He held her until it was over. And she didn't want him to let her go.

He slowly put her down, his eyes scanning her nakedness as he did so, lingering on her breasts, his fingers lightly touching them, and she took a sharp intake of breath as his thumb scraped over her nipple.

'Jim, I…'

He shook his head, tilting her chin up so her eyes met his. 'You can't come in here and distract my players, not on a day like today.'

She reached out and touched his face, letting her fingers trail lazily over his rough, stubbled chin. 'What *is* this, Jim?'

He said nothing, he just continued to stare into her eyes as he slid a hand around the back of her neck, sliding his fingers into her hair, pulling her head back slightly before kissing her slowly. And every movement of his lips against hers made Amber feel more and more confused. The taste of him, the feel of him, it was all so familiar, something she craved like a drug she just couldn't kick. But it was confusing.

'I need to go,' she whispered, running her thumb over his slightly open mouth. 'I shouldn't be here.'

He took a step back, tucking his shirt back into his pants as Amber quickly got dressed, her head spinning with a million and one things she didn't really want to think about.

'How did everything get so screwed up, Jim?'

He looked up, digging his hands back into his pockets as his eyes met hers. 'That's what we do, Amber. Me and you. We screw things up.'

She shook her head. 'No. No, Jim, we don't.'

'We do. We're no good together, baby. It just doesn't work.'

'Then what the hell was *this*?'

'I look at you and I still want you, Amber. I always have, that's just the way it is. I look at you and I fall in love all over again and I need you so much it hurts, so badly I can feel it, like the most cruel, physical pain imaginable. But we… we can't do this.'

She stared at him, her stomach sinking so deep she almost felt sick. 'This is why I can't deal with you,' she whispered, her voice quiet but surprisingly steady. 'You come into my life, every time, and you do this. You fuck me up and I hate you for it, Jim. Because I just can't deal with you; what you do to me, how you make me feel. I can't deal with it.'

'I'm sorry.'

'I love you. I never stopped loving you, I never did that, and I need you to know that and I need you to believe it. I never stopped loving you.'

'I know.'

'Then don't do this. Don't mess with my head, don't fuck up my life all over again. Don't make me want you and then walk away. Because I don't think I can take that again. Not any more.'

'I'm confused, Amber.'

'And you think *my* head is straight? Huh? You think *I'm* dealing with all of this okay?'

'You're a mum now, Amber.'

'And that means, what? That I can't feel the things I used to feel? That I just instantly stop loving you; is that what you're saying? Because, if anything, Jim, having Rico has only made me see more clearly what I really want.'

Her eyes locked with his again, nobody saying anything as they stared at each other.

'I need you to go, Amber.'

It was a few seconds before she could tear her gaze away from his, but when it finally happened it was as if a curtain had come down on everything, cutting her off from this man in front of her. Closing down those feelings, blocking them out. Or trying to.

Walking calmly out of his office she closed the door behind her and leaned back against it, breathing in deeply as she tried to regain the composure she'd just lost in there.

'*Come on, Amber, you can do this,*' she whispered, inwardly berating herself for letting Jim get so close to her – too close – all over again. For repeating that age-old mistake, that continuous, heartbreaking mistake she'd been making for over two decades now.

Breathing out, she pushed her hair back off her face and strode down the corridor, knowing she had only seconds to pull herself together. She was at work, she was a professional – she was trying to be, anyway.

'What's up with *you*?' Ronnie asked, joining Amber as she hovered around the entrance to the tunnel that led out onto the pitch.

'Nothing's up with me.'

'Liar.'

Amber said nothing. She continued to stare out at the rapidly filling stadium as people made their way to their seats, the noise of an overexcited derby-day crowd echoing around the ground.

'What have you done to piss Ryan off?'

Amber swung around to look at Ronnie. 'Sorry?'

'You've told him about London, then?'

'Jesus Christ…'

'Today, Amber? You told him *today*?'

'Alright, I know. I know, okay? I know my timing was crap.'

'Understatement. Although, come to think of it, if he's pissed off enough he might have that fire underneath him that all players should have on a derby day.'

Amber just shook her head and turned to walk back up the

tunnel. 'I'd better get up to the studio. We're on air in a few minutes.'

'Yeah, I know the running schedule, thank you.' Ronnie gently grabbed her wrist, stopping her from running ahead of him. 'I thought Amber Sullivan was coming back.'

Amber looked at her best friend, taking in another deep, deep breath. 'She's trying, Ronnie. It just isn't that fucking easy.'

His hand slipped into hers, squeezing it tightly while his smile calmed her slightly. She really had no idea what she would do without this man. He wasn't just her best friend, he was her rock. That one person she could rely on when everything else was turning to crap. He was the one person she couldn't afford to lose.

'Maybe telling him – telling Ryan – maybe today wasn't the best day to tell him I'm leaving. It wasn't my finest moment, but… I need to do it, Ronnie. I need to move away, to get some space, because I'm going crazy here. I'm going fucking crazy.'

He leaned over to whisper in her ear, letting his lips brush gently and discreetly over her cheek as he edged closer to her. 'I know, sweetheart. I know. Come on. Let's get this over with, then we can get out of here.'

*

Ellen watched from one of the hospitality boxes as Brandon Palmer ran rings around the Newcastle Red Star defence, leaving Gary Blandford for lost and the goalkeeper no chance at all of saving a goal that thundered past him, rocketing into the back of the net, sending the Wearside Spartans fans wild. On derby days it wasn't just points that were being played for – pride came into it, too. But with both teams so close together in the league, both of them fighting for a top-five position and one of those coveted European cup places, points were all of a sudden becoming more important to play for, which was why both teams were playing like their lives depended on it.

Ellen smiled to herself, letting her mind wander back to

yesterday afternoon, when she'd successfully persuaded Brandon that sex the day before a big match could only be a good thing. All that rubbish about it draining players of all their energy; she'd just proved how wrong that theory was, because her boyfriend was on fire. And anyway, when she'd been with Ryan they'd never given that old theory much thought. But then, Ryan never had been one to play by the rules.

Thinking about Ryan was something Ellen never had been able to help. Ryan Fisher wasn't a man you let into your life and then let go of easily. He made sure of that. But his one downfall, the one thing that made him such a frustrating man to be in love with was his obsession with Amber Sullivan. She was his Achilles heel; the one thing that stopped him from moving on. She was the one thing that had made sure Ellen's relationship with Ryan had never stood a chance. And even though it was quite obvious to anyone but Ryan that she was still very much in love with his boss, still he couldn't seem to let her go. But Ellen didn't give up easily. She might be living with one of football's newest and most talented stars, but he wasn't Ryan Fisher. Brandon Palmer might be handsome and rich; he might be the son of one of football's most respected and successful players and managers, and he might be quite a few women's walking fantasy, and she loved him, she did. He was a good man, a kind man, and he cared about her. He just wasn't Ryan. And Ellen wanted Ryan. She wanted him back, and when Ellen wanted something, she usually got it. In the end. Even if it meant undergoing one hell of a fight to get there.

*

Jim stood at the edge of the technical area, his hands deep in his pockets, his eyes covered by the aviator shades he always liked to wear as he watched the final few seconds of a tough match play out. The game was deadlocked at two goals apiece, which, under normal circumstances would be a welcome result for a derby game. But this one was different. This one needed to be won to make sure Newcastle Red Star climbed above Wearside Spartans in the league table, because ever since Brandon Palmer had joined Spartans he'd made sure they were no longer the region's poor relation as far as football teams were concerned. How ironic that Jim's own son should be the one to make sure Newcastle Red Star had stiff competition so close to home.

Keeping his composure, which was something Jim Allen was famous for, he shouted over to Ryan, issuing instructions for one final push forward. Ryan immediately retrieved the ball from a Spartans player and ran with it, at a blistering speed, and with a determination Jim was glad hadn't been overshadowed by his earlier distraction.

Overcoming an attempted tackle from a Spartans defender on the edge of the penalty box, Ryan carried on towards the goal, the ball remaining at his feet as though it were glued there, and even Jim couldn't help but be in awe of the talent Ryan possessed. When he was on his A-game, he was one of the greatest players of his generation; Jim couldn't deny that.

Stepping back towards the dugout, Jim watched as Ryan cannoned what was probably the final kick of the match past the Wearside Spartans' goalkeeper and into the back of the net. The ecstatic Red Star fans filled the stadium with a roar so loud it was deafening. And when the final whistle, just seconds later, sealed that late winner for Newcastle Red Star, that roar grew louder as both the points, and the pride, went to the team that played north of the Tyne.

After quickly shaking the hand of Billy Bishop, Wearside Spartans' manager, Jim quickly headed off into the tunnel, almost running back up the stairs, making his escape into his office. He had just minutes before he had to be back out there, giving post-match interviews and press conferences, but he needed this few seconds alone, to think about everything. To think about his next move; to make sure he knew what he was doing. What had happened with Amber had thrown him slightly. It hadn't been planned; he'd never intended to have sex with her or embark on any kind of conversation with a woman he loved beyond anything. He just couldn't be with her. He couldn't. Even though that was all he wanted. He wanted to be with her so much he felt that pain cut right across his chest again as he remembered how she felt, how she tasted. How he fitted her so perfectly it was almost as if they'd been created purely to be together.

Pouring himself a small shot of whiskey he knocked it back in one mouthful before throwing his head back and letting out a heavy, laboured sigh. His heart felt as though it was breaking, but that was a feeling he was used to now. Ever since he'd allowed himself to love her, he'd felt this pain, an intense, burning pain. And he'd thought he could handle it because he was Jim Allen. He could handle anything. Except this. This was killing him, and he couldn't let that happen again. He couldn't let it almost ruin him, like it had once tried to do before.

Resisting the urge to take another shot of whiskey, he put the glass down and looked in the mirror on the wall above the sideboard. Pushing a hand through his hair, he stared at his reflection, blinking slowly as he noticed eyes that were tired, a face that was still impassive but a little more worn than he felt comfortable with. He had to get himself back on track. What had happened this afternoon with Amber had been a lapse he couldn't allow to be repeated. He couldn't let this distract him from what really mattered – his career; making sure this club was more successful than it had ever been. He had his sights set high, and he couldn't let anything detract from that.

Inhaling deeply he turned around and headed for the door, hesitating slightly as his hand reached out to open it. He could do this. Love not only broke your heart, it made you weak. And if there was one thing Jim Allen wasn't, it was weak.

Chapter Four

'Are you serious?' Debbie asked, sipping demurely on a large gin and tonic as the post-match Players' Lounge began filling up with girlfriends, wives, friends and family.

Amber leaned back against the wall, staring out ahead of her, smiling at people who waved hellos or smiled in her direction. 'I don't know, Debbie. I just know that I can't stay here.'

'And I thought things were okay with you and Ryan.'

'They are… they were.' She looked at her friend. Debbie Hogan – glamour model, gossip columnist, and wife of Ryan's best friend, Newcastle Red Star defender Gary Blandford. 'Things were fine. But fine isn't enough, Debs. Fine isn't how I want to live my life.'

'And running away from things is?'

'Oh, don't you start. Just – don't. Okay? I've had enough from him.' She jerked her head towards Ronnie, who was standing over by the bar talking to one of his fellow pundits.

'You don't even like *working* in London, never mind living there.'

Amber threw her head back, sighing heavily, and probably rather more loudly than she'd intended. But sometimes frustration got the better of her. 'It's hardly like I'm upping sticks and emigrating, is it? I have a house down there anyway, and like I told Ryan, I'll probably be up here just as much as I usually am. I'm just… I'm just swapping bases for a while, that's all.'

Debbie took another sip of gin and tonic. 'Sounds like a pointless waste of time, then, if you ask me.'

'I'm not. You brought up the subject.'

'Because I don't understand, Amber. If things aren't working out with Ryan, why not just tell him?'

'I *have* just told him,' Amber sighed, sliding her hands into the pockets of her jeans.

'So what's the prob… oh, hang on.'

Amber turned her head to look at Debbie, but she didn't say anything.

'You haven't?'

'I haven't, what?'

'You and Jim.'

'There *is* no me and Jim. We're divorced, remember?'

'That means nothing where you two are concerned.'

'Why do people keep saying that?'

Debbie narrowed her eyes as she continued to stare at her. 'You've slept with him, haven't you?'

'No, I…' Amber let out another sigh, this time one of resignation.

'When?'

'What *is* this? You'll be reading me my rights next.'

'When did you have sex with him, Amber?'

'I'm not sure that's any of your business.'

'You're my friend. It's very much my business. When?'

'Just before the game.'

'Okay… and, what happened after that?'

'Newcastle Red Star beat Wearside Spartans 3 – 2.'

'Oh, Ronnie is so right about your tendency to be flippant when faced with something you don't want to talk about. So, let me get this straight, you have sex with your ex-husband, and then you decide to move down to London to get away from him, is that right?'

Amber just stared at Debbie for a second or two. 'No. That is *not* right. I'd already made the decision to base myself down south before all this shit happened…'

'This shit? Oh, so, it wasn't good, then? Sex with Jim.'

'Now who's being flippant? I'm being serious here, Debbie. Ronnie told me I needed to sort myself out, so, that's what I'm trying to do.'

'By moving away from everything you know?'

'Jesus, Debbie, come on. I've been working down there for over a year now, it's hardly the end of the earth. And I just need the space, alright? I need the space.'

'Why?'

Amber stared at her again, knowing all too well she was trying to get her to admit to something she already knew. 'I'm moving to London, end of subject.'

'Okay. That's me told,' Debbie huffed, sucking up the last of her gin and tonic. 'I'm off to get a refill.'

Amber watched her walk over to the bar, whispering something to Ronnie that caused him to look over, and Amber could only hope it wasn't enough to make him come and talk to her. She really wasn't in the mood to discuss this any more, not today.

'So you're moving to London?'

She felt her heart skip a ridiculous beat as the familiar American accent once more filled her head, but she didn't look at him. She couldn't. She didn't think she was strong enough.

'Why didn't you tell me?'

'It wasn't really the right time, was it? When you were fucking me up against your office door.'

'I would have thought it was the perfect time.'

Still she said nothing. She just dug her hands into her pockets and stared down at the ground.

'You thought it was the perfect time to tell Ryan, though. Didn't you?'

She slowly looked up, raising her head so her eyes met his. 'I wasn't thinking straight, Jim. I haven't been thinking straight for a while now. Ever since you walked back into my life my head's been a fucking mess.'

It was Jim's turn to look away. 'I don't want you to go.'

'You have no say in the matter. And I don't want to hear you say that, okay? I don't want you to say something like that when you don't really mean it.'

'I mean it.' His eyes were back on hers, staring at her with an intensity that was quite frightening. 'I don't want you to go. I don't want you to be so far away I can't see you or talk to you or…'

'Hang on…' That confusion that seemed to be omnipresent at the minute washed over Amber once again, but she couldn't tear her eyes away from him. It was like some weird and invisible force was keeping them locked on his. 'You have absolutely no right to stand there and say those things. None. You… you divorced me, Jim. *You* left *me*.'

'Because you were sleeping with one of my players.'

Amber laughed, a small, cynical laugh. 'This is crap. All of it, it's crap.' She pushed a hand through her hair and turned away, knowing that she needed to leave here. She needed to walk away and leave this crazy situation that she couldn't understand. Before it killed her.

'Amber, please…' Jim reached out, his fingers gently circling her wrist, stopping her from going anywhere. 'I'm sorry, okay?'

She looked at him again, her head telling her one thing, and her heart screaming something altogether different. 'For what, Jim? For sleeping with me when I was just a teenager? For making me love you my entire life? For messing with my head every single, fucking day? What *exactly* are you sorry for?'

'Letting you go. I'm sorry for letting you go, and there are reasons, believe me, Amber, there are reasons why I… why…'

She frowned slightly as she noticed emotion clouding his usually impassive and stoic expression. This was a side of him she'd very rarely seen, and it confused her even more. 'Jim?'

He shook his head. 'Not here.'

'No. No, don't ask me to go somewhere more private or make

me listen to any more excuses or…'

'I have to go.'

'What the…? Jim!'

She watched as he just turned and walked away, pushing through the crowded Players' Lounge until she couldn't see him any more.

'You alright?'

She turned to look at Brandon, who'd suddenly materialised beside her. Handsome, hot and talented – a frighteningly younger version of his father. A constant reminder of a man she would always love. A man who was destined to spend the rest of his life fucking up hers.

'What the hell is wrong with him, Brandon?'

Brandon looked down at the bottle of lager he was holding, scuffing his heel against the wall behind him. 'He's got a lot on his mind.'

'Haven't we all?' Amber sighed, her mood brightening slightly as she saw Ryan walk in carrying their baby boy. Her father had been looking after Rico but he'd obviously brought him to Tynebridge to see his mum and dad, and for that Amber could only be grateful. She badly needed the distraction.

'Do you want me to talk to him?' Brandon asked.

'Do whatever you like.' Amber's attention was elsewhere now. 'I'm past caring.' Not entirely true. She turned to look at Brandon, suddenly realising that his father's odd behaviour was nothing to do with him. 'You were great out there this afternoon. Without you on their side, Red Star would have annihilated Spartans.' She smiled, standing up on tiptoes to kiss his cheek. 'See you later, okay?'

Brandon smiled back, but Amber was done there now. She didn't want to talk about Jim or even have to think about him, not when she had way more important things to be concentrating on.

'And what are *you* doing here, gorgeous?' She had the biggest grin on her face as she reached out to take Rico from Ryan's arms.

'I've brought our son to see his mum.' Ryan grinned back, and

Amber couldn't help but smile.

'I was talking to Rico.'

'I know. Your dad brought him in, thought you might want to see him seeing as you've been away from him all day.'

'Well, Dad was right.' Rico was her steadying influence, the one thing that could stop her from making any more crazy decisions that were nothing but a way of deflecting her real feelings. With him in her life, she had to make sure every decision she made was the right one. For both their sakes. 'Hello, baby! Has Granddad got you all dressed up in your daddy's team's colours?'

Rico was dressed in the cutest of baby football strips, with the number nine on the back and the name Fisher above it. A tiny replica of his daddy's strip.

'Oh, you are *too cute!*' Debbie cooed as she tottered over on her four-inch heels. 'Amber, he gets more beautiful every day.'

'Just like his mum,' Ryan said, his eyes instantly meeting Amber's.

'Jesus, do you ever give that flannel a rest?' Gary rolled his eyes, and Debbie nudged him hard in the ribs. 'Ouch! What the fuck was *that* for?'

'We need to get home to check on Jodi.'

'Do we?'

It was Debbie's turn to roll her eyes. 'Just get your arse out of here, come on,' she said, ushering him quickly away from Amber and Ryan.

'That was subtle,' Ryan sighed, leaning back against the wall, his hands in the pockets of his doubtless very expensive jeans.

'You can talk.'

He looked at her. 'I meant it. You *do* get more beautiful every day.'

'I bet you say that to all the girls.'

He shrugged, a slight smirk on his handsome face. 'Once upon a time I did, yeah.'

Amber couldn't help smiling again. 'And didn't I know it.'

Neither of them said anything for a second, they just let the silence between them hang in the air as they both watched their son play with Amber's hair, wrapping it around his tiny hand and pulling at it gently. This perfect little man had been created in the midst of a not-so-perfect relationship. And Amber doubted it could ever be anything but that. Too much had happened, too many things had been said. Too many truths had been told.

'We had something, Amber. You and me. Remember? We had something.'

'I know we did, Ryan. It's just...' She was distracted by Jim's reappearance in the room, her grip on Rico tightening as her eyes followed him, watching the way he walked, the way he smiled at everyone who acknowledged him. She'd allowed this man to take over her life all those years ago, and now there was no way back.

'I'm going to get a drink,' Ryan sighed, pulling himself away from the wall.

'Ryan...'

'Later, Amber.'

She threw her head back, stroking her son's soft, dark hair as he snuggled into her.

'Do you want to get out of here?'

She opened her eyes to see Ronnie standing there. He was the only person who could bring some sanity and sense into this rapidly deteriorating situation.

She nodded, kissing the top of Rico's head.

Ronnie smiled. 'Okay, well, I've just got a couple of things to tie up here, but I'll only be a couple of minutes.'

'I'll wait for you out in the main reception. I'd better let Ryan know I'm going.'

Ronnie leaned over to kiss her quickly before retreating back over to the bar, smiling at Freddie Sullivan as he approached Amber.

'Everything alright, kiddo?'

'I'm trying to make it that way, Dad.'

Freddie frowned at his daughter, taking Rico from her. 'Something you want to tell me?'

She looked at him. 'Like what?'

Freddie raised an eyebrow. 'Like, London?'

All of a sudden that move to London wasn't sounding like such a good idea. And a huge part of her wished she'd given it a lot more thought before mentioning anything to anyone. So much for leaving the days of rash decision-making behind.

'Look, Dad, forget London, okay?'

'So, you're not moving down there, then?'

'I don't know...'

'What's happened?'

'What do you mean, what's happened?'

'Something going on between you and Ryan?'

'Nothing's going on between me and Ryan.' And that's where the problem lay. 'I just wish it was,' she said quietly. 'Then none of this crap would be happening.'

Freddie frowned again. ''I don't understand, sweetheart.'

She leaned over to gently kiss Rico's warm cheek, stroking his hair. 'No. Neither do I.'

'Do you want to talk about it? Whatever it is you've got on your mind? Would that help?'

Amber smiled at her dad. He was the best dad a girl could ask for, and she loved him beyond words. But she really didn't want him getting mixed up in any more of her turbulent and complicated love life. He didn't need that, and neither did she. 'No, it's okay. I'm gonna go with Ronnie, grab something to eat.'

'Do you want me to take Rico?'

'Oh, no, Dad, it's alright. He can come with us.'

'He doesn't want to do that, do you, little fella? You'd rather spend some more time with your old granddad. He can stay the night, can't you, kiddo? If your mum doesn't mind.'

'Dad, are you sure? You've had him all day, and I... I can't just...'

'Amber, it's fine. I love having him, you know I do. You just go with Ronnie, okay?'

'Okay.' She smiled, kissing first Rico, then her dad. 'I'll call you later. You be a good boy now, baby, you hear me? No acting up for granddad.'

'He'll be fine. You go, go on.'

She made her way out of the Players' Lounge, keeping her head down because she didn't really want to stop for any small talk. She just wanted to leave Tynebridge and go somewhere away from it all. Just for a little while.

'Hey, Amber, hang on!'

She'd put one foot outside of the door when he caught her, giving her no choice but to stop and face him. 'What do you want, Ryan?'

'I thought we were taking Rico home together?'

'And when was *that* decided? I don't remember making any plans. I didn't even know Dad was bringing him in until ten minutes ago.'

'You're leaving him with Freddie, again?'

'What do you mean, "again"? You make it sound as though Rico's never with me. It's one night, Ryan.'

'Why?'

She narrowed her eyes as she stared at him. 'Why, what?'

'Why are you leaving him? Come on, Amber, you haven't seen him all day…'

'Can you just quit with the lectures and the guilt-tripping and anything else that has very little to do with you.'

'He's *my* son, too, Amber. So I think it has quite a bit to do with me. Jesus, I don't even know how we got to this. To here. To the point where we can't even have a frigging conversation without it ending in an argument. And it really doesn't have to be this way, you know that, don't you? It doesn't have to be this way.'

She looked at him. A man she'd once thought she'd loved so much, but was Ronnie right? Had she ever really loved Ryan Fisher? Or had he always been nothing but a distraction. Something to hide behind because she was scared of giving in to someone she really should have left behind a long time ago.

'Everything's just so confusing, Ryan. And I'm sorry; sorry that it's all turned to this so quickly, but… I don't know. I just don't know any more.'

He closed the door of the Players' Lounge behind him, moving so he was standing in front of her, and she reluctantly leaned back against the wall.

'Can't we just talk, Amber?'

'About what?'

'About us. About how we can make this work – you, me and Rico. We're a family now, babe. The three of us. We're a family.'

She shook her head, looking down at her feet because meeting his eyes was painful. 'It wouldn't be fair, Ryan.'

'Why not let *me* be the judge of what's fair and what isn't?'

'Because that in itself isn't fair, don't you get it?'

'What I get, Amber, is that you're pushing me away because you can't move on. You can't fucking forget him, and I know that's hard, because he's here all the time…'

'Which is why I need to get away, Ryan.'

'You need to get over him. If he doesn't want you, why are you wasting your time? Why are you even bothering to give him any thought at all. Amber, I love you. I *love* you, and I want this to work… I want *us* to work. I don't want you to leave because you need to get away from him, I don't want you to do that.'

'Ryan…' His mouth touching hers stopped her mid-sentence. Not that she'd had any idea what she'd been going to say anyway. And it felt nice, his kiss. His mouth was soft against hers, their lips moving together in a perfect rhythm, and for a few seconds Amber once more lost herself in that kiss. She allowed herself a few seconds to think about how it could be, if she was to just let it happen. The past few months had been good. Ryan had changed so much from that man she'd first encountered a couple of years ago. He was different now. He'd grown up, learnt to control himself;

overcome his demons. And she was proud of him. He'd helped her through a crazy, unpredictable time in her life when, at times, she'd thought it was all crashing down around her. And she'd honestly thought she could love him again and that they finally stood a chance after everything that had managed to get in the way before. But now she wasn't so sure. She just couldn't be sure any more. And what he didn't deserve was her making him think something could happen, if it really wasn't going to.

'I love you,' he whispered, tucking a strand of hair behind her ear.

'I know, baby. I know you do.' Why couldn't she love him back? Why couldn't she do that? It would make everything so much easier if she could just do that.

'Then let's go home and talk about this. Rico can stay with your dad and we can…'

She shook her head, pulling away from him. 'No, Ryan. I'm sorry… Look, if you want to take Rico tonight, just talk to my dad. He's got all the baby stuff, and if you want to take him…'

He grabbed her hand as she started to walk away, stopping her in her tracks. But she didn't turn around when he spoke. She couldn't. She wasn't even sure she could look at him now without the guilt overwhelming her. 'I love you, Amber. Just remember that.'

She gently pulled her hand away from his and almost ran down the corridor, pushing open the doors that led out into the main reception so hard she almost flung them off their hinges, so desperate was her need to get away from that situation.

Stepping out into the almost empty, and thankfully cool, reception area, she walked over to the huge floor-to-ceiling windows that looked out over the main entrance, watching as the last of the derby-day crowd hung around outside, waiting to see if they could catch a glimpse of any of the players leaving.

'Did that kiss mean anything?'

She felt a shiver run up her spine as his hand lightly touched the small of her back, staying there for a brief second or two. But he stayed behind her; she could feel him standing there, even if he wasn't touching her now.

'He loves me, Jim.'

'But you don't love him back.'

She couldn't argue with that. She couldn't lie, what would be the point? 'I do love him.'

'But you're not *in* love with him. Are you?'

She kept her gaze on the now-dwindling crowd outside. 'Not here, Jim.'

'Then come with me. Somewhere we can talk.'

'You still think there's something to talk *about*?'

She felt him lean in towards her again, his breath warm on her cheek as he whispered in her ear. 'Yes. I do.' His hand was resting in the small of her back again, and she felt that shiver return, her stomach diving down and flipping over. 'I shouldn't have touched you, Amber. Before. I shouldn't have done that. Because now I need to do it all over again. I need to hold you, to feel you – to come inside you. All over again.'

She closed her eyes, hoping that when she opened them he'd be gone, that he'd never really been there because she didn't need this. She didn't. This wasn't how things were supposed to have worked out. She was supposed to have stayed with Ryan, had his baby and tried to make a go of it. Tried to settle down. But she should have known, from the second Jim Allen had walked back into her life, that that was never going to happen. How could it? When he took over everything, invaded her every waking thought, whether she was aware of it or not. When he was always there. Always. And he'd been there for over twenty years now. How was she supposed to forget all of that?

'Don't do this, Jim. Please.' She turned around, looking up into his eyes. 'This has come out of nowhere…'

'Has it?' His eyes never left hers, his hand reaching out to gently touch her cheek. 'You know where I am. If you need me.'

She felt that all-too-familiar wave of confusion wash over her once more as she watched him walk away, out of the ground. Her first love. Her ex-husband. Her obsession.

'What did *he* want?' Ronnie asked, sidling up beside her, his gaze following Amber's.

'Nothing.'

'You use that word a lot, as far as answers to questions are concerned.'

She turned to face him. 'Okay. Well, maybe I should expand on that answer, then. It's got *nothing* to do with *you*.'

'Nice.'

She threw herself down into one of the chairs that graced the huge entrance atrium, leaning her head right back and letting out a quiet but heavy sigh. 'How the hell did I end up here?'

Ronnie sat down on the arm of the chair, clasping his hands together. 'Because you never really were as strong as you thought you were.'

Amber glared at him.

'As far as men are concerned. As far as *one* man is concerned.'

She sat up, dropping her head into her hands and burying her fingers in her hair, letting loose another frustrated groan. 'Two years ago I was happy, Ronnie. I had a great job, independence, a life I could control… and now look at me. I'm nothing but an over-emotional wreck with a complicated, fucked-up life!'

'You've got an incredible career, Amber. And you've got Rico. There's nothing fucked-up or complicated about that.'

She looked at him again. 'Rico is the best thing that ever happened to me, Ronnie. He's the only thing I've got right in the past few months. But I'm not talking about my career, or my baby. They're good, I know they are. It's everything else that's fucked-up.'

'So, like I said, do something about it.'

'Like what?'

'Jesus, Amber, what are we on here? Some kind of loop? I don't know, kiddo. Just… follow your heart, okay?'

'Follow my heart…' She trailed off, looking outside. Jim was standing at the bottom of the steps that led up to the entrance, talking to a small group of fans. He was laughing, and she felt her stomach twist and turn again as he threw his head back, laughing some more.

Ronnie's eyes followed her gaze again. 'Maybe following your heart isn't such a good idea.'

'I can't leave him alone, Ronnie. I'm like a schoolgirl with this ridiculous, obsessive crush.' She trailed off again as she realised just what it was she was saying. That was how it had all started in the first place, wasn't it? Jim Allen, an American twenty-seven-year-old, hotshot football player who'd walked into her life when she'd been nothing but a teenager and rocked her entire world. Forever. That schoolgirl crush had never gone away. It had never really faded. And he knew that. So, was she doing the right thing by letting him think she was always going to be there? Even if she was. 'I can't let him go,' she whispered.

'You should try.'

'You told me to follow my heart.'

'I know.' Ronnie sighed, standing up, his tone one of defeat now. 'I know I did. I just thought you'd be more sensible than to head off in *that* direction, considering you know where it's going to take you.'

She looked at him, something akin to guilt mixed with a hint of fear swamping her. She really didn't have a clue what she was doing here. She only knew she was going to do it, and to hell with the consequences. 'You think I'm making a mistake, don't you?'

Ronnie held her gaze for a few, long seconds. 'The biggest one of your life.'

Chapter Five

'Jesus, Brandon, what do you want?'

'Good to see you, too, Dad.'

Jim sighed, standing aside to let his son through into the hall. 'I'm sorry. It's just been a long day. Derby matches always seem to drain me more than any others.'

'At least your side won.'

Jim couldn't help but smile as he followed Brandon into the living room. 'You did your best to stop that from happening.'

'Yeah. I did my best.' He walked over to the fireplace, turning around and folding his arms as he looked at his father. 'Who's Carrie Jackson?'

Jim almost dropped the glass of whiskey he was holding, then leant back against the sideboard to steady himself.

'Who is she, Dad?'

Jim poured himself another drink, turning his back on Brandon. 'It's none of your business.'

'Is she the reason you can't let yourself be happy? The reason you *won't* let yourself be happy?'

Jim turned back around, his expression telling Brandon he was in no mood to talk about this. 'I'm shutting this conversation down, Brandon. Right now.'

'Is she the reason you push people away?'

'I won't tell you again, son.'

'Like you pushed Amber away?'

'She was pregnant with another man's baby.'

'That wasn't the fucking reason, Dad, and you know it.' Brandon's eyes were holding Jim's gaze now, refusing to let go. 'You are still crazy-in-love with her, but you just can't let yourself be happy.'

'If you know all of this…'

'All I know is the name, Dad. All I know is you were once in a relationship with a girl called Carrie Jackson. That's all I know. Because I wanted *you* to tell me the rest. I wanted *you* to tell me the reason why she affected your life so much you won't let your-self be happy with a woman you are so obviously in love with.'

Jim narrowed his eyes as he stared at his son. 'Have you… have you been checking up on me?'

'The internet is a wonderful tool, Dad. You'd be amazed at what you can find out after just a half hour of searching.'

'I don't believe this…' He downed his whiskey, slamming the glass down onto the sideboard behind him, a mixture of panic and fear washing over him. He was losing control again, and he didn't like that. It never made him feel comfortable. Losing control wasn't something Jim Allen liked to make a habit of. 'You need to go, Brandon. Now. Please. I really need you to go.'

Brandon held up his hands in defeat, shaking his head as he walked over to the door, stopping when he reached Jim. 'You can't keep doing this to yourself, Dad. Acting like some kind of robot who pushes his feelings to one side. Someone who finds happi-ness – who actually has it right there in his hands, and then just lets it go, as though it means nothing. When it actually means everything. You can't keep on doing this, because it'll destroy you.'

Jim grabbed Brandon's arm as he walked out of the door. 'I get scared, Brandon.'

'Who was she, Dad?'

Jim looked down, letting go of Brandon's arm, signalling the end of the conversation. It was over. Done. Finished. For now.

Brandon left without saying another word. Jim waited until he heard the front door slam shut before pouring himself yet another drink, the alcohol doing little to numb those feelings that short conversation with his son had caused to resurface.

As he felt totally unexpected tears fill his eyes, he furiously blinked them back, refusing to let this bring him down. He just had to put it back where it belonged, out of his mind, out of reach, and carry on. Just like he had been doing ever since. Just like he needed to do again.

*

Amber closed the car door and leaned back against it, shutting her eyes as the cold north-easterly wind whipped across her face. But it was a reality she needed to feel before she stepped back inside a bubble she knew full well she should be steering clear of. It had burst so many times she couldn't really keep count any more, but it was a bubble she needed to be in right now. She needed him, needed his touch, his kiss; she needed to feel him inside her. She needed that.

Walking slowly up the driveway, she ran her fingers lightly along the side of his car, already feeling the forecasted frost begin to form on the cold surface. She began to shiver, the temperature was rapidly falling as the night wore on, and for a brief second she wondered if the fact she'd spent the last two hours just driving around – was that a warning sign? Should she be listening to those alarm bells, no matter how quietly they were ringing? If she'd needed him that much, why hadn't she just come straight here when she'd left Tynebridge?

Finally reaching the front door she watched her fingers as they hovered over the bell. Pressing it was going to restart something she wasn't sure she was ready for. But it was something she couldn't stop from happening, because Ronnie was right. She was weak.

Where Jim Allen was concerned she was weaker than any human being should ever be.

Pressing down on the bell she took a small step back. She still had a couple of seconds left to run away, to get out of there. To grow up and do what she'd said she was going to do – leave here and try and make a new start in London. But nothing could make her turn away from this, and she knew that. Now. She knew that.

Her heart fluttered wildly in her chest as the door slowly opened, her stomach doing that same old dip and dive as she looked up and saw him standing there. He was wearing faded, battered jeans and a dark t-shirt, his hair a little longer than he usually wore it, and the only thing she could think about was burying her fingers in it and messing it up as she lay underneath him.

'I need you,' she whispered, unable to do anything about the zillion and one butterflies that had just started flying around inside her.

He smiled the same smile that had reeled her in and dragged her into his world over twenty years ago. That same smile that could do it all over again, because she'd let it.

Closing the door behind her she looked at him, letting every memory of this man wash over her. Every beautiful kiss, every tiny touch – every heartbreaking goodbye. They all came back to visit, all at once, making her twice as confused, but it didn't matter. They could stay there, embed themselves in her brain on a permanent basis and she knew she still couldn't walk away from this. He was too much a part of her, and even if he broke her heart a million times more she was always going to love him. So, what did that say about her? What did that say about Amber Sullivan – that feisty, strong, independent woman who'd once thought she could take on the world. What did that say about her?

She walked over to him, taking the glass he was holding out of his hand, their eyes locked together. Reaching out to touch his mouth with her fingertips, she felt an altogether different kind of shiver engulf her as his hand rested lightly on her hip, pulling her just that little bit closer to him. Once more, the invisible cord she couldn't seem to cut had brought her back here, back to him, and there was nowhere else she wanted to be.

Standing up on tiptoes she closed her eyes as her lips touched his, so gently they just brushed over them at first, but it was enough to cause those goosebumps to break out, that wave of confusion to be washed away by something far harder to understand. And as his arm snaked around her waist, pulling her against him, his mouth pressing down harder on hers, she shut out everything else – Ryan, Ronnie; even Rico. She shut them all out, because she wanted nothing to spoil this. She wanted nothing to get in the way of what she was about to do.

They were never going to make it upstairs, she knew that. They were never going to make it that far. It was going to happen right here, but it wasn't going to be the quick and harsh encounter they'd shared earlier. She didn't want that. She wanted to feel him properly, to take in every touch of his fingers on her skin. She wanted to sink deep into his kisses, feel him move inside her as their bodies once more became one. She wanted all of that. She wanted *him*.

Stepping back slightly, she smiled as he leaned back against the wall, folding his arms, his eyes on her as she slowly stripped. And all that did was heighten everything she was already feeling, turning her on even more as all those things she was trying to push to the back of her mind slowly started to fade away.

'Leave the boots on,' he said, his eyes still boring into hers. 'Jesus, baby, please leave those boots on.'

She couldn't help smiling as she walked back over to him, now wearing nothing but black, knee-high boots, pressing her naked body against his still fully-clothed one.

'I'd forgotten how much you kill me, Amber.' His voice was low and oh-so-sexy as his mouth rested on hers. 'What you do to my head, honey, it's crazy.'

'I shouldn't be here,' she whispered, slowly pulling his t-shirt off over his head, flinging it aside like a used rag.

'Then why are you?'

'Because I need you.' She began pulling the belt away from his jeans. 'I already told you that. Because I can't get you out of my head, no matter how much I try.' She ran her thumb over his cheek, his stubble rough beneath her fingers. 'And because I'm weak.'

He took hold of her hand, bringing it up to his mouth and kissing it. 'I can't stand here and promise I won't hurt you again, Amber...'

She shook her head. 'Don't say anything, Jim, please. Just... just don't say anything.'

His hand tightened around hers, their eyes still locked together. 'I don't *want* to hurt you...'

'It's too late for that.'

He finally broke the stare, but only for a brief second. 'I'm glad you came. I didn't think you would.'

'Oh, you knew I would, Jim. You knew I would come.'

He bowed his head, once more breaking the stare. And when he finally raised it he said nothing, just wound his fingers into her hair and pulled her forwards, kissing her slowly. And Amber felt herself falling again, faster and faster, deeper and deeper into that web of pain and heartache that she couldn't stay away from. It was almost as if everything he put her through was a turn-on.

As he gently lowered her down onto the stairs she felt a tiny twinge of reality nip at her conscience, the image of her beautiful baby boy swimming before her eyes and she squeezed them shut, pushing that image away. Rico was fine, he was good. He was safe and he was loved and he would always come first in her world. Always. And yet, how could she say that, when she was here? When she was about to do this and reopen every old wound Jim Allen had ever inflicted.

'Are you okay?'

She opened her eyes, stretching her arms up above her head. 'I'm fine. I was just thinking, that's all.'

'About what?'

She took a second or two to look at him. He was naked now, as he stood there in front of her. For a man of his age he still had the body of someone twenty years younger; tall and lean, toned and hard, and every memory of the first time she'd seen him like this came rushing forwards, flooding her brain, making her almost breathless. She could feel her chest rising and falling, faster and heavier than it had done just seconds before, her heart beating wildly against her ribs, her fingers entangling themselves in her own hair. 'About why I shouldn't be here.'

He lowered himself down over her, the heat of his body as it touched hers almost burning her skin and she breathed in deeply, letting him pull one of her hands away from her hair, his fingers intertwining with hers.

'I thought we weren't talking,' he whispered, his mouth moving closer to hers.

'We aren't,' she breathed, her chest now rising up to touch his as her legs pulled up around him, keeping him close.

'Okay...' He kissed her slowly, and she stretched out more as she felt his other hand slip between her legs, touching her gently, checking she was ready for him. 'No more talking.'

'No more talking,' she repeated, opening her legs wider now, letting him in, inviting him to do whatever it was he needed to do.

As the kiss got deeper his fingers played harder, touching her, sinking into a wetness he'd created, and she found it difficult to hold back, to stay quiet, because what he was doing to her was everything she'd dreamed of him doing since the day he'd told her it was over. It had only been a few months ago, the last time he'd broke her heart, yet it seemed like an eternity had passed. She'd missed him so much, and although she hadn't always been aware of that – the months leading up to Rico's birth had given her more distractions than she'd been able to handle – she knew that the second her son had been born, that was when reality had kicked in. That was when she'd realised things had never really changed. That was when she'd realised it was this man she needed to be with. He just hadn't wanted her. He'd pushed her away. But was all that changing now?

His mouth was still resting on hers as his fingers slid slowly inside her and she moaned quietly, bucking her hips up as she pulled him in. And it felt good to have him back there, to feel him where she needed him to be. Everything else felt wrong. Only he'd ever felt right, despite everything. Despite it all. Only he'd ever felt right.

Moving his head down, he covered one of her nipples with his mouth, flicking his tongue over it, causing her to moan out loud again as she buried her fingers in his hair. He was making her dizzy; her head was spinning with a hundred different reasons why this was wrong, but still she didn't want to be anywhere else. She didn't want him to leave or stop doing this; she didn't want him to go.

He let go of her hand, pushing her legs a little further apart, and as he slowly pulled his fingers out of her she gasped, closing her eyes as she prepared for what was going to happen next, the anticipation both exciting and terrifying. But when he finally made that move, gently pushing into her so carefully, the complete oppo-site of the sex they'd had earlier, she felt nothing but a wonderful warmth spread through her entire body, from the tips of her toes to the top of her head. An incredible, mind-blowing feeling of warmth and safety. Yet she was anything but safe. Jim Allen was the epitome of danger as far as relationships were concerned. But she was trapped, in a world she wasn't willing to leave.

Pushing her hips up to meet his again she took him deeper, angling her body so he fell into her, and he held onto her as though his life depended on it as they moved together in an erotic dance, their rhythm perfectly synchronised.

His moans merged with hers, soft and quiet yet loaded with an intensity that circled around them, filling the hallway, turning up the heat on an already burning atmosphere as bodies crashed together and feelings were torn apart under waves of confusion and pain. But Amber wouldn't have it any other way. She didn't want to feel anything other than what she was feeling now as he thrust in and out of her fast, then slow, keeping that rhythm going, holding out for as long as he could but he was sinking quickly, she could tell. His breathing was heavier, his body tensing up as he got ready for that final push, and Amber almost held her breath as she waited for the inevitable to happen, wanting it yet dreading it, because she didn't want this to end. She didn't want to end this closeness. She didn't want to let him go. But she couldn't stop that rush of beautiful, white-hot pain that flooded her body as he spilled out into her with a cry so loud it seemed to shake the room. And when he reached down to touch her, to help her to her own climax before he'd finished his, she thought she might pass out with the sheer weight of feelings he was making her experience in the space of those final few seconds.

And when it was over, all she felt was a crashing emptiness that seemed to wash over her at breakneck speed.

'Stay with me,' he whispered, stroking the hair from her eyes, which she didn't want to open just yet, in case he disappeared the second she did. In case this was just a dream. She felt sixteen all over again, and she wasn't sure she liked it. It made her feel vulnerable, out-of-control, when she should be grown up and strong.

'I… Jim, I don't know…'

'Stay with me.' He took hold of her hand, gripping it tight, his eyes now staring deep into hers. 'Please. Because I can't let this go… I can't let *you* go. Not yet.'

She wanted to hear him say *not ever*; that's what she wanted to hear him say. *Not yet* signalled that he was willing to let her go at some point. And once more she could hear those alarm bells ringing. 'What are we doing, Jim?'

'I need you, Amber.'

'For what? For a few days? A couple of weeks? For sex and nothing else? Forever? For what, Jim?'

He sat up, pushing both hands through his hair, letting out

a quiet sigh, but Amber could see the weight of the world right there on his shoulders. 'I can't do this. Not with Ryan still here. That constant threat...'

She sat up beside him, slipping her hand into his, kissing his shoulder lightly. 'He isn't a threat, Jim. He never was, not really.'

He looked at her, smiling a small smile, but even she could see it hadn't reached his eyes. 'You say that, but then something happens and he's there, back in your life. And now you've got Rico... Amber, you and him, you have a child together.'

'I'm not in love with him, Jim.'

'But he's always going to be a part of your life. He's always going to *be* there.'

'And I can't help that. I can't. He's Rico's dad, and that's a job he's got for life.'

Jim looked down at their joined hands. 'It still tears me apart that I couldn't give you what you wanted. That you had another man's child when I... when I loved you so much it broke my fucking heart every day to see you... to see you carrying his baby. You were my wife, Amber.'

'And *you* divorced *me*, Jim.'

He let go of her and dropped his head into his hands. 'Because I just couldn't face losing you.'

'Baby, that doesn't make any sense. You were the one that left *me*. I didn't want to go anywhere.'

He raised his head, his eyes tired and heavy with tears, and Amber didn't know what to do. This was a side of him she'd very rarely seen, if ever. 'But you might have done. You were pregnant, with a baby that wasn't mine. Pregnant to a man who meant something to you, Amber. You say you're not in love with him, but, Ryan Fisher – he meant *something* to you. Once.'

She got up, finding his t-shirt that she'd thrown on the floor. And he watched as she pulled it over her head, watched as she covered that beautiful nakedness with his own clothes.

'I'll go get us something to drink,' she said, heading off into the kitchen, a fresh wave of confusion sweeping over her now.

She found a bottle of brandy on the counter and pulled two clean glasses from the dishwasher before filling them both with a generous measure.

'We really do need to talk, Amber.'

She turned around, unable to stop a sharp intake of breath as she looked at him standing there, dressed only in jeans that hung low on his hips, his hands in his pockets. 'When did you get so paranoid, Jim? When did you let anyone get in the way of anything you wanted?'

'You aren't just *anything*, Amber. You're not just a winning football score or some defender I desperately want before the transfer window closes. You're my whole fucking world, and the thought of you...' He trailed off, turning his head away for a second. 'We need to talk.'

She watched as he walked over to her, taking the glass she held out for him and putting it straight back down on the counter.

'There are reasons why I did what I did. Reasons why I pushed you away.'

'So, tell me what those reasons are. Help me to understand just what's going on here, Jim, because, right now, I don't understand any of it. I don't get it. None of it makes any sense.'

'I can't, Amber. I can't explain...' He slowly slid his hand up under the t-shirt she was wearing, causing her to gasp as his fingers touched her skin. 'I can't.' He leaned forward, his lips brushing over her neck and she threw her head back. She let herself fall into him all over again until a glimmer of reality pushed its way forward and she gently pushed him away.

'Because sex will solve everything, won't it?'

'It helps.'

'I need you, Jim. Because without you I'm a wreck. I can't think straight, I can't function, because you not being there, it's wrong. It's not how it should be. But if we're... if we're even thinking about being together again I need you to be honest with me. For the first time in your life. I need that more than anything.'

He leaned back against the counter beside her, digging his hands back into his pockets, taking the deepest of breaths before he spoke again. 'Before I came over to the UK, I was… I was involved with… I was involved with someone.'

Amber felt her stomach tighten as he spoke. Was he about to reveal yet another secret he'd kept from her for all these years?

'We'd met at a party, some awards ceremony a friend of mine had gotten tickets for. She was an up-and-coming country singer, someone the music industry had tipped for the big time, even though she was so young. We both were…'

Amber watched him as he spoke, watched the way his eyes filled with those tears she very rarely saw; a look on his face that scared her, because it was so alien, to see him like this.

'I was only twenty, she was nineteen… but we fell in love. Hard. We fell in love hard.'

Amber felt her stomach tighten even more now. To watch him talk this way about someone else hurt with a pain she couldn't explain. And it felt strange, almost as if she was listening to someone else completely. Someone she didn't know. As though the Jim she'd once known had left the room to be replaced with someone more vulnerable. Someone she was having trouble recognising.

'And for almost five years we were happy. We were so happy. My soccer career was taking off, and her music was going places, we had it all. We had everything. We had a future…'

Amber took a deep breath, wanting to reach out and take his hand but not knowing if that was the right thing to do. Did he want her intruding on something that was obviously so emotional for him?

'But somebody made sure that future was never gonna happen.'

Amber was willing him to look at her now. She wanted to see his eyes, to feel what he was feeling because she could tell it was breaking his heart. Whatever he was about to tell her, it was breaking his heart.

He turned his head, his eyes finally locking onto hers. 'She died, Amber. She was on her way back from a gig in L.A., and there was an accident. Her van collided with a car that was speeding. It had cut the lights, swerved out of control…'

Amber reached out and took his hand, her fingers tightening around his, and he responded, clinging onto her as tears started streaming down his face.

'I was in New York. I'd been playing in some soccer tournament and they didn't tell me until… until it was over. For some reason. I don't know why they left it. I just remember this numbness taking over, a pain so intense it cancelled out anything else I might be feeling. My whole world shut down that night. She was gone. She was my world, and she was gone.'

He turned away from her again, and Amber didn't know what to do. Watching him fall apart right there in front of her was something she'd never seen before, and it scared her. Jim Allen was strong. Jim Allen was always in control. Jim Allen didn't break down.

'I changed that night.' His voice was quiet, but there was a tougher edge to it now. 'The person I'd been before, he was gone.'

'Jim, baby, look at me. Please.'

His eyes met hers, tears still streaming down his face and she couldn't help but reach out and brush them away with her thumb. 'I couldn't fall in love again, not like that. I couldn't do it. I wouldn't let myself. So I changed. I threw myself into my career, made the decision to play football over in the UK. It was the only way I could deal with it all. And I… I vowed never to fall in love again, because the pain you feel when your world is suddenly ripped away from you and you know you can never get it back… nobody deserves to feel that.' His fingers tightened around hers once more, their eyes locked together. 'But then came you. Beautiful, sixteen-year-old Amber Sullivan. From the very first second I saw you I knew. I knew I had to have you. I had to. And maybe I should have walked away, because you were so young, too young. But there was something telling me…' He stopped talking, turning his head away for another brief second, causing another wave of confusion to wash over Amber. 'The reason I spent all those years acting the way I did; the reason why I kept pushing you away.' He turned back to face her, his eyes boring deep into hers. 'I loved you too much, Amber. It was … it was like Carrie all over again, those same, uncontrollable feelings that I knew I couldn't ignore. They were back, and they were real, and they scared the hell out of me. I wanted to be with you so much it hurt, but I couldn't let myself get too close because that fear of losing you was just too great. Too overwhelming. And I know I hurt you, I know that, and I'm sorry. I'm so, so sorry, because we wasted so much time.'

Amber felt her own heart start to break as she watched him wipe those still-falling tears away, once more turning his head so he wasn't looking at her.

'I thought I'd be able to handle it better, you know? When I took the Red Star job. When I came back up here. All those years apart, but I still couldn't get you out of my head. I couldn't forget you. I was still so much in fucking love with you, Amber.' He looked at her again. 'You know I took the manager's job at Newcastle Red Star because I needed to be near you again. You know that. And I thought I'd be able to handle it better after all that time away, I really did. I was wrong. Because I didn't bank on Ryan Fisher. I didn't bank on you still hurting so much because of what I'd done to you…'

'Jim.'

He bowed his head, his hand still clinging onto hers. 'We almost had it, Amber. You and me. We almost had that future I wanted. We were together, you were my wife…' As his eyes met hers again she felt her heart beat so fast she almost couldn't breathe. 'And still I pushed you away. Because that fear of losing someone I loved so much just wouldn't leave me. I couldn't forget how losing Carrie almost broke me, I couldn't let that go. So I *had* to push you away. I had to pretend I didn't care about you when you're the *only* thing I care about. The only thing. And I should have been man enough to face up to everything and tell you the truth.'

She reached out and cupped his cheek in her hand, her own eyes filling with tears as everything she'd ever felt for this man collided and merged into one huge, emotional mess. Who she'd thought he was, and the actual man underneath, were two completely different people.

'Why didn't you just talk to me, Jim?'

'You were so young when we first met, Amber. Too young to understand all the crap going on inside my head. And back then – back then I just wanted to be this hotshot footballer who was suddenly having women falling at his feet, giving him every distraction he could possibly wish for. I didn't want to talk about it. Not back then. And I know that wasn't fair on you...'

She leaned forward and kissed him, the salt from his tears dampening her lips. 'You should have talked to me. When you took the Red Star job, when you came back here... you should have talked to me.'

He tried to smile, wiping his eyes with the back of his hand. 'I know. Jesus, I know that now. I've been so stupid.' He pulled her into his arms, holding her loosely around the waist. 'I acted the way I did because I was scared, Amber. And I'm so sorry, baby. So sorry I hurt you, so sorry for everything I put you through because throughout it all... throughout it all I loved you so much it killed me. And I had to put on that front, create a mask to hide behind because if I hadn't done that, I would've fallen apart. But now? Now I just wish I'd been stronger. We wasted so much time.'

'Sshh, it's okay. It's okay. Let's not think about the past any more, alright? And let's mean it this time. None of that matters now.'

He threw his head back, releasing a long, slow sigh. 'I don't deserve to have you in my life, Amber. Not after everything...'

She shut him up with another kiss, letting it build, her mouth opening to accept him more, his tongue sliding inside and she pushed against him, all those confusing feelings filling her head and she just wanted to forget them. For a few, short minutes she wanted them to go away.

He turned her around, lifting her up onto the countertop, pushing her legs apart with a gentle force that signalled the beginning of something Amber needed now. She needed sex with a man she'd never really known, but he was a man she couldn't walk away from. She'd known that before, and she knew it even more now.

Leaning back, she placed her hands palm-down behind her, wrapping her legs around him as he pushed into her once more, so hard and so quick it rocked her whole body back, causing her to cry out loud, but it was a beautiful pain, and one she welcomed. To feel him back inside her was the only thing she wanted right now.

He slid the t-shirt she was still wearing up over her breasts, his mouth covering them in tiny, almost feather-light kisses, sending her beyond crazy as the rhythm suddenly changed, and everything slowed down. Everything became calmer. He was kissing her so softly it was making her cry all over again, his arms holding her so tightly, as though she'd break if he let her go. And she just wanted to stay there, in his arms, feeling him move inside her as he kissed her. She wanted to feel that, forever.

So when they both finally came, in a climax that was so beautiful yet understated in its intensity, once again she didn't want to open her eyes. She didn't want to step back into reality.

'The next time, I want you to look at me when you come,' he whispered, gently stroking her cheek with his thumb. 'I want you to look at me.'

She stared into those green eyes of his; eyes that she'd never really been sure of. Eyes that had never really told her the truth, until now. Now she could see something in them she'd never seen before. Honesty. A whole new start. A different man.

'I love you so much, Jim. But I never really knew you, did I?'

He rested his forehead against hers, his fingers now lightly stroking the back of her neck. 'You know me now.'

She smiled. 'I'm beginning to.'

He kissed her again, his lips soft and damp against hers as those tears still fell from his eyes, more slowly now. 'Stay with me tonight, Amber. Please. Stay with me.'

And if there was one thing Amber knew for certain now, it was that she wasn't going anywhere.

Chapter Six

'You look happy.' Freddie smiled as he handed Amber her son, clean and freshly changed.

Amber breathed in Rico's beautiful baby smell, kissing him gently. 'That's because I am.'

'So, what's changed since yesterday? Because when *I* saw you last you looked like you had the weight of the world on your shoulders.'

'Jim and I, we're back together.' It was probably best to just come out with it. There was no sugar-coating the situation or waiting for a right moment that may never come. She was in love with Jim and he was in love with her. End of story.

Freddie just looked at his daughter, an expression of not-altogether-unexpected surprise covering his face. 'I… Amber, I… When did *this* happen?'

'Last night.'

'I thought you were with Ronnie last night?'

'It's complicated, Dad.'

'It always is, kiddo. And I have to admit, this isn't something I was ever expecting to hear. I'd thought you and him were finally over.'

'We've never been over, Dad. I don't think we ever *will* be over.'

Freddie sat down on the arm of the couch, clasping his hands between his knees. 'Well, I just hope you know what you're doing,

Amber. Because it isn't just you and him any more. You've got that baby to think about now. And speaking of which, does Ryan know about you and Jim?'

Amber shook her head, cradling Rico in the crook of her left arm as she gathered all of his things together. 'Not yet, no. I'm going to see him this afternoon. I suppose we do, kind of, need to talk.'

'And how do you think he's going to take it?'

She threw her father a look. 'How do you *think* he'll take it, Dad?'

Freddie sighed. 'Amber, sweetheart, I have no idea how you make your life such hard work.'

'I love him, Dad.'

Freddie looked at her, his expression softening slightly. 'I should have seen what was happening all those years ago. I should have stopped it. You were so young. And I should have stopped it.'

'How could you? You didn't know any of it was going on, so how could you have stopped it? I fell, Dad. I fell so hard and so deep and it's impossible to let go or walk away now, but… believe me, there are things about Jim Allen… there are things you know nothing about. He's not the man I thought he was. He's different. It won't be like every other last time. It won't be like that any more.'

Freddie's head shot up, a fleeting expression of something verging on suspicion sweeping over his face.

'He told me things last night that explained everything – why he acted the way he did all those years ago, why he did what he did…'

'And you believe him?'

She stared at her father, cuddling her baby boy closer to her. 'I do now.'

*

Jim sat back in his chair, staring up at the ceiling for a few seconds before sitting up, re-reading the email that had just arrived in his inbox. Things were changing so quickly it was difficult to take it all in, but maybe this was a sign – a sign that things were *meant* to change and that his life was meant to go in this direction. And it was what he wanted, after all; Amber back in his life, back in his bed – that was all he'd ever wanted.

A knock at the door made him jump, pulling him out of his thoughts. 'Come in.'

'Work on a Sunday?' Brandon asked, closing the door of Jim's Tynebridge office behind him.

'Did you want to see me about something?'

'I'm not one of your players, Dad. And yeah, I do want to see you about something, as it happens. I tried calling you at home but you weren't there, so I figured there was only one other place you were gonna be.'

'That predictable, huh?'

Brandon shrugged, perching himself on the corner of Jim's desk. 'You okay?'

Jim looked at his son, raising a surprised eyebrow. 'Any reason why I shouldn't be?'

'Last night, when I came round… Maybe I shouldn't have gone in so heavy-handed. I'm sorry.'

'I've spoken to Amber and I've told her everything. About Carrie, about how that had affected the way I loved *her*; how it had caused me to push her away when… when all I wanted was to be with her.'

Brandon took in a sharp intake of breath. 'Okay.'

'I'm assuming you went straight back home and tried to find out more for yourself.'

Brandon held up his hands. 'Guilty. Of course I did, Dad. You weren't saying much, and… well, there wasn't an awful lot there if I'm honest. You guys must have kept that relationship of yours pretty much a secret back then.'

'Neither of us were big enough or famous enough in our fields to be that interesting at the time, Brandon. But, yeah. We deliberately kept things quiet, kept ourselves to ourselves. It was the way we wanted it.' Jim looked away as he felt a wave of pain return. It was pain he'd thought he'd seen the last of last night.

'Dad, I'm sorry. For what happened. When she died it must have…'

'It was hard.' Jim didn't really feel much like talking about this or going over it all again. He'd done all the talking he'd needed to do with Amber. That was the only conversation that really mattered. 'It was a difficult time, and that caused me to do a lot of things I'm not proud of. I pushed Amber away because I couldn't face losing someone I loved so much all over again, but that was the wrong thing to do, Brandon. I know that now. And I really don't want to go over everything again, but let's just say that last night a lot of things that were broken got fixed.'

'I'm glad.' Brandon smiled at his dad. 'I'm glad that you might finally start to believe that being happy isn't something to be scared of.'

Jim stood up, walking around the front of his desk. 'Shouldn't you be spending the day with that pretty girlfriend of yours?'

'Ellen? She's still in bed. And all she's got planned for today is shopping. No, I'm meeting some of the guys from the squad in town. We're going for a few drinks, something to eat, maybe even the cinema later. We're making the most of having a day off.'

Jim frowned. 'Is everything alright? Between you and Ellen, I mean?'

'Yeah. Why shouldn't it be?'

Jim shrugged, digging his hands into his pockets. 'No reason. I just thought a young guy of your age would rather spend his free time with a beautiful woman than teammates he spends the best part of every day with.'

Brandon slid down from the desk, pushing a hand through his dark hair. 'Things are fine between me and Ellen. What about you and Amber?'

Jim smiled, a smile he hadn't felt much like smiling for a long time now. 'We're gonna be okay. We're gonna be just fine.'

'You're definitely back together, then?'

'We're definitely back together.' It felt good to say those words out loud. It felt really good. It felt like a whole new start, and Jim couldn't stop a frisson of excitement from surging through him.

'Good. Dad, that's great! But, what about Ryan...?'

'I can handle Ryan. He isn't a problem any more. Now, go on, go. Get out of here and enjoy your day off.'

Brandon started walking towards the door, stopping and turning around before he opened it. 'Are you sure everything's alright?'

'Everything's fine, Brandon. I promise you.'

'Okay, well, I'll call you later. And don't spend all day in here, huh? Try having some fun now and again. It won't kill you.'

Jim couldn't help smiling again as he watched his son leave. Maybe things *were* finally starting to look up. So maybe he should heed Brandon's advice and start having some fun. After all, hadn't he told Amber last night how they'd wasted so much time? Did he really want to waste any more?

'Can I come in?'

He looked up at the sound of her voice, his smile growing wider as she walked through the door, her baby son nestled in the crook of her arm. 'Hey! I wasn't expecting to see you... sorry. Is he asleep?'

'No, but he's getting there. I just saw Brandon outside. Is every-thing okay?'

'Everything's fine. He's on his way into town so he just stopped by to say hello.' Jim watched as she placed Rico's carry-seat on the couch and gently lowered him into it, kissing his forehead gently. A stab of pain cut across his chest so fast it almost left him breathless – why couldn't that baby be his? Why couldn't he have given her the one thing that could have stopped this latest round of crap from happening? 'The complications don't go away, do they?' Jim said quietly.

Amber slowly turned around, her eyes meeting his. 'Is Rico a problem?'

'No, baby. No. He isn't a problem, of course he isn't. But his daddy might be.'

She looked down at the ground, folding her arms against herself. 'I'm on my way to speak to him. I just…' She looked back up at Jim. 'I needed to see you first. I needed to make sure that what we're doing… that we both still feel the same way. That we're both sure this is what we want. That we can handle it all this time around, because that little boy over there, he's involved in all of this now. And I can't… I won't mess up his life the way you…' She pushed a hand through her hair, looking away for a second before meeting Jim's eyes once more. 'I won't mess up his life, Jim. I won't do that. And I won't let anyone else do that either. You take *me*, you take him, too. Do you understand? And if you can't handle that…'

Jim walked over to her, pulling her into his arms and kissing her gently. And all she could do was fall against him, giving into a kiss she craved like a drug. 'I can handle it, okay?'

She returned the smile he gave her, running her thumb lightly over his mouth. 'Good. Because I love you both. And I need you both. But I can't promise it's going to be easy…'

He shut her up with another kiss. 'Will you stop bringing up negatives that may never actually be a problem?'

'I'm just being realistic. Jim, this is hard, okay? I mean, last night, it was a shock. And my head's still all over the place.'

'One day at a time, baby. One day at a time. And we'll get there. I promise.'

'No promises, Jim. Please. You know how I feel. No promises.'

'Okay. No promises. Just know that everything I said last night, it was the truth. Every word, I meant them.'

'And that's all I need to know.'

She closed her eyes again as his mouth lowered down onto hers, pulling her back under his spell, but it would be different this time. Everything would be different. It had to be. Circumstances had changed and nothing was the same any more. So it had to be different.

'I love you so much,' she whispered, her fingers running lightly over his rough chin. 'So much. You have no idea.'

He took hold of her hand. Suddenly he felt like a kid again; could he really wind the clock back and try to make everything better? He needed to correct those stupid mistakes he'd made that had almost ruined everything for him. For both of them.

'I'd better go,' she said, reluctantly pulling away from him. 'I need to talk to Ryan.'

'You gonna be okay?'

'I never made him any promises, Jim. I never pretended there'd be any kind of happy-ever-after, so, yes. I'll be fine.'

'And what if he has a completely different take on things?'

She sat down on the arm of the couch, reaching over to stroke Rico's dark mop of hair. 'I hate what I'm doing to him, because he doesn't deserve it. When all's said and done he's just an innocent victim of all the crap you and I created. All the crap we couldn't cope with. He got caught in the middle, and that wasn't really fair. So I hate what I'm doing to him.' She sighed, picking up Rico's carry-seat. 'But, this is it.' She turned to face Jim, her eyes determined as they stared into his. 'No more running to Ryan Fisher. Because you won't give me cause to any more. Will you?'

*

'Looks like my dad and Amber are getting back together.' Brandon sat down at the kitchen table, watching as Ellen emptied the dishwasher. 'I've just been to see him, and I swear, it looked like some great weight had been lifted off his shoulders.'

Ellen slowly turned around, leaning back against the counter and folding her arms. 'Your dad and Amber are getting back together? When… when did *this* happen?'

'Last night, apparently.' Brandon didn't really want to go into the ins and outs of why it had happened. Jim had quite obviously managed to keep his past a secret for this long, which probably meant he wanted as few people to know about it as possible. Which was fine with Brandon. All he cared about was that his father was finally learning to live – and love – again.

Ellen frowned. 'And does Ryan know about this?'

Brandon shrugged. 'Not as far as I know. I'm assuming Amber's gonna tell him, though. I mean, if her and Dad really *are* getting back together then they aren't gonna be able to keep it under wraps for too long, are they? Given the circumstances.'

'No. I suppose not.' Ellen's mind had wandered now. This was all happening a little faster and a lot sooner than she'd anticipated, but, if what Brandon was telling her was true then this left the door wide open for her to put her own little plan into action. It was time for her to begin making Ryan see sense. And Amber Sullivan had just made it a hell of a lot easier for her to start doing that.

*

'Hey! How's my little man? You all ready for a day with your dad?' Ryan took the carry-seat from Amber and walked into the living room of the new home he was still getting used to. But having a kid, it really had changed him. And all of a sudden that quayside apartment hadn't felt like such a great place to be. He'd wanted a house, with a garden and space for Rico to run around in. He'd wanted a home. A family home. So he'd moved to a new place on an exclusive estate just outside Newcastle, a lot more suburban but still close enough for him to be near the centre of town. It was everything Ryan had run a mile from when he'd first arrived back in the north-east. But now it was everything he needed.

It wasn't exactly your average family home, though. He was Ryan Fisher, one of the most famous top-flight footballers around, and he had a reputation to keep up. He hadn't changed *that* much. And although the house wasn't exactly something straight out of *Footballers' Wives*, it was still large and detached, with a back garden the size of a football pitch and four huge en suite bedrooms. And it was right next door to Gary and Debbie's place. He'd needed to be near friends, to make sure that the life he was trying to get right stayed very much on track.

'He's had a feed, and he's just been changed, and he managed a little sleep on the way here, but, I can't promise he won't be wide awake for a while now.'

'That's okay, isn't it, kiddo? We'll find something to do.' He looked up at Amber. 'When do you head back down to London?'

'Tomorrow afternoon. We're recording a few episodes of *Back of the Net* on Tuesday, then I'm in the studio for the League Cup games on Wednesday night… Can I trust that between you and my dad you'll make sure Rico's alright?'

Ryan raised an eyebrow. 'I think we'll manage. Somehow.'

'Yeah, well, my Aunty Kim's on board, too, just in case you need her. I know my dad's got to work, he's got a home game midweek, and you might get waylaid… You know, I could just take him with me…'

'Amber, Jesus, will you just calm down? Why are you suddenly so nervous of leaving him with me? This whole set-up has worked pretty well since you decided you weren't even going to give maternity leave a try, so why are you panicking now?'

'I'm not panicking, Ryan.'

'Well, you're not exactly calm, either. What's up?'

She walked over to the window, staring out at the array of large, expensive houses, most of which were occupied by other big-name footballers and their WAGs, local celebrities, and the odd TV presenter. It wasn't somewhere she'd ever really wanted to be, surrounded by all that glamour and extravagance. She preferred her own little home, not that far away from here. It felt more cosy, more homely. And it had been her safe haven for so many months. But would she be leaving it soon? To go back to Jim? Back to the home that carried memories, good and bad, despite the fact she'd only lived there for a matter of months.

'Amber?'

She swung back around to face him. 'Sorry? Did you say something?'

'You were miles away. You alright?'

She folded her arms, looking down at the wooden floor because she didn't think she could meet his eyes when she told him what she was about to tell him now. 'Ryan, I...' But she knew she owed him that. She owed him the truth, and she should look at him when she told him. She should look at him and she should feel the guilt she deserved to feel because Ryan didn't deserve this. 'I didn't make you any promises, Ryan. Did I?'

He felt his stomach sink, a feeling that told him he wasn't going to like what was coming next. 'No. No, you didn't.'

'I never said this was all going to work out or that having Rico would guarantee we'd stay together.'

'We were never really together, though, Amber. Were we?'

Her pale-blue eyes locked onto his as she shook her head, and that guilt she knew was coming swept over her like a cruel tidal wave. 'I thought it would happen, Ryan. I really did. You have to believe that. And I *do* love you... I do, but... I'm in love with Jim. I'm in love with him, and I can't change that. No matter how hard I try, and I *have* tried. I have. I really have. I tried so hard to move on, but, I can't. I can't do it.'

Ryan knew this had been coming. He wasn't stupid; he wasn't naïve enough to think that he'd had her forever. But a little more time would have been nice. Because, who knows what could have happened, with a little more time?

'He'll hurt you, Amber. Again, and again. He'll hurt you.'

'No.' Amber shook her head. 'Not this time. No.'

'Are you really that blinkered?'

'Don't make this harder, Ryan.'

'For who? You? What about me, Amber? Huh? What about *me*? You're taking my son away from me...'

'No, Ryan, I'm not. I would never do that. Never.'

'Are you moving back in with him?'

'I don't know. I don't know what's happening now.'

'I guess those plans to move to London have changed, then, huh?'

She looked at him. 'I don't know what's happening, Ryan. Okay?' She leaned back against the wall, pushing a hand through her hair. 'I don't know.'

'You will. You'll move back in with him. One day. And what does that mean, huh? That means *my* son will be brought up by Jim Allen.' Ryan couldn't help but let out a laugh dripping with cynicism. 'And that's going to take some getting used to.'

'I'm sorry, Ryan. Really, I am. I never meant for any of this to happen…'

'What did he promise you this time?'

She stared at him. 'He didn't promise me anything.'

'So, what was it, then? A chance meeting in the corridors of Tynebridge yesterday and all of a sudden you're back together? For the past few months you've done your level best to avoid being anywhere near him, Amber. What the hell changed?'

She turned her head to look back out of the window, watching as Debbie climbed into her pale-pink Range Rover, Gary carefully fastening Jodi into her car seat. They were a family now. A proper family. Why couldn't she have given that a chance?

'What happened after I left yesterday, Amber?'

She slowly turned to face him again, but she said nothing.

'What happened?'

'I didn't plan it, Ryan. I really didn't plan it.'

'Another one of those quick fucks up against his office door, huh? Is that what it was?'

'Ryan, please…'

He walked over to her, his dark-blue eyes never leaving hers. 'So, it's okay for *him* to touch you, is it? It's okay for *him* to fuck you, because you sure as hell didn't want *me* in there.'

'Ryan…'

'Jesus, Amber!' He turned away, pushing both hands through

his hair. 'Knowing it's coming really doesn't make it any easier to deal with.'

'I'm sorry.'

He swung back around to face her. 'And that makes it all okay, does it?'

She shook her head, desperately trying not to cry. What good would that do?

'You never even gave us a chance.'

'And if I had, would that have made this any better? No. All it would have done is make this situation ten times harder to deal with.'

'Oh, so, you think this is the easy way, do you?'

'You're not being fair.'

'Neither are you, Amber. Neither are you.' He walked over to Rico, crouching down in front of his carry-seat, taking his tiny hand in his. 'We made this little guy, you and me. And look at him. He's incredible!' Ryan stood up, walking back over to Amber. 'Without him I really don't know where I'd be now. And *you* did that, Amber. You gave me my reason for changing. You gave me Rico, and for that I am so grateful – so grateful that he's here. Because you alone were never enough.'

Amber turned her head away from him, tears pricking the back of her eyes and she blinked hard to try and stop them from falling. 'Things are different now, Ryan. Between me and Jim. They are so, so different.'

'How?'

She faced him again, not caring that she was crying now. What did it matter any more? 'I can't tell you.'

'He's spouting crap, Amber. Whatever he's told you, he's fucking lying. Because that's what he does.'

'That's not true… This isn't some game…'

'Isn't it? That's exactly what it is. And the last person Jim Allen wants to see win is me.'

Chapter Seven

'Amber, can I have a word?'

Amber looked up from her desk in the Cloud Sports office to see Max standing there. 'Yeah. Sure. Is something wrong? I didn't know you were coming down here today.'

'One of your guests on *Scoreline* tonight is a new player on my books so I'm here to provide a bit of moral support.'

'Is that all?'

He fixed her with a look, smiling slightly. 'Nothing gets past you, does it?'

She turned her attention back to her emails. 'You've heard Jim and I are getting back together, then?'

'It's definite?' He perched himself down on the edge of her desk.

'Well, we haven't sent out a press release or done a five-page spread in *Hello*, but it's on the cards. Yes.'

'And you've told Ryan?'

'You know, I've told Ryan or you wouldn't be here.' She looked up at him again, chewing the end of her pen; a habit she'd never really grown out of. 'Is he okay?'

'He's fine.'

'Really?'

'I'm not in the habit of lying to you, Amber. I've seen a new side to Ryan Fisher since he became a dad.'

Amber sat forward in her chair, the end of the pen still in her mouth. 'We haven't made anything public yet, Max. Me and Jim. We're still playing it very much by ear, but, I think we're gonna be okay this time around.'

Max raised a more-than-cynical eyebrow. 'You think?'

'I know.'

'You seem very sure.'

She sat back in her seat, swinging her jean-clad legs up onto the desk. 'He isn't the man everyone made him out to be.'

'Oh yeah? Care to enlighten me?'

'You're my agent, Max, not my therapist.'

'And that's another reason I'm here. You got time for another photo shoot while you're down in the capital?'

'What kind of photo shoot? I'm not doing *Ice* magazine again. Once was enough.'

'I'll be sure to let them know.'

Amber pulled a face, still chewing on the end of her pen.

'It's another men's magazine, though. And before you start, it's not one of those where they're asking you to get your tits out.'

'Such an eloquent way with words you have there.'

'It's one of the bigger ones. One of the more classy ones.'

It was Amber's turn to raise a surprised eyebrow. 'I've just had a baby, Max, so this had better involve me wearing clothes.'

'Can you do sexy power woman with maybe just a hint of cleavage on show?'

'Are you kidding me here?'

'No, I'm being deadly serious.'

She looked at him, narrowing her eyes slightly.

'They want to do a piece on you and your rise to the top of football broadcasting.'

'I'm at the top of football broadcasting? Nobody told me.'

'Do you ever turn that flippancy level down?'

She sat back up, finally removing the pen from her mouth, throwing Max another look.

'I'll leave it with you, then,' he sighed, standing up and slipping his phone into his top jacket pocket. 'Oh, and Amber?'

'What?'

'Think carefully about what you're doing.'

She knew that sentence was loaded with so many meanings, but she let it go. Of course people were going to question this latest decision of hers to go back to Jim, but did it matter what anyone else really thought? As long as she and Jim were together.

She picked up the pen again and returned it to her mouth, sitting back and staring out around the office she called home at Cloud Sports, grateful it was empty. She was glad of the peace. It wasn't usually so quiet, but this morning had seen something going down at Endleigh United, one of the big London clubs – the club Jim had managed for all those years before he'd made the decision to move up north and take the manager's job at Newcastle Red Star. So most of her colleagues had shot off down there to see what was happening. Amber had preferred to make the most of the peace and catch up with any updates via the Cloud Sports News Channel on the large, flat-screen TV on the wall beside her desk. She was due to do a spot of presenting on Cloud Sports News later that afternoon, in between filming a couple more episodes of *Back of the Net* and preparing for her evening stint on *Scoreline*. Just thinking about the amount of things she had to fit in before she got the chance to switch off and relax almost made her shudder. But at least being busy kept her mind occupied.

'What I wouldn't give to be that pen.'

Her stomach suddenly flipped over and she couldn't help smiling as she heard his voice behind her, felt his hand on her shoulder, his fingers lightly stroking the back of her neck. She quickly stood up, slipping her arms around his waist, unable to stop herself from kissing his mouth, falling against him as though she hadn't seen him in months, instead of just a couple of days ago. 'What are *you* doing down here, handsome?'

'It's a long story.'

Amber frowned. 'Oh yeah? Well, I've got time to listen.' Sort of. She had a little bit of time, but not all that much. And now he was here she wished she had more.

'I've just come from Parkfield.' Parkfield Stadium was the home of Endleigh United. But why had Jim been down there? Shouldn't he have been back in Newcastle, preparing for this weekend's game? 'They've sacked Ken Hollins. My replacement.'

'Yeah, I know who Ken Hollins is, in case you've forgotten what I actually do for a living. So, they've sacked him? I know it's sort of been on the cards for a while now… Is that what all this commotion is down at the stadium this morning?'

'The ground's surrounded by press and fans. Heaven knows how I managed to get in and out without anyone seeing me.'

'Seeing you? Jim… what's going on?'

He sat down on the edge of her desk, pulling her in between his legs, his hands on her hips. 'They want me back.'

Amber's frown deepened. 'Who do?' That was a rhetorical, not to mention stupid, question. Because she knew exactly what the answer was.

'Endleigh United. They want me back in charge.'

'Hang on… you've got a contract with Newcastle Red Star.'

'Contracts can be broken, Amber, and you know that.'

She was confused now. 'And, when… when did all this kick off?'

'Well, you just said yourself Hollins' job has been on the line for a while now. The club hasn't really done all that great since I left…'

'Big yourself up there, why don't you.' She couldn't help smiling, a smile he returned and she felt her stomach dip and dive all over again. She loved this man so much it was ridiculous.

'I got an email a few days ago, kind of giving me a heads-up on what was about to happen, but I didn't want to say anything until I knew for sure what was going on. And then, late last night, I got a call, asking me to come down and talk to them, and… Baby, I know this seems like it's come completely out of the blue, but it couldn't have come at a better time in reality.'

'How do you work that one out?'

'We can make a fresh start down here, Amber, don't you see? You were already thinking about moving away from the north-east anyway, and I hated that idea because I didn't want you to leave me. I didn't want you to be so far away I couldn't… I couldn't see you. But things have changed now, baby. We can make a new start here. Together. And maybe that's just what we need.'

'Whoa, hang on. Slow down there. They've offered you your old job back?'

'More money, more power, a relocation package you wouldn't believe. Honey, this is so perfect. It's almost like fate has thrown this at us and I… I really think we should consider it. Seriously consider it.'

Amber couldn't say anything. All of a sudden this whole situation had just got real, and she didn't know what to do, or what to say.

'Most of your work is down here now, Amber. You're in London far more than you're up north these days, and if I stay at Red Star we're hardly gonna see each other. But if I take the Endleigh United job, and we make London our base…'

'I never wanted to live in London, Jim. Not really. All that talk of moving down here, it was only because I couldn't think of another way to distance myself from a situation I…'

He stood up, pulling her closer, kissing her quickly, but long enough to make Amber's knees go weak. That's how easy it was for him to draw her back under his spell. One kiss. That was all it took. 'A new start, Amber. And don't tell me you don't think we need that.'

'Do they want you straight away?' she asked, running her fingers over his cheek, her eyes watching their every move.

'Pretty much. You know how badly their season's gone so far, and whether I say yes or not, Hollins is out and someone new is coming in, regardless. They can't afford to waste any more time.'

'And when do they need a decision from you?'

'As soon as possible. A couple of days, max.'

She let go of him, suddenly aware that anyone could walk in at any given moment. And the one thing she didn't want was their rekindled relationship announced on the gossip grapevine. 'Ryan won't be happy.'

'What's Ryan got to do with it?'

'He's Rico's dad, Jim. And I promised him I wouldn't take Rico away from him. I promised him that.'

'You aren't taking him away from anyone, Amber.'

'That's not how Ryan'll see it. He thinks any move to London is off now.'

Jim reached out and took her hand, pulling her back against him, and she didn't fight it. Not this time. If anyone saw them, so what? It was all going to come out anyway. Eventually. And if Jim took the Endleigh United job then it was going to come out sooner rather than later.

'Our lives are not gonna revolve around Ryan Fisher, baby. Not any more. It's time to think about what *we* want now. Because we need to make it work this time, Amber. We need that. Because I don't know how many chances we've got left.'

She looked at him, into those beautiful green eyes, her fingers still lightly trailing over his cheek. 'I know,' she whispered. The love she felt for this man was all-consuming; confusing. Unbearable, at times. But she needed him, no matter what. She needed him. And no matter what it took, she'd do it. If it meant they could finally be together.

'What do *you* want to do, Jim?'

'I want to do whatever's best for us, Amber. And if that means taking the Endleigh United job and moving down here, then that's what I'll do. But only if you want that too.'

She felt his fingers slide between hers and she looked down at their joined hands, at his thumb gently rubbing her knuckles. 'I only know I want *you*, Jim.'

He tilted her chin up, kissing her long and slowly, and once more she let herself become lost in him, her body falling against his like that rag doll she always became in his arms.

'You do realise that if it had been anyone other than me who'd just walked in here, you two would be all over Twitter by now.'

Amber broke away from Jim, turning to see Ronnie standing in the doorway.

'I'll leave you to it.' Jim smiled, quickly squeezing her waist.

'Are you going straight back up north?' She didn't want him to go. She really didn't want him to go, not now he was here. She wanted him to stay, at least for one night.

He smiled again, moving his mouth close to her ear, his hand resting on her hip. 'I'll see you at home. Then we can get naked and talk some more.'

She breathed in deeply as she watched him leave, unable to stop her stomach from somersaulting so fast she almost felt dizzy.

Ronnie stood aside to let him through the door. 'They've offered him the job, then?' His tone was matter-of-fact as he threw the newspapers he was holding down on his desk next to Amber's.

'I… that isn't common knowledge, is it? I mean, he's only just left the stadium after talking to them…'

'Chill out, will you? It *isn't* common knowledge. But I'm not stupid enough to think he's come all the way down here on a Thursday just for sex. He's too professional for that.'

Amber threw him a look as she leaned back against her desk. 'People are gonna put two and two together, though, aren't they? If he's seen down here.'

'Probably, yes. His name's already being touted around by the bookies as favourite to be Hollins' replacement so I wouldn't think it'll be too long before the rumour mill is well and truly up and running.'

'He wants us to move down here.'

Ronnie stopped what he was doing and looked at her. 'He's *taking* the job?'

'I don't know. No. I mean, he hasn't come to a decision yet. *We* haven't come to a decision yet.'

'A fresh start, huh?'

Her eyes met Ronnie's, and once again she wondered how different her life would have been if *they'd* stayed a couple. When she thought about it now, those few months they'd been together back when he'd been a player in Manchester and she'd been working as a reporter for New North East, they'd been good. Fun. Uncomplicated. If she'd just let that ride, given that relationship a chance to evolve, could it not have turned into the perfect life she'd been looking for? But she already knew the answer to that. It never would have happened. Because she'd never have left Jim behind. Ryan was right – nobody else had ever stood a chance. 'Would that be such a bad thing?'

Ronnie said nothing, he just kept his eyes locked on hers for a few seconds longer before breaking the stare.

'You still think I'm making a mistake, don't you?'

'I don't know *what* to think any more, Amber. Everything's changing so quickly, and I'm just scared you're getting lost in all the crap he surrounds you with. So much that you can't see the reality.'

'I can see the reality, Ronnie.'

'Can you?' He walked over to her, his hands dug deep in his pockets. 'Twenty-two years, Amber. He's been doing this to you for twenty-two years and you had a chance to let go and move on. To leave him and all his shit behind. You had more than one chance to do that.'

'But I can't, can I? I tried, remember? For almost sixteen years I stayed away from him, avoided him. Did everything I possibly could to make sure our paths never had a chance to cross. And yet, now… now I regret doing that. Because after what he told me…' She stopped talking, turning her head away.

'What did he tell you, Amber? Come on. What was it he told you that's suddenly changed everything and turned you back into that lovesick kid he prefers you to be?'

'Do you know what? I don't need this. And I especially don't need it from you.' She turned to leave, but Ronnie grabbed her wrist, swinging her back around to face him.

'I'm not doing this to be cruel, Amber. Or because I wish it was me instead of him that you just can't leave alone. I'm doing it because I care about you, and because I've been through way too much crap with you, all of it caused by Jim Allen. And every time he does that to you, it kills me. It fucking kills me to see you put yourself through it, time and time again.'

'He won't hurt me any more, Ronnie.'

'Has he promised you that, huh? Has he promised you he won't hurt you again? Has he promised you he won't put you through any more shit? Has he promised you that?'

'He doesn't make me promises. I won't let him.'

Ronnie let out a small laugh, full of nothing but cynicism tinged with scorn. 'Well, there you go, then. And how convenient is that? When it all turns to shit again he can just turn right around and tell you he never made you any promises.'

'You're supposed to be my friend,' she whispered, trying to pull her arm free but his grip on her was firm.

'I *am* your friend, Amber. That's why I'm saying these things. Because I love you too much to see you dragged down again. You've got Rico now…'

She finally pulled her arm free. 'I am tired of people throwing Rico at me as some sort of reason as to why I shouldn't be with Jim. That isn't fair on me, it isn't fair on Rico, and it certainly isn't fair on Jim.'

Ronnie laughed that laugh again, pushing a hand through his hair. 'Jesus, Amber, he really has got you reeled in hook, line and sinker, hasn't he?'

She stared at him, their eyes locked together for what seemed like an eternity. 'For all my life, Ronnie. For all my life.'

*

Ryan flung open the door and let out a heavy sigh.

'And I'm really happy to see you, too,' Ellen said. 'You look like crap, by the way. Baby been keeping you up?'

'He's with his granddad.'

'So why do you look like you haven't slept in days?'

'Because I haven't. What do you want, Ellen?'

'I thought you might like a bit of company.'

He leaned against the doorpost, folding his arms. 'Why would I like some company? I've just spent the best part of a day with a whole lot of people and, to be honest, I'd quite like to chill out on my own now.'

'That's not very sociable, is it?'

'I'm not feeling particularly sociable. And haven't you got a boyfriend who needs your attention?'

'He isn't some puppy I just picked up from the shelter.'

Ryan rolled his eyes and walked back inside. Ellen took this as a sign to follow him, seeing as he hadn't exactly slammed the door in her face.

'I hear Amber and Jim…'

'I don't want to talk about it, Ellen.'

She followed him into the living room, slipping off her coat and throwing it over the back of the sofa. 'If you want *my* opinion…'

He turned around to face her, his eyes dark and determined. 'I don't.'

'You deserve better than Amber Sullivan.'

'I said, I don't want your opinion, Ellen. I really don't care what you or anyone else says or thinks because your opinions mean fuck all to me. Do you understand? Your opinion is pointless.'

'Okay. If that's the way you feel.'

Ryan frowned as he looked at her. 'Why *are* you here, Ellen? I mean, I thought you were all loved-up with Brandon Palmer.'

'Have I ever said that?'

'I kind of got the idea that you were, seeing as every time I see you you're hanging off his arm like some WAG.'

She smiled slightly as she walked over to him. 'That's not very nice, Ryan.'

'I'm really not in the mood, Ellen. Just go home, will you?'

'I wanted to make sure you were alright, that's all.'

'What am I? Some twelve-year-old who's had a row with his best friend? I'm fucking fine, okay? Now, can everyone please get off my back and leave me alone?'

'You're certainly acting like a petulant child,' Ellen said, turning her back on him as she walked away.

Ryan reached out and grabbed her by the waist, swinging her back around to face him, pulling her against him and kissing her so hard and so quickly she almost forgot to breathe. 'Is that what you wanted, huh?' he sneered, keeping a tight grip on her. 'Is that what you came for?'

Ellen didn't struggle to free herself. She stayed right where she was, smiling as she gently stroked his face, letting her fingers run over his chin, which was rough with heavy stubble. 'I care about you, Ryan. More than I've ever cared about anyone. And the way you've been treated by Amber, it's wrong.'

'I loved her, Ellen. I still *do* love her.'

'But you're wasting your time, baby, don't you see? Because she will *never* love you back. Not the same way you love her. She isn't capable of doing that.'

'How do *you* know what she's capable of?'

'Because I see the way she looks at Jim Allen. The way *he* looks at *her*. And anyone else just doesn't matter. They're two selfish people who deserve each other.'

'And what does that make you, huh? I mean, here you are, with me, when you've got a boyfriend at home who has no idea his girlfriend is after another man.'

Ellen laughed quietly, taking a small step back, but not far enough away to be out of his arms. 'Is that what you think? That I'm after you?'

'Aren't you?'

'I think you deserve someone who really cares about you.'

'And that's you, is it?'

'You could do a lot worse.' She moved a little bit closer, sliding a hand around the back of his neck. 'You could do a *lot* worse.'

He pressed his hand harder into the small of her back, pushing her against him, kissing her again, only slower this time. And she responded with the tiniest of moans, her fingers burying themselves in his hair as the kiss became deeper, longer.

'We shouldn't be doing this,' Ryan whispered, even though every inch of him was crying out for something to take his mind off Amber. And if Ellen was quite happy to sleep with him, the way he felt right now he was more than up for it. Or he would be, if he could just get rid of that last, lingering feeling of guilt. What the hell was wrong with him? The old Ryan Fisher wouldn't have hesitated for even a second over this decision. 'We shouldn't…'

She put a finger to his lips, shaking her head. 'We shouldn't, what? Follow our hearts?'

Was he really following his heart? Because this wasn't exactly the direction he wanted it to go in. Not really.

'Come on, Ryan. What happened to that hot, sexy player I used to know? The one who wouldn't think twice about making his move, especially if someone's holding it right there on a plate for him.'

That person felt like a lifetime ago for Ryan. 'Have you got no self-respect?'

Ellen smiled, slipping a hand up under her dress and wriggling out of her knickers. 'Just fuck me, Ryan.'

And who was he to argue?

*

'I really do have to get back to Newcastle,' Jim groaned as Amber slid back into bed beside him. 'But when a beautiful, naked woman is lying right beside me, what am I supposed to do?'

'Have some willpower?'

He laughed, pulling her against him, kissing her slowly. She tasted of mint and toothpaste, and a life he wanted. 'I'm done with willpower. Maybe I want to give reckless and spontaneous a go.'

'You're the least spontaneous person I know, Jim.'

'Yeah, well, times are changing, baby.'

She smiled, closing her eyes as his mouth lowered down onto hers again, and she held onto him tightly because she was truly scared to let him go. All the pain and the hurt of the past year wasn't forgotten; it was still there, and she still felt it all with a fresh reality every time she looked at him. Even now, as they made plans for a brand-new future and the life they'd tried to make together for so long, she still felt that fear that she'd lose him again. She probably always would. She'd just have to learn to fight harder, that was all. To make sure she didn't lose her grip quite so easily this time. To make sure she never gave him a reason to doubt them ever again.

'So, we're gonna do it, then?' he asked, his forehead resting against hers, his thumb lightly stroking her cheek.

She nodded, laying her hand over his, their eyes locking, her stomach turning over and over with a mixture of nerves, fear and excitement. 'Yeah. We're gonna do it.'

He smiled, that wonderful, beautiful smile of his which lit up his face and made her fall in love with him a hundred times over. 'Okay. I'll call Gavin Kilpatrick at Endleigh this morning, and get the ball rolling. Then I'd better go and talk to the board at Newcastle Red Star. It won't be pleasant, but it's gone way past being just about football now. This is what I need to do. What *we* need to do.'

Amber felt her stomach flip over again as the reality of what they were doing hit home for her. This was really happening now. Her life was about to change all over again. But it wouldn't just be her life that was changing; Ryan's was going to change, too. Because, no matter how much Jim tried to tell her she wasn't taking Rico away from him, she was. That was exactly what she was doing. Hundreds of miles would soon separate father and son, instead of the few that kept them apart now. Dropping in at any time to see his baby would cease to be something he could do, and Amber felt that guilt hit her head-on.

'He has no say in this, Amber.' It was almost as if Jim had read her mind.

'Doesn't he? Rico is his son, Jim.'

'And nobody will ever stop him from seeing him. Nobody.'

Amber sighed, turning over onto her back, flinging one arm up above her head. 'Nothing is ever simple, is it?'

'Life would be pretty boring if it was.'

She closed her eyes again, as though blocking out everything she was going to have to deal with would just go away if there was nothing but blackness in front of her.

'You do realise that you're also taking on my child, and not just me, don't you?' she whispered, aware that his fingers were trailing lightly up her legs now, his breath warm on her cheek as he kissed her neck. 'And you do realise that Rico comes first now. I love you, Jim, but you ceased to be the most important man in my life the second I gave birth to that little boy.'

He stopped what he was doing and Amber opened her eyes.

'What's wrong?'

'What was it like? Giving birth, I mean.'

'Painful. Next question.'

'Was Ryan there? Was he with you, when it happened?'

'Only just... look, do we have to talk about this? I don't really want to...'

'Did he see his son come into the world, Amber?'

'Did you see yours? Were you there when Brandon was born?'

'You know I wasn't. And that was a completely different situation. There were no feelings involved, I didn't love his mom...'

'But you love your boy.'

'You're changing the subject, Amber.'

She reached up and gently touched his cheek, stroking his skin, her eyes staring deep into his. 'This has nothing to do with *us*, Jim.'

'You and Ryan, you shared one of the most special experiences two people could ever share. And that kills me, Amber.'

'Do you regret it? Not being there when Brandon was born?'

He took her hand, bringing it up to his mouth and kissing it gently. 'Now I do, yes. Which is why it hurts even more to know Ryan was there with you when Rico arrived.'

'It still couldn't make me love him the way I love you, Jim. Do you understand that? Yes, it was an incredible experience, but I would give up everything I have to have shared that experience with *you*. Not Ryan. Even through the most painful of contractions I wanted *you* there with me. You. Not Rico's dad. I wanted *you*. The first alarm bell rang that night, Jim, drowning out everything else my head was trying to tell me. It rang out loud and clear; even when I was holding Ryan's child in my arms, I wanted *you*.'

'Jesus, Amber, we handled all this so fucking badly.'

'Oh, baby, don't cry. Don't cry...' She leaned over to gently kiss his tears away, tasting the salt, hating the way all the pain and the hurt still refused to go away.

'He could have been *my* baby, if we'd just tried that little bit harder.'

She shook her head, her hand still resting against his cheek. 'Don't go back there, Jim. Please. Don't go raking over the past. What happened, happened. And there isn't a thing we can do to change it. All we can do is try to move forward and deal with all the problems and complications that are going to be thrown at us in the best way we can. And if we love each other, we can do that. We can do that, Jim. Together.'

He threw his head back for a second, and Amber watched as fresh tears fell from his eyes, her heart physically aching as everything he was feeling seemed to flood through into her.

'I love you so much,' she whispered, her voice faltering as she watched him almost fall apart in front of her. She'd never seen him like this before; never seen him so vulnerable, so real. But the pressure of keeping up that controlled and slightly harsh front was quite obviously becoming too much now.

He smiled and she wiped away yet more tears, sliding a hand around the back of his neck, pulling him down for another kiss, opening her legs to let him lie between. She needed to feel him close, to feel him against her before she had to let him go. Before he left her to start making the plans that would change their lives, plans that still scared her, but it was all she wanted now. A new life with the only man she could ever let herself love. And this time she wasn't going to fight it.

'I am so, so sorry, for everything,' Jim whispered, his eyes staring deep into hers, and she gasped quietly as she felt him gently push inside her.

'It doesn't matter,' she breathed, pulling her legs up around him. 'None of it. It doesn't matter.' Maybe that was a little lie. Some of what had happened mattered a great deal, but right now she meant it. Right now it didn't mean a thing. All that mattered was that he was with her, beside her, inside her. He loved her. And how badly had she wanted that only a few months ago? How badly had she wanted that, forever?

Arching her back she moved her hips up against his, wrapping her legs around him as he pushed harder, his hands in the small of her back pushing her up towards him, and she cried out as she felt him touch her so deeply it sent the most incredible shivers coursing through her entire body. For over two decades this man had been her life. Her world. Yet only now did she feel he was truly hers.

Chapter Eight

The freezing north-east wind whipped around Amber's ears and she wished she'd put a hat on. It was December, and the Christmas lights and festive feel filled the city of Newcastle. And she should have been excited. This Christmas she had the baby she'd so badly wanted, and the man she loved beyond anything. Last Christmas she'd had neither. But it wasn't that simple, was it? Her baby belonged to another man, and she was about to tell him that, this time, she really was taking his son hundreds of miles away to another city, to be with the man he'd fought against for so long.

Walking past Fenwicks, one of the oldest and largest department stores in the centre of the city, she stopped to look at the beautiful Christmas window display the store put on every year. Ever since she'd been a little girl she remembered her mum and dad bringing her here, to see what theme the store would be displaying that year – from traditional to fairytale, she'd always loved standing there with her nose pressed up against the glass, staring in awe at the colours and the moving puppets and the sheer magical feel of everything. And now that she had a child of her own she wanted him to experience that, too. But maybe it wouldn't be here, in her native north-east. Maybe he'd experience that elsewhere. And anyway, London was full of this kind of thing. There'd be plenty of places to take him over all the future Christmases she'd have with her son.

'Here. I thought you could do with this.'

She turned to see Ronnie holding out a takeout cup of coffee. 'Thank you.' She smiled, taking a much-needed sip.

'So, it's all going public today, then.'

Amber stared back at the window, concentrating on a Christmas elf, who was banging a wooden hammer up and down on a bright-red brick. 'There's a press conference at 5 o'clock. At Tynebridge.' She looked at Ronnie. 'I should have told him sooner, shouldn't I? Ryan, I mean. I should have told him about this sooner.'

So far only her father and Ronnie knew about Jim's imminent departure from Newcastle Red Star for his old London club, Endleigh United. Her father wasn't exactly over the moon at this sudden turn of events, but he also knew there wasn't much he could do to change Amber's mind. He just wanted her to be happy, when all was said and done. And Jim made her happy. Simple as that.

'Ryan Fisher is still unpredictable, Amber. He's still a loose cannon, no matter how much you think he's changed. If you'd told him this sooner, there was every chance he'd kick off and the secret would have been out way before now.'

'I've been lying to him, though.'

'Think of it as sparing him the truth before he needed to know it. And anyway, you could have just let him hear about it at the same time everyone else was going to hear about it.'

'Oh, yeah, that would work, wouldn't it?' She took another sip of coffee, staring back at the window, her eyes now focused on a mechanical Rudolph chewing on a carrot. 'Maybe if Rico wasn't involved… maybe then I *would* have left it to the press conference to let him know about it.' She threw her head back and sighed. 'Oh, what kind of person does that make me?'

'Come on, Amber. He's just going to have to deal with it, isn't he? And anyway, you're telling him now, aren't you?'

She checked her watch. 'Yeah. I'm telling him now.'

'Come on. I'll drop you at his place.'

She slipped her arm through Ronnie's as they walked away from the crowd that was building outside Fenwicks' window. 'I'm scared, Ronnie.'

'Of what?'

'Of everything. It just feels as though it's all out of my control now. When I think back to the way things used to be...'

He slipped his arm around her shoulder and she clung onto his waist as they walked past the imposing Theatre Royal, the cold wind showing no signs of letting up. 'You're gonna have to stop thinking in the past now, kiddo. Things have moved on. Your life has changed inextricably over the past couple of years and I...' He stopped walking and turned to face her. 'I really want to tell you to stay here, to forget about going with Jim.'

'Jim's only going *because* of me, Ronnie. But we need a new start if we have any chance of making it work this time, and that just isn't going to happen here. It isn't. That's why he's cited conflict of interest in his get-out clause. The whole set-up is so complicated nobody really wants to get involved.'

'So that's why it's all happening so quickly, then.'

'That's why it's all happening so quickly. Jesus, my whole frigging life is so complicated that Newcastle Red Star are quite willing to let the best manager they've ever had go without a fight. I'm probably single-handedly killing this club! The fans are just gonna love me.'

'Okay, okay. Enough of the self-pity. And forget the fans.' Ronnie sighed, sliding his arm back around her shoulders as they continued walking towards his car. 'Maybe it *is* time to start thinking about what *you* want. For a change. And before you say anything, I still don't think Jim Allen is good enough for you.'

'But you are?' She couldn't help smiling as she said that, and Ronnie smiled back, squeezing her shoulders.

'Yeah. Of course I am. Actually, I'm probably way *too* good for you.'

'Cheeky sod,' she laughed, playfully punching his arm.

He stopped as they reached his car, leaning back against it.

'I'm serious, Amber. He really isn't good enough for you. And I'm scared history is gonna repeat itself all over again.'

'It won't.' She stuck her hands in her pockets, burying her chin into her scarf as the wind whipped up once more.

'Because he told you that?' Ronnie arched a sceptical eyebrow.

'Because he told me that,' she repeated. 'Come on. Take me to Ryan's and let's get this over with.'

*

'You think I *knew* about this?' Ryan didn't know what to feel. Everything from anger to upset to a searing pain was clashing together inside him, making his head spin.

'She hasn't told you?'

'Do you think I'd be reacting like this if she'd told me, Max?'

Max sat down on the arm of a nearby chair, pushing a hand through his hair. 'Jesus… I'm sorry, Ryan. I thought you knew. I just wanted to see how you were doing before the press conference makes it all official.'

'It's all happening *today*?' He didn't know what to do. He seriously didn't know what to do.

'Red Star have called a press conference for 5pm, at Tynebridge…'

'I'm going down there,' he said, grabbing his jacket from the back of the couch.

'Hey, hey, calm down. Ryan, calm down!' Max stood up, grabbing his arm. 'You're not going anywhere. Now, I'm sorry you had to hear it like this, but she hasn't exactly been open with me, either. I only heard about it an hour ago.'

'*You're* not the father of her child, Max. A child she is planning to take all the way down to London, away from me, to be brought up by Jim fucking Allen! Jesus Christ, I can't believe this…'

'She was talking about moving down to London anyway, Ryan, so this can't have come as a complete surprise.'

'She didn't say anything about shacking back up with *him*,

93

though, did she?'

'But even *you* said that was on the cards, kiddo.'

'I didn't think… I… They've planned a whole new life together in a matter of weeks, Max. With *my* son!'

'Okay. Okay, I understand how much…'

'You understand nothing. Nothing. I loved her. I loved her so fucking much, and I thought… I thought that when Rico was born… I thought he'd bring us closer.' He was pacing the floor now, pushing a hand through his hair, backwards and forwards in an almost nervous action.

'You always knew he was never going to go away, Ryan.'

He stopped pacing for a second and swung around to look at his agent. 'But maybe I always hoped he would. Somehow. Jesus!' He slammed himself back against the wall, resuming the repetitive motion of raking his hand through his hair, stopping only when the doorbell echoed through from the hall. He looked out of the window, catching sight of Ronnie's burnt-orange 4x4 on the driveway. 'That's her.'

Max held up his hand, a silent order for Ryan to stay exactly where he was. 'I'll get it. And Ryan? Don't blow this, okay? Don't start acting like a petulant kid who thinks the world owes him a living.'

'She's taking my child away, Max.'

'She's doing what she needs to do to be happy. And you're just going to have to deal with that. I'll call you later.'

Ryan watched Max walk out into the hall; he heard the front door open and muffled voices before she finally appeared in the doorway. She looked as though she'd been crying, and her dark-red hair was all mussed up and windswept. She was beautiful, and to look at her broke his heart more than he cared to admit.

'I'm sorry, Ryan. I should have told you sooner. I should have told you before now.'

'Yeah. You should have.'

She looked down for a second, digging her hands deeper into

the pockets of her cream coat. 'It's all happened so fast…'

'No, it hasn't, Amber. It hasn't. Because it never *stopped* happening. You and Jim Allen, you never stopped being together, even when you were apart.'

'You don't know…'

'I know it all, Amber. I know you never really loved me; I know I was always just some kind of buffer between you and him, someone to run to when he was treating you like crap. I know that's all I ever was to you.'

'That's not true.'

He looked at her, her eyes shining with fresh tears, and yet still all he could feel was love. He wanted to hate her for what she was doing, but he couldn't. He couldn't hate her. 'Just admit it, Amber. Please. No more pretending, okay?'

She leaned back against the doorpost, pushing a hand through her hair as she stared up at the ceiling for a couple of beats. 'Why does everything always end up so complicated?'

He wasn't even sure she was directing that question at him. She wasn't really directing it at anyone, she was just thinking out loud, or that's what it seemed like.

'When are you going?' he asked, his voice calmer now. That anger he wanted to feel just wouldn't come.

She wiped her eyes with the back of her hand. 'Jim's last match in charge is New Year's Day. He wanted to finish on a home game.'

'That's big of him.'

Amber threw Ryan a look, telling him his sarcasm wasn't something she appreciated. Tough. He didn't appreciate her taking his son hundreds of miles away, but he wasn't being given much choice in the matter.

'I wanted to leave sooner,' she whispered, her eyes staring down at her black ankle boots.

'That desperate to get away from me, huh?'

Her head shot up and she glared at him. 'Grow up, Ryan.'

'What do you expect, Amber? Did you think I'd be happy for

you? Really? Did you think I'd be jumping for joy at the thought of my son – *my* son – being brought up by a man who has basically taken from me the one person I wanted to spend the rest of my life with?' He walked over to her. His head was all over the place, and that anger he'd wanted to feel earlier was now creeping in, spreading slowly. 'And now he's not only taking *you* away from me, he's taking my son, too. So I can't be happy, okay? I can't do that.'

Her eyes locked onto his, and all that guilt she knew she deserved to feel flooded through her, like someone had just opened a flood-gate somewhere inside her. 'I'm sorry. I'm so sorry. But I can't… I need him, Ryan. I need him.'

'Like shit you do, Amber. You don't need anyone. The Amber Sullivan I first met, where's she gone, huh? Where's *she* gone? Because *she* wouldn't have let herself be dragged down by a man she knows she should have left behind a long time ago. She wouldn't have done that.'

Amber shook her head, taking a deep breath, her eyes still locked on Ryan's. 'But she did, Ryan. Don't you see? That's exactly what she did.'

*

Jim leaned back against his desk and looked around the office he was about to vacate in just a couple of weeks' time. Part of him felt a little sad about that, because he'd come here to Newcastle Red Star, and turned this club around. He'd given them the success they'd craved for decades; he'd helped them become league champions, seen them through several good Cup runs and stints in Europe they could only have dreamed of before. So his decision to leave and go back to Endleigh United wasn't going to be a popular one. He knew that. Only a matter of weeks ago he'd been determined not to let anything get in the way of ensuring this club stayed right where it belonged, at the top of the League. That memory just intensified the guilt he was already feeling at leaving them like this, in the middle of a season in which they were doing well. They were doing really well. And he was leaving them. But he had no choice. He was a different man now. Things had changed; his life had changed. He had Amber back. And if he wanted to keep her; if he wanted to make sure it worked this time, something had to give. And that something was Newcastle Red Star.

Thinking about Amber also made Jim realise that it was going to be his private life under scrutiny at this press conference just as much as his professional one, which made him slightly uncomfortable. Anything to do with his personal life becoming public made him uncomfortable. For years Jim Allen had been a very private man, an enigma, almost. The most anyone knew about him was that he was better at his job than any manager of his generation. But then everything had come out about his past relationship with Amber, about Brandon Palmer being his son – about his marriage ending because Amber was pregnant with Ryan Fisher's baby, even though that had only been part of the problem. And now – now it was going to happen all over again. Today wasn't only about telling the footballing world he was making the trip back down south, it was also about telling the world he was back with the woman he loved. And for once he wanted everyone to know that. He wanted them all to know how much Amber meant to him. He was quite willing to expose himself emotionally if that's what it took to show just how much he loved her. If that's what it took to prove that, this time – this time it was for keeps.

'You okay?'

He looked over towards the door, a smile spreading across his face the second he saw her. 'I am now. Come here, come on.'

She walked over to him, stepping between his legs as his arms circled her waist. 'I just thought I'd pop in and see how you were feeling.'

'I'm fine. Is it busy out there?'

'You could say that, yeah. The place is teeming with press and media, as you'd pretty much expect.'

'And who's covering this exclusive for Cloud Sports, then?'

'Ronnie. He's already got a front-row seat in the Press Lounge, so be nice to him, okay?' She winked, and he laughed, that low, deep, sexy laugh that made Amber's stomach flip over and over.

'And where are *you* going to be?' he asked, his hands sliding down over her bottom.

'I thought I'd just stand at the back and keep my head down.'

'Are they mad at you? The bosses at Cloud Sports, I mean, for not letting on that you already knew about this?'

'Well, I can't say they were happy. I seem to make a habit of harbouring secret stories from the world of football, most of them concerning you.' She shrugged. 'But I walk a fine line between being professional and being personally involved with the people who make these headlines, so, they kind of understand why I had to keep it a secret, why I didn't want Cloud Sports to claim some big exclusive just because I'm your... Jesus, Jim, what *am* I, exactly?'

He stared right into her eyes, and for a few seconds he didn't say anything. 'Marry me. Again. Marry me, Amber.'

She couldn't stop a small laugh from escaping. 'Sorry?'

'Marry me. And let's do it properly this time. Jesus, honey, if I'm gonna make a habit of putting my private life out there, then let's do it in style, okay?'

'Are you serious?'

'Like you wouldn't believe.' Jim laughed, pulling her even closer, his mouth gently brushing over hers. 'Just say you'll marry me, Amber. Please. And this time... this time we'll make it work. Both of us. We'll make it work.'

She smiled, her stomach flipping a ridiculous amount of somersaults as she closed her eyes, letting his kiss take her over, loving the feel of his body pressed hard against hers.

'I want you, right here, right now,' he whispered. But he was telling her something she already knew. She could feel him hard against her thigh and a familiar ache for him spreading through her body.

'You've got a press conference to go to,' she murmured, her mouth moving closer to his.

'And they can't exactly start without me, can they?'

She smiled again, already slipping out of her shirt. 'Well, they *could*, but there wouldn't be much point.'

'Turn around.' His mouth was almost touching her ear as he spoke, and Amber felt that ache grow more intense, her breathing becoming more rapid by the second. 'I won't hurt you, I promise.'

She stared up at him, reaching out to touch his face, her fingers running lightly over his cheek, down over his slightly open mouth. 'Kiss me,' she whispered. 'Just kiss me.'

The electricity between them was almost ricocheting off the walls, and the intensity that had suddenly filled the room seemed to make the heat rise and the temperature almost unbearable, despite it being freezing outside.

And when his mouth touched hers she felt her stomach take a leap so strong her knees literally gave way and he had to hold her up, catch her in his arms, all the while his mouth never leaving hers. His fingers were loosening her jeans, pulling them down slightly, his tongue flicking across the back of her teeth, sending her stomach into yet more spasms.

He pulled away only to gently turn her around, and she leaned forward, her hands palm-down on his desk, knowing exactly what was coming now, the anticipation verging on unbearable. She could hardly breathe; every breath was shallow and ragged as it tried to escape, mingling with the small gasps the touch of his hands on her naked skin were causing. Gripping the edge of his desk she closed her eyes as she felt him pull her jeans down around her ankles, his hands sliding back up her legs to slowly pull down her knickers, and she gasped again, louder this time, desperate for him to take her, to push inside her so hard she'd feel that beautiful pain she so badly wanted to feel. Her whole body was on fire, just waiting for him to come inside her, to give her that relief she needed now. And when she felt his knee nudge her legs further apart, his hands on her hips keeping her still, she bit down on her lip as she waited for the inevitable, crying out quietly as he pushed into her with an almost violent thrust that rocked her forward, causing her to grip the desk even tighter.

But then those thrusts became more gentle, a little slower, and she pushed back against him, wanting him deeper, needing to feel every inch of him. And it was just minutes before his actions grew faster again, his movements in and out of her speeding up, pushing harder, until neither of them could hold on any longer. But the inevitable endgame was every bit as beautiful as she'd wanted it to be, that white-hot pain searing through her as she felt him flood out into her, filling her with everything she needed from him. Everything she'd ever wanted. He was making himself a part of her all over again and she was taking him, and loving him, and keeping him close this time.

She felt his grip on her hips loosen slightly as he slowly pulled out of her, and she stood up, quickly yanking her knickers and jeans back up her legs as she leaned against the desk.

He smiled, and she felt her stomach embark on another round of somersaults. Would it never let up with those acrobatics? Was she going to feel this way about him forever? 'You know, there's a perfectly respectable office down there in the Parkfield Stadium. And I'm sure my desk was bigger there, too, if I remember rightly.'

Slipping her shirt back on, she returned his smile, running her fingers through her hair and shaking it out. She was absolutely positive people were going to be able to tell what she'd been doing in here. She was sure of it. And she didn't care. 'You get off on this, don't you?' She pulled him towards her by his shirt collar. 'Fucking me, in your office. You really get off on it.'

His arm snaked around her waist, his smile widening. 'I could be fucking you anywhere, Amber, and I'd get off on it. Jesus, just thinking about you gives me an instant hard-on.'

'Well, try not to let that happen out there, okay?'

'Can't promise.'

She moved her mouth closer to his as she spoke. 'Try.'

'Still can't promise.'

She was lost in him again, falling into his kiss like the lovesick teenager he was constantly going to make her feel she was. Almost forty years old and still she couldn't stop herself from feeling like that sixteen-year-old kid she'd been when this man had first walked into her life.

The sound of someone clearing their throat made them both jump apart, and Amber looked over toward the door. Max was standing there, arms folded, a look of something bordering on slight amusement on his face.

'You two finished?'

Jim took another step backwards, his hands now in his pockets, his head down as he gave a small laugh. 'Yeah. Yeah, we are.' He raised his eyes slightly, giving Amber a look that only made those stomach somersaults start up all over again. 'I'd better go. I've got a big announcement to make.'

Amber straightened his collar, quickly kissing him before he grabbed his jacket from the back of the couch and slipped it on.

'I'll see you in there?' he asked, turning back around to look at her.

She nodded, folding her arms and smiling at him. 'Yeah. I'll see you in there... Jim?' He turned around again, his eyes fixed on hers. 'You *are* sure about this, aren't you?'

He didn't know whether she was talking about him taking the Endleigh United job, or whether she was talking about them, but either way, he couldn't be more sure about anything. 'I'm sure.' He smiled, and she leaned back against the desk to steady her already weak knees. 'I love you, Amber.'

'Yeah. I love you, too,' she whispered, watching as he left the room.

Max closed the door behind him. 'Well, thanks for making me sit through something bordering on some schmaltzy scene from a Hollywood movie.'

She looked up and poked her tongue out at him.

'Nice. You know, if you took *Ice* magazine up on their second, much more lucrative offer, and did exactly that whilst wearing nothing but your ex-husband's suit jacket you'd make sure they sold so many copies they'd have to order a dozen reprints.'

'I'm going to start ignoring you. I'm almost on the wrong side of forty now, and I've just had a baby. I think my days of doing glamour shoots are over.'

'You've only done the one.'

'Exactly.'

'But you've got a body kids half your age would kill for.'

'So? Does that mean I have to get it out for all and sundry to look at? And why are we talking about this?'

Max walked further into the room, stopping to check out the array of Manager of the Month awards that lined the wall of Jim's office. 'This has shattered Ryan.'

'I can't help that, Max.'

He turned to face her. 'Maybe you should have trusted him. Given him a little more credit. Told him about this before now.'

'Don't lay the guilt trip on me, Max, please. I feel bad enough as it is.'

'Was he okay? When you left him?'

'He seemed fine.'

'*Seemed?*'

'He seemed fine, Max. Okay? What do you want me to say? I can't spend the rest of *my* life worrying about his, I can't do that. Not any more.'

'I know. I know you can't.'

'I care about him, believe me. And what I'm doing, I'm not proud of it. I didn't want any of this to happen. But Jim, he's… he's like some drug I just can't give up. He's a lifelong addiction, Max. And I can't kick it.'

Max looked at her. 'Then Ryan's just going to have to deal with that, isn't he?'

'Yeah. Yeah, he is.'

*

'Have you seen this?' Gary stared up at the huge, oversized TV screen that hung on the wall in his pristine white kitchen. 'What the fuck…?' He looked at Ryan. 'Did you know about this?'

Ryan didn't look at the TV. He just continued to sink mouthful after mouthful of beer from the bottle Gary had just given him. 'I didn't know a fucking thing, mate. Not until a couple of hours ago.'

'Jesus…' Gary looked at the TV again, turning the volume up so he could hear Jim Allen as he spoke.

'Does that have to be so loud?' Debbie stopped in her tracks as she joined them in the kitchen, her eyes automatically going to the screen. 'Has he just said he's leaving Newcastle Red Star?'

'Shut up, Debbie, will you? I'm trying to listen.'

'What about Amber?'

'What about her? Can you just zip it for a second, huh? Just let me listen.'

Debbie sat down at the breakfast bar that separated the functional part of the kitchen from the family room area. Not that any area of Debbie's kitchen was particularly functional. She very rarely cooked anything that needed more than a quick re-heat, so it was little wonder that every one of her many expensive appliances were still sparkling and brand new.

'When the fuck did *this* all kick off?' Gary sat back down, taking a big swig from his own bottle of lager. 'And who told *you*?' He directed that question at Ryan, who was still refusing to look up.

'Max. Well, he didn't tell me, as such, he mentioned it and… Look, does it matter who told me?'

'So, it wasn't Amber who told you?' Debbie asked.

Ryan finally looked up, his eyes meeting Debbie's. 'No. It wasn't Amber who told me. And before you start giving me the Spanish Inquisition, yes, I've spoken to her, and no, everything isn't fine.'

'That's why you're round here, then, is it?' Gary took another swig of lager, smirking slightly at Ryan, who ignored him.

'Do you want me to go?'

'That's not what I said, mate.'

'She never said anything to me…' Debbie's voice trailed off as she fished her mobile phone out of her pocket.

'Well, it would seem she didn't say much to anyone,' Ryan sniffed. 'And I wouldn't bother trying to call her. She'll be in there.' He cocked his head toward the TV, where questions were now being fired left, right and centre at Jim Allen.

Debbie put her phone down and sat back on her stool, looking over at Ryan. 'I can't believe this. I'm assuming, because of the state of you, that Amber's going with him?'

'Why else do you think he's leaving, Debbie?' Gary got up to fetch two more bottles of lager from the imposing double fridge at the back of the room.

'Okay. Don't start on *me*.' She looked back over at Ryan. 'I thought you would've been glad to see the back of Jim Allen.'

He threw her an almost withering look. 'Yeah, and I would have been, if he hadn't been taking my girlfriend and son with him.'

Debbie bit down on her lip, scrunching up her nose. 'Oh. Sorry. I didn't think…'

Gary put the beers back and shut the fridge door. 'Look, instead of hanging round here looking at your miserable face, let's go out. Have a few drinks in town.'

'Is that a good idea?' Debbie nudged her head in the direction of Ryan, trying to keep her voice low.

'I am *here* y'know.' There was a slightly irritated tone to Ryan's voice now.

'He'll be fine. You're a big boy now, aren't you, mate?' Gary winked, grabbing his phone from the countertop. 'You just need to get out, have some fun. Take your mind off everything. It'll be just like old times.'

'It better not be,' Debbie muttered, slipping down from her

stool and picking up the pile of ironed baby clothes that were lying on the breakfast bar. 'And try not to make too much noise when you come back in, Gary, okay? Because, if you wake Jodi, I don't care how much you've had to drink, you're the one that'll be settling her back down.'

Gary ran over to Debbie and picked her up in his arms, swinging her round before putting her back down and kissing her quickly. 'I won't be late, and I won't be drunk.'

'Yeah.' Debbie threw him a sideways smile, retrieving the baby clothes she'd dropped when he'd picked her up. 'And where have I heard *that* one before?'

*

Amber stood at the back of the room, her hands in the pockets of her skinny jeans, her eyes never leaving Jim as he spoke, his expression sincere, his voice steady as he spoke of how much Newcastle Red Star meant to him, not only as a manager, but as a player, too.

A wave of guilt stabbed her chest and she briefly looked down at the floor. If it wasn't for her, he wouldn't be going anywhere. If it wasn't for her, this club wouldn't be losing the best manager they'd ever had – the best manager the game had seen in a long, long time.

She briefly closed her eyes, silently scolding herself for giving in to another bout of self-pity because she didn't deserve that luxury. She'd helped cause this mess. She'd done that.

Looking over at Jim again she felt her stomach contract as his eyes locked onto hers, and he smiled – at *her*. A smile that may have been brief but it was meant only for her, she knew that. It was a smile that was trying to tell her it was all going to be okay, because that's what Jim Allen did. He told her how things would be.

He broke the stare and turned his attention back to the room, but that smile he'd aimed directly at her hadn't gone unnoticed by a few of the more eagle-eyed journalists and reporters in the room, some of whom had now turned around to look at her, which made her feel more than a little uncomfortable. She still wasn't a fan of being anywhere near the limelight. She may be what they classed as a minor celebrity now; a famous face in the world of sports presenting. And she may have appeared on more than a handful of magazine covers and done photo shoots that had caused more than a few eyebrows to be raised, but sometimes she felt as though someone else entirely had done all of those things, because it was still hard for her to get her head around everything that had happened to her. But being the centre of attention, having people interested in every move she made, having them write about her personal life and ask questions that nobody but those closest to her should ask, that still wasn't something Amber could get used to. Nor did she want to.

'You okay?' Max asked, sidling up next to her.

She nodded, staring out a particular journalist she was familiar with; a hack who'd twisted stories about her and Jim on more than one occasion to make them sound more sordid or interesting than they really had been. 'I'm fine.'

'You didn't have to come in here, if you didn't want to.'

'I wanted to be with Jim.' She turned her head to look at Max. 'I wanted to make sure he told them what he'd told me. I wanted to make sure he was really leaving; that's how bad things have got, Max. I actually need to hear him say the words, to hear them for myself as he tells the football world he's leaving here. To start a new life. With me. I needed to hear him say those words to someone other than just me. That's the only way I can believe him; believe that he means it. That's how paranoid and obsessive I've become.'

Max reached out to quickly squeeze her hand. 'You know this isn't the end of it, though, don't you? This is just the beginning of the questions and the speculation about you and Jim, you and Ryan... This isn't the end, Amber.'

'I know,' she whispered. 'I know that.'

'And I'll be there, sweetheart. Every step of the way. I'll be there to help in any way I can. To make this easier, for all of you.'

She couldn't help smiling at him, squeezing his hand back. 'I knew I'd made you Rico's godfather for a reason.'

Max grinned at her. 'Yeah. It means I get to him first when he becomes one of the most famous footballers this country has ever seen.'

Amber laughed quietly, shaking her head. 'As long as he's got his daddy's talent, and not his mother's ability to fuck up everything.'

Max gave her fingers one more squeeze before letting go of her hand. 'You'll get through this, Amber. You're a Sullivan. You'll get through this.'

Once upon a time she would have believed that. But now she wasn't quite so sure.

Chapter Nine

'Jesus, Ryan, slow down, mate. Debbie's gonna kill me if I take you back home wasted.'

'You my babysitter now?'

'Do you need one?'

'Fuck off.'

'Yeah. Really good to see the old Ryan back. I'm going to the bar. And if you want another one, you can get it yourself. I'm not being responsible for you getting into a state. Those days are frigging over.'

'Good to know who my real friends are.'

Gary turned around and leaned over the table, his face close to Ryan's as he spoke. '*I'm* a real friend, Ryan. I was there when you were throwing your life down the fucking toilet, remember? I was there when you were lying in the gutter because you were too frigging pissed to even stand up, or off your fucking head on coke. I was there when you were so fucking low you didn't think you'd ever drag yourself back up; when you were *this* fucking close to losing everything, *I* was there. Me. Your real fucking friend. *I* was there, Ryan. But if that's what you want to go back to, you're on your own this time, you got that? Because I refuse to go there again. I refuse to watch you piss it all away because you still can't fucking deal with something you should have learnt to deal with a long time ago.'

Ryan watched as Gary walked back over to the bar. But even after listening to those words and after seeing the look on his best friend's face, all he wanted to do was get so drunk he didn't know what time of day it was. He wanted to forget he was losing the only things that mattered to him, and he couldn't do that by being mature and dealing with it, because he couldn't deal with it. He couldn't. Not yet. He didn't want to.

'On your own tonight, Ryan?'

He turned his head to see an extremely pretty dark-haired girl sit herself down beside him. 'Not any more.' He knew her face, and he vaguely recognised her. He knew he'd probably fucked her once or twice at some point during his time with Newcastle Red Star, but that only meant she was one of many, and he never had been all that great at remembering names.

She smiled, sidling up closer to him. 'So, you looking for some company tonight?'

'You offering?'

'Well, you're a free man now, aren't you?'

He frowned slightly, not quite drunk enough yet to have lost the ability to focus as he looked at his pretty companion.

'Your ex-girlfriend,' she explained, her perfectly manicured, baby-pink fingernails trailing lightly over his tattooed forearm. 'She's gone back to her husband, hasn't she? I saw the press conference earlier this evening on the local news. He's taking some other manager's job down south, and she's going with him.'

Hearing someone else say those words out loud was like a dagger to Ryan's heart, the pain almost physical. 'They're divorced. He isn't her husband.'

'Yeah, but, they're getting married again. He said so, at the press conference.'

Ryan's frown deepened. 'Sorry?'

She rolled her eyes, her fingernails still running slowly up and down his arm, not that he was noticing. All he cared about was clarifying what she'd just told him.

'Your ex-girlfriend, Amber Sullivan, or whatever she calls herself these days, and Jim Allen. They're getting married again. That's what he said.'

Ryan reached for his drink, draining the last of his pint. Now he needed something stronger that would take the pain away for a lot longer than just a few hours. Something that would wipe away everything he'd just been told and let him believe it was all okay. He needed that. Again. He needed that. Everything he thought he'd left behind, he wanted it back.

'You up for a good time?' He gently removed her hand from his arm and slid his fingers between hers, his eyes asking her another, silent question he hoped she understood.

She smiled slowly, and he felt a strange kind of relief surge through him. An excitement he hadn't felt in a long time. 'As good a time as you like,' she drawled, leaning forward so her mouth was almost touching his. 'You call the shots, Ryan. Whatever you want, whatever you need, I can get it. You know that.'

He smiled, too, reaching into his pocket for his phone. 'I'll call The Goldman. Let them know we're on our way.'

She grabbed her bag and stood up, wiggling her hips as she pulled the already-too-short hem of her barely-there dress down over her thighs. 'I'll make a couple of calls myself. Make sure we've got everything we need.'

'You're an angel.' He gave her the full-on Fisher smile, feeling a sense of freedom he hadn't felt in so long. It was almost exhila-rating, as though someone had just opened the cell he'd been locked inside for too many years, and now he was free to do whatever the hell he liked. 'I'll meet you in the lobby.'

'I won't be long.' She blew him a kiss, and he watched as she sashayed over to the bar, throwing his head back and letting out a laugh that was almost maniacal.

'What's up with you?' Gary asked, his eyes narrowing in suspi-cion as Ryan stood up, slipping his jacket back on and pushing both hands through his hair.

'Nothing, mate. Absolutely nothing is up with me.'

'Where you going?'

Ryan looked at his friend. A friend he knew cared about him. And he'd never forget how instrumental Gary and Debbie had been in making sure he hadn't gone too far down a road that had almost ruined him, but he could handle all of that now. He didn't need looking after, not any more. 'I'm going to enjoy myself, Gary. That's where I'm going.'

'Ryan…'

He swung around to face Gary. 'I can look after myself, Gary, okay? I don't need you or anyone else hanging over me, waiting for me to do something stupid, I don't need that. I don't. I can look after myself.'

'You sure about that?'

Ryan said nothing for a couple of beats, his eyes boring into Gary's as a brief but fleeting moment of doubt flashed through his mind. But then he remembered what he'd just been told – Amber and Jim were getting married. Again. And the only sound he could hear was the hammering of that final nail into the coffin of a relationship he knew he could never have now. It was over. And he couldn't deal with that right now. Not sober. Not clear-headed. 'I'm sure.'

*

'Did we do the right thing? Announcing our engagement during that press conference?' Amber wrapped her arms around Jim's waist from behind as he slid his tie off, throwing it over the back of the chair.

'We're doing this properly, Amber. No more secrets, no more lies. No more pretending.'

She rested her head against his shoulder, closing her eyes as his fingers slid between hers. 'No more pretending…' she whispered,

111

trailing off as he slowly turned her around, his mouth meeting hers in a kiss so gentle it was hard to believe he was the same man who'd caused her so much heartache for most of her life. Any sane woman would have walked away decades ago. But she obviously wasn't sane. And she could never walk away. She'd tried, and she'd tried hard, but she couldn't do it. She couldn't walk away.

'No more pretending.' He smiled, and she felt her heart dance that dance reserved only for him as his handsome face lit up and those eyes she'd found so hard to trust for so long were conveying nothing but honesty. Truth. Something she'd found so difficult to get from him. Dare she believe that, this time, everything really was going to be okay?

'I love you so much, Jim.'

'I love you, too, baby. You have no idea…' She closed her eyes as his lips touched hers again, and she buried her fingers in his hair, pushed her body against his as the kiss deepened, the intensity growing by the second. But then, for some reason she just couldn't fathom, she pulled away.

'You okay?' Jim frowned, watching as she walked away, into the en suite.

'I guess all of this, the press conference, me and you…' She turned to look at him as he leaned against the doorpost. 'It's a lot to take in, Jim. The speed at which it's all happened…'

'Do you want to slow things down?' He'd smiled as he'd asked that, and she couldn't help but return that smile, leaning back against the sink as she brushed her teeth.

'No,' she replied, through a mouthful of toothpaste.

'Okay…' He walked into the bathroom, his hands in his pockets as he stood in front of her. 'So, what's up?'

'Nothing's up, Jim.' She turned briefly to spit toothpaste into the sink, quickly wiping her mouth with a tissue before turning back to face him. And she couldn't stop another slow smile from escaping. 'It's strange, that's all.'

'What is?' He reached out to tuck a strand of hair behind her ear, his eyes locked onto hers.

'Feeling like I can finally trust you.'

'That's strange?'

'Yeah, that's strange.'

He moved a step closer, and all she was aware of now was the smell of his cologne and the warmth of his body as it almost touched hers. 'Well, I guess we've both got a few new things we need to get used to.' His voice was low, practically a whisper, and she felt her breath catch in her throat as he moved even closer, his hand on her hip now, resting gently on the thin material of her short nightdress.

'I guess we have,' she murmured, her fingers gripping the sink behind her as his body finally touched hers, his hand sliding up and under that nightdress, making her gasp as it came into contact with her skin.

'All I've ever wanted is this, Amber.' His hand was moving higher now, cupping her bottom as he kissed her neck, covering it in tiny, tiny kisses, each one making her gasp out loud, again and again, until she could stand it no longer.

Slipping her hand around the back of his neck she pushed his head down so their lips met, at the same time pulling herself up onto the edge of the sink, opening her legs to let him in between, wrapping them around him the second he was there. He held onto her tightly, keeping her steady as he tried to manoeuvre inside her, and he was there within seconds, one hand on her bottom the other in the small of her back as he pulled her forward slightly, pushing her further onto him.

Amber couldn't stop the cries from escaping as her legs gripped him tighter, her hands behind her as she leaned back slightly, trying to avoid the taps digging in because she wanted nothing to detract from what was happening. It was a little uncomfortable, but he was inside her so she didn't care that her bottom was numb or that her arms ached with the effort of keeping herself steady. All she cared about was that feeling of complete calm he was giving her. That was all that mattered.

His hands had moved now, sliding further up under her night-dress, his thumbs flicking over her nipples, sending her crazy, and she bit down on her lip as he stripped her naked before lowering his head to kiss her breasts.

She could feel it now, the almost burning sensation that began at the tips of her toes and travelled slowly up her body, creating that white-hot pain, that beautiful rush she couldn't get enough of. She could feel it already beginning its journey and even though it was far sooner than she would have liked, she gave into it, pushing her hips against him, taking him deeper as she leaned back further, screaming out his name as he came fast and hard, his fingers digging into her as his body tensed up, his face buried in her shoulder; until he'd given her all he had to give. Until he was spent.

'Jesus, Jim…'

He pulled back slightly as he slowly withdrew, shaking his head, smiling as he sank to his haunches and Amber gripped the edges of the sink even tighter. She knew what was coming next, her eyes closing as his mouth touched her, and she bit down on her lip again, flinching just a touch as his tongue flicked over the most sensitive part of her body, causing her to moan out loud. She could feel those tingles returning, coming back to give her another wave of intense pleasure and she closed her eyes, her head thrown right back as his hands pushed her legs further apart, his tongue probing deeper, pushing harder, until she had no option left but to give in, to let it happen, her cries echoing around the white-tiled bathroom, her whole body shuddering with the most exquisite shivers, despite the fact she was probably the most uncomfortable she'd ever been during sex.

She kept her eyes closed as those tingles slowly subsided and the shivers wore off, until she was left with nothing but the most beautiful feeling of calm.

'You okay?'

She opened her eyes and smiled at him as he gently lifted her down, his arm staying firmly around her waist. 'Oh, I'm just fine.'

He returned her smile, and she felt those stomach flips and those erratic heart beats and every other cliché in the book take over as he looked at her. She was sixteen all over again, in the arms of her handsome footballer, her first love; her world. She was sixteen all over again.

'We're really doing this, aren't we?' she whispered, stroking his cheek with her fingertips.

He nodded, kissing her slowly, pulling her back inside that web she'd never quite managed to fully escape from. 'We're really doing this.'

She stared up into his eyes, cocking her head slightly. For so long, this man had been her life, and for a brief second or two she wondered what it could have been like if she'd tried harder to give others a chance and if she'd really tried to push him to the back of her mind in the way she should have done. Could she have made herself forget him? Could she have saved herself years – decades – of pain and heartache? Could she have stopped hating him for being the man she thought he was, when he didn't really seem to be that man at all?

'I love you, Amber.'

She blinked rapidly as his voice broke into her thoughts, his eyes staring deep into hers. 'I know you do.'

'Do you? Baby, do you really believe that now, because...'

She put her fingers to his lips, shaking her head. 'I'm not going to do anything that could mean I lose you again. I'm not going to do that. Because I love you, too, okay? I love you so much I can't even think straight some days. And the thought of you...' She looked down, watching as his hand caught hers, holding it tightly against his chest. 'It's just going to take time, that's all.' She raised her head slowly until her eyes once more met his. 'Everything you kept from me, all the things you did when... when there was no need, Jim. We could have been together all those years ago if you'd just talked to me.'

She had no idea why all this was spilling out of her now, but suddenly she felt almost angry that so many years had been wasted. Years they could have spent together. Years in which they could have been happy instead of all the fighting and the anger and the hurt. All that pain could have been avoided.

'You should have just talked to me.'

He looked down briefly, watching as his thumb gently stroked her knuckles. 'We can't change the past, Amber.'

'And I can't help feeling cheated out of a life I could have had.'

'We can have that life now, baby. I'm sorry for what I did, and I'm sorry for what I didn't do. I am so, so sorry. But that life we could have had, we can have it all now, and I will do everything I can to make it up to you. I promise.'

She shook her head again, looking away. 'No promises, Jim. I still don't want promises.'

She pulled away from him, picking her nightdress up off the floor and slipping it back on before she walked out into the bedroom.

'Amber…'

'I'm tired, Jim. It's been a long day.'

She sat down on the edge of the bed. She couldn't get the image of Ryan out of her head now, the expression on his face when she'd walked in the door, and it pulled at her heart. It made her sad because he didn't deserve this. He didn't deserve any of it. And she understood how upset and angry he was feeling at the thought of being so far away from Rico, because she knew *she* just couldn't do it. She couldn't be away from her baby for days on end with no idea of when she'd be able to see him again. Ryan loved Rico more than even he realised, she could see it whenever she saw the two of them together. That baby boy had changed him, but was what she was about to do going to undo all of that?

'This is why we need to get away from here,' Jim said quietly, sitting down beside her.

She turned her head to look at him, but she didn't say anything. She didn't need to. She knew what he meant.

'He's a constant distraction, to both of us.'

'He isn't a distraction…'

'He is, Amber. Honey, he is. As long as we stay here he is always gonna be there, messing with your head…'

'He doesn't mess with my head, Jim.'

'That's *all* he does, Amber.'

'And you never did that? You never messed with my head?'

'I just want us to be able to have a chance this time. That's all I want.'

She looked at him. 'And you don't think that's all *I* want, too? But I can't just wipe the past away, Jim. Too much has happened. Ryan and I have a child together now. And that guarantees that he will never really be out of my life, no matter how far away from here we are.'

'You having second thoughts?'

She stared at him, taking in his handsome face, that strong jawline, that stubble he always seemed to carry that was greying slightly now as he got older, but that only seemed to make him all the more sexy in her eyes. 'No, baby, of course not. Like I said, I'm just going to need time, that's all.'

He slipped his hand into hers and she leaned in against him, closing her eyes as she breathed him in. The only man she'd ever wanted. The only man she'd ever really loved. The only man she wanted to be with. And she couldn't allow anything else to come between them, not now. Not ever.

Chapter Ten

Jim stood on the touchline, his hands in the pockets of his track-suit bottoms as he stared straight ahead of him, out onto the training pitch, where every player except Ryan Fisher was busy training hard for the forthcoming matches taking place over the Christmas period. One of those games would be Jim's final game in charge of Newcastle Red Star before he and Amber made the move down to London.

'Colin!' He shouted over to his tough-talking Scottish head coach. Jim's hands remained in his pockets, his eyes still focused on the training pitch. 'As soon as Fisher gets here send him up to my office, okay?'

'No word from him this morning, then?' Colin asked, kicking a stray ball back onto the pitch.

Jim shook his head. 'Is Blandford here?'

'Over there.' Colin indicated one of the goals, where Gary was practising defending free kicks. 'Do you want a word?'

'Get him over here.'

'Blandford!' Colin yelled. Gary stopped what he was doing and turned around, his hands on his hips as he squinted at Colin. 'Over here, now! The boss wants a word!'

Gary jogged over to the touchline, stopping just in front of Jim, whose stance hadn't changed. He still had his hands in his pockets, his expression stoic. 'Something up, boss?'

'Where's Fisher?'

Gary let out a small laugh. 'How the hell should *I* know? I'm not his frigging babysitter.'

Jim's eyes narrowed as he stared at his defender. 'You live across the street from him. You're best friends. He talks to you.'

'Does he?'

Jim raised an eyebrow. 'Where is he?'

Gary rolled his eyes and sighed, folding his arms. 'We went out last night, okay?'

'Out?'

'Yeah. He…' Gary stopped mid-sentence, not sure he should be telling Jim any of this. Despite Ryan being a total pain in the arse at times, a sense of loyalty to his friend would always be there.

'He, what? Come on, Gary. He's late for training, nobody's heard from him all morning, and now you're telling me you were out with him last night. Out where, exactly?'

'Is that really important?'

'If he's fucking about again, then yes, it's important.'

Gary let out another sigh. 'He didn't take it too well. Hearing about you and Amber…' He stopped talking, still not sure he should be saying any of this, but Jim just fixed him with a look, raising that eyebrow again. 'He didn't take it too well, okay? So, I thought I'd take him out, take his mind off it. But…'

'But what, Gary?'

'Jesus… He pissed me off, okay? He started being an idiot…'

'An idiot?'

'Yeah. An idiot. Knocking back the drinks, mouthing off…'

'And you didn't think to stop him?'

'Like I said, boss, I'm not his frigging babysitter. He's old enough to look after himself.'

'You'd think, wouldn't you?' Jim sighed, throwing his head back. 'And what state was he in when you got him home?'

Gary looked down at the ground, stabbing the pitch with his

football boots. 'I left him to it.'

'You what?'

Gary looked up, his voice tinged with more than a hint of agitation now. 'I can't be there all the time, boss. I can't be with him twenty-four hours a day. If he can't handle real life then that isn't my fault.'

'Do you know where he went?'

Gary shook his head, looking down at the ground again. 'He was with some woman. I don't know who she was, I just saw him leave with her. My guess is they were going to The Goldman.'

'Jesus fucking Christ,' Jim sighed. 'Okay, Gary, thanks. Go on, get back out there.'

'Everything okay?' Colin asked, walking back over to Jim.

'It appears Fisher may have briefly reverted to his old ways.'

'Really? Do we have a problem here?'

Jim sighed heavily again, finally removing a hand from his pocket and pushing it through his hair. 'Just send him up to my office the second he gets here.'

'You got it.'

Slipping his aviator shades on to shield his eyes from the low winter sun, Jim made his way back over to the administration block, checking his phone as he walked, smiling as he read a message sent just seconds ago from Amber. She was on her way to London to record a *Back of the Net* Christmas special and cover the weekend's main matches in the Cloud Sports studio. Jim was just glad Newcastle's televised Sunday game was down south, at one of the big north London clubs. It would be his penultimate game in charge of the north-east side that was in his blood, both as a player and a manager. But leaving was the only thing he could do now, the only option left to him if he wanted Amber.

He'd no sooner arrived in his office when Colin called him from the training pitch to tell him Ryan Fisher had finally turned up and was on his way to see him. Jim leaned back against his desk, folding his arms against him as he waited, deliberately leaving the door ajar slightly so he could see Ryan arrive.

'Get in here,' he said the second he saw his young and temperamental striker approach his office. 'And close the door behind you.'

'What've I done now?' Ryan asked, not flinching in the slightest at the look Jim threw him. 'I mean, shouldn't I be down there getting some training in? We're leaving for London in a couple of hours, aren't we?'

'We are, Ryan. Whether *you* are is another matter entirely, though.'

Ryan frowned, and immediately wished he hadn't because even that small action hurt like hell. He should have taken a stronger painkiller before he'd left the house because this hangover was a killer.

'Look, do you want me down there training? Or are you just gonna waste more frigging time pulling me up here for no reason.'

Jim stayed silent for a few seconds. All of a sudden the old Ryan, the one who knew no boundaries and cared about little other than his own selfish feelings was standing there in front of him. 'I wanted you in training an hour and a half ago, Ryan. I wanted you down there with every other player who gives a fuck about this club...'

'Like you, you mean?'

Jim's eyes hardened as he stared at Ryan. But he ignored the comment. A reaction was exactly what Ryan wanted; Jim could see that, it was written all over his face. 'But instead you choose to walk in here almost two hours late, looking like crap, stinking of booze, and talking to me in a way I don't appreciate.'

'And maybe *I* don't appreciate you taking my son hundreds of miles away from me.'

Again, Jim fixed him with a look that said he wasn't doing this, he wasn't giving him what he wanted, not here. But Ryan was in no mood to hold back.

'I stayed out last night because I needed to forget, just for a few hours, that my life is fucking falling apart, and it's falling apart, again, because of *you*. And her. And the fact that all you two do is play with the emotions of every other poor fucking idiot who dares go anywhere near either of you. That's what you do, do you know that? You, and her… you…'

'You don't talk about Amber like that, do you hear me?'

Ryan couldn't help but let out a low, cynical laugh. 'She tore my fucking heart out; she killed me, that's what she did. That's what she's *doing*. And that's why I walk in here almost two hours late, looking like crap. *That's* why this shit is happening, all over again.'

'You're not my problem any more, Ryan.' Jim's voice was quieter now, calmer. Controlled. Because what he was saying was the truth. Once he walked out of this club in just over a week's time, Ryan Fisher would be somebody else's problem. 'You do whatever you need to do, okay? You throw your life away, you kill it for no reason other than you aren't man enough to grow up and deal with things. You do that. You do whatever you need to do because you will cease to be my problem.'

Ryan looked at Jim, a man who'd taken it all, and would continue to do so for the rest of his life. But he'd come prepared. He might look like crap and feel even worse, but last night hadn't just been a time to forget everything that was going on, it had also been a time to focus and think about what he had to do to make it right. And there was really only one thing he *could* do.

'Go and tidy yourself up in the dressing room, go on. Grab a shower, wake yourself up, and get out there for whatever's left of this training session.' Jim had walked back behind his desk, already busying himself with jobs he had to do before they left for their journey down south.

'You're taking my child away,' Ryan said quietly, everything suddenly falling into place so simply he couldn't believe he hadn't thought of it earlier.

Jim slowly turned around, his expression telling Ryan he was rapidly tiring of this conversation. 'Nobody is taking anyone away, Ryan. Now, will you just go. Please.'

'I don't want my son living hundreds of miles away. I don't want that. I want to be close to him, and if he's down there and I'm still up north...'

Jim looked at him, a feeling of uneasiness creeping up from somewhere deep inside.

'But I don't have to stay up north, do I?' Ryan went on, his eyes locked upon Jim's. 'Because, the second that transfer window opens in January, I'm putting in a request. I'm moving, Jim. I want to be where my son is, and there isn't a fucking thing you can do to stop me.'

*

'This is ridiculous,' Amber gasped as she stood in the large and open, round hallway of the new north London home she and Jim had been given by Endleigh United. 'What the hell do we need with all this space? I mean, we've got a perfectly decent home not all that far from here.'

'They've *given* you this?' Ronnie asked, turning a full three hundred and sixty degrees on his heels as he took it all in.

'Apparently so,' Amber sighed. 'Part of the relocation package they've used to woo Jim back down here.'

'You don't like it, then?'

'I didn't say that, Ronnie. I just think it's... it's a bit ostentatious. I mean, it's very nice, I can't deny that. The décor's good, but then it should be, seeing as they've just had it all redone and new flooring put down and... this isn't me, Ronnie.'

'Why not?' He sat down near the bottom of the long, winding staircase that led up to the first of three floors. 'Jim's in the big league now, sweetheart. He's one of this country's – if not one of the world's – most sought-after managers. People would kill to have him in charge of their club – you know that. So of course Endleigh United are gonna throw everything they can at him to get him back. And they can afford it. This is nothing to them.'

Amber sat down next to him, resting her head on his shoulder. 'Why can't I just let myself be happy instead of feeling guilty all the time?'

Ronnie tilted her head up so she was looking straight at him. 'What are you feeling guilty about? Oh, don't tell me. Ryan.'

'I can't help it, Ronnie. Here's me with this brand-new life ahead of me, moving into an incredible new home with a man I am so crazy-in-love with I can't even begin to explain; I've got my beautiful baby boy and a job I absolutely adore. I have it all, Ronnie. I have everything I have ever dreamed of. My life is so close to perfect it actually scares me. And I'm leaving Ryan on his own. I'm taking his son and I'm leaving him…'

'Okay, that's enough, do you hear me?'

Amber looked at him, blinking in surprise at his rather harsh change of tone.

'Enough of the whinging and the moaning and the feeling sorry for yourself, alright? Enough. The self-pity doesn't suit you, and I'm sick of having to listen to the same old thing, over and over again. You have put your life on hold for Ryan Fisher – for both of them, Amber – way too many times, and it stops, now. It stops. Ryan is a grown-up, although, to be fair, at times it might seem like otherwise, but he is quite capable of dealing with this. He just has to grow up. And as for Jim…' Ronnie looked at Amber, whose expression was still one of surprise. 'Don't let him change you, Amber. Don't do that – don't let him change you. Please.'

'Ronnie, I…'

'Be the Amber Sullivan I used to know. I need her back, I really do, because I've stood and I've watched you change from the person you used to be – every time one of them hurts you or gets to you or makes you fall in love with them so hard you lose yourself. You lose yourself, Amber. And I can't stand around and watch that happen any more.'

'Jesus, Ronnie… I had no idea…'

'That I felt that way? That I care about you?' He stood up, pacing the tiled hallway, running his hands backwards and forwards through his hair.

'No, I… I know you care about me, I know that, I just…' She frowned, looking down at her clasped hands. 'Is that what happens to me?' She raised her head to meet his eyes.

He crouched down in front of her, taking both her hands in his. 'Look, kiddo, I know I haven't been the biggest fan of either Ryan or Jim, and that's probably confused you rather than helped you, and for that I'm sorry. I'm sorry, baby, I really, truly am. I'm sorry. But now it's time to put all of that behind you. It's time to move on, and if Jim makes you happy…' He looked down at their joined hands, pausing for a beat or two. 'I know he makes you happy. I'd be lying if I said I couldn't see that. So, love him, by all means, Amber. You love him with every inch of your heart, but… just don't lose who you are, okay? Bring Amber Sullivan back. Please. Bring her back.'

She felt stupid, unexpected tears start to prick the back of her eyes and she had to look away for a second. Suddenly the air was filled with an intensity she just hadn't been expecting.

'I need a drink,' she said, pulling herself up off the stairs.

Ronnie followed her into the huge and airy kitchen with its floor-to-ceiling windows and skylights that flooded the room with winter sunshine. 'I didn't mean to upset you, Amber. That was the last thing I wanted to do.'

'I'm not upset,' she sniffed, tearing off a piece of kitchen roll and blowing her nose.

'You sound upset.'

She swung around, wiping her eyes with the back of her hand. 'I'm fine. I'm just tired of it all, you know? Tired of all the emotion, it's so bloody exhausting! I'm missing my baby, I'm going crazy without Jim, and I just want it all to be okay, Ronnie. I just want it all to be okay. But it isn't, is it? It isn't all okay.'

He walked over to her, pulling her against him, hugging her tightly, rubbing her back gently. 'Just let it happen, Amber. Please.

Stop thinking about it, stop analysing everything to within an inch of its life; stop worrying about things you don't need to worry about any more. It's a new start, you said so yourself. A chance for you and Jim to finally work everything out and make a go of it. A proper go of it.'

She pulled away from him, walking over to the French doors, folding her arms against her as she stared out at a garden so huge she couldn't even see where it ended. 'Rico is going to love this place.'

'He's going to love this garden, no doubt about that,' Ronnie said, joining her as she continued to stare outside.

'Am I being selfish, Ronnie?'

'Selfish?'

She turned to look at him, her arms still folded tightly across her chest. 'I'm doing all of this because I need to be with Jim. I'm moving away from the north-east, away from my dad and a part of the country I vowed never to leave, no matter what job I was doing. And I'm doing all of that because *I* need to be with Jim. But is that what's best for Rico?'

'Do I have to go over this again, Amber? Rico is four months old, sweetheart. He's a baby so he doesn't know what's going on. And by the time he's old enough to do that, the life he'll have will be the life he's used to.'

'I don't want him to lose his dad, Ronnie.'

'And that isn't going to happen. You know it isn't.'

She looked back out of the window. 'It's all so complicated.'

'Not really. You think you're the only people bringing up kids this way?'

'I'm probably going to have to get a nanny now, too. Now that my dad and my family aren't just around the corner. And I vowed I'd never have a nanny.'

'Things never really turn out the way you plan.'

She turned to face him again, smiling slightly. 'No. I don't suppose they do.'

'You should be grateful that you can finally be with the one person you love more than anything.' His eyes bored into hers and she pulled her folded arms tighter against her chest. 'You should be grateful for that, Amber. Because, for some of us, we just know that isn't ever going to happen.'

Chapter Eleven

'You busy?'

Amber looked up from her laptop, her smile becoming instant and wide as she saw Jim standing there in the doorway, leaning against it in a way that made Amber certain he was the most incredibly sexy man she'd ever laid eyes on. And he was hers. He was finally hers. No more false starts.

'Not any more.'

'Good.' He walked slowly over to her, his hands in the pockets of his jeans, and it was only then that it struck Amber how much more casually he'd started dressing lately. Sure, the well-cut suits and expensive shirts were still a staple on match days for him. That was the kind of manager he was. That was the image he projected. But at the training ground he'd started to show up in tracksuits, or shorts and a football shirt, and out of work she'd seen him wear a lot more jeans, t-shirts and boots. It was almost as if, since getting everything off his chest, a weight had been lifted from him and he was finally allowing the man he really was to come through and show himself. A more relaxed, a more approachable, Jim Allen. 'Because I've got something for you.'

She swung around on her chair, sliding her pen into her mouth as she crossed her legs, her eyes meeting his. 'I know I'm the only one here at the minute, handsome, but anyone could come back in at any time.'

He laughed that low, sexy-as-hell laugh and she felt a delicious shiver course right through her that made it hard for her to catch her breath for a second or two. 'As much as I would like nothing better…' He pulled her up out of her chair and into his arms, stroking her cheek with his thumb as he continued to stare into her eyes, 'than to slide my hand up under that dress you're wearing, slip those panties down and pull you astride me, I really think it'd be best if we left that until we get home, don't you agree?'

Amber swallowed hard, her knees suddenly feeling so weak she thought her legs might actually give way. 'Yeah,' she breathed, but it was taking every ounce of strength she had left not to do it anyway. Her mind had been quite focused on nothing but that evening's stint she was due to do in the Cloud Sports studio later, until he'd walked in. Her beautiful, handsome all-American fantasy. Now all she wanted to do was get naked and have lots of dirty sex with the man she wanted to marry so badly it was almost like a physical pain. 'Actually, no. I don't agree. *I* think we should go straight to the bathroom and fuck so hard I won't be able to walk for the rest of the day, because you have no business coming in here and distracting me with that sexy laugh and those beautiful eyes. You have no business, Mr. Allen.'

His stare intensified, and she swore she could feel her thighs burning up as he pulled her just that little bit closer. Oh, God, she wanted him to kiss her so badly – *so* badly. And she didn't even care if anyone saw them. She was past that point now. He was the drug she couldn't kick, that fix she needed, and she needed it right now, before she could even think about carrying on.

'You want to do that?' he asked, raising an eyebrow, an action that only made Amber's knees even weaker.

'You have no idea how much I want to do that,' she groaned, pushing herself against him as his hand gently rubbed her lower back. 'But I suppose I'd better be a good girl and wait.'

'As long as you're a very, very *bad* girl when you get home tonight,' Jim whispered, his mouth almost touching hers as he spoke.

'That's it,' she sighed, throwing her head back as she gently pushed him away. 'I can't do this any more. Get away from me before I do something I'll enjoy way too much.'

He smiled that heartbreakingly beautiful smile of his, sitting himself down on the edge of her desk as Amber quickly tried to compose herself before any of her colleagues came back into the large, open-plan office she'd spent most of the day in at the Cloud Sports complex.

'Anyway, you said you had something for me.' She ran her fingers through her hair, shaking it out before leaning back against the wall, resting one stiletto-heeled boot up against it to steady herself.

'I've got something for you, yeah.' He stood up, slowly walking over to her, and a part of her wished he wouldn't do that. If he got too close again she really would be tempted to drag him off to the nearest rest room and do the dirty in the first free cubicle. 'This is what I've got for you.' He took her left hand, reached into his pocket and pulled out a white-gold, yellow-diamond solitaire, slipping it slowly onto her third finger. 'I was going to wait until tonight, when you were naked and wet and lying underneath me… but I kind of want you to be wearing this when you're live on air tonight. I don't know, call me slightly possessive here, but I want everyone to know once and for all that you're mine. That we're together. That I'm head-over-heels, crazy-in-love with you and we are getting married, baby. We are getting married!'

She closed her eyes and gave in to his kiss, almost collapsing in his arms as his mouth moved against hers gently and slowly, her fingers burying themselves in his hair. She wanted to stay there all evening now. She wanted to stay in his arms, kissing him and holding him and knowing that it was all going to end in hot and heavy sex. She wanted that. She wanted him.

'We are getting married,' she whispered, resting her mouth against his, smiling, because he made her do that now. He made her smile. Gone were the days when he made her wary and confused; the days when she couldn't trust him and needed him gone. Now he just made her smile.

'I love you, Amber Sullivan.'

'Oh, God, I love you, too… you have no idea,' she gasped, biting down on her lip as his hand slid just a touch up under her dress, briefly stroking her thigh before pulling away. 'I love, love, love you, too!'

He kissed her again, another long, slow kiss that caused her stomach to flip, her head to spin, and her body to melt against him. But she knew if she didn't stop this soon she'd be nowhere near ready for live TV. So no matter how little she felt like doing it now, she had to leave him alone and switch back to being the sports reporter she had to be tonight.

'Everything okay with the squad?' she asked, changing the subject as she gently pushed him away again, going back over to her desk.

Jim looked at her, frowning slightly. 'Why wouldn't it be?'

'Well,' she began, turning around and leaning back against her desk. 'You have precisely three games left in charge of Newcastle Red Star, so, I just wondered if that's unsettling anyone.'

By anyone, did she mean Ryan?

'No. It isn't. Everyone's focused on the job in hand. The fact the club have a replacement ready to take over as soon as I leave is a bonus. It means it won't be too long before they're all used to a new manager.'

'He's not as proven a manager as you are, though, is he? I mean, Dave French has a great reputation, but he hasn't won any titles or any silverware for any of the clubs he's been in charge of before.'

Jim shrugged. He didn't really feel much like talking about this right now. 'He's a good manager. And he's bringing some great backroom staff with him.'

'Just as well, seeing as you're bringing all of yours with you to Endleigh.'

Jim watched her as she buzzed around the office, checking over papers, her pretty face bent over her running order, her mind now focused on her work, and he still marvelled at the way she could do that – switch from being the sexiest woman alive to the most professional presenter he'd ever seen in an instant. It was a huge turn-on.

'Colin's my right-hand man, Amber. I need him.'

She looked up from her papers and smiled. 'Yeah. I know you do.'

He really didn't want to tell her what Ryan had told him yesterday. Part of him hoped he was only calling his bluff, but Jim wasn't naïve enough to think that was the case any more. Rico was very real, and Ryan loved that baby, even Jim could see that. If Rico didn't exist then, yes, maybe Ryan could be accused of playing mind games. But not this time. This time Jim knew he was serious. And he knew he couldn't really keep it from Amber. She worked within the world of football. Her job meant that she was going to be one of the first to hear about Ryan's intended transfer request, and he needed her to hear it from him, not through information sent to her via email.

'Amber?'

She looked up again. 'Yeah?'

'Ryan's going to put in a transfer request.'

Her eyes lowered back down to the papers she was holding, as though she'd just dismissed what he'd told her as nothing important.

'Baby, did you hear what I said?'

She nodded, carefully laying the papers down on her desk. 'He wants to move down here.' It wasn't a question, because it didn't have to be. She already knew the answer.

'He wants to be closer to Rico, yes.'

She looked up, her eyes meeting his. 'Then what is the point of us doing all of this, Jim? If he's just going to follow us down here, then what is the point of us leaving the north-east?'

'Come here.'

She let him pull her between his legs as he stayed sitting on the edge of her desk.

'There is *every* point, Amber. This is still a brand-new start for us…'

'I want to get married in Vegas.'

He looked at her, completely taken aback by what she'd just said. 'You… want to get married in *Vegas*?'

'I don't want a big celebrity wedding, Jim. I don't want any of that; the whole idea fills me with utter dread. I don't want to be under the spotlight on a day that is supposed to be about you and me. And I know you said you wanted to do it properly this time but that isn't doing it properly, not really.'

'Okay…'

'So, let's go to Vegas. You've got a few days off between your last game at Red Star and your first with Endleigh, so, let's go to Vegas. And let's get married. Let's have a day that's just about you and me before we have to start dealing with any more crap, because I need that, Jim. I really need that.'

That totally unexpected outburst had taken him completely by surprise, but the more he thought about it, the more he realised she was probably right. Some time alone, just the two of them, would be good. Because they weren't going to get all that much of it once he took over the reins at Endleigh United. 'Then we're going to Vegas, baby!'

She laughed, and it was a sound that made Jim realise he just couldn't lose this woman, not again. He wasn't strong enough. Ryan Fisher may have once more moved the goalposts, but Jim had every intention of putting them right back where they belonged.

*

'Are you out of your fucking mind?' Max stared at Ryan as though he'd just told him the most ridiculous thing ever. Which he had, in Max's eyes.

'You want me to stay at Newcastle Red Star? Hundreds of miles away from my son? Is that what you want?'

'I want you to have a career, Ryan, that's what I want. Something which you seem intent on fucking up – again.'

Ryan stared at his agent through narrowed eyes.

'Oh, don't give me that innocent look, son. I know. I know you had "one of those nights." I know you turned up late to training looking like you hadn't slept, which you probably hadn't, because you were up all night playing blackjack and fucking random women in one of The Goldman's more expensive suites, flashing cash around like it was going out of fashion. Are we revisiting those old days, Ryan? Hmm? Are we?'

Ryan couldn't say anything. He felt like he'd just been reprimanded by a particularly irate head teacher. 'Jesus, Max, you might take a percentage of my earnings but it doesn't give you the right to talk to me like I'm twelve years old.'

'Then stop acting like it. Grow the fuck up, Ryan, and get back to acting like an adult. You were well on your way to actually doing that, so let's not have another relapse, okay?'

'It was one night, Max.'

'And one night leads to another. That's how it all started before…'

'I'm not going there again, alright? It was one night.'

Max raised an eyebrow, but said nothing.

Ryan sighed, pushing a hand through his hair. 'I'm still putting in a transfer request.'

'You're crazy. You are a superstar in the north-east, Ryan, a local hero. Your future is sorted with Newcastle Red Star. And I can completely understand why you feel you need to be…'

'There must be at least one of the big London clubs interested.'

'Oh, I have no doubt that quite a few of them would probably pay a ridiculous amount of money to bring you back down south, but I don't think you should be going anywhere. And besides, you're still under contract until the summer. Look, if you really want to move why not wait until the end of the season? You can just walk out of Red Star and into any other club you want, because they'll be standing there waiting with open arms, I can guarantee that.'

'I don't want to wait, Max. I can't hang on until the summer, I can't.'

Max sighed. 'You really don't make my life easy. You're settled in Newcastle, Ryan. You have a life there, why uproot it all and start all over again? Because I'm not stupid. I know you want to be close to Rico, I get that. But is he the only reason you want to move?'

Ryan sat down on one of the oversized black suede couches that graced the bar of the hotel the team were staying at. 'She's his mum, Max. She comes with him whether I want that or not.'

'And? *Do* you want it?'

Ryan looked at Max, an expression of total bewilderment on his face. 'What the hell are you talking about? I've just told you…'

'You still in love with her?'

'No.' A lie.

'Then deal with the fact she's bringing your child down here, know that she isn't taking him away from you…'

'I can't deal with Jim Allen bringing him up, Max. I can't deal with that.'

Max sat down on the coffee table opposite Ryan, clasping his hands between his knees. 'You're going to have to, kiddo. Whether you like it or not.'

Ryan sat forward, copying Max's stance. 'Y'know, you can sit there and lecture me all night about how nothing's really going to change and how Amber won't ever let Rico forget I'm his dad and any other crap you want to tell me, but it doesn't matter. If I stay up north, I lose a certain amount of control, and I'm not willing to do that. So, as my agent, I'm asking you, Max, to put the word out and find out who's interested in Ryan Fisher. You got that?'

'You're playing this all wrong, Ryan.'

'It's the only way I know *how* to play it, Max. So just put the word out, okay? Please.'

Max sighed again, getting up and shoving his hands in the pockets of his immaculately cut suit trousers. 'Get to bed early, alright? If you're putting yourself in that transfer shop window then you're gonna need to show everyone out there you're worth the money they should be paying for you.'

Ryan threw himself back against the couch cushions as he watched Max head out of the bar. Checking the time, he saw it was only eight-thirty, but it wasn't like he could go anywhere. Jim Allen had them all on hotel lock-down the night before a game, and it wouldn't be long before he'd have Colin trawling the place to make sure they were all safely ensconced in their rooms, getting their heads down ready for the match tomorrow.

Sighing heavily he pulled himself up off the couch and headed upstairs to his room. What else was there to do? He might as well try and chill out, watch a movie or something. Anything was better than sitting in a bar full of people he didn't feel much like talking to, staring at alcohol he couldn't drink.

Once in his room he switched on the TV, kicking off his boots before throwing himself down on the bed, flicking through the channels until he arrived at Cloud Sports. And there she was, sitting on that familiar cobalt-blue couch in the *Scoreline* studio, dressed in a ridiculously sexy, knee-length, figure-hugging yellow dress and black, skyscraper-heeled ankle boots, those crazily long legs of hers crossed as she talked to Dave French, the man who was about to become his new boss once Jim Allen left Newcastle Red Star. He watched as she absentmindedly flicked that dark-red hair of hers back behind her shoulder, smiling at her interviewee, and Ryan felt a stabbing in his heart he was fast getting used to. Once again that urge to lose himself in a haze of alcohol and other substances crept over him, because it would never really go away, but he could control it now. He had to. Sure, he'd had that one night of reliving the bad old days, but even then he'd managed to keep it in check; he hadn't taken it as far as he could have done, as he would have done in days gone by. But in days gone by he hadn't had Rico. He hadn't had a reason to be sober and in control. And now he did. So, although he felt like breaking every pre-match rule Jim Allen imposed, he'd suck it up and stay strong. For his boy. But it was hard, because Rico's beautiful mum was looking down the camera now, those pale-blue eyes of hers staring into his as she spoke about Newcastle Red Star's forthcoming televised game, leaning forward slightly over her still-crossed legs, the pen she was holding hanging loosely from her fingers – fingers that had touched him and held his hand and taken away all sorts of pain that he had to deal with alone now.

He closed his eyes and remembered the day Rico had been born. He'd been at the training ground, knowing Amber had been about to go into labour any day and he'd thought he'd been prepared. But getting that call, hearing she was already at the hospital and being told that Rico wasn't hanging around had made him realise just how unprepared he really had been. He'd driven like a maniac, and it had only been luck that he hadn't been pulled over. He'd have done anything to make sure he didn't miss seeing his child come into the world. And he'd only just made it. When he'd got there Amber was already pushing, her face tired but oh so beautiful. At that moment Ryan had never seen her look so beautiful. She'd been sitting up on the bed, wearing a bright-pink t-shirt, and the first thing she'd done when she'd seen him was hold out her hand, her eyes begging him to take it. And he'd held onto it; he'd held onto *her* as she'd pushed their baby boy into the world – the most incredible experience of his life. And he'd only just managed to be there to see it happen.

A sharp rap at the door pulled him back from his thoughts, and he sighed, keeping his eyes closed. 'I'm not in the mood for company, Gary.'

'Then it's just as well I'm not Gary, isn't it?'

His eyes shot open and he sat upright, pushing both hands through his hair as he got up off the bed. He walked over to the door and opened it slightly. 'You're playing a dangerous game, aren't you? Hanging around here when you're – allegedly – living with the boss' son.'

Ellen pushed past him into the room, closing the door quietly behind her. 'As far as I'm aware, Jim Allen isn't even here. He's at home, with his fiancée.' She turned to look at Ryan, flinging her jacket over the back of the chair next to the bed. 'Isn't he?'

Ryan shoved his hands in his pockets. 'What are you doing here?'

'I really can't be bothered to play hard to get, Ryan. I want you, you're a free man now, so I might as well lay all my cards on the table and see where they fall.'

Ryan frowned. 'And what does *that* mean, exactly?'

She walked over to him, playing with the collar of his shirt. 'It means, if you want me, Ryan, I'm here. I'm all yours. Do what you want with me because…' She moved her mouth closer to his, 'I'm willing to try anything.'

He pushed her away, but only with a touch. 'You're with somebody, Ellen.'

She couldn't help laughing. 'And when has *that* bothered you?'

'I'm a different man now, sweetheart.'

'Oh, really?' She folded her arms as she noticed his gaze wander back to the TV. On-screen, Amber was busily wrapping up that evening's edition of *Scoreline*, smiling down the camera as she said *goodbye*. That had been the hardest word Ryan had ever had to hear from her, and he felt his stomach dip as he knew she'd be leaving that studio and going back home to Jim. She'd be sleeping in his arms; he'd make love to her and hold her, and tell her everything Ryan still wished he could tell her but he swallowed it back, and turned to face Ellen again.

'You shouldn't be here,' he said, his eyes focusing on anything but her.

'The boss isn't around, Ryan, in case you hadn't realised.'

'Colin's twice as bad for making sure we stick to the rules.'

'You're just throwing excuses around now.'

Maybe she was right. She was there. Right there in front of him, offering him a chance to forget, to lose himself in something that would, for a short time anyway, numb the pain and stop him from thinking about things that were only confusing him. She could be the brief escape he needed right now.

She moved closer again, gently stroking his face with her fingertips. 'Look, I won't tell if you won't, okay? It can be our little secret.'

He was ceasing to care now. This might be wrong, and the guilt would probably hit him head-on in the morning, but he needed the distraction.

'I never have agreed with this no-sex-before-a-match rubbish anyway,' she whispered, slowly sliding the belt out of his jeans. 'I mean, does it really matter?'

He couldn't help smiling as he slipped an arm around her waist, pulling her against him. 'No. It really doesn't matter.'

She returned his smile, sliding her hands inside his shirt. 'Well, let's start breaking some rules, then, shall we?'

And he wasn't really in the mood for arguing.

*

Amber threw her bag down onto the table in the small and cosy hallway of the semi-detached house she and Jim had bought in north London just after she'd landed the job at Cloud Sports. The house they were now selling, because they had a new London home, thanks to Endleigh United's generosity. A new home they'd be moving into very soon. But she liked this one. She liked the fact it was small and compact and felt cosy and comfortable. This house felt like a home. She wasn't altogether sure that new one could ever feel that way.

Giving out a small sigh, she turned to look at her reflection in the mirror over the hall table. She looked tired, but it had been a long day and tomorrow wasn't looking as though it was going to be any shorter. She was in the Cloud Sports studios all day again, covering two out of the three live matches the network was featuring, and even though it was what she loved doing, her mind was on so many other things that she was finding it exhausting trying to concentrate at the minute. Christmas was just around the corner, Jim's last match with Newcastle Red Star was less than a fortnight away, and then there was Vegas. She looked in the mirror again and smiled at that last thought. Las Vegas. She'd had no idea where that had come from, or why she'd suddenly decided that a Vegas wedding was what she wanted; she'd just known that she didn't want a big, extravagant event where all eyes were on them. She really didn't want that.

She could hear the shower upstairs and she smiled again, running her fingers through her long, loose curls before making her way up to the bedroom.

Jim was out of the shower when she got there, with just a towel wrapped low around his strong, toned hips. 'Hey.' He smiled at her, and she felt her stomach contract in that wonderful, warm and fuzzy way it always did when he smiled that way. Especially when he was dressed in next to nothing.

'Hey yourself.' She slowly slipped her dress down over her shoulders, wiggling her hips until it fell to the floor, kicking it away with the heel of her ankle boot, leaving her in nothing but fuchsia-pink underwear.

Jim whistled as he looked her up and down, watching as she unhooked her bra, tossing it aside.

'I need sex like you wouldn't believe,' she sighed, backing up against the wall, running her hands slowly over her breasts.

'Tough day?' He couldn't take his eyes off her as she stroked those perfect breasts, his body responding in the only way it could.

'You could say that,' she breathed, her fingers buried in her hair now, her arms raised above her head.

He moved closer, reaching out to touch her waist, moving his hand down to her hip, sliding his fingers into the side of her knickers. Her breathing was heavier now, and he watched as her breasts rose and fell quicker, his body aching to be inside her. It had been aching to be there all day, ever since he'd seen her earlier at the Cloud Sports complex. It was an ache that never left him. A constant ache that needed to be eased.

She closed her eyes as he slowly slid her knickers down and she stepped out of them, opening her legs slightly to give him permission to do whatever he wanted. It didn't matter what, she'd take anything. She just needed to be satisfied, and however that satisfaction came, she didn't care. She just needed that fix, the shot that calmed her down and made everything feel better.

Reaching out to pull the towel from around his waist she gasped as he slipped a hand between her legs, touching her briefly, but long enough to see how ready she was for him. And when his mouth finally met hers, she let herself fall, let herself tumble deeper and faster into his world, because that's where she wanted to be. Where she *needed* to be.

He lifted her up and she wrapped her legs around those strong hips of his, clinging onto him as he took her slowly, sinking into her so gently it was the most perfect feeling. She could feel her entire body relaxing as he pushed deeper, filling her with that wonderful calm only he could give her, that feeling of peace, that dose of something beautiful that only came from him.

He truly was her world, and she should have realised that sooner, not allowed him to waste so much time. But she had him now. He was hers, she was his, and nothing would ever come between them again. She was going to begin the new year married to this man, and this time she was going to make sure it stayed that way.

Chapter Twelve

'Do you think he enjoyed his first Christmas?' Amber smiled at her dad as he took Rico from her, laying him gently over his shoulder.

'I think he had the best first Christmas any baby could have wished for,' Freddie said, rubbing his grandson's back in slow, circular movements. 'What about you?'

Amber sat down on the arm of one of the bright-red couches in the Players' Lounge at Tynebridge. 'It was good. We got through it.'

Freddie looked at her, raising an eyebrow.

Amber returned the look. 'At least there was no niggling, no getting at each other. And I couldn't deny Ryan the right to be with his son on Christmas Day, could I?'

'No, sweetheart. You couldn't.'

It hadn't been the easiest of Christmas Days, but with Newcastle Red Star's Boxing Day match being a home game at least it meant they could all spend it in the north-east, and Amber had been truly grateful for that. Having both Ryan and Jim together in the same house for all those hours hadn't been something she'd looked forward to, but having her dad and her family around her took a lot of the pressure off. By and large Jim and Ryan had stayed away from each other, and the day had passed without any kind of unease or tension, although she'd breathed the biggest sigh of relief when they'd both headed off for the team's afternoon training session. For once she'd been glad to have the better part of her Christmas Day given over to Boxing Day match preparations.

'Are you sure you're doing the right thing?' Freddie asked, his voice pulling Amber back to reality.

'Hmm? Sorry, Dad, I was just thinking… Am I sure about what?'

Freddie Sullivan raised that questioning eyebrow again, and Amber briefly looked down at her clasped hands.

'We're leaving straight after the match today,' she said, smiling as she watched Rico pull at Freddie's hair, gurgling away to himself, completely unaware of the complications going on all around him. 'Because this is Jim's last game in charge of Newcastle Red Star, we kind of want to get away as soon as possible. Avoid all the media interest. And once we get to Vegas, we'll be getting married as soon as we possibly can, and almost immediately after that we come back home – to London – so Jim can prepare for his first match in charge of Endleigh United on Sunday. It's happening, Dad. This is real. So, yes, I'm sure.'

'And this is the way you really want to get married? In secret? Again?'

'At least I've told *you* this time.'

'That's something, I suppose. And you really don't think any media will get hold of what's happening? All eyes are on Jim at the minute, you know that.'

'There's no secret we're taking a few days away before he starts back at Endleigh. We just haven't mentioned where.'

Freddie moved Rico from his shoulder and nestled him in the crook of his arm. 'Well, you know I've still got my reservations about Jim. About the kind of man he is.'

'He's changed, Dad. Believe me, he's changed.'

'And if he hadn't? Would you still be with him?'

Amber looked down again, watching her fingers as they fiddled with the strap of her watch. Of course she'd still be with him. She'd have fought tooth and nail to get him back, she had no doubt in her mind about that. As much as she'd tried to believe she could love anyone else, she was only ever going to be in love with Jim Allen. End of story.

'I'll take that as a yes,' Freddie sighed. 'Amber, sweetheart…'

'No, Dad. No more lectures, okay? I know what I'm doing and don't you dare raise that eyebrow again, do you hear me? Get to know him again, Dad, please. I know things are gradually getting better between the two of you, but, you used to be such good friends…'

'He slept with my teenage daughter.'

'And she's thirty-nine now. The age difference isn't even an issue any more, so, can we just try and get back to normal?'

Freddie kissed his grandson's tiny forehead, and Amber watched as Rico slowly closed his eyes, snuggling into his granddad.

'Yeah, well, if he doesn't look after you this time…'

'He will. I promise you, Dad, he will…'

Freddie just looked at her, picking up Rico's baby bag. 'I'm taking this one up to the box. You watching the game with me or are you down with Jim?'

Amber wasn't covering Jim's final match with Newcastle Red Star. Ronnie was doing the honours for Cloud Sports that afternoon. She was now officially on holiday for a few days.

'I'm watching the match from the dugout. But if you need me I'll have my phone with me.'

'We'll be fine, won't we, kiddo?' Freddie smiled at a now-sleeping Rico, and Amber felt her heart ache at the thought of leaving her baby behind, even if it was only for the shortest time. Throughout the entire Christmas period she'd been splitting her time between the north-east and her work in London, but she'd had Rico with her constantly, which had been hard, but she'd wanted to know she could do it. She didn't want a nanny, she was adamant about that now. She wanted to bring her baby up herself. But she also wanted to work, and Cloud Sports had been incredibly helpful in making sure she could do that. She was lucky. Very, very lucky.

Amber stood up, leaning over to kiss her son's warm cheek,

smiling at his bunched-up fists and his slightly open mouth and his cuter-than-cute Newcastle Red Star t-shirt.

'You okay?' Freddie asked, looking right into his daughter's eyes, his voice softer now. Because no matter what he thought about the decisions Amber might be making, he only wanted her to be happy.

'I'm fine.' She smiled, folding her arms against her. 'Go on. Go get settled.'

She watched him leave, although it took him a while to get out of the Players' Lounge because everyone wanted to take a look at her beautiful baby boy, and who could blame them? He was utterly gorgeous. Amber had a feeling he was going to take after his daddy in that department.

'I hope you're not having an Elvis wedding.'

Amber swung around and smiled at Debbie, one of the few people who knew where she and Jim were going straight after this match, and what they were doing once they got there.

'No. But I *am* making him dress up as a cowboy, and I thought I'd do the whole Wild West prostitute thing.'

Debbie just looked at her, her false eyelashes blinking furiously as she tried to work out whether Amber was being serious or not.

'I've got a gorgeous little dress and heels and Jim's going to wear suit pants and a shirt. Nobody's getting dressed up in anything.'

Debbie put a hand to her chest and let out a heavy sigh of relief. 'Thank Christ for that! I know you say Jim's loosened up slightly since you guys got back together but even *I* doubted he'd loosened up *that* much.'

Amber threw her friend a sideways smile as she leaned back against the wall.

'I'm still annoyed, though.'

'And why's that?' Amber asked, quickly checking her watch. She wanted a few minutes alone with Jim before kick-off. And there wasn't long left.

'This is the second time you're marrying this man and both times you've given me nothing I can put in my column.'

'No, and you'd better not sneak anything in there whilst I'm away, either. I want this to stay as much a secret as possible. Until we get back, anyway. Then you can put anything you like in your column.' She threw Debbie another smile. 'Within reason, obviously. I mean, I'm sure nobody wants to know about the wild, Vegas sex I plan to have with my new husband once I'm over there.'

'Too much information, missy. And, actually, you'd be surprised how many people *would* want to know about that. Can I have a photo?'

'What? Of Jim and I having wild, Vegas sex?'

'Jesus… no! Although, on second thoughts, that *would* sell copies, and my editor would love me… You're not being serious, are you?'

Amber just raised an eyebrow.

Debbie stuck her tongue out. 'I don't know why I'm friends with you sometimes.'

Amber smiled again. 'You love me really.'

'I'll love you more if I can be the first to have a wedding photo.'

'You can be the first to have a wedding photo, yes. I promise. Although I wouldn't be expecting anything fantastic. We're going to a wedding chapel in Las Vegas at some ridiculous time of the night so Christ knows who'll be taking the pictures.'

Debbie smiled a huge smile, mouthing '*thank you*' as she fluffed up her baby-blonde hair with her perfectly manicured fingers. 'I still don't understand why you don't want the whole big celebrity thing. There are magazines out there that would pay a fortune to feature your wedding.'

'I've never wanted that, Debbie. You know I haven't.'

'I loved all that fuss when Gary and I got married,' she sighed. 'It was an amazing day… Anyway, how's Ryan taking it?'

'How's Ryan taking what?'

'You and Jim, getting married in Vegas.'

'Jesus, Debbie, he doesn't know. And I don't *want* him to know. You haven't told Gary, have you?'

'No, babe, of course I haven't. I just assumed you'd have told Ryan.'

'Why? He doesn't need to know. Not before the event, anyway. Once we're back home I know it won't stay a secret for long, but, I just want some time with Jim, on our own, before the media circus starts up all over again. You know, I can remember a time when nobody gave a crap about anything I did. And now suddenly every move I make is attracting attention.'

'Someone will know where you're going. That's the way it works, chick.'

'Yes, thanks for that, Debbie.'

'Oh, I'm sorry, babe, I didn't mean… You work in the media, Amber. You should know that you marrying Jim in a secret Vegas wedding will probably be old news by the time you land back at Heathrow.'

'You're making me feel so much better, do you know that?'

'Yeah… my mouth does run away with me, I'll admit. Gary's always telling me so.'

Amber couldn't help smiling. 'Well, that's why I love you.'

Debbie moved to give Amber a hug, enveloping her in a mist of expensive perfume and hairspray. 'And I love you, too. Even if you do have the most complicated life I've ever witnessed.'

'It's what I do best,' Amber sighed, pulling away from Debbie. 'Anyway, I'd better go. Will I see you before we leave for the airport?'

'Of course you will. Amber?'

She swung back around to face Debbie. 'Yeah?'

'Just… don't let him hurt you again, okay?'

Amber smiled, absentmindedly twisting her engagement ring round and round her finger. 'We're gonna be okay this time, Debbie. I know we are.'

*

Jim leaned forward, resting his forehead in the palm of his hand as he listened to the voice on the other end of the line, waiting a beat or two before he spoke himself. 'Tomorrow at the earliest, okay? At least wait until I've landed in Vegas. And one word about why I'm over there and… okay… Yeah, I trust you… Thanks. I owe you one.' He put the phone down and sat back in his chair, interlocking his hands behind his head, letting out a heavy sigh.

A knock at the door almost made him jump. Was he really that on edge? 'Who is it?'

He knew it wasn't Amber. She didn't bother knocking any more.

'It's Ryan. Can I have a word?'

Jim sat up, clasping his hands together on the desk in front of him. 'Come in.'

Ryan closed the door behind him, leaning back against the wall, not even bothering to walk any further into the room. 'It's the first day of the transfer window, and until this match is over I'm assuming you're still my boss.'

Jim stood up and walked around the front of his desk, leaning back against it. 'Shouldn't you be outside warming up?' He checked his watch before folding his arms against him. 'It's getting close to kick-off, and yes, you're right, until that final whistle blows I'm still your boss. So, what do you want?'

'I'm putting in that transfer request.'

'And I'm rejecting it.'

Ryan shrugged, a slight smile on his face as he stared out his soon-to-be-ex boss. 'Fair enough.'

Jim narrowed his eyes as he returned Ryan's stare. 'I think you should get back outside instead of wasting time in here.'

Ryan laughed quietly, digging his hands deeper into his pockets. 'You'll hurt her again, I know you will. It's what you do. You hurt her, the way she's hurt me, so I know how exactly how she feels every time you fuck up her life…'

'I'd stop there if I were you.'

'I'm not scared of you any more – Jim. I'm not worried that you're gonna drop me from the team or cut my wages or anything else you've ever threatened to do because you just couldn't handle me being around. Those days are over. You have no hold over me now. None. Just know that you'll never be rid of me. Amber and me, we have a baby. We have Rico. I have a bond with her that you'll never have…'

'Get out,' Jim said quietly, a slow anger beginning to bubble up inside him.

'Just saying.' Ryan smirked, something he knew would aggravate Jim even more, but he didn't care. Like he'd said, Jim Allen had no hold over him any more; he held no power over his life. He just wanted him to be aware of what *he* had that Jim didn't. That was all. 'I'll see you out there, then, Boss.'

Jim watched him leave, grinding his teeth as the door shut behind him, that anger that had been building showing no sign of subsiding just yet.

He stood up, banging his fist down hard on the desk, rattling everything that stood on it with the force of the thud.

'Everything okay?'

He turned quickly to see Amber standing in the doorway, her fingers looped into the belt of her skinny jeans, a confused expression on her pretty face.

'Everything's fine, honey. It's just fine.'

'Really?' She frowned, and Jim held out his hand, smiling at her.

'It's just a bit of an emotional day, baby, that's all.'

She took his hand, allowing him to pull her into his arms. 'You regretting any of this?' she asked, running her fingers gently over his rough chin, her eyes following their every move.

'No, Amber, I'm not regretting any of this.'

'What was Ryan doing in here just now?'

'Saying goodbye.'

'Is that all?'

He closed his eyes for a second, resting his forehead against hers as he took her hand, squeezing it tight. 'It's a new start, Amber.'

'You keep saying that, Jim, but if the old life is just gonna keep following us…'

'There's no guarantee any London club will want him.'

She looked at him, her expression telling him that she wasn't stupid.

He sighed, throwing his head back, his hand still holding tightly onto hers. 'Baby, I have recommended to the Newcastle Red Star board that they do their utmost to keep Ryan Fisher here, and not just because I'd rather he didn't make the move down south. I care about this club, Amber. I've been a player here, I've managed it, and a little piece of my heart will always *be* here. I want this club to do well, and since Ryan Fisher arrived… they need him. This club needs him, and they know that. They won't let him go anywhere without a fight.'

'And what if he just decides to stop playing? He wouldn't be the first player to act like a spoilt child just because they couldn't get their own way.'

'Amber, baby, we are getting married tomorrow. Tomorrow. *That's* what I want to be focusing on now, not Ryan Fisher. In less than two hours he ceases to be my problem…'

'Professionally. He ceases to be your problem professionally.'

'He ceases to be *our* problem, Amber. So let's just concentrate on us, okay? And whatever he decides to do, we'll handle it. Together.'

She smiled, and he wished with all his heart that he could promise her it would be easy. So it was just as well she didn't listen to his promises.

'Together,' she whispered.

'Together.' He smiled, and be breathed an inner sigh of relief as her smile grew wider. She was his beautiful girl, his life. She was his world, a world he wasn't about to let Ryan Fisher invade. 'I love you, Amber. So much, you have no idea…'

She reached out to touch his cheek, running her fingers lightly over it, her eyes locking with his. 'I love you, too, Jim.'

He pulled her closer, needing to feel her body against his, to feel her warmth, to hold her one more time in the place where this whole journey had kicked off a second time. A place they were leaving behind. A place they *needed* to leave behind. And as her lips touched his, her fingers fanning out across the back of his neck, pushing him down onto her, he knew he was doing the right thing. Because he was doing it for them. For their future. And that was all that mattered.

*

'Well, I have to say, if that was you showing the footballing world what you're capable of when you're playing at your best they're gonna be falling over themselves to get your signature on a contract.'

Ryan grinned at Max as they celebrated Newcastle Red Star's 5-2 win over Midlands club Glendale Rovers. Four of those goals had come from Ryan himself, the fifth one coming from a penalty gained when an overzealous Glendale defender had floored Ryan as he'd headed towards an almost open goal. 'I've got to get my transfer request finalised first, though. Jim Allen rejected it.'

'Oh, Jesus, Ryan, what are you doing aggravating Jim today?'

'Who's aggravating anyone? At the time I asked him he was still my boss.'

'And you knew that mentioning any transfer request to a London club was going to aggravate him. Are you really so stupid that you feel the need to wind people up? People you really should avoid upsetting.'

'Why, huh? Why, Max? Finding out he's going to be bringing up my son with the woman I'm still…' He stopped, but he didn't miss the look Max gave him.

'I thought you said you weren't in love with her any more.'

'So I lied. Come on, Max. Only weeks ago I thought me and Amber had a chance, y'know? We had Rico, we'd been happy for weeks, and I was certain…' He leaned back against the wall, pushing a hand through his hair. 'He'll hurt her again, Max. I know he will.'

'They're going to Vegas.'

Ryan looked at Max, frowning slightly. 'Vegas?'

'Yes. And they've only told a handful of people because it's all very hush-hush until they get back home, but I'm telling you now because I think you need a reality check.'

'Why… why would I…?'

'Why do people usually run off to Vegas in secret, Ryan?' Max watched as the penny slowly dropped, Ryan's expression changing within seconds.

'Why is she rushing into it, Max?'

'Because she loves him. She loves him like she could never love you, and I'm not saying that to be cruel, I'm saying it because I care about you. More than you'll ever know, kiddo.'

Ryan stared down at his boots, his stomach lurching, a sickening feeling taking over.

'You keep this to yourself, Ryan, do you hear? It really wouldn't be wise if you were the one named as leaking this news.'

'I'm not gonna say anything,' Ryan said quietly, looking up at Max. 'But I think she's making a mistake.'

'And I'd be lying if I said you were the only person to think that. But you've got to let her go, Ryan. She'll do what she has to do, and you need to move on with your life. You've got that little one to think about now.' Max eyed Ryan carefully, trying to read his expression as he looked around the room. There was no doubt he was looking for Amber, and Max hoped he didn't find her. Not this afternoon, not after what he'd just told him. Maybe it would be better if Ryan and Amber didn't see each other again until after she returned from Vegas, but given their parental situation Max feared things weren't going to be that simple. 'You gonna be okay?'

Ryan's head shot round. 'I'm not a child, Max.'

Max just hoped he remembered that when it came to following through any actions he might be thinking of taking. 'Okay. I'll see you later.'

'Yeah,' Ryan mumbled, his eyes back scanning the room. 'Later.' His mind was on other things now. And he wasn't going to settle until he'd talked to her.

*

'I am so happy you and Hayley are hitting it off,' Amber sighed, squeezing Ronnie's hand as they shared a post-match drink at the bar in the Players' Lounge, which was the busiest she'd seen it in a long, long time thanks to an impromptu farewell party that had started up for Jim. 'She'll be good for you. And you look gorgeous together.'

Ronnie had recently started dating another Cloud Sports reporter, Hayley Samson, and from what Amber could gather, things were going better than okay. And even though Hayley was a good friend of Amber's she hadn't even had to set them up. They'd got together all by themselves after a night in the Cloud Sports bar following an evening stint presenting *Scoreline* together.

Hayley had joined the Cloud Sports team a few months after Amber, and they'd hit it off immediately. Both were northern girls, both were daughters of ex-professional football players, and both of them loved the sport. Amber couldn't be happier for Ronnie. Hayley made him smile, and seeing Ronnie smile made Amber happy; it was as simple as that.

'Yeah. She's a great girl.' Ronnie looked at Amber, a slow grin spreading across his face. 'And she's fucking hot!'

'I never had you down as the shallow type, Ronnie White.' Amber tried to look shocked, but she was only messing. Hayley *was* pretty hot with her long auburn hair and big brown eyes, but she was also one very savvy young woman. She didn't take any crap, and that's what Amber liked about her. She reminded her of herself, before she'd let Jim Allen back into her life. Before she'd allowed Ryan Fisher into her world. Before she'd let those two men change her.

153

'What's up?' Ronnie asked, noticing Amber's expression, her eyes now down on the floor.

'Nothing,' she sighed, pushing a hand through her hair.

'Okay… now do you want to tell me the truth?'

'There's nothing up, Ronnie. I was just thinking, that's all. About everything that's happened. Everything that's taken me up to this point.'

'And?' He was looking at her with eyes that told her he wasn't going to go away until she'd told him something that convinced him she was absolutely fine about everything that was going on.

'And it's just, it's unsettling, that's all. The way I've…' She leaned back against the bar, staring out ahead of her, watching as Jim moved around the room, saying his goodbyes, talking to the players and board members and staff he was leaving behind. She remembered the day she'd heard he was coming back here, to Newcastle Red Star. The way her stomach had dipped so low she'd almost been physically sick. The way her heart had broken all over again as a million memories had flooded into her head. How she'd known she was going to fall in love with him all over again – because she'd never really fallen out. So she should have been prepared for everything that had followed, but instead she'd handled it all so badly. 'You were right, Ronnie. I've changed. And I don't always like the person I've become – this weak woman who's let one man rule her life for so long.'

'So, do something about it.'

She looked at him, right into his eyes. 'I can't,' she whispered, her shoulders sagging in an almost resigned way. 'I can't.'

'Can't, or won't?' Ronnie held her gaze.

Amber shook her head. 'If I walk away from him now, I fall apart. It's as simple as that. I walk away from him and I fall apart. Because, despite everything, I am so in love with that man I've lost all sense of reality. He walks out of a room and I can't breathe. When he touches me everything feels better, everything feels right, and he's different now, you have no idea…' She trailed off, breaking the stare to look over at Jim again. He was laughing, talking to one of the American owners of the club, the beautiful smile lighting up his handsome, handsome face, and she felt her world flip upside down as she watched him. 'He touches me and I don't even want to be that person I used to be any more,' she whispered, her eyes not leaving Jim as he continued to move around the room. 'Even though I know...' She finally turned to look back at Ronnie. 'Even though I *know* I need to be her again. I need to be that woman I used to be.'

'Then do something about it, Amber. Before it's too late.'

She shook her head again, her eyes back on Jim, and she found herself smiling as he turned around, his eyes meeting hers. That switch had been flicked. And there was no returning to normal now. 'It's already too late,' she said, her voice so quiet it was barely a whisper. 'It's already far too late.'

*

'I can't believe you're doing this, Dad.'

Jim looked at his son. 'How's that injury?'

Brandon was out of action for a couple of games after an incident on the training pitch over Christmas had done some minimal damage to a tendon in his foot, which was why he'd been able to come to Tynebridge to see his father's final game with Newcastle Red Star. He was heading off to join the rest of the Wearside Spartans squad for their match in Hull later that evening. He wouldn't be playing, but he still wanted to be a part of the team and watch from the bench.

'It's fine. I'm back on light training and you're changing the subject.'

'I'm not getting into it, Brandon. Everyone knows my reasons for going back to Endleigh, and anyway, I thought you were happy Amber and I are back together.'

'Of course I'm happy you're back together, that isn't the...

Dad, I came here, to Wearside Spartans, because *you* were based in the north-east. I came here to be closer to you, and now you're moving away...'

'Brandon, I'm moving a few hundred miles down the motorway. That's all. And you know why I need to do this. You know that.'

'I know, I do, and I understand, it's just that... Jesus! I'm gonna miss you, that's all.'

Jim pulled his son in for a hug, holding him tight. 'And I'm gonna miss *you*, kiddo. But you're gonna be just fine, you hear me?' He pulled away slightly, looking Brandon in the eye, smiling at his handsome boy. 'You are one extremely talented young man, Brandon Palmer. You've got your whole soccer career in front of you, and who knows where that career is going to take you? For the time being, you just know that Wearside Spartans is the place you need to be right now. Since you've been there I have never seen you play better, and believe me, I know talent when I see it. I'm not just saying that because you're my son, trust me.'

Brandon smiled, his attention distracted only slightly as he saw Ellen walk into the room, looking pretty and perky in her match-day work outfit of tight black pencil skirt and sexy white shirt, her heels high, accentuating those incredible legs of hers.

'I'm proud of you, Brandon. Never forget that.'

He looked at Jim, trying to ignore the fact Ellen had made a beeline for Ryan Fisher. 'I know you are, Dad. Look, I'm sorry, I didn't mean to put a downer on your move to Endleigh. This is a great opportunity for you, to go back there. They're one of the biggest clubs in the world and... and I'm happy for you. Happy that you've got this amazing job, happy that you're marrying Amber again. Just try to make sure you *stay* married to her this time, okay?'

Jim couldn't help smiling at that. 'Yeah. I'll do my best, son. And remember, keep that information to yourself for now, okay?'

'You got it.' Brandon grinned, hugging his dad one more time. 'I love you, Dad.'

'Yeah, I love you, too, kiddo. I'd better go say some more good-byes, okay? I'll call you soon. And you take care of that injury, you hear me?'

Brandon nodded, his attention now focused fully on Ellen as he watched her sidle up to Ryan Fisher. He watched as she tried to be as discreet as she possibly could, but she wasn't very clever at hiding her body language. Brandon may be young – and he was a good few years younger than Ellen – but he wasn't stupid. He could see exactly what was going on.

Narrowing his eyes slightly he continued to stare at her, at the way her fingers trailed over Ryan's arm, and the fact Ryan didn't pull away. In fact, as Brandon looked harder, he could see Ryan's hand fall quickly onto her bottom, and Ellen giggled, forgetting herself for a second as she leaned in towards him. And it was then that, for some reason, she turned her head, her eyes meeting Brandon's from across the room, the expression on her face sealing it for him.

He turned around and walked away. He was done here. He had another match to get to.

*

'Amber, can I have a quick word?'

She stopped in her tracks, turning to look at Max. 'Yeah. Of course you can. What's up?'

'I've told Ryan.'

She frowned. 'You've told him what?' Then she realised. 'Oh, Jesus, Max! I specifically asked you to keep that quiet. What the hell did you tell him for? I really don't need this…'

'He's Rico's dad, Amber.'

'And that does not give him the right to know every single fucking move I make. I can't believe you told him.'

'Look, he's living in some kind of parallel universe where he's under the impression that you and him might have some chance of getting back together. I just thought he needed a reality check.'

She widened her eyes as she stared at him. 'What? And you thought telling him I was marrying Jim, in Vegas, in the next couple of days; you thought that was the best way to do that, did you? Jesus, Max. I thought you were the intelligent one amongst us.'

'I'm sorry. In hindsight maybe I was wrong.'

'You think?'

'I'm worried about him, Amber.'

'I can't do this now, Max, I really can't. I am done with caring about what state he's going to get himself into or how he's going to deal with any little problem that might come his way. He told me that since Rico's arrival he's grown up, he's changed, and I have to believe that he's adult enough to actually mean that, because I am done with worrying about him. I can't do it any more. It's draining and exhausting and it takes up too much of my time. Time I want to spend with Jim. And Rico. So if you think he's on the verge of doing something stupid then stop him, okay? Stop him. Because I can't. I can't, Max.'

'Amber…'

'No, Max.' She started to walk away from him, then stopped, turning back around to face him. 'Just make sure he doesn't say anything. About Jim and I going to Vegas. Please.'

She began pushing her way through the crowded Players' Lounge, suddenly needing some fresh air. All she'd wanted to do was escape from this place and go somewhere far away, just for a few days, somewhere where all the complications and the problems that just wouldn't seem to disappear couldn't touch them. But they still kept piling up, filling her head with crap she didn't want to have to deal with yet.

Stepping outside into the bright winter sunshine, she leaned back against the wall, closing her eyes and wishing, just briefly, that she hadn't stopped smoking. Because she could certainly do with a cigarette right now.

'Want some company?'

'No, Ryan, I don't.' She opened her eyes, but she didn't look at him. 'And before you start pretending you don't know, Max told me. He told me that he told you about Jim and me getting married.'

'Why are you doing it so soon?' Ryan didn't miss a beat.

'Because I love him.'

'As simple as that, huh?'

She turned her head to look at him. 'As simple as that.'

'You're making a mistake.'

'I didn't ask for your opinion.'

'I'm giving it to you anyway.'

'You have no right…'

'No, Amber, I have every right. That man is going to be bringing up my child…'

'Oh, for Christ's sake. He is a good man, Ryan. He's made mistakes, but he's changed and he isn't that person any more.'

Ryan laughed, he couldn't help it.

Amber stared at him. 'Excuse me…?'

'Have you heard yourself, Amber? You're making him sound like a fucking saint. Jesus, the man almost destroyed you! Have you forgotten what he put you through last year? Have you? I saw the state you were in, I was there; I watched you break down. I held you when you cried and I wanted to kill him for doing that to you. For making you so unhappy. Do you remember that, huh? Do you remember the things you told me, the way you just fell apart, because he ripped you in fucking two, Amber. He did that to you, and you stand here and you tell me he's a good man?'

'Don't do this, Ryan. Don't.'

'He'll hurt you again, and I don't know when and I don't know how but he *will* hurt you, again, and even though I want to tell you… even though I really want to say don't come running to me when he does, it's the only place I want you to come running. I *want* you to run to me. Because I love you, and I care about you…'

She held up her hands, her head down as she willed him to stop talking. To just stop.

'Please don't do this, Ryan. Please.'

'What happened to you?' he whispered, shaking his head as she raised hers, their eyes locking together. 'That beautiful, strong, independent woman. What happened to her, Amber?'

'Please, Ryan…'

'I'm taking Rico home with me, like we arranged. I take it that's still okay with you?'

She held his gaze, willing herself not to cry. She was so sick of crying. 'You're his dad.'

He looked at her, right at her, his eyes never wavering for even the briefest of seconds. 'And let's not ever forget that.' He finally broke the stare, turning away from her, but he'd only taken a couple of steps before he turned back around. 'Oh, and I almost forgot. Good luck, okay? Because I really think you're gonna need it.'

Chapter Thirteen

Clinging tightly onto Jim's waist, Amber stared down at the white-gold band that now nestled perfectly below the yellow diamond engagement ring on the third finger of her left hand. She'd been Mrs. Amber Allen for all of five minutes, and it was still sinking in.

'Did we just do that?' she laughed, looking up at the huge clock in the foyer of the hotel. It told her it was twenty-nine minutes past midnight on a cool, January night in Las Vegas. And she'd just married the man she was hopelessly in love with. For the second time.

'I think we really just did that.' Jim smiled, pulling her around to face him, kissing her quickly. 'We just did that!'

Amber couldn't stop smiling as she looked at her heartbreakingly handsome husband, so sexy and hot in his black suit, his tie now loose as it hung around the collar of his open-necked white shirt. He looked gorgeously bedraggled, his hair slightly mussed up, his face carrying that light, rough stubble she loved so much. He looked like the man she was going to spend the rest of her life with.

From the second she'd said "*I do*" she hadn't been able to stop smiling. For a ceremony that had been so quick and hurriedly organised, it had been surprisingly romantic, with dozens of candles and a wonderfully calm and friendly official who'd made them feel like they were the only two people in the world at that moment in time, despite the fact they were just one in heaven knows how many couples who'd done exactly the same before them.

'So, Mrs. Allen. What do you want to do now?'

She reached out to touch his cheek, running her fingers over that light stubble as she stood up on tiptoes to kiss his mouth, sighing inwardly as his lips moved against hers. This was the first day of the rest of their new lives, and she didn't think she'd ever felt happier or more alive.

'I want to celebrate.' She smiled, pulling away from him only slightly. 'I want to do something me and you have never actually done before. Not together, anyway.'

Jim frowned, keeping his hand firmly in the small of her back. 'Oh? And what's that? Because, beautiful, I'm sure there aren't all that many things we haven't done together. And if there are, maybe we can try some of them out once we get back to our room.'

She laughed quietly, her mouth almost touching his. 'I want to party, Jim. I want to go to a club and I want to drink and dance and then scream out loud because you're fucking me so hard in the ladies' rest room, and I've got my dress up high around my waist and my legs wrapped tight around your hips, and you're so deep inside of me... and then I want you to do it again, from behind, whilst everyone outside wonders just what the hell you're doing to me on the other side of that closed cubicle door.'

'Jesus Christ, Amber... what books are you reading these days? You're killing me here, baby.'

'I want to party,' she whispered, her fingers playing with the hair at the back of his neck as she moved closer, pressing her body lightly against his. 'All night long.'

'Who am I to disappoint my crazy, beautiful new wife?'

'You'll get so many brownie points if you give me exactly what I want tonight.'

'Do I have any choice?'

'None,' she whispered, her mouth now touching his.

'Then let's get out of here.'

Within minutes they were inside the hotel's huge and ultra-modern nightclub as everything from nineties club tracks to classic seventies disco pounded out through concealed speakers, and all around them people danced and partied and drank like tomorrow was never going to come. Amber had only ever been to Las Vegas once before, and that had been a long time ago, when she'd worked for News North East. She'd been over there covering a Wearside Spartans pre-season tour of the US, spending most of that trip, when she hadn't been working, in her room, talking to Ronnie on the phone or watching TV, feeling slightly intimidated by the whole feel of the place. But not now. Now she felt different. Now she wanted to embrace the excess and the fact you never really knew what time of day it was; she wanted to throw herself into everything and live the next couple of days to the limit before they had to go back home to another media circus and a never-ending round of questions about their private life.

'I'm not sure I'm cut out for this,' Jim breathed, throwing himself down into an empty booth by the side of the dance floor. 'Baby, you are wearing me out!'

'You're doing just fine, handsome. And anyway, you'd better find some energy from somewhere because we aren't even near done yet.'

He looked at her as she lifted herself up off the banquette just a touch, sliding a hand up under her dress. 'What are you doing?' He felt his heart start to beat a little bit faster as he watched her slip off her knickers, stuffing them into his jacket pocket, then felt his breathing speeding up even more as she straddled him, her fingers quickly unzipping him.

'Fuck me,' she whispered, her mouth close to his ear, her hand now grasping him gently, guiding him inside her before he'd even realised what was happening, leaving him no choice but to do what she said. Jesus Christ! He was fucking his wife in a crowded Las

Vegas nightclub and nobody was batting an eyelid!

'Amber, honey, you really are freaking killing me here,' he groaned, his hands resting on her thighs as she ground against him, as discreetly as she could.

'It's my job.' She took a swig of beer straight from the bottle, and the sight of her doing that, along with the feeling of him deep inside her, in a place about as public as you could get, he'd never felt so turned on despite himself. 'Nobody cares, Jim. Not here. Nobody cares who we are or what we're doing.'

'Since when did you become such a bad influence, Amber Allen?'

She smiled, taking another swig of beer. 'Since we landed here.'

'So, I don't get anything like this once we're back home?'

She leaned over to kiss him, running her thumb over his slightly open mouth first before touching it with her own, lightly to begin with before allowing the kiss to go deeper, pushing down onto him, gripping him tight. 'Oh, you'll get plenty, mister. I can promise you that.'

'You really are gonna kill me.' He groaned again as she once more rotated her hips just a little, pushing down and leaning back slightly, and he watched as she bit down on her lip, her body trying its hardest not to show any signs of the fact he was coming inside her so fast it was making his head spin. And it was the biggest turn-on. The most incredible rush. 'Shit, Amber, baby, you are one bad girl.'

'So punish me,' she whispered, bringing her hand down to discreetly touch herself underneath her dress, her fingers gently bringing her to her own quiet but glorious climax. 'Teach me a lesson.'

Jim couldn't help smiling, biting down on his own lip as he slowly withdrew, holding in a moan as she ran her hand over him before zipping him back up and climbing off him, shaking out her hair as she settled herself back against the banquette, taking a long swig of beer.

'You're crazy, do you know that?' He grinned at her, feeling as though she'd just knocked twenty years off him and he was now ready to go all night, to live the next few hours exactly how she wanted to live them. To do all the things she wanted to do before they had to go back to a reality that was going to leave them precious little time for anything like this.

'I've never really been all that crazy,' she said, tucking her legs up underneath her as she took another swig of beer. 'I've always been in control – cold, almost. My world was always so ordered, so compartmentalised, to the point where any change used to terrify me. Which is why you walking back into my life... you fucked it all up, Jim. All that control, all that order; you fucked all that up. And I can't ever go back there now, so, I'm doing crazy. I'm seeing what it feels like, and so far I'm liking it.'

He leaned over to give her a long and slow kiss, tasting the beer on her lips, the intense sexual chemistry hanging in the air so heavily he could physically feel it.

'I think you need to come with me.'

'You don't want to punish me in public?' she breathed, feeling that tingle between her thighs return with a vengeance. Although, maybe it just hadn't had time to go away just yet.

He smiled, shaking his head, trying his hardest to hide an erection that was desperate to show itself as he took her hand and pulled her up, almost dragging her out of the booth. 'Come on. We're out of here.'

As the thumping beat of Donna Summer's *I Feel Love* filled the club, they headed along the wide, dimly lit corridor that led to the various restrooms, almost falling through the door of a fairly empty ladies' room, not even stopping to check out the curious faces of the few women who were in there.

Kicking open an empty cubicle door Jim pulled her inside, slamming the door shut with his back as Amber leaned forwards, her hands out in front of her against the wall to keep her steady, her legs stood apart, her bottom sticking out. Jim didn't hesitate, didn't even miss a beat as he pulled up her dress, exposing her naked behind, unzipping himself so quickly he couldn't even remember doing it, all he could remember was that feeling of calm as he sunk into her. She was warm and she was wet and she was enveloping him in a beautiful fantasy so unreal he could barely breathe for fear that if he did, he would wake up and find her gone. He might find that the past few months had been nothing but a dream. So he held his breath and pushed deeper into her, letting her cries and her moans bring him to a quick and crashing climax, the likes of which he'd never experienced before, and it scared him and it terrified him, but he never wanted to let it go. And as he gave in to the rush he slid his hand around to touch her, his fingers sinking into that warm, wet heaven as she shuddered to her own endgame, pushing back against him so hard she almost knocked him backwards.

'Oh, Jesus, that was fucking incredible,' Jim gasped, pulling out of her, watching as she stayed where she was for a second, her breathing heavy and ragged as she tried to get back to normal. Whatever that was. He wasn't altogether sure any more.

She stood up straight, turning around to face him and he reached out for her, pulling her against him, their bodies crashing together as their mouths met in an almost violent kiss it was so hard, so desperate. His hands were up and under her dress, diving back into that heaven she'd opened up for him, his fingers pushing into her, and she buried her face in his shoulder as he touched her deep, moving around inside her.

'Crazy is so good,' he whispered, smiling as he pulled out of her just a touch before delving back in there, causing her to cry out but stop herself by once more burying her face in his chest, her fingers gripping his shirt tightly as her legs almost buckled underneath her. 'It's so–fucking–good.'

She raised her head and looked up at him, closing her eyes and kissing him deep as the sound of Donna Summer still thudded hard and heavy from the club outside.

'Pull out,' she whispered, her mouth not leaving his as she spoke.

'I don't want to,' he said, biting down gently on her bottom lip.

She took his hand and pulled him out of her, moving him away from the cubicle door and turning around so she had her back to the wall. He knew where this was going now. He knew, and he was just going to roll with it and know he was going to be so fucking tired in the morning and he wouldn't give a shit.

Lifting her up he slammed her back against the wall as her legs wrapped around his hips, and even though he had no idea how he was doing this, he was hard all over again, ready to sink back into that beautiful warm place he never really wanted to leave. She was still so wet, still so ready to take him any which way he was willing, and as he thrust in and out of her, every one of those thrusts pushed her back against the hard wall so violently he could almost feel the bruises on her back begin to appear, but she didn't seem to care as she clung onto him, her legs gripping him so tightly he didn't think she'd ever let go.

'I love you so much,' he breathed, feeling that familiar rush begin its journey, even though he had no idea if he had anything left to give. She'd practically squeezed every last drop out of him, but he still felt it, felt something about to explode as her legs gripped him even tighter, pushing everything he had in him out into her. 'So fucking much.'

'I love you, too,' she gasped, her fingers buried in his hair as she continued to squeeze him with her legs and muscles so taut and tight he felt another wave flood out of him just thinking about it. 'I love you, too.'

'Jesus, baby girl, you really have fucked with my head tonight.' His throat was sore with the sheer exertion of breathing so hard and heavily for what had felt like an eternity, but had only really been for a few minutes. Minutes he was never going to forget.

She kept her fingers in his hair as he gently put her down, his hand sliding up under her dress again, but only to stroke her naked thigh as he kissed her slowly, enjoying the feeling of calm that followed the most insane few minutes of his life.

'If we weren't already married I would be down on bended knee right now begging you to make me the happiest man that ever walked this earth. But you've already done that. Baby, you are my world, and I can't believe we're here and we're doing this and I am so freaking high I can't even explain.'

'It wasn't too much?' she asked, those beautiful pale-blue eyes of hers so wide as they looked into his.

'Too much? Oh, honey, no. No. It was my freaking fantasy wedding night. Like I prayed to God and he just made every dream I ever had come true!'

She smiled, gently stroking his face with her fingertips. 'I love you so much, Jim.'

'Hey, I love you, too. And right now, I don't think I ever want to leave this place.'

And right at that second he meant that. So much shit was about to hit the fan when they got back to the UK, and as he looked at Amber, at her beautiful face with its olive-toned skin and those baby-blue eyes, he hoped with every fibre of his being that this was it for them. That this time, forever really was a possibility because any other option scared the hell out of him.

'I've really got to pee,' she said, removing his hand from underneath her dress, kissing him quickly before sitting down on the toilet.

Jim leaned back against the cubicle door, folding his arms. 'Everything *will* be okay, Amber. You know that, don't you?'

She looked at him. 'Yeah, I know. We'll make sure it's okay, won't we?'

'Yeah,' he said quietly. 'Yeah. We will.'

She flushed the toilet, letting her dress fall back down over her thighs as she reached into Jim's pocket to retrieve her panties. 'I should probably put these back on.'

'Do you have to?' He threw her a smile so sexy she really could have hoisted that dress back up and opened her legs so wide for him he wouldn't have been able to refuse, but she had other things she wanted to do tonight. They were living on Las Vegas time, and in this world it was still early. There'd be plenty of time for more of what they'd just done here later.

She smiled, wiggling back into her knickers, kissing him slowly as she did so.

'Jesus, Amber, even you putting clothes back on is a fucking turn-on.'

'*You* did this to me,' she whispered, still smiling, her mouth resting on his. 'You. You did this.'

He grinned, sliding an arm around her waist. 'I knew I was good at something.'

She closed her eyes as he kissed her again, her body melting against his, and there really was a part of her that didn't want to go anywhere just yet. But there was another part that still wanted to party.

'How about we hit the casino?' he said, his hand dropping down onto her bottom.

'I think you just read my mind, handsome.'

He reached out behind him, unlocking the door to a sea of impressed faces and a round of applause, and for the first time in her life Amber saw Jim Allen in a whole new light as he took in the praise and the applause and fended off the outrageous flirts women were throwing his way, grabbing the opportunity gladly while Amber quickly washed her hands.

He was loving it, and at that very moment in time she'd never seen him so animated, so alive. She'd never seen him look so sexy. And as she grabbed his hand, letting him pull her out of there, she couldn't help but mouth "*he is HOT!*" back at everyone, and nobody disagreed. Not one of them.

'I can't believe we just did that,' he laughed, stopping for a second outside in the corridor, leaning back against the wall as he tried to catch his breath.

'I don't ever want to forget this, Jim. I don't ever want to forget how this place made us feel.'

His arm circled her waist again, pulling her against him, his fingers intertwining with hers down by their sides. 'I don't think we'll ever forget this, do you?'

She smiled, her stomach flipping over at the thought of him touching her, his fingers on her skin, his body deep inside hers. 'No. I don't.'

He pushed her harder against him, kissing her slowly, mouths opening, tongues touching, and Amber felt so happy, so in love; she'd had no idea she could feel anything more for this man than she already did, but right now, as he held her hand and kissed her gently, she knew she was still falling in love with him. She was still falling deeper and deeper and there really was no way back now.

'Let's go hit that casino, huh?' Jim smiled, stroking her cheek with his fingers, his eyes staring deep into hers.

'Jim – thank you.'

'For what, honey?'

'For opening up to me. For coming back to me.'

'Baby, I never went away. I never went away.'

'If I lost you...'

He silenced her with a kiss, and once more she just fell against him, a ridiculous need to be constantly close to him taking over. 'I'm not going anywhere, Amber. Believe me, baby. I'm not going anywhere.'

And all she had to do was believe him.

Chapter Fourteen

'You should go.' Ryan stood at the back of the room, watching as Ellen pulled on her clothes, running her fingers through her hair.

She looked at him. 'Now? Don't I even get the option of staying for breakfast?'

'I need to see to Rico. He'll be awake any second now and…'

'I get it.' She cut him off, her tone quite abrupt. But then, this wasn't working out quite the way she'd planned. She hadn't banked on Brandon being at Tynebridge for Jim's final game in charge, and she certainly hadn't banked on him seeing her with Ryan. And even though Ryan had asked her to come home with him last night, and she hadn't even had to think twice about her reply, despite what had happened with Brandon, she hadn't expected to share him with his four-month-old son. 'I'll be out of your hair as soon as I've got my things together.'

Ryan threw his head back and sighed heavily, shoving his hands in the pockets of his jeans. 'You can stay for a coffee. I'm not gonna throw you out on the street, I just meant that I really need to be with my son today, that's all. Amber's back home tomorrow, and I want to spend as much time as I can with him before she takes him down to London.'

Ellen looked at him. He was just-stepped-out-of-the-shower handsome in nothing but the sexiest of low-slung jeans, with those incredibly hot tattoos on show. All she wanted to do was throw him back on that bed and spend the morning underneath him. She was desperate to have him again, to feel him making love to her, as he had done for most of last night. But that baby of his was becoming a major form of extremely unwanted contraception. As cute as he was, she wished Amber would hurry up and take him away so she could concentrate on winning this man back.

'Don't you feel in the least bit guilty?' Ryan's voice interrupted her daydreaming of endless sex with one of the country's hottest football players.

'Guilty?' She knew what he meant, she just couldn't quite get her brain into gear quickly enough today.

'Brandon. Don't you feel guilty about what you're doing to him?'

'He doesn't want to speak to me,' Ellen said, rummaging around in her bag for her phone.

'That's not what I asked, but, can you blame him?'

Her head shot up as Ryan said that, agitation suddenly flooding her. 'When the hell did *you* get so holier than thou, huh?'

'I'm not...'

'You're seriously going to stand there and take the moral high ground with me after everything you've done? After everything you're still going to do?'

He narrowed his eyes as he looked at her. 'I'm sorry? And what the hell is *that* supposed to mean?'

'Oh, come on. The world and its frigging mother knows you can't leave Amber fucking Sullivan alone. The second she sets foot back in this country you'll be there, hanging round her ankles like some lovesick puppy...'

'Like I said, Ellen, I think you should go.'

She closed her eyes for a second, breathing in deep, desperate to claw some composure back. The last thing she should be doing was pushing him further away. She'd just killed her relationship with Brandon Palmer. Was she going to allow all that to be for nothing? 'I'm sorry, Ryan, I just... I'm just tired. I didn't get much sleep.'

'Yeah, well, that's what babies do for you. They don't always let you sleep.' The sound of Rico's crying immediately turned Ryan's attention to the baby monitor on the sideboard. 'I'd better go get him. Help yourself to coffee but then I really think you need to go.'

Ellen watched as he walked out of the bedroom, along the hall to the nursery. She listened as he spoke softly to his baby boy, so quietly she couldn't hear exactly what he was saying but she felt a pain, a stab of jealousy so strong it cut into her chest that it shocked her. This baby meant Amber Sullivan had a hold over Ryan. She had something that meant Ryan would never be out of her life, and Ellen wished with all her heart that she had that same kind of hold over him.

She heard Ryan's voice grow a little louder and she watched through the slightly open door as he made his way downstairs, his baby son balanced on his hip. He was still talking to him, and Ellen felt that jealousy burn even hotter now.

Taking a minute to compose herself, to try and get some rational thought back into her muddled head, she finally picked up her bag and made her own way downstairs. She could hear the sound of the TV coming from the family room adjacent to the kitchen, and the faint muffle of Ryan's voice. Jesus, just what kind of conversation could you have with a four-month-old baby?

Walking through the archway that led to the kitchen and family room, she stopped, leaning against the wall with her shoulder as she watched Ryan, his son still balanced on one hip as he moved around the room, taking Rico's bottle out of the microwave and checking the temperature by quickly drinking a bit. She watched as he smiled the biggest smile at his baby boy, leaning back against the counter as he cradled Rico in his arms, staring down at him as he took his bottle.

He leaned over and gently kissed his son's forehead, and Ellen felt that pain, that jealousy rush through her all over again. She couldn't watch any more. She turned on her high heels and walked out into the hall. This was going to be a lot harder than she'd ever thought it would be. But maybe there was a way to make it that little bit easier. Maybe there was a way…

*

The sun was just beginning to rise, but even at that early hour the Las Vegas streets weren't exactly deserted, although they were far quieter than they had been a few hours ago, which was the last time she and Jim had ventured outside.

But, after a night of doing things they'd never dream of doing back home; of partying hard, fucking even harder, and playing the roulette wheel like their life had depended on it, the only thing they both wanted now was some fresh air. They hadn't even known what time it was when they'd walked out of the hotel, but the fact that the sun was coming up told them the night was now over, and that another new day was dawning. Their last few hours in Vegas lay ahead of them, and even though she should be feeling like the only thing she wanted to do was sleep, Amber had never felt so awake. To sleep would be to waste what precious little time they had left in this place, a place that had made sure they forgot everything else and concentrated only on themselves. And she wasn't sure she wanted to leave that behind just yet.

Leaning into Jim as she held onto his waist, his suit jacket flung loosely around her shoulders as they walked along the Strip, she felt like her sixteen-year-old schoolgirl self again. Her stomach was filled with butterflies, her heart couldn't control itself whenever he looked at her; all she wanted to do was be with him.

'Everything looks so different in daylight,' she said quietly, her head resting against him as they walked.

He squeezed her shoulders, quickly kissing the top of her head. 'Everything?'

She looked up at him, smiling slightly. 'Not you. You look just as hot as you did when this night began. I mean this place. It looks different at this time of the day, when all the lights are turned off and the streets are quiet. I kind of like it. I've always liked this time of day, those early hours of the morning when so few people are out and about. It feels almost ethereal.'

'We should be in bed. We've got a plane to catch in a matter of hours.'

'I'm not tired.'

He smiled at her, pulling her into his arms, gently stroking the hair from those beautiful pale-blue eyes of hers. 'No. Neither am I. We should still be in bed, though.'

She returned his smile, tipping her head back slightly as he kissed her slowly, his hand lightly rubbing her back. 'I couldn't have wished for a more perfect wedding,' she whispered, and she meant it. Just the two of them, nobody else there to invade their time, nobody else trying to hide disapproving looks or congratulate them when they really didn't mean it. It was just the two of them. The way she'd always wanted it. 'But we're going back to things that aren't perfect, Jim.'

He shook his head, pulling her in against him as they started walking back towards their hotel. 'Don't, Amber. We're still here, and while we're still here I don't want to think about what's going on back home or what may or may not happen once we're there. Because we're still here.'

She clung tightly onto his waist, holding her left hand up in front of her, smiling as she looked at her wedding ring against the backdrop of the early-morning Las Vegas sun. 'I'd get used to this time of day if I were you.'

He kissed her forehead, rubbing the top of her arm as they walked. 'And why's that? You planning on waking me this early every day for some pre-dawn exercise?'

She laughed quietly, stopping for a second to slip off her heels, not caring that the sidewalk was actually quite cool against her bare feet. 'Oh, you wish, handsome. But I think you'll find your stepson will have one or two things to say about that.'

He stopped walking again, pulling her back into his arms. 'My stepson…'

'Yeah. We're kind of equal on that one now. I've got Brandon, you've got Rico. Although, yours isn't all that great as far as conversation goes at the minute.'

'I'm gonna do my best to look after you both, Amber. I mean that. I… I know Rico's not mine, but… I'm gonna love him as though he were.'

She smiled, reaching up to touch his face, that once-light stubble now forming a darker shadow on his strong jawline. 'And he's gonna love you right back, I know he is.'

'But, right now…' Jim squeezed her waist, his mouth moving closer to hers as he spoke. 'Right now, I'm gonna take his mommy to bed, and love her like nobody else has ever loved her before.'

'You're such a sweet-talker,' Amber breathed, closing her eyes as his fingers tangled in her hair, pulling her head back slightly as their mouths touched, his kiss plunging her deeper and deeper into a web she now never wanted to break free from.

'Let's go,' he whispered, his hand slipping into hers as they resumed a pace that was almost a run now, both of them realising how little time they had left in this place. And neither of them wanted to waste any of it. 'Six hours and counting.'

Chapter Fifteen

Max threw his head back and closed his eyes, letting out a heavy sigh. He needed this the day news had broken about Amber's 'surprise' Vegas wedding to Jim Allen. His phone hadn't stopped ringing since the crack of dawn, and this was probably going to swamp anything else out there. And both stories breaking on the same day was just destined to give him a headache he could really do without.

He got up and walked over to the windows of his plush Covent Garden offices, staring down at the crowds of people darting this way and that, rushing to work or heading off early to the next tourist attraction London had to offer. He checked his watch before sticking his hands in his pockets. Amber and Jim were due to land back in the UK within the next hour or so – should he ask her to come in? Did he have time before his flight up to Newcastle? She wasn't going in to work until tomorrow, he knew that, although he also knew Freddie Sullivan was arriving in London later that day with the baby. So dragging her away from home when she hadn't seen her son for days wasn't going to go down well. But he really needed to see her. However, Max knew he was just going to have to wait.

Giving up another heavy sigh he turned and walked back over to his desk, sitting down on the edge of it as he picked up his phone, scrolled down his list of speed-dial numbers and pressed *call*. It was answered within seconds, the voice on the other end of the line a little muffled. Probably because he'd woken them up.

'What do you want, Max? Have you seen the frigging time? Even Rico doesn't wake me this early.'

'It's twenty past eight, Ryan.'

'I know, Max. That's my point. What's up?'

'I'm assuming you haven't seen the papers today? Or switched on your TV yet?'

'No. Because I was asleep. And because Freddie now has Rico I assumed I'd get a bit of a lie-in this morning seeing as training isn't starting until ten... why? Oh, hang on... is this to do with Amber? Shit! She's gone through with it, hasn't she?'

Max closed his eyes for a beat, rubbing the bridge of his nose with his thumb and forefinger. 'Yes, she's gone through with it. But that's the least of your worries, kiddo.'

'You think? Jesus! I can't believe she's married him – again!'

'What did you think would happen, Ryan? That she'd arrive in Las Vegas, suddenly realise what a massive mistake she was making, get on a plane back home and run straight into your arms?'

'What the fuck is wrong with *you* this morning?'

'Switch your TV on, get on the laptop, read a newspaper... then call me back. I won't go anywhere until I hear from you.'

'Max? Do you want to tell me what's going on here?'

'Just do it, Ryan. Then, please, call me back.'

*

'Did you organise this?' Amber gasped as she walked into the nursery of their new London home. When she'd last seen it the room had been a canvas of beige, with nothing but a chest of drawers and a wardrobe filling the emptiness. But now the walls were painted a vibrant yellow, a huge wooden cot sat in the centre of the room, an oversized chocolate-coloured corner couch rested against one wall and on the other side of the room was a long sideboard decorated with cuddly toys and assorted baby paraphernalia. There was a new changing table, a large flat-screened TV on another wall, and yet more toys and baby clothes were piled up in boxes next to the couch. It was too much for Amber to take in.

'I wanted him to have a perfect place to come home to.'

Amber smiled as Jim walked around the nursery, making sure everything was in place. 'Thank you.'

He looked at her, returning her smile, and once again Amber felt her stomach contract in a barrage of waves that made her feel weak – both physically and mentally. That was what this man did to her, and she was just going to have to learn to deal with it.

'We're a family now, Amber. And I want this to be a perfect family home, for all of us.'

She walked over to him, sliding her arms around his waist. 'I love you, Jim Allen.'

He pulled her closer, kissing her gently, and just that brief touch of his lips on hers caused her to fall against him, like some invisible magnet was drawing her to him. 'I love you, too, honey.'

She looked up into his eyes, touching that beautiful mouth of his with her fingertips. 'I guess we're back to reality now, huh?'

He took hold of her hand, his fingers closing around hers as he lifted them to his mouth and kissed them. 'Nothing is going to tear us apart again, Amber. Nothing.'

'Promise?'

'I thought you didn't want me to ever promise you anything?'

'Do you promise, Jim? Do you promise me that nothing will ever tear us apart again?'

He stared into her eyes so deeply he felt as though he was falling. But he wanted her to believe him this time, he needed her to do that; to believe him. 'I promise,' he whispered, his mouth lowering down onto hers again, his thumb gently stroking her cheek. 'With every beat of my heart, I promise.'

Amber felt her own heart skip those proverbial beats and those butterflies fly loose inside her as his lips touched hers, and she pulled away only briefly to let out a tiny gasp as he pushed her back towards the couch.

'In the nursery?' she asked, raising an eyebrow, a slight smile on her face.

'Hey, come on. His mommy and step-daddy have got to make sure this couch is comfortable.'

'Seriously?' But she wasn't really putting up much of a fight. She was already pulling the belt out of her jeans, her eyes telling him she wasn't exactly going to object.

'Seriously.' He pushed her gently back onto the couch, that smile of his almost sending her crazy.

'What are you waiting for, Mr. Allen?' She smiled back, pulling off her t-shirt and whipping off her bra, throwing her arms above her head, arching her back as he slowly pulled her jeans down over her legs.

'I have no idea,' he groaned, his hands on her knees, pushing her legs apart. 'You know, we really have to start behaving ourselves, beautiful. Or neither of us are gonna get any work done.'

'Just get inside me, handsome. Before I get bored and do the job myself.'

He grinned, lying over her, his hand covering her breast, and just the touch of him set her skin on fire. 'Baby, as long as I can watch, you can get there any which way you want.'

'I want *you* inside me,' she breathed, burying her fingers in his hair as she moved her mouth close to his. 'All that solo stuff, I'll leave that for the days when you're not with me, when the only choice I have is to think of you and touch myself. But right now you're here, and I want *you* inside me.'

'Oh, Jesus, I love you so fucking much.'

'I know. Now stop talking and show me how much you love me.'

'You're such a turn-on when you're like this, do you know that?'

She couldn't help smiling, reaching down to take him in her hand, their eyes still locked together. 'Yeah, well, I'm back home now, aren't I? So I need to lose that lovesick wreck of a woman and bring back the professional presenter the rest of the country sees.'

He looked at her, his fingers slipping between hers as he gently pushed inside her. She was his beautiful girl, his necessary escape; his whole fucking world. And as he sank deeper into her, losing himself in that warm and welcoming heaven, he never wanted to leave. Never wanted to stop feeling how she made him feel. He never wanted to lose this.

'Don't, baby,' she whispered, stroking his cheek as she stared into his eyes. 'Whatever you've got on your mind right now, forget it. For the next few minutes just forget everything. Please. Because we don't have all that much longer left of this. Of it just being you and me. We don't have long left. And I don't want to lose that yet.'

She bucked her hips up against him and he groaned quietly, his eyes diverting briefly from hers to look down at her perfect breasts as they rose and fell quickly, inviting him to touch them, and who was he to say no?

For the next few minutes, at least, he was exactly where he wanted to be. With the only woman he wanted to be with. And he'd promised her, hadn't he? He'd promised her nothing would ever tear them apart again, and that was all he'd done. He'd made sure nothing would ever do that. All he could hope was that he'd played the game to the best of his ability, and that his opponent had no comeback.

*

'I need you here, Max,' Ryan said, a feeling of panic enveloping him, and he wasn't used to that. He didn't panic, he handled things. That's what Ryan Fisher did.

'I'm on my way, Ryan. My flight's just landed and I'm on my way to the training ground right now.'

'The new boss wants me in his office, Max, and I…'

'Wait until I get there, okay? Don't do or say anything until I get there. I'll call Dave, make sure he knows the score. Ryan, it'll be okay. It'll be okay, do you hear me?'

'I didn't do this, Max. I didn't. I mean, I…'

'It'll be okay. I'll sort it.'

'Who the hell leaked this? Huh? I thought we'd covered all those bases, made sure that had been the end of it when I left London. I came back up north to leave all this shit behind, Max, because they promised me it wouldn't get out. So who the hell went back on that, huh?'

'Ryan, just calm down, alright? I'm sorting it, and that's all you need to know.'

'Jesus! As if I haven't got enough to fucking deal with.'

Max waited a beat before asking the next question. And even though it was probably a subject he shouldn't have brought up, if it took Ryan's mind off what was going on right now, that could only be a good thing. 'Have you spoken to Amber yet?'

Ryan sighed, throwing himself back against the dressing room wall. 'No. Not yet. Is she home?'

'She's home.'

'Have *you* spoken to her?'

'No.'

'Does she know about this?'

'I have no idea, Ryan. As soon as I'd called you I went straight to the airport, but I haven't heard from her. So I'm assuming she hasn't heard anything yet.'

'She'll be too busy playing mummy and daddy with Jim fucking Allen.'

'Jesus, Ryan, grow up.' Yeah. Bringing up Amber had been a bad move.

'My son is living with a man who… Max, my head is so fucked up right now, I don't think I can do this.'

'Ryan, listen to me. Listen to me! I'm almost there, so just stay where you are and I promise you, I'll sort this.'

'I need to speak to her, Max.'

Max sighed, rubbing the bridge of his nose again as he stared out of the window. Familiar sights flashed by in a blur as his car headed towards the Newcastle Red Star training ground, reminders that he was back up north; back to sort out yet another chapter in the ridiculously complicated life of Ryan Fisher. 'Leave it for now, son, okay?'

'I really need her, Max.'

'Five minutes, Ryan. I'll be there in five minutes.'

Ryan slid his phone back into his pocket and slumped down onto the bench, dropping his head into his hands.

'Hey, mate, you alright?'

Ryan looked up, shaking his head. 'It's all turning to shit again, Gary. I thought it was bad enough Amber leaving me, bad enough that she had to go and marry him, again. Because she's broken my fucking heart, she really has. The way it happened, I thought I'd be okay about it, y'know? I mean, she's never really made it a secret that she and Jim Allen – there was always something there. And I should have known this was going to happen, and maybe I could have handled it so much better if Rico hadn't arrived, but he has, and now she's taking *him* away from me, too, and she's breaking my heart all over again, Gary. She's breaking my fucking heart...' Ryan quickly wiped away a stray tear as it slid slowly down his cheek. 'But this... this could finish me.' He looked at his best friend, an almost defeated tone to his voice. 'This could be the fucking end, Gary.'

Gary gave Ryan's arm a gentle squeeze. 'I don't know what to say, mate. I mean, I knew you had stuff going on when you were playing down in London, but surely...'

'I didn't do it, Gary. What they're saying. I didn't do it.'

'Were you involved? In any way?'

Ryan sat back, pushing both hands through his hair, letting out the longest and heaviest of sighs. 'Not in the way they're saying.'

Gary leaned forward, hanging his head. 'I'm assuming the new boss wants a word?'

'Max is on his way. I can't deal with this on my own. Max was there; he knows the truth.'

'Then he'll sort it, won't he?'

Ryan said nothing. He just stared straight ahead, at the untidy dressing room, the bag of footballs sitting in the corner, the various bits of kit that were thrown over the benches that lined the walls. And he felt sick at the thought of losing the life he had – a life that enabled him to play the game he loved. When all was said and done, you could take away the money and the fame and the endless string of women that could all be his if he so chose; you could take all of that away, as long as he was still able to play the game. Take that away from him and who was he? He was nothing.

'Ryan? Max *will* sort it, won't he?'

Ryan turned to look at Gary. 'I don't know, Gary. I really don't know.'

*

Amber stared at the TV, watching the yellow ticker as it scrolled across the bottom of the screen, signalling *Breaking News*. She kept reading it, over and over again, unable to take in what it was saying.

'Is this true?' She'd heard Jim walk into the room, but she didn't turn around to look at him. Her eyes were still focused on the TV, although she wasn't really listening to the words coming out of her fellow presenter's mouth as he broke the news live on air.

Jim dug his hands deep into his pockets, staring at the TV. 'I don't know, Amber.'

She turned around, her legs crossed underneath her as she sat on the couch, dressed in one of his t-shirts and a pair of cut-off denim shorts, her dark-red hair piled up messily on top of her head. She looked beautiful, devoid of make-up and fresh out of the shower. And he'd never been more in love with her than he was right now.

'I need to speak to him.'

'Why? Anyway, your dad's on his way here with Rico.'

'Yeah, I know. But I just want to see if Ryan's... what? What's the matter?'

'Max will be with him, Amber.'

'No, that look you just gave me. Jim, this is serious. If Ryan is involved in some kind of illegal betting ring...'

'Was.'

'Sorry?'

'He *was* involved in an illegal betting ring. That's what they're saying.'

'Are they?' She got up from the couch and started walking over to the kitchen, but Jim stopped her before she could get there, slipping an arm around her waist.

'Amber?'

She looked at him. That carefree Amber he'd seen in Vegas was slipping away from him; he could see it happening, right there in front of his eyes. Exactly what he'd been afraid of. Exactly what he'd known was going to happen the second they'd set foot back in the UK.

'This isn't something you need to be worrying about, honey.'

'He's Rico's dad, Jim. So, yes, it *is* something I need to be worrying about.' She broke free of his grip and walked into the kitchen, turning around and folding her arms as she leaned back against the counter. 'I know he's not my problem any more, but...' She pushed a hand through her hair, turning her head away from Jim to look out of the window. 'Oh, I don't know. I think I'm just overtired. We haven't had much sleep since Vegas, have we?'

Jim smiled at her as her eyes met his. 'No. We haven't.' He walked over to her, resting a hand on her hip as he gently stroked her cheek, kissing her softly. 'I didn't want to sleep. I wanted to stay awake, I wanted to make love to you; that's all I wanted to do. It's all I *still* want to do.'

She pulled him a little closer by his shirt, kissing him quickly, but long enough to let the feel of his mouth against hers calm her slightly. 'Yeah, well, there's a little thing called *work* getting in the way of that.'

Jim groaned, throwing his head back, his hand still resting on her hip. 'I wish I didn't have to go in today.'

'It's your first official day in charge of Endleigh United, and you've got a big press conference this afternoon, so you can't exactly miss all of that, can you?'

He cupped her cheek in his hand as he kissed her again, and all Amber wanted to do was slide up onto the counter, slip out of her shorts, open her legs and let him back inside. But that fantasy was soon forgotten as the doorbell ringing signalled the arrival of her dad and Rico.

'And there's another reason why we have to start behaving.' Amber smiled, planting one last kiss on her husband's lips before running off to answer the door.

She almost flung it off its hinges, letting out a tiny squeal at the sight of her beautiful baby boy. 'Has he been okay?' she asked Freddie, taking Rico straight from him and kissing her son's warm cheek. He snuggled in against her, pulling at her t-shirt, and all Amber wanted to do now was sit down and cuddle him and not move until she had to.

'He's been fine,' Freddie replied, quickly kissing Amber before closing the door behind him, throwing his bags down onto the hall floor. 'So, how was Vegas?'

'It was perfect.' She was looking down at Rico as she spoke, watching as his tiny hand wrapped itself around her finger.

'You certainly look happy,' Freddie continued, following Amber into the kitchen where Jim was making some fresh coffee. 'You okay, Jim?'

'I'm good, Freddie, yeah.'

Amber watched as two men who'd once been the best of friends tried their hardest to regain that friendship. Two men she loved very much. And even though she knew their relationship could never be the same as it once had been, she really hoped they could carry on growing closer.

Freddie turned his attention back to Amber. 'You looked beautiful, by the way. The photo in Debbie's column, the one you released? You looked beautiful.'

She smiled at her father, Rico still gurgling away in her arms.

'That's because she is,' Jim said, and Amber turned to look at him, her eyes locking onto his, a smile passing between them that promised so much. 'She *is* beautiful.'

Amber broke the stare, turning back to her father, and it didn't escape her notice how uncomfortable he still looked whenever Jim spoke about her in that way. She guessed it was always going to be hard for Freddie to get his head around what had happened between her and Jim all those years ago.

'This house… it's something else,' Freddie said, quickly changing the subject.

'It's going to take a while before I can start thinking of it as home,' Amber sighed. 'But, now that Jim and I are married, and Rico's here, well – it feels more like a family home, that's for sure.'

Freddie looked at her, his face expressionless for a second or two, before he allowed a slight smile to appear. 'I'm going to miss you, kiddo. And that little one. I was just getting used to having him around.'

'We'll be up north all the time, you know that,' Amber said, although her eyes were back on Rico, who was now pulling gently on her t-shirt. 'Because you'll miss your granddad, won't you, baby?'

'And you're sure that taking him with you to work – you're sure you're okay with that? You're sure Cloud Sports are okay with that?'

She looked up sharply. 'Yes, I'm okay with that. And yes, Cloud Sports are absolutely fine with it. And no, I'm not getting a nanny, okay? It's not happening.'

'Amber, sweetheart, all I'm saying is…'

'It won't be easy, I know that. I'm not naïve enough to think this is all gonna work out perfectly, of course there'll be problems,

I know that, too. But I'll work through them.' She looked at Jim, his smile giving her all the support she needed. '*We'll* work through them.'

'Okay, I'm sorry. I just worry about you, that's all. Now that you're based down here and I won't see half as much of you as I used to… I just want you to know that, if you need me or your Aunty Kim, or any of us – if you need *any* help you just call, do you hear me?'

'Yeah, Dad, I hear you.' She gave Rico to Jim before going over to her dad, giving him the biggest hug. And only then did she realise just how much she was going to miss him. Ever since her mum had died they'd spent so much time together, and now that time was going to be limited.

'Yeah, well, no being all stubborn and thinking you can cope. If it all gets too much, you know where we are.'

Amber let him go. 'Do you want some coffee?'

'Please.' Freddie's eyes focused on the TV still playing away at the other end of the family room. 'You've heard about Ryan, then?'

Amber nodded as she spooned sugar into her father's mug. 'I should speak to him, really.'

'Why?'

'That's what I said,' Jim muttered, cradling Rico in the crook of his arm.

Amber swung around to face them both. 'He's Rico's dad. What's the problem here?'

'Now's probably not the best time, Amber.' Freddie leaned back against the counter, folding his arms. 'I know Dave French, and I know that the last thing he'll want is something like this blighting his early days in charge of Newcastle Red Star.'

'And your point is?' Amber asked, copying her father's stance as she folded her own arms.

'My point is, kiddo, that Ryan probably has other things to think about right now. Max'll be with him…'

'I said that, too.'

Amber turned her stare on Jim.

He just raised his eyebrows and shrugged. 'What?'

She shook her head but said nothing, turning her attention back to making coffee. 'You're in one of the back rooms, Dad. The one at the end of the first-floor landing. What time do you have to be back in Newcastle tomorrow?'

'As soon as possible. I'll be getting up early, I'm afraid. Got myself on a 7.15am flight back up north in the morning. Are you going in to work today?'

Amber shook her head. 'No. Ronnie might be coming over later, though. Before he heads off to Parkfield for the press conference.'

'Okay if I come with you to that press conference, Jim?' Freddie asked.

'Of course it's okay.' Jim gently lay Rico over his shoulder, and Amber felt a pain cut right across her heart as she watched Jim kiss her baby's forehead, smiling down at him. And as Rico reached out to touch Jim's face, she felt her heart break just a little bit more. As much as she would never, ever take Rico away from Ryan, she still wished with every beat of her breaking heart that he was her husband's.

'Is it alright if I go and take a shower?'

'Of course it is. I've put fresh towels out for you in the en suite, but if you need anything else just shout.' She waited until she could hear her dad making his way upstairs before she said anything to Jim. 'You okay?'

He looked at her. 'Hmm? Yeah, I'm fine.'

'You okay to keep a hold of him while I finish making this coffee?'

Jim nodded, reaching out to stop her from walking away from him. 'Hang on, Amber… Look, I know you want to speak to Ryan and – and I understand why. I do.'

'Do you?'

'I do. But your dad's right. Now really isn't the time. It isn't our problem, baby, okay? And he's got plenty of people around him, you know that.'

'I also know the kind of person he is, Jim. I know the way he handles things.'

Jim slid his arm around her waist, pulling her closer. 'This isn't our problem.'

She reached out to stroke his cheek, kissing him gently. 'I know,' she sighed.

'Then let's just concentrate on us, okay? Me, you, and this little guy here.' He kissed Rico's cheek and Amber felt her stomach flip for a whole different reason this time. 'What do you say, kiddo? Should your mommy stop worrying about your daddy and concentrate on you and me?'

Amber couldn't help smiling. If this was her life, then she was in love with it already. 'Well, if you two are gonna gang up on me…'

Jim kissed her again, a little longer and a little harder, but Rico had other ideas, pulling on Amber's t-shirt in an obvious attempt to gain his mum's attention.

'Okay, baby boy, I'm all yours now.' She took Rico from Jim, cradling him gently in her arms. 'I'm all yours.'

'I've got competition, huh?' Jim smiled.

Amber looked up, returning his smile. 'You're a very close second, handsome.'

'I'll take that. Look, I'd better go make some more calls, get myself ready for that press conference, so, I'll be in my office if you need me.' He kissed the top of her head, ruffling Rico's hair. 'I'll see you both before I leave.'

Her attention was back focused on her son, but, as far as Jim was concerned, as long as Rico was the only competition he had to face, things were going to be just fine.

Chapter Sixteen

'He's fucking dropped me from the squad, Max! Jesus…'

'Yes, I was there, Ryan. I heard what he said.'

'I thought you were gonna sort this.'

'And I will, but it's all going to take time.'

Ryan threw himself back against the wall outside the training ground administration block. 'Shit! This is a fucking nightmare… I don't know what to do, Max. I really don't know what the fuck to do.'

'You do nothing. Okay? *You* do nothing. You lie low, you don't say anything to any reporters, you speak to no press, you keep quiet. Do you hear me, Ryan?'

'Yeah, I hear you.'

'Well, I'm not sure you do.'

Ryan stared at his agent. 'You're treating me like a kid again.'

'I'm just making sure you know the score, that's all. Because there is going to be so much digging into your past now… you got anything else I don't know about that you might want to share with me?'

Ryan held that stare, shaking his head slowly. 'You know all there is to know.'

'You better be telling me the truth, Ryan. Because the last thing I need is some new "surprise" coming from out of nowhere giving me problems I really don't need.'

'For fuck's sake…' Ryan sighed, turning his head away from Max.

'This isn't a game, Ryan.'

'I'm well aware of that, thanks.' Ryan pushed a hand through his hair before facing Max again. 'What about Amber?'

'What about her?'

'*She's* a reporter. And I can't not speak to her; she's Rico's mum. I *need* to speak to her.'

'Not about this you don't. I'm serious, Ryan. I know you care about her…'

'I love her, Max.'

'Jesus Christ,' Max sighed. 'Have I got *this* to deal with, too?'

'What?'

'You. Behaving like a fourteen-year-old.'

Ryan threw Max a look.

'Don't create more problems for yourself, kid. You've got enough going on. Come on. Let's get you home.'

'I don't fucking want to go home, Max.'

'Well, there's no point in you staying here. Besides, the police need to speak to you some time soon, so we might as well get that over with.'

'Is it gonna go against me, Max?'

'Is what going to go against you?'

'The fact we covered up my association in all of this. That betting ring was being investigated; it was all over the news at the time I signed for Red Star. So, is that gonna go against me?'

Max dug his hands into his pockets and sighed. 'I honestly don't know. All I know is…' He looked at Ryan, and he could quite clearly see the panic in the young man's eyes before he hung his head. 'All I know is we've got some of the best lawyers working on this, and they'll do everything in their power to limit the damage, I promise you that. But that's all I can promise you right now.'

'I told her she wasn't enough.'

Max frowned slightly. 'What?'

Ryan raised his head, his eyes meeting Max's. 'Amber. I told her she wasn't enough. I told her if it wasn't for Rico… I lied, Max. I fucking lied, because she was all I ever needed, and I just couldn't fucking make her love me too. I couldn't do that. Why couldn't I do that?'

'Oh, Jesus…' Max moved closer to Ryan, gently squeezing his shoulder. 'Hey, come on. Where's that cocky, arrogant, self-obsessed Ryan Fisher we all know?'

Ryan's eyes were full of tears, and he didn't even know if he was crying because he was terrified of what was happening now, or because of what he was telling Max; he had no idea. It just felt as if all the control was slipping away from him. He was beginning to feel helpless.

'He was the one who drove her away, Max. The old Ryan. He was the one she couldn't live with, and even when I tried to tell her I'd changed… even when…' He couldn't get the words out; they were stuck in his throat, the emotion taking over everything until he felt as though he couldn't breathe.

'Come on,' Max said kindly, putting his arm around Ryan's shoulders as they walked towards the car park. 'Let's get out of here.'

'I don't know what to do, Max.'

'I'll sort this, Ryan, I promise you. Somehow, believe me, I'll sort this.'

*

'You're not worried about him, are you?' Ronnie asked, watching Amber closely as she moved around the living room, straightening curtains, nudging items of furniture around and generally doing anything possible to avoid sitting down.

'Worried about who? Jim? No, he'll be fine. It's not like he hasn't done this kind of thing before. He had just as much hype surrounding him when he came to Newcastle Red Star.'

'Yeah, but back then he didn't have all this personal drama surrounding him, did he? And I wasn't talking about Jim. I was talking about Ryan.'

'Yes, I'm worried about him.' Amber moved a large brown table lamp a centimetre to the left of the sideboard it was currently sitting on. 'I'd be lying if I said I wasn't.'

'Amber, will you just sit down, please? You're making me nervous with all this unnecessary flitting about from one end of the room to the other.'

'I'm not "flitting about", as you put it, Ronnie. I'm trying to make my new home feel more lived in, that's all. Because it's taking some getting used to.'

'Well, considering you've only been living in the thing for about five minutes I reckon you're expecting a bit too much, to be honest.'

She flung herself down onto the couch beside him, throwing herself back against the over-stuffed cushions. 'It's too big. This place, I mean. It's way too big.'

'It's frigging amazing, that's what it is. You still not feeling it?'

She looked at her best friend. 'I don't hate it. But I'm not in love with it.' She looked away, leaning forward to push the glass bowl sitting in the centre of the coffee table a little bit more to the right. 'But I'm in love with Jim. And if he's here, then I'll learn to love this place.'

'You heard from Ryan since all this kicked off?' Ronnie asked, taking her hand and pulling her back against the cushions. 'And stop doing that, will you? Everything looks fine.'

'No,' she sighed, running both hands through her hair. 'I haven't heard from him. I really want to talk to him – or a part of me really wants to talk to him, anyway, but I'm not sure I should.'

'Why not?'

She looked at Ronnie. 'I don't know.'

'Maybe you shouldn't get involved.'

'Don't you start. I've had enough of that from Jim, and my dad, but what people don't seem to understand now is that things are different. Before I could have just tried to ignore this. I could have pushed it to the back of my mind and believed that Ryan Fisher really wasn't my problem any more. But I can't do that now. He's Rico's dad, and that means he's still a part of my life and because of that connection I… I still care about him, Ronnie. I can't just switch that off because it doesn't work like that.'

'So call him.'

She frowned, slightly confused by the fact he was telling her to do something everyone else had told her to leave well alone. 'Maybe now *isn't* the right time.'

Ronnie shrugged, getting up off the couch. 'Your decision.'

She sat forward, narrowing her eyes as she continued to stare at him. 'Is it? Ronnie, why are you pushing me to do something everyone else is so against?'

'Because you listen to other people way too much. More than you think you do. Look, Amber, if you want to call him, call him. Ask him how he is, make sure he's okay, then get back on with your life. That's all you have to do. And whether you do that or not is entirely up to you. Besides, the Amber Sullivan I used to know would never have waited for someone's permission to do anything. Would she?'

Amber looked at him as he raised an eyebrow and threw her a small smile before leaving the room. No. She wouldn't. And that's what confused her even more.

*

'I'm going down there,' Ryan said as he sat at the breakfast bar in Gary and Debbie's stark white kitchen nursing a cup of strong coffee.

'Down where?' Debbie asked, not looking up from her laptop. Her nanny had taken Jodi to playgroup and she was making the most of the time she had alone to get some work done. Or she had been, until Ryan had turned up.

'London.'

Debbie's head shot up, her eyes meeting Ryan's. 'Is that a good idea?'

'What the fuck do people expect me to do? Sit on my arse doing nothing until all this blows over? *If* this all blows over.'

'It'll blow over,' Debbie said, her eyes now back down on her keyboard. 'You've got one of the best agents there is. He'll sort this.'

'You know, everyone keeps saying that as though all he has to do is have a word with a few people and it'll all go away. Well, we tried that, didn't we? And look what happened. And what are you doing anyway?'

Debbie looked up again. 'I'm working, Ryan. Believe it or not, I do actually have a career, despite what some people might think.'

Ryan took a sip of coffee, ignoring the edgy tone to her voice. 'If I'm being forced to take a break from playing I might as well use that free time to go and see Rico.'

'Well, there is that, I suppose.'

Ryan frowned. 'He's my son. And if I want to go and see him I'll go and see him, and there isn't a lot anyone can do to stop me.'

'I wasn't stopping you from doing anything, Ryan. But Amber's just got back from Vegas, Jim's started his new job, not to mention the fact that they're both trying to settle into a new home.'

'And the last thing they need is me turning up, is that what you're trying to say? Besides, Jim Allen isn't exactly starting a *new* job, is he? He's just going back to his old one, and…'

Debbie rested her chin in her hand as she looked at Ryan. 'And, what? Come on, what's the matter?'

Ryan stood up, walking over to the window, looking out over Gary and Debbie's huge back garden with its swimming pool, purpose-built kids' play area and manicured lawns that seemed to go on forever. 'I think Jim Allen's got something to do with this.'

It was Debbie's turn to frown as she swung around on her stool, her eyes not leaving Ryan. 'You think Jim Allen's got something to do with your involvement in an illegal betting ring?'

Ryan turned away from the window to face Debbie. 'I think he's got something to do with the fact that my involvement is all over the media.'

Debbie's frown deepened. 'You got any proof of this? Because you can't just go throwing accusations like that around.'

'He's got something to do with it, Debbie, I'm telling you. I've got this feeling, right here in my gut. He's not content with taking my girlfriend and my son away from me; he's now hell-bent on taking my career, too. And why? Because I'm in love with Amber?'

Debbie sighed, sliding down from her stool. 'Ryan, are you sure you're not just being paranoid? I mean, I know you and Jim have never really got on... Hang on, you're still in love with Amber?'

'Of course I'm still in love with Amber. I've always been in love with Amber. I just wasn't always mature enough to realise that.' He leaned back against the French doors, shoving his hands deep into his jeans pockets, his eyes staring down at the black-tiled floor. 'I owe her so much because she changed me, Debbie. She made me see the kind of man I could actually be; she gave me my amazing baby boy.' He looked back up, his eyes meeting Debbie's. 'I watched her give birth to my son, and she has no idea what that did to me, not really. She became everything to me that day, and yet still I couldn't tell her that. I just kept banging on about sex and how much I wanted to...' He turned away again, taking a deep breath. 'But, do you know what? The day she gave birth to Rico, I think that was the day it all ended for us.'

'How can you possibly know that, Ryan?'

He closed his eyes for a second, breathing in deeply again. 'Jim Allen never did walk away from her, did he? Oh, on paper, yes, that divorce was final. Their relationship was over.' He opened his eyes and looked back over at Debbie. 'But it wasn't, was it? He broke her down and he tore her heart out but he never really walked away. Because Amber wouldn't let him. She'll never let him, Debbie. Will she?'

'She loves him, Ryan. They've just got married, they're making a new life together.'

'And that's all proof that he's changed, is it? Look, don't tell Amber any of this, you got that? Everything I've just told you… everything. It stays between you and me, okay?'

'You really think Jim's involved in all of this?'

'Somehow. I mean it, Debbie. I don't want anyone to know about this, not even Gary.'

Debbie held up her hands, the look on Ryan's face more than determined. 'Okay. I won't say a thing. I promise. But I still think you're being paranoid. I mean, why would Jim do that? He's got what he wants now, hasn't he? He's got Amber back, they've got a whole new life ahead of them – what would he gain by trying to wreck your career?'

'I'll never be out of her life, Debbie. Because of Rico I will *always* be a part of Amber's life.'

'Yeah, I get that, but I still don't see why that would make Jim feel the need to ruin your career.'

'Because he wants me down in the gutter. He wants me on my knees with nothing left. He wants to destroy me because it makes him feel better, that's all. That's the kind of man he is. In his eyes I'm always going to be a threat to what he and Amber have. In his eyes, that's never gonna go away.'

Debbie leaned back against the counter, that frown still present on her face. 'I still don't get it. I mean, surely, if that was the case, then isn't there a risk that this could push Amber closer to you, rather than further away? If she thought Jim was trying to do that to you… I think you're wrong here, Ryan.'

Ryan stuck his hands in his pockets, a slight smile now forming on his handsome face. 'Yeah, well, you can think what you like. But I know what I'm feeling, and that feeling is telling me that Jim Allen may not be quite as clever as he thinks he is. Because you're right – if he really *is* going all out to destroy me, and Amber finds out, that isn't gonna be pretty, is it?'

Debbie shook her head. 'No, Ryan, come on. You have to have

some proof here, you can't just go marching down there throwing accusations around. That's only gonna cause more trouble. Surely it'd be better if you kept your head down for a bit until all this really does blow over?'

'And that's exactly what I plan to do, Debbie. I'm not stupid. But once my suspicions are confirmed, believe me, she isn't gonna want to know him any more. And this time… this time I'll make sure she never goes back to him.'

'You're talking about wrecking a marriage here, Ryan. And I can't let you do that. Amber's my best friend, and she's happy with Jim.'

'With a man who still lies to her? With a man who's trying his best to bring down the father of her baby? Do you really think she wants to be with a man like that?'

'She loves him, Ryan. And I really don't think anything you can do… Come on! Everything you're talking about here is purely hypothetical because you have no proof. The only reason you think Jim has anything to do with this is because of your history. That's all. You have no other reason.'

'She *thinks* she loves him, Debbie. She thinks she does. But Jim Allen is on his last life with Amber, and he should have realised that before he started all of this. He should have realised that.'

'Should have realised what? Ryan, please, don't go down there. Don't start any trouble when you have nothing to back it up with. Can't you just let her be happy?'

'Oh, I want her to be happy more than anything, Debbie, believe me. I just want her to be happy with *me*. And now… now I just might have all the ammunition I need to finally make that happen.'

Chapter Seventeen

'He's been suspended,' Amber sighed, throwing the newspaper down onto her desk.

'Well, I wouldn't feel too sorry for him, Amber. He's still on full pay. I don't think your child-support payments are gonna suffer, somehow.'

Amber threw Ronnie a sideways glance, folding her arms as she leaned back against the desk. 'And I still haven't spoken to him.'

'Because you're afraid of what anyone else might say if you do?'

'No. Because I haven't been able to get in touch with him, that's why. He won't answer his phone… Oh, just the man I want to see,' Amber said, directing her attention to Max as he walked into the Cloud Sports office.

'That's handy, because you're just the woman *I* want to see. Morning, Ronnie.'

'Max.'

'So, how's my most beautiful client today?' Max smiled. One of those smiles that told Amber he definitely had some kind of ulterior motive.

'Sorry, are you talking to me?'

Max rolled his eyes. 'Take a compliment, sweetheart, will you?'

'I would if I thought it was sincere, so, whatever it is you're about to ask me, the answer's no.'

'You don't even know what it is yet?'

'The answer's still no. Where's Ryan?'

'How the hell should *I* know? I'm his agent not his babysitter. Although sometimes those lines get more than blurred, I agree.'

'He's not answering his phone when I call him, Max.'

'I wouldn't get involved, kiddo.'

'Too late. Why isn't he answering his phone?'

'Look, Amber, I really have no idea why he's choosing to ignore your calls because he's answering mine, and believe me, sweetheart, I wish it were the other way around. He's killing me right now.'

'Is he alright?'

'As much as he can be, given the circumstances.'

'So, what exactly went on, then?' Ronnie asked, folding his arms as he looked at Max.

'I really can't say, Ronnie. It's all in the hands of our lawyers right now, and I can't risk anything more getting out into the media that could be twisted into something it's not. The last thing we need is anything jeopardising Ryan's position.'

'And what *is* Ryan's position, exactly?'

Max laughed, his hands digging deep in his pockets as he looked down at the ground for a beat or two. 'Yeah, you're good, Ron. You're very good.'

'Worth a try,' Ronnie sighed.

'Ronnie!' Amber exclaimed.

'What? Oh, come on, Amber. People are falling over themselves to get the truth about this story. And when all's said and done I'm a sports reporter. We report on the big sports news, and this – *this* is big sports news.'

'Can we just quit this subject now? I'm not saying anything, alright? If you want a statement, contact our lawyers. But I can tell you, all you'll get is the stock "no comment." Now, can I get back to what I came here to do?'

'Which is?' Amber wasn't really in the mood for another battle with Max over lads' mags and photo shoots that she didn't think were wholly appropriate, so she was glad when the sound of the door opening again distracted her. And when she looked up and saw who'd just walked through it, she knew Max had lost any chance of any kind of conversation with her for the foreseeable future.

'I went and got him from the crèche, was that okay?' Ryan asked as he sauntered into the room, full of cocky arrogance and swagger, carrying his baby son in one arm.

Amber couldn't help smiling. No matter what she did or didn't feel for this man, he still looked as hot as hell with his messed-up dark hair, heavy stubble that was back to verging on the beard he'd used to sport, and those deep-blue eyes. 'Of course it's okay. What are you doing here? I've been trying to get hold of you for days now.'

'Yeah. What *are* you doing here, Ryan?' Max asked, not even trying to hide the fact that he didn't appreciate Ryan turning up down here without letting him know.

'I didn't want to speak to you over the phone, Amber. I wanted to see you in person. And, seeing as I don't have a whole lot to do at the moment, I thought I might as well come down here and see my beautiful boy.' His eyes locked with Amber's. 'And his just-as-beautiful mum.'

'Okay. Ryan, can I have a word?' Max said, not missing the look Ronnie threw Ryan – a look Ryan didn't see, but one he surely must have felt because if looks could kill then Ryan would most certainly be pretty much lifeless right now.

'Jesus, Max, all I've done these past few days is *have words* with you. Can I talk to someone else now?'

Max sighed, throwing his head back, and Amber was almost certain she heard a small string of expletives just making themselves audible above the sound of that heavy sigh. 'Just remember what I said, Ryan, okay?'

Amber looked at Max, frowning slightly.

'Don't look at me like that, Amber. You know the state of play here.'

She just raised her eyebrows, turning her attention back to Ryan, the smile reappearing back on her face as she watched their son pulling at the collar of his daddy's black-leather jacket. 'Hey, baby! Look who's come to see you.'

'You free for lunch?' Ryan asked, his eyes now focused solely on Amber. Everyone else could just fuck off.

'Yeah, of course I am.'

'We need you back here at three, Amber,' Ronnie said, his stance one of suspicion as he eyed Ryan warily. He knew Amber too well, and he could read those warning signs better than anyone. 'We're recording two episodes of *Back of the Net*, remember?'

'Yes, I'm well aware of my schedule, Ronnie.' She leaned over and kissed the top of Rico's head, smiling at Ryan again. 'I'll just grab my coat and we'll get out of here, okay?'

*

'You're looking well, considering.' Amber watched Ryan from across the table as he fed Rico his bottle. And it didn't escape her notice how many of the restaurant's adoring female eyes were on him. He did look pretty sexy, though, even she had to admit that. And the addition of a gorgeous baby only served to make him ten times more attractive.

'What? Considering I've currently got fuck all to do because some bastard's spreading lies about me that could threaten my career? And did you never consider breast-feeding?'

'I considered it, but it was never really gonna work.'

'Why? Because those incredible tits of yours are reserved for one man only? And I wish that man was me because, Jesus, I know exactly what I'm missing.'

'You know, just when I begin to think you really have grown up, you come out with something like that.'

Ryan looked at her. 'So, how *is* everything with the not-exactly-new husband?'

'Do you want me to get up and leave?'

He looked back down at Rico. 'No. We don't want your mum to leave, do we, kiddo?'

'Then stop making *him* look like the adult.'

Ryan said nothing for a second or two as he put Rico's bottle down and laid his son over his shoulder, gently rubbing his back. 'He's settled back in at Endleigh United, then?'

'Like he's never been away. Why are you here, Ryan?'

'I wanted to spend some time with my son, seeing as I appear to have quite a bit of it on my hands at the minute. And I wanted to see you, I told you that. I want to explain things, in person.'

'Max doesn't seem to think you should be telling me anything.'

'That's because he's thinking of you as Amber Sullivan, sports reporter, rather than the mother of my baby. The woman I used to sleep with.'

Her eyes stared straight into his. 'I would never betray your trust, Ryan.'

'I know.' He held her gaze maybe a little longer than he should have done because she eventually broke the stare and looked down, her eyes focusing on her wedding ring.

'Is any of it true?' she asked, twisting the wedding band round and round.

Ryan waited a second before answering. 'I don't know why I got involved,' he began, his hand still gently rubbing Rico's back. 'I mean, it wasn't as if I needed the money. I guess I just got off on the idea of having even more. It was at the height of my – of my problems, Amber, you need to remember that.'

'Height of your stupidity, you mean.'

Ryan laughed as Rico let out a tiny burp. 'Hey! There you go, little fella. Do you want your mum now?'

Amber couldn't help smiling. 'I think he's quite happy with you.'

Ryan nestled Rico in the crook of his arm, his eyes once more locking with Amber's. 'I met this guy – a pretty prominent businessman, does a lot of his work out of south-east Asia, where most of these betting rings are…'

'I know all about these betting rings, Ryan. I want to know what *your* involvement with this particular one was.'

Ryan sighed, breaking the stare briefly to look down at his now-sleeping son. 'It was some charity function the club I was playing for at the time was throwing. I met this guy, this businessman, there. We got talking, and he obviously knew a lot about me, about the fact I liked to take risks, the fact I wasn't scared of breaking the rules or…' He broke off for a second, his eyes now back on Amber. 'He told me they were looking for players, top-flight players, to help fix some of the bigger matches. He made it sound so easy, Amber. I told him I didn't need the money, but I *was* gambling quite heavily at the time and what this guy was offering me – the kick it could give me was just too much to turn down.'

'Jesus, Ryan, I don't believe you…'

'All I had to do was fix things like yellow cards, bookings – if they wanted someone sent off in, say, the second half of a match then all I had to do was make sure I got in the way, so to speak, of an opposing player; make sure they tackled me badly enough to get that necessary red card. They'd bet on the most ridiculous things, the smallest of things, it was crazy! Two yellow cards in the first fifteen minutes of a match? It was easy money, Amber. And don't think some of the referees weren't involved either, believe me, it's…'

'Did you do any of it, Ryan? Did you actually have anything to do with fixing any matches?'

His eyes locked with hers again, and this time he was determined no one was going to break that stare. 'No. And that's God's honest truth, Amber. I thought about it, I listened to them, I even watched videos of some of the matches where players *had* been involved, and they really made that shit look easy. It was nigh-on impossible to tell what the hell was going on, so I thought about it, of course I did. We're talking hundreds of thousands of pounds here,

Amber. They were willing to pay me hundreds of thousands of pounds because that was nothing to them. It was frigging peanuts compared to the amount they'd be winning when those matches were played. But I couldn't do it. When it came down to it, I just couldn't go through with it.'

'How far down the line did you go?' she asked, her eyes never leaving his.

Ryan took a deep breath, exhaling slowly, looking down at the table only briefly before raising his head to meet her gaze. 'I was in the tunnel. I was about to go out and make sure I was booked as close to the tenth minute of the game as I could make it, and that would have earned me more money than I made in a week, believe it or not. But I couldn't do it. I couldn't. I love this game too much to sell it down the river and for once my head ruled my pathetic, materialistic heart and it said no. I couldn't do it.'

'So, you didn't actually *do* anything that could constitute fixing a game in any way?'

He shook his head. 'I swear, Amber, I couldn't do it. Oh, they weren't happy, believe me. And there were threats and recriminations and for a time I really thought it was all gonna come out there and then. But Max, he… he stepped in. Oh, he dragged me over the fucking coals first, for being a bloody idiot, but he stepped in. He took it out of my hands and, somehow, he managed to get them to back down. I don't know how he did it, or who he used to make sure that outcome was reached; I didn't ask. Because I didn't really want to know, I was already too involved. But he made sure my name was left out of it. He made sure my involvement was wiped clean, erased. Even when that particular betting ring was exposed, my name was never mentioned.'

'Is that why you moved back up north?'

'It was one of the reasons. You know the others. It was time to get away, to try and get my head straight because I'd just let those problems build up and I – I needed the space. I needed the distance.'

'And that's everything now, is it? No more skeletons waiting to fall out of the closet?'

'That's all.'

'So why is your name suddenly coming out now? If they'd promised to keep your involvement out of it?'

Ryan wasn't going to tell her what it was he was really thinking. What good would that do? To sit there and tell her he thought her husband was behind all this would only push her away, and that was the last thing he wanted. 'I don't know. Max has got people trying to find out just what's going on, but...'

'But, what? Do you think you *know* who might be behind this?'

'No. No, I've got no idea. But this could ruin me, Amber. And I'm scared.'

'But if they can prove you didn't do anything... have the police spoken to you?'

He nodded, leaning over to kiss Rico's forehead. 'I told them exactly what I've told you.'

'And?'

He looked at her. 'And, that's it, for now.'

'For now?'

'They're speaking to more people. Going back over the case from a couple of years ago. So I had to tell them the truth because they're going to be speaking to people I was involved with. But the fact my involvement was covered up...'

'Why didn't you just tell the truth back then, Ryan?'

'All I could think about was coming home. I'd been in London since I was fourteen years old, Amber, but all of a sudden I felt like a stranger. Newcastle seemed like a safe place to run to, back to my northern roots. Back to where I belonged.'

'I still don't understand why you couldn't just tell the truth.'

'Because it wasn't that simple. There was all the other shit going down with my addiction, the depression, the drinking... I couldn't handle it all, I couldn't handle any of it, if truth be told, and even though it was wrong, I know that now, I just wanted it all to go away. I wanted to get out of London and come back home and forget that any of it had happened. But I couldn't leave it alone, could I? And the only way I seemed able to forget was to immerse myself in the crap that had caused all my problems in the first place. And the rest, as you know, is history. But now…' He looked down at Rico again. 'Now I know I should have just faced up to everything. I should have dealt with it all and not let it follow me to Newcastle. I was weak and I ignored everything Max and you and Gary… I ignored it all. But if I'd listened…'

'Hey, come on. Look, it's pointless going over old ground now, it's happened.'

'I wanted the fame and the women and this ridiculous life of excess that just isn't fucking real, Amber. It's all a smokescreen for people who can't face up to the things they really need to deal with, but it isn't real.' He bent his head to kiss Rico again, stroking his tiny cheek with his finger. 'This little guy – *he's* real. You…' his eyes were back on Amber's, and there wasn't a thing Amber could do to break that stare, even if she'd wanted to. 'What I felt for you – what I still feel for you, *that's* real. That is so fucking real.'

'Ryan…'

'I love you, Amber, and I don't care that you don't want to hear that, I don't fucking care because *I* need to say it. I need to say it and know that you heard me, okay? I need that, right now, more than at any other time.'

Amber shook her head, but still her eyes wouldn't leave his.

'I'm scared,' he whispered, and Amber felt a little piece of her heart break for this man in front of her. Because he really was so different to the person she'd first encountered just a couple of years ago. 'Football is my life. It's all I've ever known, and if that's taken away from me I don't know what the hell I'm gonna do. I don't know who I'll be any more.'

'It won't come to that, Ryan.' She reached across the table, taking his hand, her fingers curling tightly around his. 'Max won't let it, I know he won't. He loves you like a son; you know that. He'll have the best people working on this, and it won't come to that. You aren't going to lose anything.'

'I lost you.'

She slowly let go of his hand, her eyes back down on her wedding ring. 'I'd better get back. I don't want to be late.'

'Amber…'

'Rico needs to go back to the crèche.'

Ryan stood up, his baby son still asleep in his arms. 'I can take him, can't I? Amber, please, hang on…'

'I need to get back, Ryan.' She slipped on her jacket, walking over to him, leaning in to kiss her little boy. 'And so does he. Make sure you get him back to the crèche soon. They'll be expecting him.'

'Amber…' He reached out and gently grabbed her hand, stopping her from walking away. 'Everything I said, I mean it.'

'Yeah.' She looked into his eyes once more. And then wished she hadn't. 'I know.'

Chapter Eighteen

'Is he going to be down here long?' Jim asked, leaning back against the nursery doorpost as he watched Amber settle Rico down in his cot.

'I don't know. They've suspended him indefinitely so it's not like he's got anything to stay up north for at the minute. And, like he said, while he's got the time he might as well spend some of it with Rico.' She walked over to Jim, flicking off the light switch so the room was bathed with the soft glow of Rico's night light. 'And that *will* actually take a bit of weight off our shoulders, for a little while, won't it?'

'He's taking him every day?'

'Most days, yes. Have you got a problem with that?' She pushed past him and made her way downstairs.

'Of course I haven't got a problem with that… Amber.' He followed her into the living room. 'Is everything okay? You've been a bit on edge ever since you got home.'

'It's been a busy day, Jim, that's all,' Amber sighed, pouring herself a small measure of whiskey. 'And I'm tired.'

He walked over to her, taking the glass out of her hand and pulling her into his arms. 'Do you want an early night?'

'Early? It's half past ten.' She pulled free of him, sitting down on the couch and switching on the TV. 'I just need to chill out for a bit.'

Jim looked at her. Something was wrong, and it didn't take a genius to work out what. 'He's not our problem, Amber.'

'Yeah, you see, you keep saying that, Jim, but, to be honest, he still *is* our problem.' Jim sat down beside her, and she turned her head to look at him. 'Because he's been down here for all of half a day, and look at me. I want it to be just you and me and Rico, but it's never really going to be like that, is it?'

He reached out to touch her face, gently cupping her cheek in his hand, his mouth brushing lightly over hers. 'It's like that now,' he whispered, his hand moving lower, sliding inside her shirt and cupping her breast, his thumb flicking over her nipple. 'It's like that right now.'

'I hate it when you do this,' she groaned, but she was already slipping out of the denim shorts she was wearing, lying back against the cushions as he unfastened her shirt before undoing his own, pulling it off and throwing it down on the floor. 'I really, really hate it.'

He smiled, and she felt the past few hours just wash away, pushed aside as he took over everything. Her strong and beautiful American man. Ryan Fisher could try, and she'd never be able to stop him from trying, but he would never, ever come between her and Jim again. She wouldn't let him, because she loved this man too much. She ached for him, constantly, with a need bordering on obsession. And all it had taken here was the touch of his hand against her skin and she was lost in him. And lost was exactly where she needed to be.

'Close your eyes,' Jim said quietly.

She did as she was told, a tiny groan escaping as he slowly pulled her knickers down, sliding them off. 'I really, really hate it when you do this.'

'But you love it, when I do *this*.' He pressed his hand between her legs, leaning over to run his tongue lightly up and over her neck.

Amber groaned again, louder this time, arching her back as his hand pressed harder against her, his thumb touching her right where she needed to be touched, sending a beautiful shockwave coursing right through her. 'Oh, baby,' she laughed, squirming underneath him, her fingers buried in his hair as his tongue reached her ear, tickling her slightly, her stomach contracting in the most incredible way as he laughed his low-down-dirty laugh that got her every time.

'You still tired?' He smiled, running a hand over her leg as she pulled it up around him.

'Hazard a guess, handsome. But let's try and keep the noise down, okay? I'd like that little man up there to stay asleep.'

'I can do quiet,' he whispered, gently pushing her legs further apart.

'You can do quiet?'

'Oh, I can do quiet, baby. Because my mouth will be otherwise occupied.'

'I knew I loved you for a reason,' she moaned, arching her back again as his hand stroked her slowly, his thumb pressing gently, circling that part of her that sent those tingles coursing through her body once more with a speed that took her breath away. He pressed harder, responding to her moans, her tiny sighs turning him on so much he almost pulled his hand away so he could dive into her properly, but he wanted to do things this way first. He wanted to touch her and watch her as he did that; he wanted to watch as he brought her to a climax that would send him over the edge, but he didn't care. Because he'd do it again, he'd come inside her and he'd do it all over again, and he had to close his eyes briefly to gain some kind of control, his erection now verging on the painful.

She opened her legs wider, pulling her knees back slightly as she felt that pressure start to build, her whole body beginning to burn up with the anticipation and she gasped quietly as he carefully slipped his fingers inside her, his thumb still rotating slowly, pushing and pressing until it all came crashing over her like the most beautiful tidal wave, washing over every inch of her as her body bucked underneath him, his fingers still inside her, and she could feel him touching her deep inside. It was the most incredible feeling.

He watched as she closed her eyes, a slight smile on her beautiful face, her hands clasped together above her head, accentuating those breasts of hers that he could look at all day, and he knew he couldn't wait any longer. The pain was physical now, the ache too much to bear.

He kept his eyes on her face as he slowly pulled his fingers out of her, watching as she bit down on her lip, her back arching even further. 'Baby, open your eyes.'

They flickered open, fixing on his and staying there as his hand held hers; as he pushed into her gently, her legs wrapping around him as he fell deeper.

'Don't close them' he whispered, noticing her eyes begin to shut. 'Please. I want to look at you.'

She stared up at him, her fingers tightening around his as their hips moved together in that same sensual rhythm, gradually picking up pace, becoming faster, his thrusts becoming harder and more frequent as that pressure built again, hitting them both within seconds of each other. And as Amber stared deep into his eyes she felt a pain so intense, so raw and so real she couldn't stop the tears from streaming down her face. It was almost as if panic had risen out of nowhere, hitting her head-on, and even though he was there, he was with her, Jesus, he was *inside* her; she knew she couldn't lose him again. She couldn't. No matter what Ryan tried to do or say she couldn't lose this man, because this time she'd fall apart and she'd never be able to keep it together, or carry on, not this time. She wouldn't be able to do that.

'I'm okay,' she whispered as he looked at her, his expression one of concern, his fingers gently wiping away her tears.

'Am I always gonna make you cry?' He'd said that with a smile, and she couldn't help but smile back.

'I really need those promises from you now, Jim. And I need them because things have changed and I need to know that we're really okay now, that we're really here and we're doing this and… and I just need those promises now. I need you to promise me you will never, ever leave me, do you understand? I need to hear you say that because I can't lose you again, I can't do that. So I need those promises now.'

His eyes bored into hers, their fingers still entwined, her breathing heavy and fast as she stared up at him.

'I need those promises, Jim.'

His mouth lowered down onto hers, resting lightly against it as he spoke. 'I promise you, baby, I am going nowhere. I *promise* you.'

She could finally close her eyes now, her breathing slowing down as he kissed her, pulling her deeper and deeper into his world but she didn't care any more. She was giving in, waving that white flag and letting Jim Allen take her, completely, totally. Everything she had was his, he could have it all – her heart, her soul; she was tired of fighting it.

'We're gonna be so good together, Amber, you and me. Finally. We're gonna be so good together.'

'I know,' she whispered, reaching up to run her fingers lightly over his rough chin, resting them on his slightly open mouth. 'I know… oh, hang on. Listen, he's awake.' She couldn't help laughing. At least the little guy's timing was good.

Jim sat up, pushing a hand through his hair, watching as she pulled on her knickers and grabbed his shirt. 'Do you want me to see to him?'

She leaned over to kiss him, lingering for just a few seconds, enjoying the feel of his mouth against hers, his hand resting on her hip. 'No. I'll get him. You go fix us some drinks.'

'Okay… Amber?'

She turned to look at him, leaning against the doorpost, and he felt his heart shudder in his chest, she looked beautiful. So, so beautiful. 'It really is gonna be alright this time. I'll make sure of that.'

She smiled, before running upstairs. It really was going to be alright. It was. There was no other option.

*

'Are you trying to avoid me?'

'No, Ellen, I am *not* trying to avoid you,' Ryan sighed, tucking the phone between his chin and shoulder as he sat down at the dining table in the kitchen of his rented home. If he was in London indefinitely, he wanted somewhere he could bring Rico back to. A hotel room just wasn't going to cut it.

'Really? Because it feels as though you are.'

Ryan ran a hand over the back of his neck, closing his eyes briefly as he tried to work out when this relationship between himself and Ellen had actually begun. Again. Because, for the life of him, he really couldn't remember.

'I'm down here seeing my son, Ellen, okay? I'm spending some time with my baby son. I wasn't aware I needed to ask your permission first before doing that.'

'Don't get smart, Ryan. Of course you don't have to ask my permission, that's not what I meant. I just wish you'd told me before you left, that's all. I was hoping… I was hoping *we* might be able to spend some time together too, seeing as you…' She stopped mid-sentence, and Ryan sat back in his chair, exhaling deeply.

'Seeing as I'm suspended?'

Ellen said nothing for a beat or two, obviously trying to gauge his mood. 'Are you okay?'

He leaned forward, resting his forehead in his hand, staring down at the table. 'I'm fine.'

'Do you want some company?' She really needed to see him. There were so many reasons that she needed to see him.

'I've got all the company…' He closed his eyes again, taking a deep breath, holding the phone away from his ear for a second

215

or two. What the hell? It wasn't like Amber was going to come running any time soon. 'If you want to come down here, Ellen…'

It wasn't exactly the most enthusiastic of invitations, but then it wasn't as if he was head-over-heels in love with this girl. He felt something for her, sure. He just wasn't sure what that was or where it was going. And just what kind of mess it was all going to cause.

'I've got a couple of free days coming up, so you won't mind if I come down and see you?'

'No. I won't mind. Look, Ellen…' He sat back, pushing a hand through his messed-up dark hair.

'Yes?'

He let out another heavy sigh, throwing his head back. Over the phone wasn't really the right place to tell her he had no intention of taking this relationship anywhere further than the bedroom. Because of their history he really needed her to understand that. But over the phone wasn't the right place. 'Nothing. It doesn't matter.'

'Oh… okay. Well, I'll see you sometime tomorrow, then. I'd better go book that train ticket.'

'Yeah. See you tomorrow. Call me when you get into London.'

He put the phone down and threw his head back again. What the hell was he doing? Was his need for some kind of distraction really this desperate?

The doorbell cut through his thoughts, saving him from sinking into some kind of self-pitying analysis of how fucked-up his life was becoming again. He stood up, kicking his chair back before heading out into the hall, checking his watch as he went.

'Do you know what time it is?' he asked, swinging the front door open and finding Max on the doorstep.

'I'm very much aware of the time, Ryan. My watch cost the best part of three grand so it's extremely accurate. Can I come in?'

Ryan stood aside to let him through. 'Something wrong?'

'No. Just the opposite, as it happens. You going to offer me a drink?'

'What did your last slave frigging die of?'

'Exhaustion. Whiskey on the rocks, please. Slice of lemon on the side.'

Ryan threw him a look.

'Okay. Hold the lemon. Anyway…' He sat down on the arm of the sofa, clasping his hands together in his lap as he waited for Ryan to fix his drink. 'I've just had word back from the police. There won't be any charges brought against you.'

Ryan swung around, almost spilling Max's drink in the process. 'Really?'

'Really. But that doesn't mean there won't be any repercussions from the F.A. or Newcastle Red Star.'

'Can I get back to playing?'

'Well, I've had a word with Dave French and he's meeting with the Red Star board tomorrow, but he can't see a problem with you returning to the squad.'

'When?'

'I don't know, Ryan. I'll let you know when I hear something from the club. But, listen, kiddo. Mud sticks, I'm sure you know that.'

'I didn't do anything, Max.'

'You almost did. You were this close, and you know that. Now, it's possible it *will* all blow over and soon you'll be nothing more than yesterday's news. But, on the other hand, as I said before, there *may* be repercussions.'

'Like what?' Ryan asked, handing Max his drink, but resisting the urge to get one of his own. Something told him he was going to need a clear head now.

'Like the captaincy being taken from you.'

'Jesus…' Ryan sighed, leaning back against the sideboard. 'They'd really do that?'

Max arched an eyebrow as he took a sip of whiskey. 'They can do what the hell they like, kiddo. And, to be quite honest with you, that's the lenient end of the spectrum.'

'Is that what they're gonna do?'

'Dave mentioned it, yes. It may only be temporary, I don't know. But if I were you I'd just shut up and take it.'

Ryan shoved his hands in his pockets, staring down at the floor. 'And what about my transfer request?'

'I'd forget that for now.'

'And what if I don't *want* to forget it, Max?'

'Listen, don't rock the boat any more than it already has been, okay? I know you want to move down here because you want to be with your baby, but right now is not the time to go demanding anything from a club that has given you more second chances than it's humanly possible to give. You hear me?'

'That's bullshit, Max.'

'It's the way it's gonna be, Ryan. You're coming out of this relatively unscathed and for that you should be incredibly relieved. So you keep your head down, you behave yourself, and you say thank you to Newcastle Red Star by becoming that model player you were well on your way to becoming before all this hit the fan.'

'Jesus, Max, I can't be up there while Rico's down here.'

'Well, you're just gonna have to get used to it. You're not the first father to be separated from their child for a job, and some people have got it a hell of a lot harder than you have. With your money you can afford to be coming down here whenever you've got a spare afternoon.'

'It's not the frigging same, though, is it?'

Max finished his drink, fixing Ryan with another of his stern, no-nonsense looks. 'I'll keep you posted on any more developments. In the meantime, you just behave yourself, alright? Nothing stupid.'

'Like what?'

'I don't know, Ryan. You've done plenty of stupid things in the past. Pick one.'

'I fucking hate you sometimes.'

'Yeah. The feeling's mutual.' Max walked over to him, quickly squeezing his shoulder, allowing the tiniest of smiles to appear. 'I'll see myself out.'

'Hang on a second, Max.'

'What?'

'Is there any… does anyone know how all this started? Who leaked it all to the press, I mean? Because somebody must have done.'

Max shrugged, digging his hands in his pockets. 'No idea. Does it matter?'

'Yeah. It matters to me. Because I think I know who's behind it.'

Max narrowed his eyes. 'I'm not sure I want to hear this.'

'I think… Jim Allen. I think he's behind this, Max, I really do…'

Max put a hand up to stop Ryan from saying any more. 'Okay, I've heard enough. Forget it, Ryan. Don't even go there.'

'Seriously, Max. I really think he's the one who started all this.'

'And why would he do that, huh? Why?'

'People keep asking me that…'

'People? Who the hell else have you been talking to?'

'I might have said something to Debbie – Debbie Hogan. Gary Blandford's wife, Amber's friend.'

'Yes, thank you, Ryan. I'm well aware who Debbie Hogan is. Why were you talking to her?'

'Because she was there, Max. She was there, and I needed to talk to someone because I just had this hunch…'

'You had a *hunch*? You're telling me you think Jim Allen is behind all this because you had a *hunch*?'

'Isn't it obvious?'

'No, not really. Look, Ryan, just leave it, okay? I know you and Jim Allen have never had the best of relationships, but do you really think he'd do something like this?'

'Yeah, I do. Look, I know there doesn't seem to be any kind of logical reason why, now. I mean, he's won, hasn't he? He's got Amber back, he's a god over at Endleigh so he's sorted there. Jesus, he's even got my son! But I just have a feeling…'

'Well, I'm sorry, kiddo, but you can't go throwing accusations around just because you've got a "feeling." It doesn't work like that. So if I were you I'd just be grateful that you've come out of this fairly well and stop over-analysing everything.' Max kept his eyes on Ryan for a second or two, watching his expression change. 'It's all in your head, Ryan. All this venom you've still got for your old boss, it's all in your head.'

'You think?'

'She married him.'

'I know that, Max. And I'm not...'

'You need to forget whatever feelings you still have for her and get on with your life. And I know that's hard now because of Rico, but for your own sanity, Ryan, just try and get it together, okay?'

Ryan said nothing; what *could* he say? That somewhere in the back of his mind he *wasn't* hoping Amber would come back to him? He'd be lying. He was always going to hope Amber would come back to him. Always.

'I'll call you tomorrow,' Max said with a kind smile, before leaving Ryan alone. With his thoughts. With his hopes. With his dreams that may or may not come true.

Chapter Nineteen

'You sound a bit odd, Debbie. Everything alright? There's nothing wrong with Jodi, is there?'

'No. Jodi's fine, everyone's fine. I'm just tired, that's all.'

'Yeah. That's the excuse I always use whenever I'm trying to avoid talking about something.'

'I'm not trying to avoid… okay, I am.'

Amber sat bolt upright in Jim's office chair, her attention suddenly piqued. 'Come on, then. Spill.'

'I don't know if I… he made me promise not to say anything.'

'*Who* made you promise not to say anything? Come on, Debbie. You're gonna have to tell me now.'

Amber heard Debbie sigh heavily down the line.

'Ryan.'

'*Ryan* made you promise not to say anything? About what?'

Another sigh.

'Debbie!'

'He's still in love with you, Amber.'

Amber threw herself back against the huge, black-leather chair, briefly closing her eyes. 'I kind of know that already, Debbie. He told me so himself only the other day.'

'He did? Did he also…?'

Amber sat upright again, resting her chin in her hand. 'Did he also, what? Jesus, Debbie, this is like pulling teeth. I've had easier conversations with Rico.'

'It's nothing, chick. Just me being stupid.'

'Did he also, what, Debbie? You're not getting out of it that easily. When did you speak to him anyway?'

'Just before he left for London. He came to see me because he needed to talk about… about something.'

'Like what?'

There was another pause. Another moment of silence that only served to make Amber nervous.

'It's nothing, Amber, really. He was just upset, about all the negative publicity, and what it might all mean for his career, but it's all alright now, isn't it?'

'Sort of, from what I can gather. Debbie, I'm struggling to understand this conversation, really I am.'

'Yeah. I kind of wish I hadn't started it myself.'

'Did he say something else to you? Ryan, I mean. Apart from the obvious.'

A longer pause this time, and Amber clearly heard another heavy sigh come down the line.

Just tell me, Debbie, will you? I'm not going to shoot the messenger, alright? Whatever he's said, it can't be that bad, can it?'

'I'm just worried he's going to go back to what he used to be, Amber.'

Amber waited a second or two before responding to that, because she wasn't entirely sure that was what Debbie had really wanted to say. 'Okay, look, I'm getting bored of this now, so, I'm gonna love you and leave you, Debs. Ryan isn't going to revert back to his old ways, I'm almost 100 per cent sure about that. And whatever it is he told you, you're obviously not going to tell me…'

'Amber, babe, I really *am* worried about him.'

'I'll speak to you soon, Debbie. Give Gary my love and Jodi a big hug from her godmummy.' She threw her phone down on the desk, once more throwing herself back against Jim's leather chair.

'What's that phone ever done to you?' Jim smiled, closing his office door behind him.

Amber looked up, returning his smile. 'Nothing. It's Debbie. Sometimes talking to her is like entering the twilight-zone.'

Jim raised an amused eyebrow. 'You two had some kind of disagreement?'

'No,' Amber sighed, getting up and walking over to him, straightening his jacket collar before kissing him quickly. 'She just starts these conversations and then backs away from telling me something she obviously wants to tell me at the last minute.'

Jim's expression changed from amusement to confusion.

'She said she'd spoken to Ryan before he came down to London, and he'd said something to her that he'd made her promise not to tell me…'

'Like what?'

'That's what I've just spent the past five minutes trying to get out of her. In the end I gave up. Whatever it is it'll be pointless.'

Jim's arm fell around her waist, pulling her closer. 'Well, it can't have been important, whatever it was. Anyway, shouldn't Ryan be heading back home soon?'

'He's going tomorrow. He wanted to spend one more day with Rico. He's not back training with Newcastle Red Star until Monday.'

'Is he okay about being stripped of the captaincy?'

'He seems fine about it. What's bothering him the most is that Max has advised him to quit with the transfer talk and just keep his head down at Red Star for the foreseeable future.' She looked up at Jim, right into those green eyes of his. 'Is it really bad of me to be relieved about that? I mean, of course I feel for him. If I had to be away from Rico for any length of time it would devastate me. But I almost breathed a sigh of relief when he told me. He loves Rico so much, Jim. And I still feel so selfish for separating them like this.'

Jim squeezed her waist, kissing her gently, and Amber felt that familiar calm start to spread through her the second his lips touched hers. That was the effect he had on her. 'Ryan Fisher is all grown up, Amber. People keep telling you that and you refuse to believe them. You keep saying that the person he was back then and the person he is now are two completely different people, so quit worrying about him and let's just get on with our lives, okay?'

'Is that an order?'

He smiled his all-encompassing, overwhelming smile and Amber felt her stomach dip and dive in the familiar, beautiful way it always did when he smiled at her. 'Yeah. If it has to be.'

She reached up and slid a hand around the back of his neck, pulling him down for another, longer kiss. 'Okay. I'll stop worrying about Ryan.'

'Promise?'

She returned his smile, running her thumb lightly over his mouth. 'I promise.'

'Good.'

She stood on tiptoes to kiss him once more, pressing herself against him and then regretting it. 'I'd better go.' She smiled again, letting her hand drop, resting it against him. He was hard, and she would have loved nothing more than to see to that for him, but her timing was more than a little off. 'Sorry.'

He laughed, shaking his head as she walked off. 'You're gonna pay for this later, missy.'

She turned around, backing up against the door, biting down on her lip. 'Have I been a bad girl, again?'

'Get out of here,' he laughed, sitting down on the edge of his desk, wincing slightly due to that poorly timed hard-on.

She blew him a kiss and slipped out of his office, closing the door quietly behind her. Jim waited a few seconds, looking down at his, thankfully, diminishing erection. She could do that to him with just one look, never mind a kiss.

Looking at the door, satisfied nobody was coming back through it any time soon, he reached for his phone, pressing *call* without a moment's hesitation. He had something to sort out. And it needed doing before kick-off.

*

'You don't mind, do you? Ellen being around Rico, I mean.'

'Well, I'm not over the moon about it, no. But I can't stop you from seeing whoever you want. Although, I wish you *weren't* seeing the woman who messed about with Brandon. What she did to him was wrong, Ryan. He's really cut up about it. He doesn't say as much, but I can tell.'

Ryan looked down at the floor, a brief glimmer of guilt making its presence felt. He couldn't really argue with the fact that how Ellen had gone about things – well, it was wrong. Of course it was. But he needed another distraction right now, and as weak as it might sound, Ellen was there, and he didn't have the energy or the inclination to go looking for anyone else. She was there. He could live with his conscience.

Amber rocked Rico gently in her arms as she watched Ryan's body language. She could tell he wasn't totally comfortable, which she was pleased to see. It meant that maybe he really did feel bad about jumping straight into bed with the woman who'd broken Amber's stepson's heart. Not that he'd do anything about it, of course. But she didn't expect that he would.

She leaned over to kiss Rico's warm forehead. He smelt of baby talc and Amber wished she could just stay there and hold him for the next hour and a half. But she was actually there to work. Endleigh United versus Wandsworth Rovers was that evening's Cloud Sports televised match and she was on interview duty. She should really be down on the pitch now, trying to grab a word with whoever was out there during the warm-up.

'You can, if you want to.'

Amber looked up at Ryan, still rocking Rico gently back and forth. 'Sorry?'

'You *can* stop me from trying to see people. I don't mind.'

225

She stared at him for a few seconds. 'Stop it, Ryan. Anyway, I've just had a really strange conversation with Debbie. She said you spoke to her, just before you came down here. She said you told her something that you'd made her promise not to tell me. Feel like sharing what that was, exactly?'

'Not really. It was nothing.'

'Yeah, that's exactly what *she* said and I didn't believe her, either.'

'It was nothing, Amber.'

She kissed Rico's cheek, carefully handing him back to Ryan. 'There's nobody else here, but there will be in a minute, so, if it's something private – although why it would be private if you've told Debbie…'

'Did Jim have anything to do with my involvement in that betting ring hitting the headlines?'

Amber blinked a few times, trying to take in what he'd just told her. 'I'm sorry?'

'I think he had something to do with it.'

'Oh, *you* think he had something to do with it? And do you have any proof to back that up?'

'No, not exactly…'

'Not exactly? Jesus, Ryan, I thought we were past all this. What the hell would Jim gain from selling you out like that?'

'I don't know, Amber. Why don't you ask him?'

She narrowed her eyes, staring him out. 'Okay. Now, I don't know what it was exactly you said to Debbie, but I don't want to hear it. Jim had nothing to do with this…'

'You sure about that?'

Amber took a deep breath, exhaling slowly, her eyes focused on the floor because she didn't trust herself to look at him and stay calm. 'Just look after Rico, and don't even think about leaving him alone with Ellen. You got that?'

'Amber, please…'

'I'll be back later.'

She left the director's box and headed back out into the corridor, bumping into Ronnie on her way. 'Whoa there! You in a hurry?'

She stopped and looked up at him. 'Do you think Jim had anything to do with all that coming out about Ryan and the betting ring?'

Ronnie frowned. 'Where's this come from?'

'Ryan seems to think Jim's to blame.'

'Look, sweetheart, Ryan is probably going to blame Jim for everything that goes wrong in his life now. Just ignore him.'

She leaned back against the wall, absentmindedly chewing on a nail. 'Maybe I should talk to him.'

'Who? Ryan? I thought you just had.'

'No. Jim.'

'So, you think he *might* have something to do with it?'

Her head shot up. 'No! Of course not. It's just…'

'Just, what?' Ronnie asked, joining her at the wall.

'Oh, I don't know. Given everything that's happened in the past… But I know he wouldn't do that now, Ronnie. Jim has nothing to gain by trying to blacken Ryan's name, not any more. Do you know? I hate it when Ryan does this. I really hate it.'

'I told you, Amber, just ignore him. His head's all over the place at the minute…'

'Yeah, well, his head's been all over the place for far too long, Ronnie, and I'm tired of it. I'm tired of all this crap between him and Jim. I moved down here to get away from all that but it's never gonna happen, is it?'

'Don't let it get to you, kiddo.'

She turned her head to look at him, a slight smile on her face. 'When the hell did *you* get so chilled-out? Don't tell me Hayley's done this to you?'

Ronnie stretched his arms up above his head, letting out a loud, contented sigh. 'Well, let's just say that I've never felt so relaxed in all my life.'

'Glad to hear it. She's a lovely girl.'

'Yeah, I like her,' Ronnie laughed, and Amber couldn't help but laugh, too, leaning over to quickly kiss his cheek.

'I don't know what I'd do without you, Ronnie White.'

'You'd survive. I just don't want you to have to.' He gave her hand a quick squeeze and threw her a smile, leaning in to kiss her mouth, ever so briefly. 'Forget Ryan Fisher, okay? He's had a bit of a rough time lately and he's just looking for someone to blame. Jim's the obvious choice.'

'Yeah, I suppose you're right,' Amber sighed, pushing a hand through her loose curls. 'Anyway, aren't you supposed to be up in the studio?'

Ronnie looked at his watch. 'Christ, yes. I'll catch up with you in a bit, okay?'

Amber watched him run off along the corridor, digging her hands into her pockets while she contemplated whether to go and see Jim, or whether she should go and get herself mic'd up, which is what she should be doing. She was already running late.

She turned and headed back towards Jim's office and the dressing rooms, not exactly sure what she was going to say to him when she found him; she just felt this was what she needed to do for her own peace of mind. Ryan had sown a seed of doubt in there and now she couldn't shift it, no matter how much she wanted to forget it.

Approaching the door of Jim's office she leaned in, her hand hovering over the handle, but the sound of his voice coming from inside stopped her from walking straight in. She could hear him talking, and the fact she couldn't hear another voice made her think he must be on the phone, so she took a step back. Maybe this was a bad idea. Maybe she should just head off down to the pitch, where she should be right now, and get on with her job. Maybe now, less than an hour before kick-off – maybe now wasn't the time to start questioning her husband over an irrational hunch Ryan Fisher was harbouring. But *was* it irrational?

The noise coming from the nearby open dressing-room door, and people coming in and out of the Players' Lounge down the corridor distracted Amber somewhat, making her lose focus slightly. She really didn't know what to do, but what she did know was that she hated herself for thinking, for even the briefest of seconds, that Ryan might be right.

Leaning in towards the door again she could still hear Jim's voice. It was raised slightly now, giving her the impression it was a conversation that wasn't going entirely her husband's way.

She knew she should just walk away, but there was another part of her that made her lean in even closer, straining to hear what Jim was saying, and she didn't even know why; it was probably just some transfer deal going wrong. They were at the back end of the transfer window now, and when it got this close to the deadline things often got heated as clubs started to play dirty and players became more demanding. He was probably just trying to level with an agent or a fellow manager as they attempted to meet somewhere in the middle and strike some kind of deal.

'No, I know there was no guarantee…'

Amber pressed her ear right against the door, cupping her hand around it in the hope it would shut out some of the ambient noise surrounding her and allow her to hear more.

'I know that… Look, I didn't know this would be the outcome… Of course I wasn't naïve enough to… I know. I know you warned me this could happen. I just hoped things might have been a bit more concrete, that's all…'

Amber heard voices growing closer along the corridor and she jumped away from the door, almost running away from it. Those few words she'd heard Jim speak were nothing, really. And she'd heard it all out of any kind of context. But they could be construed as pretty ambiguous, if she thought too much about it. Damn Ryan Fisher for putting thoughts into her head that would never have got there if it hadn't been for him.

Jim was different now. There was no way he'd have had anything to do with that story about Ryan. He was different now. He was a different man. She only wished Ryan was, too.

Chapter Twenty

'Jesus, Ellen, what's with all your crap lying all over the place?' Ryan was slightly agitated by the fact Ellen seemed to be moving her stuff into his home bit by bit. Ever since he'd arrived back in Newcastle she seemed to bring more things with her each time she came over; bags full of underwear and perfume and make-up that she left lying around every available surface in every one of his bathrooms. 'I hope you're not getting any ideas about moving in,' he huffed, sliding up onto a stool at the breakfast bar.

'Would you like some tea?' Ellen asked, ignoring his rude behaviour.

'Yeah. Go on.'

'And a good morning to you, too,' she sighed, turning around to pour some boiling water into a mug.

Ryan looked at her, a sudden wave of guilt washing over him, causing his shoulders to sag. 'Look, Ellen, I'm sorry. Okay? I'm just a bit stressed, alright? I didn't mean to take it out on you.'

She turned back around and smiled at him, handing him his mug of tea. 'Don't worry about it.'

'No, listen, I really am sorry. It's just – it's hard, y'know? Having the captaincy taken away from me and all the crap that's still going down in the press.'

She leaned forward, resting her elbows on the breakfast bar, throwing him what she hoped was a warm and reassuring smile. 'You knew it wasn't going to go away overnight, babe.'

'It's been two weeks now.'

She just raised an eyebrow, leaning further forward to kiss him quickly. 'What time you got to be at the training ground today?'

'Half ten. Shouldn't you be at Tynebridge by now? Isn't the entire P.R. department over there still on red alert, ready to divert all that unwanted media attention away from the place?'

She looked at him, throwing him a sarcastic smile. 'Newcastle Red Star doesn't just revolve around you, mister. You're not the only thing we have to concentrate on, you know. Anyway, I've got the morning off. So, how about we go back to bed and I try to ease some of that tension you still seem to be feeling?'

Ryan pushed a hand through his hair, sighing quietly. 'I dunno, Ellen… I'm not really… Jesus! Was I about to turn down the offer of sex there?'

Ellen couldn't help smiling as she watched his face break into a grin; watched as he slid down from his stool and walked over to her, slowly sliding the short, baby-blue robe she was wearing down off one shoulder, leaning over to kiss it gently.

'Now *that's* the Ryan Fisher I recognise,' she groaned, throwing her head back as he loosened her robe, sliding a hand inside to cup one of her breasts. 'And I need to see more of him.'

He looked at her, his grin showing no signs of disappearing. What the hell was wrong with him? Was he really going to let all the crap that had happened fuck up *everything* in his life? Ellen was beautiful and smart, and willing. Loyalty might be an issue, because he still wasn't comfortable with the way she'd treated Brandon Palmer, but who the hell was *he* to start preaching about morals and loyalty? She was here and she was willing to take his mind off everything that just made him want to kick out right now. Something he couldn't afford to do. 'You said something about going back to bed. That offer still open?'

Ellen pushed herself closer against him, sliding her hands up the back of his t-shirt, touching his warm skin, letting her mouth brush gently over that space just below his ear; a place she knew he liked to be touched, and she smiled as she felt his body give an involuntary shiver. 'You bet your life it is.'

This was the Ryan Fisher she wanted. A man who might not be completely hers just yet, but she was working on it. The wheels were in motion. And this time, she knew exactly what she was doing.

*

Amber pulled her knees up to her chest and hugged them tightly, resting her chin on them as she looked out over an empty Parkfield. It was a cold February morning and she was supposed to be busy setting up for the live televised match that evening, but her mind was on other things. Her mind had been on other things for a while now.

'Talk to me.'

She turned her head to see Ronnie sit down beside her, gratefully taking the mug of tea he held out for her. 'No.'

'Oh, so we're in that kind of mood, are we?'

She took a sip of tea, staring out ahead of her again. 'Is everything okay in there?'

'You and Jim had a row?'

She turned her head slowly to look at him. 'You really didn't have to ask that with such a hopeful tone of voice. And no, we haven't had a row.'

'So what's the face for, then? Has Ryan been throwing his weight around or something?'

Amber took another sip of tea, turning back to look out over the quiet stadium, her attention focused on a lone groundsman down by the touchline who seemed to be giving the grass there some close examination. 'Everything's fine, Ronnie. I've just got a bit of a headache, that's all.'

'Do you want me to go away?'

'I'd prefer to be on my own right now, yes.'

'Tough. I'm going nowhere. Not until you talk to me, anyway.'

'I *am* talking to you.'

Ronnie threw his head back and let out a loud sigh. 'You know, you used to be so much better at hiding what you were really feeling.'

She looked at him again, cocking her head slightly. 'Am I not allowed an off day?'

'Of course you are.'

She just raised an eyebrow and turned her attention back to the groundsman, who was now poking the grass down by the technical area with a rake.

'Why don't you just talk to him, Amber?'

Amber closed her eyes, taking in a long, deep breath, but she didn't say anything.

'It's over now, and you know that.'

She stared down into her mug of tea. 'Is it?'

'Ryan's back at Newcastle Red Star, it doesn't look like any criminal charges are going to be brought against him…'

'I'm scared, Ronnie. I'm scared to talk to him because I don't know if I want to hear what he has to say.'

'Have you been feeling like this for all these weeks?' Ronnie asked, leaning forward, clasping his hands together between his knees.

Amber nodded, her eyes still fixed firmly on her tea. 'I feel… I feel like crap. Because I'm doubting him, and I'm only doing that because of the things he's done in the past. I'm still assuming he's that man, and what does that make me, Ronnie?' She finally looked up, her eyes meeting his. 'What kind of wife does that make me? If I can't trust my husband. If I can't believe that everything he told me was the truth. If I'm still doubting that he really has changed. What kind of wife does that make me? Because I hate myself for it.'

Ronnie reached out and took her hand, squeezing it gently.

'You really do need to talk to him, Amber. I can't believe he hasn't already noticed you've got something on your mind.'

'Well, maybe I'm a better actress than I give myself credit for.'

'Talk to him.'

'Not before the match. That isn't fair.'

'Just talk to him. Today. Before this gets out of hand, because you have absolutely no proof that Jim had anything to do with all of that coming out about Ryan and the betting ring. You have no proof, Amber. You're worrying yourself stupid purely because of something Ryan said. So you really need to talk to Jim.'

'How's that going to make him feel? How is making him think that I still don't trust him going to make him feel?'

'Just talk to him, Amber. Because you know as well as I do that this can't carry on. If you were any other kind of person I'd tell you to just brush it under the carpet and forget about it because no damage appears to have been done. But I know you too well, and I know this will only grow into some kind of obsession if you don't sort it out. Come on, kiddo. Don't let Ryan's paranoia spill over onto you. You know how he feels about Jim. And he needs someone to blame. Jim's the obvious choice, I've already told you that.'

It was Amber's turn to sigh. 'I know I'm being stupid, but I just got scared, Ronnie. Something could damage what Jim and I have finally found, because I'm happy. I'm so much in love with that man that sometimes I feel as though I can't even breathe if he isn't around, it's that bad. He's so far under my skin that he is never going to go away. But if he's lied to me, after everything he's told me...'

'And what *has* he told you, Amber? Because you seem so sure that he really has changed this time.'

'He has. I know he has, but I also know that him and Ryan...' She stood up, digging her hands into the pockets of her jacket. 'I'm going back inside. It's freezing out here.'

'Amber...'

'I'll talk to him, Ronnie. I promise. I'll talk to him. Tonight.'

*

Ryan put the phone down and frowned. Rico was staying with his granddad for a few days, and although it was great that he had his son back up north for a totally unexpected visit, he couldn't help wondering why Amber had done that. Why had she allowed Rico out of her sight for no particular reason, because that wasn't usually the case. Sure, she was working tonight, he knew that. She was reporting live for Cloud Sports from Parkfield for Endleigh United's top of the league match with a rival London club, but he knew that she had nights like this covered – nights when both she and Jim were working. Family members usually travelled down south to help her out, he knew that. So why had she suddenly decided to change the rules?

Freddie had told him he was reading way too much into it; that she was probably just snowed under and it was better for Rico to be back in the north-east for a while. But Ryan wasn't totally convinced. He knew Freddie wasn't lying to him; if something *was* going on then he'd be one of the last people Amber told. But Ryan just had a feeling that Rico's visit up north wasn't quite as simple as it might sound.

Picking up his phone again he quickly searched for Amber's number, pressing *call* before he had a chance to change his mind.

She picked up after three rings. 'What do you want, Ryan?'

'Why didn't you tell me Rico was back in Newcastle?'

'Has my dad not called you?'

'Yes, he has, but why didn't *you* tell me?'

'Ryan, I really haven't got time for this, I'm busy.'

'Yeah, I know you are, I just…'

'I thought you'd be happy to have your son with you for a few days.'

'Amber, baby, I'm frigging ecstatic, I just don't understand…'

'It's pretty simple, Ryan. Both Jim and I have got a lot on this week, and I just thought it would be better for Rico if he stayed with my dad for a few days. But I told him to make sure you saw him whenever you wanted, has he told you that?'

'Yes, he has…'

'Then what's the problem here?'

'There isn't one. I'm really grateful that I'm going to get some time with my boy, but… why, Amber?'

'What do you mean, why? Ryan, I really don't have time for this, it's almost kick-off…'

'You don't usually do anything without at least a week's planning, so, I'm finding this really hard…'

'Maybe I just got all spontaneous. Now, will you get off the phone? Please? And go and do whatever it is you've got planned tonight.'

'I haven't got anything planned.'

'Ellen not coming over? Or has she fucked about with you, too, the way she fucked about with Brandon?'

Ryan closed his eyes, rubbing the bridge of his nose with his thumb and forefinger. 'She's really sorry about the way she treated him, Amber.'

'Yeah. I'm sure she is. But you're not one to turn down a free fuck, huh? Even if it's with a woman who's quite willing to rip the heart out of my stepson the second you show her the tiniest hint of interest.'

'It wasn't like that, Amber.'

'I don't actually care *what* it was like, Ryan. Because sometimes I think the pair of you deserve each other.'

'What the frig's *that* supposed to mean? And when the hell did we start pulling *me* apart?'

'I've got to go. I'm working, and I haven't got time to stand here and argue with you.'

'Hey, sweetheart, I didn't call you for an argument. I called because I was worried about you.'

'I'm fine.'

'Yeah. You always are, Amber.'

'Give Rico a kiss from his mum when you see him.'

Ryan stared at the phone as she hung up, before throwing it down onto the counter. Jesus, she was hard work sometimes. So why did he still want to do nothing but rip every item of clothing from her body so fast it would make her head spin, then fuck her like tomorrow was never coming? Shit! He really didn't need this. Even when she was being a first-rate bitch she gave him a hard-on he knew he was going to have to deal with. It reminded him of the day he'd first met her – when she'd interviewed him for News North East on the day he'd officially signed for Newcastle Red Star. She'd been all hard-faced attitude with the sexiest legs he'd ever seen and a body he'd dreamed of diving into, even though she'd been nothing but an ice queen who'd seemed to ooze contempt for him. But, oh boy, once he'd managed to break her down, melt that cool exterior…

He threw his head back, closed his eyes, and let out the loudest groan. His erection was straining to break free now, and even though he wanted to rid himself of these thoughts of the woman he still wanted more than anything; a woman who, no doubt, would be fucking his old boss at some point tonight, he couldn't. All he could think about was her.

He made his way into the downstairs bathroom and sat down on the closed toilet lid, reaching down to pick up a magazine from the pile beside the sink. The magazine was months old now, but he couldn't throw it away. He was never going to throw it away, because she was in there, long legs and perfect tits and eyes that locked onto yours and made you think she wanted you as much as you wanted her. And he wanted her. He wanted her so fucking bad he could taste it. He could taste *her* because he'd been down there, hadn't he? He'd been to that heaven that lay between her legs and it was a place he needed to visit again.

He threw the magazine down onto the floor, open at a

double-page spread of Amber lying naked across a bench in the Newcastle Red Star home dressing room, her back arched, those perfect tits covered only by her strategically placed forearm, one leg pulled up slightly, only just hiding something many would kill to get a glimpse of, but he knew what was there. He knew everything about her.

Reaching down, he took himself in his hand, taking his pleasure the only way he wanted it tonight. Just him and the woman he was still hopelessly in love with. Just him and those memories of the nights he'd lived inside her, the feel of her skin against his, his mouth touching her in all those private, secret places. But even when that relief came, she was still there, in his head, invading every thought he was going to have tonight.

He sat back, closing his eyes as his breathing slowed down. Was this the way it was always going to be now? Was she back to being a bitch towards him, and he'd spend the rest of his life staring at naked pictures of her while he wanked off and remembered the times he'd fucked her senseless? Was he really going to let that happen?

Zipping himself back up, he stood up, washed his hands, and splashed his face with freezing-cold water, pushing his hands back through his hair. As he stared at his reflection in the mirror above the sink, he couldn't help smiling. He was one good-looking bastard. Was he really going to deny other women the chance to spend their time with him just because he couldn't forget someone who really didn't want him any more? Fuck that! He was Ryan frigging Fisher. And it was about time he remembered that, put all the crap of the past few months behind him and started over.

Reaching out to grab the towel from the heated rail, it slipped through his fingers, landing on top of the small white bin beside the sink. Crouching down to retrieve it he accidentally stepped on the pedal, flipping the lid open, and he was about to push it shut again when his eyes were drawn to something sticking out of the pile of make-up remover wipes and cotton-wool balls that were in there. It was something that someone had quite obviously tried to hide, and Ryan reached into the bin to pull it out, staring at the packet in his hand, blinking a couple of times as he tried to focus on what it was he was holding. And then he realised. It was a full, unopened and unused stack of contraceptive pills. Pills that belonged to Ellen, because her name was on the packet, right there in black and white. Unused contraceptive pills.

He sat back down on the closed toilet lid, his fingers gripping the pills tightly as a million and one thoughts raced around his head. But only one thought was shouting the loudest.

Chapter Twenty-One

'Is everything alright, Amber, only… only, you seem to have been in a whole other place today. In fact, if I'm being honest here, I'd say you've been a bit distant for a couple of weeks now. Is there something you want to talk about? Is something wrong?'

Amber looked up slowly, her eyes meeting Jim's. 'No. Everything's fine. It's just been a busy few weeks, that's all. And it's been a long day today. That was a pretty stressful game tonight, you have to admit.'

Jim shrugged, leaning back against the chest of drawers and folding his arms. 'It was a bit tense, at times. But I've got a great squad at Endleigh. They're doing their job and they came through in the end. But I don't want to talk about football any more. Not tonight, anyway.'

Amber shrugged off her shirt and threw it onto the bed, reaching out to take her robe from the back of the open bathroom door, but Jim gently grabbed her wrist, stopping her from taking it. She stared at him. 'I'm practically naked here, Jim.'

'And you think that bothers me?' he asked, raising an eyebrow.

'I'd really like a shower before bed. It's late…'

'I know what time it is, Amber. Baby, just talk to me, please. I'm your husband and I want you to be able to talk to me.'

Like he'd talked to her?

He let go of her wrist and she dropped her arm, leaning back against the wall. 'I'm really tired, Jim.'

'And that's why Rico's back in Newcastle for the next few days, is it? Because you're tired?'

Her eyes locked onto his again as he stood in front of her. He was so heartbreakingly handsome, still dressed in dark suit pants and a white shirt, and she really didn't want to do this tonight. All she wanted to do was lie in his arms, let him make love to her and fall asleep as he held her. She didn't want to do this now.

'Look, forget that shower.' He moved closer, reaching out to tuck a strand of her hair behind her ear. 'I'll run us a bath. And if you're really tired then just let me do all the work, okay?'

She shivered slightly as he kissed her slowly, his fingers pushing her knickers ever so slightly down over her thighs. Just a touch, but it was one of the sexiest actions Amber had ever known. 'Jim…'

'Sshh. It can wait. Whatever it is, it can wait.'

She watched as he went into the bathroom and turned on the taps, sitting down on the edge of the bath as the water splashed out into the tub.

'Is it something to do with me?'

Amber stared at him again, swallowing hard. 'You said it could wait.'

'Is it something to do with me?'

'I love you, Jim.'

'I know you do, baby, and I love you, too. So much that this is scaring me, but I don't want to know what it is. Okay? Not yet. Whatever's on your mind, honey, the details really can wait. I just need to know if it's something to do with me.'

She held his gaze for a few more beats before she nodded slowly.

He hung his head briefly before standing up, walking over to her, pushing her back against the wall before she even had time to realise what was happening, kissing her so hard and with so much force it literally took her breath away. His fingers intertwined with hers above her head, their bodies so close it would have been impossible to get even the thinnest sliver of paper between them, and she could feel herself falling, deeper and deeper, faster and faster, even though she didn't really know what was going on here. She just knew she wanted it; she wanted *him*.

'Two minutes,' he whispered, backing away from her, leaving her gasping for breath, and all she could do was close her eyes and bury her fingers in her hair as she tried to gain some composure. Some measure of calm. But it wasn't coming. Not any time soon.

She kept her eyes closed as she felt him close to her again, felt his fingers trail down over her collarbone; she kept her eyes closed as she felt him strip what few clothes she still had on away from her body, every inch of her skin breaking out in a million tiny goosebumps with every brush of his fingers against her.

'Look at me, Amber.'

She slowly opened her eyes, her fingers still entangled in her hair, her breath catching in her throat as she realised he was naked now, too. Tall, toned, and naked and ready to take her anywhere she needed to go. Oh, God, she loved this man so much. So, so much.

Her eyes locked with his, the intensity now flying around the room, making it almost claustrophobic, and she had to take the deepest of breaths before she could feel herself breathe anywhere near normally again.

It was crazy, what he was doing to her – what he'd always done to her. What he would continue to do to her, no matter what. It was all crazy, but she'd take crazy right now. She'd take all that and anything he was about to throw at her because all she could think about now was him.

'Are you going to walk away from me, Amber?'

She took another deep breath. What was happening here? Because her head was spinning now; she couldn't think straight. 'I don't know,' she whispered, her eyes still locked on his. 'Jim…'

But it was useless; any attempt at a conversation was pointless now as he lifted her up, his mouth crashing against hers, and all she could do was cling on and wrap her legs around him as he carried her over to the chest of drawers, sitting her down on it before unwrapping her legs from his hips.

Part of her was scared, and yet another part of her was filled with so much excitement it was bordering on the manic as she felt him gently push her legs apart, his hand lightly running over her, touching her, moving back and forth until she could feel herself becoming wet, and she gasped quietly as he pulled his hand away, pushing into her almost immediately, holding onto her knees to keep her legs apart.

Amber threw back her head, her fingers gripping the chest of drawers as he thrust in and out of her, fast then slow, his mouth covering her breasts, his tongue working a magic she would never get tired of, but all it seemed to do was make the confusion already swimming around inside her ten times harder to deal with.

'Whatever it is, Amber, I don't want to know,' Jim breathed, his hand cupping her cheek, his eyes staring deep into hers and she felt her stomach dip so low she couldn't catch her breath. 'Baby, I don't want to know.'

She couldn't say anything. She couldn't get any words out; all she could do was close her eyes again as she felt that beautiful climax begin its journey up her body, washing over her in a succession of waves, causing her to cry out loud as she felt him come, felt him flood into her, and it brought with it a feeling of calm so intense but so brief it was painful.

He pulled her back into his arms and she clung onto him, wrapping her legs back around him and, for some reason she just couldn't explain, she'd never felt closer to him. Not since Las Vegas had she felt that bond between her and this man so strong she doubted anything could break it.

'Come on,' he whispered, pulling away slightly, helping her down from the chest of drawers, his arm remaining firmly around her waist. 'We'd better go make sure that bath hasn't run over.'

'Jim...'

He stopped her from saying anything else by kissing her so

slowly she just fell against him. It was as though, with every movement of his mouth against hers, he was erasing every ounce of
strength she had left until there was no other option but to give
in to him. 'Not now, okay? Not yet.'

She looked up at him, into those green eyes that had messed
with her emotions so many times. And still she couldn't let him
go. 'Okay.'

He took her hand and she clung onto him as he led her back
into the bathroom, her body shivering once more with a heady
dose of anticipation and nerves. Excitement and fear. Confusion.
They were all emotions she was all too familiar with as far as Jim
Allen was concerned.

And as she sank into the warm water, leaning back against him,
his legs pulling up around her, she closed her eyes and just let it
all wash over her. All the confusion and the doubt and the fear
that Ryan just might be right. But he could also be wrong. And
she inwardly berated herself for automatically thinking the worst
of her husband – a man who'd sworn to her that he'd changed.

She rested her head against his shoulder, closing her eyes as she
felt his breath warm on her skin, his fingers touching her breasts,
sending a shiver right through her.

Reaching back behind her, she buried her fingers in his hair,
pushing his head down as his lips brushed over her neck, sending
more of those shivers coursing through her so fast she almost
couldn't breathe. And when his hand moved down, resting against
her stomach for the briefest of seconds before slipping beneath
the water, she took a sharp intake of breath, her fingers sliding
between his as he touched her.

She kept her eyes closed as their hands moved together, his
lips still touching her neck, her shoulder, his other hand on her
knee to keep her legs wide open, and she let his hand guide hers
as he slowly brought her to another, beautiful climax. A quiet,
understated climax that caused her fingers to grip his tight, her
body shuddering slightly as he held her against him.

'I need you in my life, Amber,' he whispered, resting his hand on her stomach, her fingers still intertwined with his. 'I need you.'

She couldn't say anything. Her eyes were closed and she just wanted to stay there, right there, feeling him hold her, knowing he'd make love to her again and everything would be alright because that's what he did. That's what she *let* him do – make love to her, and let her believe that everything was alright.

'Amber, baby, I love you, and if I've...'

She pulled her hand away from his and pushed herself up, climbing out of the bath and grabbing her robe from the door, covering herself up. 'Maybe we need to get some sleep now. It's been a long day.' She walked out into the bedroom, the need for an alcohol hit suddenly quite overwhelming.

Making her way downstairs to the kitchen, she could hear him moving around now, and she knew he'd follow her, of course he would. But was now really the right time to confront him?

Finding a bottle of whiskey in one of the kitchen cupboards she poured herself a small measure, just enough to give her that hit she needed. And as she felt that warmth she'd craved flood her stomach she knew he was there now, with her. The man who'd vowed he'd changed. The man she loved beyond anything else, and now the fear she was feeling wasn't really about what he was going to say to her, it was about her reaction. Did she really have the strength to walk away? If what he told her wasn't what she wanted to hear, was she strong enough to walk away?

She slowly turned around, putting down her glass and folding her arms as she looked at him leaning back against the wall, hot and handsome in nothing but jeans that hung so sexily on those slim hips of his, his dark hair damp and pushed back off his face.

'Did you have anything to do with Ryan's involvement in that betting ring being made public?' The words were out before she'd even had time to think about whether it was the right thing to do or not. They were out now.

She watched his reaction; watched as he hung his head briefly, his hands dug deep in his pockets. And then he looked up, his eyes meeting hers and she held his stare. To keep her eyes on his would be the only way she'd know if he was telling her the truth.

'Yes,' he whispered. That was all he said. Just that one, small word. Yet, for Amber, it was a word that had just kick-started a barrage of feelings all jostling for space inside her. A word that said a thousand things. A word that could change everything. Again.

She couldn't say anything. All she could do was look at him, and know that, this time, he was being honest. Of course he was being honest, he'd just admitted to doing exactly what Ryan had accused him of doing. Yet she couldn't decide just how that was making her feel.

'Amber, I…'

'Why?' Still she couldn't break the stare, and he was the first to look away, just for a brief second, before his eyes once more met hers.

'I can't lose you, Amber. Not again…'

'Why, Jim? Why did you do it?'

This time he broke that stare for longer, his eyes down on the floor, his hands still deep in his pockets. 'I don't know. And that's God's honest truth.'

'He didn't deserve that.'

Jim raised his head slowly. 'No, maybe he didn't. But he's a threat, Amber. To me, to a future I've now got within my grasp. A future I'm just not willing to jeopardise any more.'

Amber couldn't help a small laugh from escaping. 'So, what? You think that by trying to bring Ryan down, by wrecking his career once and for all, you think *that's* going to make sure we stay together? He's the father of my baby, Jim. Do you get that yet?'

'Yeah, I get it, Amber. I get it every, single, fucking day, and do you know what? Every day it kills me. Every day it tears me apart that you have that bond with him, and I just lost it, okay? I panicked. I saw a way to get to him, to make him vulnerable, and I just went with it. But I fought against doing it, I fought so hard, you have to believe me…'

'Not hard enough.' Her voice was quiet, an almost resigned tone to it. 'You know, there was a time when, despite anything else that was going on, you would never have jeopardised a player's career. Not a player as talented as Ryan. You would have tried anything else, Jim, I know that. I realise that. But you would never have tried to kill their career.'

'He's not my player any more, Amber. He's not my player and he's not someone I care all that much about….'

'But *I* do. I have to, don't you see that? I have to care about him, for Rico's sake. Because I am not having that baby grow up without his father being a big part of his life. And if you really can't get used to that…'

'He's still in love with you.'

'And that isn't my problem.'

'You think?'

'It isn't my problem. Because I'm not in love with him… Jesus, I am so tired of having to explain this. Especially to you. And I'm not sure I can deal with the insecurity and the paranoia right now.'

'Don't walk away from me, Amber. Please.'

She looked at him, her eyes locked on his as he walked towards her. 'I can do what I like.'

'Please,' he whispered, stopping right in front of her. 'I can't lose you, baby. I can't go through that again. I can't.'

'You don't think you're strong enough? Oh, you're strong enough, Jim. You can cope with anything, no matter what you think. And you could deal with me walking away.'

He shook his head, his eyes boring deep into hers and she could clearly see the tears building up, which only served to pierce her heart with a pain that was almost unbearable.

'When did you do it?'

'Just before we left for Vegas.'

'Jesus.' She turned her head away, pushing a hand through her hair.

'Amber, please…'

She looked at him. 'When we over there, getting married? When we were over there, you knew…'

'Amber, baby, I regret ever even thinking about it now, and I need you to believe that, I really need you to believe that.'

'You lied. Again. After everything you promised me…'

'And I'm sorry.'

'Such an empty, meaningless word, Jim. Because it means nothing.'

'Ryan he… he's gonna be okay. It wasn't as bad as I…' He stopped talking, hanging his head, rubbing a hand over the back of his neck.

'I heard you,' she whispered, her eyes still on him. 'On the phone. I was outside your office, and I heard you talking to someone… you sounded as though you were almost disappointed that things weren't quite as bad as they could have been. Disappointed that Ryan wasn't quite as involved as you'd hoped he would be. Oh, at the time I didn't really know what you were talking about, not for sure anyway. But Ryan, that seed of doubt had been sown, Jim, and thinking back…'

'Amber, baby, please…'

'You don't change. You'll never change, I don't think you're capable. I don't even know if what you told me about Carrie was even true…'

His head shot up and he fixed her with a look that almost scared her. 'That was true. Every heartbreaking fucking second of what I told you about her was true, Amber. And if you think for one minute that I could lie about something like that…'

'You've lied before, Jim. About so many things.'

'Not that,' he whispered, shaking his head. 'Never that.'

It was her turn to bow her head, just for a couple of beats. 'You're hurting Rico, too, do you know that?' Her eyes met his again. 'By hurting his dad you're hurting him, too. And I can't let that happen. That baby comes first, before anybody. My son

comes first, and you don't get to hurt him, in any way. You don't get to hurt him the way you've hurt me.'

Amber watched as tears started to stream from his eyes, and she was surprised at how little she actually felt like crying herself.

'But I'm not going anywhere, Jim.'

He frowned, quickly wiping his eyes with the back of his hand. 'I… I don't understand.'

'You really think I can walk away from you? Again? You don't hold the monopoly on being so much in love with someone it hurts like no other pain you've ever felt. So, no matter what you've done, we'll get through it. Because *I'm* the one who isn't strong enough to walk away. You'd cope, Jim, and you know you would. You'd cope. Because you've walked away from me before, remember? But I'd fall apart.'

'Amber, baby…'

She shook her head, reaching out to touch his cheek, brushing away tears with her thumb. 'Don't say you're sorry, because I'm not sure that you are. Not really. You and Ryan, I'm just going to have to accept that you two are never gonna get along. But for Rico's sake, you're really gonna have to try. For *my* sake you're gonna have to try. Because I can't deal with any more crap, Jim.'

He put his hand over hers, tears still streaming down his face. 'I love you so much, Amber. So, so much, and with every beat of my heart I will make sure…'

She shut him up with a kiss. Because she needed to touch him, to feel his mouth on hers and his body against her. She needed that.

His hand fell into the small of her back, pushing her closer to him, their mouths now moving together in a faster, harder rhythm. She was falling under his spell, letting him drag her deeper and deeper under until she knew, one day, there'd be nothing left of her. Nothing of the old Amber who'd once had the strength to walk away from this man, because he was killing her – the woman she'd used to be, she was disappearing fast. And she couldn't stop it from happening. He pulled her apart and he messed with her head, but he also completed her. And there wasn't a thing she could do to change that.

Chapter Twenty-Two

'Something you want to tell me?'

Ellen's eyes widened as she looked at the packets of pills in Ryan's hand. 'You'd better come in.'

He kicked the door shut behind him, throwing the pills down onto the hall table, his eyes burning into hers. 'Please tell me this isn't what I think it is.'

'I can explain, Ryan, if you'll…'

'Were you *deliberately* trying to get pregnant? Huh? Is that what you were *seriously* trying to do?'

'Ryan, no, it was…'

'You told me to ditch the condoms… Jesus! You told me you were on the pill, you *promised* me. How the hell could I have fallen for that one, huh?'

'Please, Ryan…'

'These are your pills? Yes, or no.'

'Yes.'

'Then it's a simple enough question. Were you deliberately trying to get pregnant?'

She leaned back against the wall, her shoulders sagging for a brief second before her demeanour changed to that of someone a little more in control. 'I see the way you are with Rico, and…'

'And, what? You want some of that for yourself?'

'That bond you have not just with Rico, but with Amber, too…'

Ryan threw his head back and laughed. 'You're frigging unbelievable. Is this all because you're *jealous*?'

'Of course I'm fucking jealous! You can't let go, Ryan. You're like some lovesick teenager who can't get over some ridiculous crush, and now? Now she's had your baby! So you're never going to let her go, are you?'

'So, you thought, maybe, if *you* had my baby too, then, I wouldn't be quite so – I dunno – attached to Amber?'

Ellen's shoulders sagged again. 'You love that baby so much, Ryan.'

'Of course I love him. I'd die for that kid; he's my whole fucking world.'

'And so is she.' Ellen's voice was almost a whisper, her eyes looking straight into his. 'So is Amber.'

What could Ryan say? She was right.

'I just thought that… that if I had your baby, too, then you'd *have* to take a step back, Ryan. You'd have to. And you would, because I can see what a great dad you are.'

He shook his head, sitting down at the bottom of the stairs, clasping his hands between his slightly open knees. 'This is mad. I can't believe I'm actually having this conversation. You can't do this, Ellen. You can't use kids as pawns in some kind of game.'

'You're using your own son as a pawn, Ryan.'

'The fuck I am!'

'Don't you see? Oh, I know you love him, that's more than obvious. But you're using him all the same, to get closer to her.'

'She's his mum.'

'And you still love her.'

'This is ridiculous.' He stood up, walked over to her and stopped just in front of her. 'This isn't about me, sweetheart. It's about you, playing crazy games with my life. And it stops, right now, do you hear me?'

She nodded, reaching out to touch his face but he gently pushed her hand away. 'Ryan…'

'So, *are* you?'

She frowned. 'Am I what?'

'Pregnant.'

She looked down, shaking her head. 'No.'

'Thank Christ for that,' he sighed, throwing his head back again, taking a couple of steps away from her. 'This is over, Ellen. Whatever the hell it was, it's over. Have you got that? All of it. It's over.'

'Ryan, please, I'm sorry…'

'It's over, Ellen. And I really don't want to hurt you, but I just can't deal with another relationship right now. It isn't even you, although, what you've tried to do…' He looked at her. 'It isn't even you. When you're not acting all psycho you're actually an amazing girl. But I just can't deal with this – with any kind of relationship at the minute, not while… I just can't.'

'Not while you're still in love with her. Is that what you were going to say?' Ellen's voice was quiet, resigned to the inevitable now.

Ryan said nothing for a couple of beats, he just dug his hands deeper into his pockets and looked down at the floor. 'I can't deal with another relationship, Ellen. I'm sorry.'

'You're going to let her ruin your life, Ryan.'

'And that's my choice.'

'You're crazy! You could have any woman you want, yet you seem determined to throw everything away on someone you'll never have.'

'You don't know that.'

She narrowed her eyes as she stared at him. 'Someone you'll never have, Ryan.'

He said nothing for a few seconds. He just stared her out, a determination growing inside him that he'd never felt before.

'I'll see you around, Ellen.'

He turned to walk away, but her voice made him turn back around.

'I've said this before, and I mean it, Ryan. You deserve better.'

'Do I?'

'You deserve someone who loves you.'

'Yeah. Maybe I do. Or maybe I just really *want* the woman I love.'

*

'Leave him, Amber.'

She looked up from her laptop, throwing Ronnie a look that told him she really wasn't in the mood. 'When I told you all of this, Ronnie, I really should have added that I don't want your opinion.'

'Leave him.'

'What did I just say?'

'He lied.'

'I'm not talking about this with you.'

'Well, forgive me, Amber, but it was *you* who chose to share this information with me.'

'And I should have remembered how you can't keep your mouth shut. I'm trying to work here.'

'So, it doesn't bother you that he lied? Again.'

She threw her pen down and sat back in her chair, swinging her legs up onto the desk. 'I'm disappointed, Ronnie, that's all. Disappointed that he did it, and yes, it bothers me. Of course it bothers me. I'm angry and confused and there was a second – a split second – when I thought I really was going to walk away. For good this time. But I can't do it. I can't.'

'You won't. And there's a difference.'

'I don't need the lectures, alright? He's my husband, and I love him. Simple as that.'

Ronnie raised an eyebrow, perching himself on the corner of Amber's desk. 'You make it sound like he just forgot your anniversary or something. Now, as I know you're all too aware, I'm not Ryan Fisher's biggest fan, not on a personal level, anyway. But for someone to want to destroy his career... Amber, Jim wanted to destroy the career of Rico's dad.'

254

'And you don't think I've made all this clear to him?'

'What did you do, exactly? Give him a light telling-off, then offer him a blow job he'd never forget?'

'I'm not listening to this.' She stood up, kicking her chair back under her desk. 'You're out of order, Ronnie. You're my best friend, and I love you, I do. But you're out of order.'

'I care about you.'

'Then start acting like you mean that, because, right now I just feel as though you're trying to make me feel guilty about staying with the man I love.'

Ronnie walked over to her, tilting her chin up so she had no choice but to look at him. 'I care about you, Amber. And all I can see in front of me is a woman who has no idea what the fuck she's doing.'

'I don't need this.'

'Yes. You do.'

She pushed his hand away and walked out of the office, but he followed her.

'Amber, wait!'

She swung around to face him. She really wasn't in the mood for this.

'Where are you going?'

'Nowhere,' she sighed, her shoulders sagging.

'Come home with me.'

'Why? So you can nag me into submission?'

He couldn't stop a smile from appearing and she backed up against the wall, unable to stop smiling herself. 'Hey, if you want to submit to anything, beautiful, you won't find me stopping you.'

'I hate you sometimes.'

'The feeling's mutual.'

He held out his hand and she took it.

'Come on. We'll go back to mine and you can talk to me. Properly.'

'Fine. But only if you've got alcohol. Because I've got a feeling

I'm gonna need it.'

*

'I shouldn't have said anything, should I?'

Ryan looked at Debbie through slightly narrowed eyes. But he said nothing.

'I mean, I might just be reading this completely wrongly, because I'm only going from how she sounded over the phone… is Rico alright?'

'He's fine,' Ryan said, gently rubbing Rico's back as he lay over his shoulder. 'And how *did* she sound over the phone, exactly?'

'I shouldn't be talking to you. Amber'll kill me. I've already said way more than I should have done to you.'

'Debbie, come on. You've opened your mouth now so you're gonna have to tell me.'

'She sounded… I dunno. She sounded a bit down.'

'Down?' Ryan frowned.

'Yeah. Like she had something on her mind.'

'Last time *I* spoke to her she was being a complete bitch.'

'Maybe there's a reason for that, then.'

'Like what?'

'You know what Amber's like. When something's wrong she can sometimes go on the defensive.'

'That's true.'

'Do you know what you two sound like?' Gary said, making his way into the kitchen. 'You sound like a pair of gossiping housewives. You ready, Ryan?'

'Yeah,' Ryan sighed, handing Rico over to Debbie. 'Look, Debbie, you said she sounded down. Did she say anything to make you think he's upset her or done something to…?'

'Jesus, Ryan, come on!' Gary's tone was slightly irritated now. 'Forget it, okay? Married people have ups and downs, it's normal.' He looked over at Debbie, who just poked her tongue out at him.

256

'Nice. Actually, you look quite sexy when you do that.'

'Are you still here?' She lifted a gurgling Rico up into the air, bringing him back down for a kiss, blowing a soft raspberry on his tiny cheek.

'She's been married to him for all of five minutes, Gary,' Ryan pointed out, watching as his baby boy let out the cutest little laugh, and he felt his heart break with love for him. He felt his heart break for Rico's mum. She was never going to go away, not now, no matter how far he ran. And he'd tried that one before, hadn't he? He'd tried running, and it hadn't really got him anywhere.

'She's been married to him forever, mate. Now start getting your head around that and come on. We're meeting everyone at the bar in an hour.'

'Debbie, are you sure…?'

'Ryan, I've told you everything I know. She didn't say all that much, really. It was just the way she sounded, and she *has* been extremely busy these past few weeks. She's probably just tired.'

'No, that's not it.'

'Look, you'll be able to find out for yourself when we play Endleigh United on Saturday, Ryan, but in the meantime can you get your arse in gear and move it, please? We're gonna be late.'

'Did she say *anything* about her and Jim?' Ryan asked Debbie, ignoring Gary's eagerness to head off into town for a night out that Ryan really couldn't be bothered with. He had far too much on his mind.

'No. And even if she had I don't think it'd be my place to tell you anything, so can you please stop putting pressure on me and take him out to play.' She nudged her head in Gary's direction as he stood in the doorway, tapping his watch. 'Amber will be fine, Ryan, okay? She can look after herself. Like I said, she's had a busy few weeks. She probably just needs some time out.'

Ryan threw his head back and sighed, pushing both hands through his hair before he turned and took his little boy from Debbie, cuddling him close. Sometimes he just wanted to sit and hold his son because it was the most incredible feeling. It was something he never thought would happen to him, but now it was something he never wanted to be without. It was better than any sex he'd ever had – except, maybe, the sex he'd had with Amber. The sex that had created their beautiful baby son. 'You gonna be good for your Aunty Debbie, huh?'

'He's gonna be just fine, won't you, poppet? And can we have less of the "aunty," please? It makes me sound old.'

'Which is what I'm gonna be if we don't get out of here,' Gary said, throwing Ryan a look that told him if he didn't make a move now he was going without him.

Ryan handed Rico back to Debbie, giving him one last kiss as he let go of him. 'I need to be with her, Debs. I need to be with her so badly it's killing me.'

Debbie reached out and squeezed his arm, giving him what she hoped was a reassuring smile. 'I don't know what to say, Ryan. I mean, I can stand here and tell you to get over it because she isn't coming back, but they're just words. I wish you would listen, I really do, but whatever I say, you're not gonna do that, are you? You're not gonna listen.'

He shook his head. 'He doesn't deserve her. He'll hurt her, I know he will…'

'Ryan!'

'Jesus, Gary, will you just leave it! Maybe he doesn't *want* to go out, did you ever think about that?'

Gary looked at Ryan, raising his eyebrows in question. 'Well? *Do* you want to go out?'

'Not really,' Ryan replied, relief sweeping through him. No. He didn't want to go out. He wanted to stay here and pour his heart out to Amber's friend and then hope, in some childish way, that she'd tell Amber everything he was about to tell her. That Amber would then know how he was feeling. That she'd think about the life she'd made for herself. And the life she could still have. The life *he* wanted.

'You sure? Because I'm out of here, right now.'

'I'm sure.'

'Okay. Well, you know where we are if you want to join us later.'

Ryan just nodded, a smile spreading across his face as Rico stretched his arms out towards him. He wanted his daddy. And Ryan didn't hesitate to take him back from Debbie. 'Hey there, little guy! Your daddy's staying in now. Who wants to go out drinking and gambling when I can stay here and be with you?'

'Well, those are words I never thought I'd hear come out of Ryan Fisher's mouth.' Debbie half-smiled as she switched the kettle on.

'Yeah, well, a lot's changed, hasn't it?'

She nodded, leaning back against the counter and folding her arms as she watched him cradle his baby boy. 'He's beautiful, Ryan. He really is.'

Ryan couldn't help smiling again as he stroked Rico's dark hair and watched his eyes slowly closing. 'He takes after his mum in that department.'

'I think you'll find that his mum actually thinks he looks like *you*.'

Ryan looked up. 'Did I fight hard enough, Debbie? To keep her?'

'It was a fight you couldn't win, Ryan.'

'What's so special about him, huh? What's so special about a man who's done nothing but treat her like crap ever since she was a teenager? I don't get it, Debs. I don't get what kind of hold he has over her, why she can't just let him go.'

Debbie shrugged, turning to pour boiling water into the mugs behind her. 'Who knows what really went on in their past or what's gone on since he came back into her life? We just don't know.'

'We know he hurt her.'

Debbie turned back around. 'You have to stop this, Ryan. Seriously. Because it's going to take over your life and you're going to let it affect everything you do. Stop obsessing about her and stop putting her on a pedestal because she won't thank you for it. She's my friend and I love her to bits, but she isn't worth you destroying your life over. Okay? You need to get a grip, and start thinking of her as someone you once shared something good with; the mother of your incredibly gorgeous son. But that's it, Ryan. That's it. You need to move your relationship on or it *will* destroy you.'

'And *he'll* destroy *her*, Debbie. I know he will, I know it. He'll destroy her. And I'm not gonna stand around and watch that happen.'

Debbie just looked at him. 'It's pointless me trying to persuade you to leave this alone, isn't it?'

He nodded, his eyes back down on his baby boy.

'Then, be careful, okay? Just, be careful.'

He looked up. 'He had something to do with that story being released, Debbie. I know he did.'

'You have no proof, Ryan.'

He held her gaze for a good few beats. 'Why else do you think Amber's acting the way she is now, huh?'

'It's a fight you can't win,' Debbie whispered.

But, as far as Ryan was concerned, she couldn't be more wrong.

*

'Does he know where you are?'

'He's not my father, Ronnie. I don't have to text him what time I'm gonna be home. He's a big boy now. He can look after himself.'

'There was a time when you'd rush home just to be with him because you couldn't bear to be apart for more than half a day. Has the sex lost its appeal already?'

She turned her head to look at him, pulling her knees up further against her chest, hugging them to her. 'You seem obsessed with mine and Jim's sex life.'

Ronnie just shrugged, looking down into his glass of whiskey. 'You're still just-married, Amber, that's all I was saying. Isn't the honeymoon period supposed to last a little longer than a few

260

weeks?'

Amber didn't answer that. 'Maybe I *should* have walked away.'

Ronnie looked at her. 'So why didn't you?'

It was her turn to shrug. 'Like I said, I can't.'

'And like *I* said, you *won't*.'

'He's been such a huge part of my life, Ronnie. It's like he's always been there, you know?'

'No. Not really.'

'I can't just turn my back on almost twenty-three years of loving him. I can't.'

'And for most of those years you hated him, Amber, remember? You hated him because he'd hurt you and he'd used you and then he just tossed you aside like you didn't really matter…'

'And there's a reason for that. There's a reason why he acted the way he did.'

'Oh, really? And what reason would that be?'

'I can't tell you. He doesn't want anyone else to know.'

'Why? Why, Amber? Jesus… he's got *you* keeping his secrets for him, now.'

'It's not a secret, Ronnie, okay? It's just personal, that's all. Personal and painful. But it explains so much…'

'I don't believe you… I don't believe you're actually keeping secrets from me now. We promised we'd never do that, Amber.' He got up off the couch, walking over to the sideboard to pour himself another drink. 'Can't you see what he's doing to you?' He turned around, leaning back against the sideboard. 'He's taking you apart, bit by bit, piece by piece, until there's nothing left of the real Amber. Just this – this empty shell that is so in love with him you can't even think straight any more. Because that's what he wants you to do. That's who he wants you to be.'

Amber stood up, too, walking over to him, a wave of anger bubbling up inside her. 'You don't get to talk to me like that, Ronnie. You don't get to dissect my life or believe that you know what's going on, because you don't. You don't.'

Ronnie just raised an eyebrow. 'Really?'

'I don't need this. Coming here was a mistake…'

He grabbed her wrist, swinging her back around to face him. 'Can't you see it, Amber? What loving him is doing to you? It's changing you.'

'And what if I *want* to change? Huh? Did that thought ever cross your mind?'

'No, because I don't believe for one frigging minute that you want to be the person you are now. Someone who gives into a man who's controlled you for over twenty years. I don't believe you want that.'

'Nobody has controlled me, Ronnie.'

He let out a loud laugh, letting go of her wrist. 'Is that what you really think? Then you need to take a closer look at your life, sweetheart.'

'Fuck you!' she spat, turning around and walking away from him, out into the hall, grabbing her coat from the rack and making her way to the front door. But he wasn't giving up.

'I don't want to lose you, Amber, that's all.'

She swung around to face him. 'He isn't the fucking devil, for Christ's sake! Why do people make him out to be this evil, controlling person who doesn't give a crap about anything except what *he* wants? Why, Ronnie?'

'You used to be strong, and independent, and ready to take on the world, Amber. And now… now you don't seem to be able to do anything unless he's right there with you. Unless *he's* in your life. But he wasn't there for sixteen years, remember? And for sixteen years you managed just fine, didn't you?'

She shook her head, folding her arms against her. 'No. I didn't.'

'You did, Amber. You just need to remember that. Because he is killing you and I can't watch it any more.'

'I really don't need this. Not from you, not from anyone. Now get out of my way.'

She tried to push past him but he caught her arm again, stopping her from going anywhere. 'I miss her. The old Amber. I miss her so fucking much.'

'Let go of me, Ronnie.'

'I miss her.'

'Let go of me!'

His mouth was on hers before she had a chance to even think about what he was doing, his fingers sliding between hers, keeping her close. But she wasn't in the mood. Once upon a time this may have got her, but she really wasn't as weak as he made her out to be.

Pulling away from him she took a step back and slapped him, her hand stinging, but she didn't feel any pain. She was way too angry for that. 'You don't get to do that to me, do you hear? You don't get to stand there and tell me I'm weak and then do that to me. You're supposed to be my friend.'

'Amber, please, I'm sorry…'

She shook her head, picking her jacket up from the floor, where she'd dropped it, finally opening the front door. 'Yeah. So am I, Ronnie. So am I.'

Chapter Twenty-Three

'Kevin! Oh my God, I had no idea you were coming down here!' Amber threw herself into the arms of Kevin Russell, her old boss from News North East, clinging onto him as he swung her around before putting her back down, pulling her in for another hug.

'Well, your dad thought it'd be a nice surprise. And seeing as I'm on the last couple of days of my holiday and I had nothing better to do, I thought I'd come down with Freddie and pay my beautiful ex-employee a visit. And it gets me out of doing any more decorating. There's only so much wallpaper a man can hang in a fortnight.'

Amber couldn't believe how excited she was at seeing Kevin again. It brought back memories of old times, when things had been less complicated and she'd been in complete control of everything in her life. Those memories seemed like a lifetime ago now.

'And I have to say, Amber, I never thought I'd see the day when you'd be pushing a pram and heating bottles at two o'clock in the morning. But that baby of yours, he is one cute kid! Hard to believe he's half Ryan Fisher's.'

Amber leaned back against the wall of the tunnel that led out onto the pitch at Parkfield, stuffing her hands in the pockets of her skinny black jeans. 'I think he looks like Ryan, don't you?'

'Sweetheart, he's only a few months old. To be fair, he doesn't really look like anyone just yet.'

Amber couldn't help smiling. 'Humour me. I'm a new mum. And anyway, despite whatever's going on between me and his daddy, Ryan Fisher is one good-looking bastard, and I'd be quite happy for our son to grow up as handsome as he is. I may have to vet every single one of his girlfriends, of course, because no one'll ever be good enough. But, yeah, I'd love him to grow up as handsome as Ryan.'

Kevin looked at her, saying nothing, just raising an eyebrow.

'What was *that* look for?'

'Nothing. How's life as one of football's better-looking reporters, then? Max Mandell treating you okay, is he?'

'Max is a superstar, Kevin. He's been brilliant.'

'We miss you back home, you know. You brightened up the office – and I'm not just talking about that hair colour – even though you could be a right temperamental pain in the arse at times.'

Oh, it was so good to see him again! Despite the myriad changes that had gone on around her over the past couple of years, Kevin Russell still seemed to be the same man he'd always been, and that was something of a comfort to Amber. And looking at him now, well, there were times when she longed for those days when she'd walk into the News North East offices and he'd be standing there ready to give her some assignment she really couldn't be bothered to do. The days when Ryan Fisher hadn't existed in her world, and Jim Allen was nothing but a memory she'd hoped to keep very firmly at the back of her mind. Yeah. And that had worked, hadn't it?

'And married. Again! You like to keep the journalistic world on its toes, I'll give you that. How *are* things with Jim?'

She fixed him with a look. 'Things are fine.'

'You sure?'

'Oh, you're *just* what I need.'

Kevin raised that eyebrow again. 'Nice to see the old Amber

hasn't left us completely.'

'Yeah, well, try telling that to Ronnie.'

'Ronnie just worries about you, Amber.'

'You been talking to him?'

'I've been talking to everyone, kiddo.'

'Is nothing in my life private any more?'

'Well, after that photo shoot you did for *Ice* magazine I'd say, no. Not really. Some of the lads back in the office had those pictures up all over the staff-room walls. Made me feel quite uncomfortable they did. I mean, you're almost like a daughter to me and I don't want to see you wearing nothing but a Newcastle Red Star scarf. I'll leave all that to Jim Allen.'

She couldn't help smiling. 'But you had a look, though, right?'

'Of course I did. I'm only human. Just don't tell your dad.' He smiled at her. 'You sure you're alright? Freddie says you've been working yourself into the ground over the past couple of weeks, and that's never a good thing.'

'I like being busy.'

'Oh, believe me, kiddo, I'm well aware of your work ethic. But even the best of us need to slow down at some point.'

'Kevin, honestly, I'm fine. There's just… there's a lot going on right now, that's all. I've just had a baby, I've got married, and then there's all this work with Cloud Sports and filming back-to-back episodes of *Back of the Net*. Not to mention all the stuff Max keeps shoving in front of me. I think it's all just caught up with me.'

'Okay. I'll quit with the nagging. I suspect you're already getting enough of that from plenty of other places.'

'You got that right,' she sighed, but then her whole demeanour changed as Jim walked over, that beautiful, heartbreaking smile covering his handsome face as he held his hand out for Kevin to shake.

'Hey, Kevin! Good to see you. Amber didn't say you were coming down here.'

'That's because Amber didn't know. It was a spur-of-the-moment thing. I haven't seen her in too long, and I had some spare time, so… anyway, what's all this about, huh? Ditching Red Star to come back down south. We're missing you up north.'

Jim slipped an arm around Amber's waist and she snuggled in against him, slipping her hand just inside the waistband of his black pants.

'Circumstances, Kevin. Things were changing, and, well… it was becoming untenable, staying at Red Star.' He looked at Amber, leaning over slightly to plant a quick, light kiss on her lips. 'I want things to work between me and this beautiful girl here. That's why we needed to get away.'

Amber stared up at him, and suddenly all the sound and the noise of a match day that had, not seconds earlier, surrounded her just seemed to melt away, to disappear. He was the only one she could see.

'I'll leave you to it,' Kevin said, and for a second Amber turned her attention from Jim back to her old boss.

'I'll see you later?' she asked, hopeful he wasn't just here to watch the match and run.

He smiled at her, reaching out to take her hand, giving it a quick squeeze. 'Of course you will.'

She watched him walk back up the tunnel, stopping briefly to chat to people who were milling about inside, before she looked back at Jim. 'Shouldn't you be in the dressing room?'

'Colin's doing his pre-match rant.'

Amber laughed, leaning into him as he hugged her waist tighter. 'Are they taking any notice?'

Jim shrugged. 'Who knows? But you know what happened when that lot at Newcastle Red Star ignored him.'

Amber turned so she was standing right in front of him, his arms falling loosely around her. 'I wish we could get out of here, Jim. Away from everything. Just you, and me.'

He kissed her quickly, and all that did was make Amber want him more. 'I know, baby. But real life has a habit of getting in the way of all the good stuff we *really* want to do.'

She slipped her arms around his neck and hugged him, resting her head on his shoulder, her eyes immediately falling on Ronnie as he hung around at the other end of the tunnel, talking to another of their Cloud Sports colleagues. He met her gaze, only briefly, but it was enough to start something up in Amber that she couldn't stop now.

'Have you got time for a little pre-match playdate?' She smiled, moving her mouth closer to Jim's as she spoke.

He grinned, letting his hand fall onto her bottom. 'What've you got in mind, beautiful?'

'Your office, five minutes.' She kissed him slowly, sliding her hand around the back of his neck, ignoring all the noise and the sound of the stadium filling up outside. All she was aware of was the sound of her heart beating and a voice inside her head telling her this was okay. What she was doing, it was okay. And it didn't matter what anyone else thought. 'Five minutes.' She smiled, watching as he walked back up the tunnel, one hand in the pocket of his black pants, the other one raking its way through his hair.

'What was *that* all about?' Ronnie asked, arriving by her side.

'What was *what* all about?'

'Public displays of affection never used to be Jim Allen's thing, so having to watch you two all over each other isn't something I'm keen to make a habit of.'

'We're not kids at a high-school disco, Ronnie. It's good to see Kevin here, isn't it?'

'It's always good to see Kevin, and please stop changing the subject. We need you up in the studio in fifteen minutes. You gonna be there?'

She looked at him, saying nothing.

He let out a heavy sigh, leaning back against the wall. 'Amber, babe, it really doesn't have to be this way.'

'You made your feelings towards my marriage very clear, Ronnie.'

'And you think I'm the only one feeling this way? Why the hell am *I* the one getting all the crap thrown at me?'

'Because you're the one whose opinion matters the most.' Her eyes were locked on his. 'You're the one I care about, the one I don't want to lose over this but if you can't accept...'

'He lied, Amber.'

'It's over, Ronnie. It's done.'

He stared at her for a couple of beats, and Amber felt her heart almost ice over. 'Yeah. Carry on like this and it will be. I'll see you up in the studio.'

She threw herself back against the wall, closing her eyes and breathing in deeply, taking a few seconds to compose herself before she almost ran the short distance to Jim's office.

Stopping outside only briefly, she turned around and leaned back against the door, listening to the sounds coming from both the home and away dressing rooms, hearing some familiar voices from the Newcastle Red Star players who were Endleigh's opponents for the Saturday evening televised Cloud Sports match. She could hear Ryan's voice, his laugh loud as it echoed around the dressing room, drifting out into the corridor, and she felt her stomach give an involuntary leap that she hadn't asked it to take.

She hadn't seen him yet. Ryan. But she knew she was going to have to face him at some point, knowing that what he'd suspected – what he'd accused Jim of. Ryan had been right. And that still bothered Amber.

Closing her eyes she swallowed hard, trying to push that to the back of her mind, instead pulling forward everything Ronnie had said. Was he right, too?

As a small bubble of anger mixed with frustration took over from the guilt, she pushed back against the door, going inside and kicking it shut behind her. Jim was leaning back against his desk, his arms folded and a slight smile on his face.

'You wanted to see me?' He raised an eyebrow and Amber felt her stomach contract in the most beautiful way. Ronnie wasn't going to make her feel guilty about loving this man. He had no right to do that. None. And as for Ryan…

She smiled, walking slowly over to him, pulling him closer to her by his tie. 'Do you have any idea how sexy I find you on match days?' she whispered, her fingers loosening his belt, playing with the zip of his pants. 'All – powerful and dominant, and so, so *hot!*'

He returned her smile, sliding a hand up under her shirt but she pulled it away, shaking her head as her fingers curled around his. 'Oh no, mister. You don't get to call the shots this time. You may be in charge of that team out there, but in here I think you'll find *I'm* in charge.'

'Well, I ain't complaining about that, baby.'

She closed her eyes as his lips touched hers, and so began the process of blocking out everything that didn't matter, and replacing it all with the only thing she wanted to think about right now. Him.

Nipping his bottom lip with her teeth she smiled at him, her fingers gripping the lapels of his suit jacket, his erection already digging into her, but that was good. That was what she'd wanted.

'What are you…?'

'Sshh. No talking, okay? You just lean back and enjoy the ride.'

'Amber…' He let out the loudest groan as she sank to her haunches, finally unzipping him, taking him in her hand and wrapping her fingers tightly around his hardness. 'Jesus, baby, you freakin' kill me!'

'I said, no talking,' she whispered, watching her hand as it moved slowly back and forth along him. She loved the feel of him there in her grasp; hot and throbbing and ready for her.

Her heart had started to beat wildly now, her breathing already faster, and she briefly closed her eyes again, once more running her fingers over his still-growing hardness, eliciting another long, deep moan from him.

Then, keeping her eyes closed, she leaned forward slightly, taking him in her mouth, running her tongue lightly over him as he tried to stifle yet more groans. She could feel him lean right back against the desk, his legs opening just a touch wider in response to her actions, his hand in her hair, pushing her closer to him. And she responded, taking him deeper, gripping his thighs tighter as her tongue continued to stroke him, the taste of him sending her stomach on another wave of beautiful contractions, her body shivering with anticipation.

'Jesus, Amber, baby… I'm gonna come, right now,' he groaned, but she already knew that, she could feel the way his whole body stiffened as that killer climax she'd wanted to tease out of him rushed forward so fast.

But she took him, all of him, keeping him inside as he came hard, and she swallowed him down, because she wanted to taste him. She wanted to capture every tiny part of him, to have him all, in any way she could.

'For fuck's sake, Amber…' he breathed when she finally released him, standing up and wiping her mouth with the back of her hand. 'What the hell brought *that* on?'

She smiled, pulling him back together. But she wasn't finished with him yet. She still had plans. 'You too tired to play some more?'

'What did *you* have for lunch today?'

'Are you too tired?' she repeated, slowly unfastening her shirt and slipping it off, tossing it aside. 'Because I'm only just getting started.' She was supposed to be somewhere else, she knew that, and she wasn't exactly being professional here, but she didn't care. She really didn't care. She was ceasing to care about much, to be honest. Apart from her baby boy and her beautiful husband, nothing else seemed to matter any more.

'When did I get so damn freakin' lucky?' Jim whispered, pulling her against him, unclipping her bra and throwing it aside, immediately lowering his head to cover one of her nipples with his mouth, his warm tongue flicking back and forth, making Amber's insides almost melt.

Stepping between his legs she pushed her breasts further towards him, arching her back slightly, letting out the quietest of moans as his tongue continued to flick over her naked skin, his fingers stroking her waist, pushing her jeans down ever so slightly over her hips.

'Jim, baby, I haven't got – *we* haven't got time for this.' She pulled away, crouching down to pick up her discarded clothes before backing off towards the door, her eyes locked with his.

He smiled, shaking his head as she leaned back against the door, her shirt hanging from her fingers. 'You playing games with me, Mrs. Allen?'

She kept her eyes on his as she unfastened her jeans, pushing them down a little further, just a touch, so they sat just below her hip bone. Sliding a hand down inside her jeans she moved her legs slightly further apart, shaking her head, their eyes still locked together as he stood up and walked slowly towards her.

'You're gonna do that without me?' he asked, raising an eyebrow, an action that made Amber's heart jump and her stomach dip.

She didn't reply, just kept her eyes on his as she continued to touch herself.

'Because, if you are, I sure as hell need to watch.'

She looked up at him, her stomach flipping over so many times it was making her feel quite dizzy. 'When we get home...' she whispered, pulling her hand away from herself, 'you can watch. In fact, I'm gonna *make* you watch.'

'Jesus–fucking–Christ!' he groaned, throwing his head back. 'And you expect me to go out there now and *work*?'

She smiled, pulling her shirt back on. 'I'm not sure you have much choice, Mr Allen.'

He slipped an arm around her waist, lowering his mouth down onto hers in a kiss that literally made Amber's knees go weak. 'Legs wide open, no panties... is that what I can expect?'

She pushed herself against him, her fingers playing with his hair. 'Do you want me naked?'

'Oh, Jesus, baby, you have got to get out of here before this gets out of hand.'

She smiled again, running her fingers lightly over his rough jawline. 'I'll see you later, handsome.'

He waited until the door was closed behind her before he sank to his haunches, dropping his head and pushing both hands through his hair. He was never going to be able to let that woman go. Every day it just got harder and harder to deal with, the thought of her walking away from him. And there'd been times when he'd wondered if he should have stayed away, never given this relationship another chance. Times when he'd wondered if he should have moved down here without her and saved himself all the pain that could still be coming his way, because Amber wasn't stupid. She'd told him she couldn't walk away, she'd told him that, and for a second he'd believed her. For a second. But out there, in his new sanctuary, was the man who could still ruin it all. A man who still had that bond with Amber that Jim could never have, and no matter how much he tried to believe that didn't matter, it did. It mattered. And it was still a problem that Jim needed to fix, before it was too late.

*

'You're very quiet,' Debbie said, turning to look at Amber. They were sitting up in one of the executive boxes, watching the last few minutes of the game play out, a game Amber's husband's team was winning. But only just. Ryan had been like a dog with a bone for most of the match, always clipping at the heels of the Endleigh defenders, trying to infiltrate their defence, managing to pull one goal back for Newcastle Red Star, but it didn't look like it was going to be enough. With only a minute of injury time left Endleigh were leading 2-1, another successive win for a side that had gone from strength to strength since Jim had returned to take over.

'I feel almost guilty, Debbie.'

'About what?'

Amber hugged a sleeping Rico against her, gently kissing his forehead. It was so good to have him back in her arms. Her beautiful baby boy. The only man who wasn't giving her any problems. 'About loving him.'

Debbie fixed her with a look. 'What's happened?'

'Nothing's happened, it's just…' She turned to look out at the pitch as the final whistle was blown, her eyes going straight to Jim as he walked over to Dave French, Red Star's new manager, shaking his hand and exchanging a couple of words, before she scanned the pitch, trying to find Ryan. And she watched as he headed off in the direction of the tunnel, watched as he and Jim briefly looked at one other before Ryan disappeared into the tunnel and back to the dressing room. 'It's nothing.'

'I hate it when you start a conversation with that.'

'It's nothing,' Amber repeated, standing up and balancing Rico on her hip, slipping her phone into her back pocket. 'Really.'

'The honeymoon period over then, is it?'

'No. Things are just… they're complicated.'

'They always are. You know the F.A. are about to come to a decision about Ryan's punishment regarding his involvement in that betting ring. They're claiming he's brought the game into disrepute, apparently. And it's rumoured he's going to get a lengthy match ban, possibly until the end of the season. Dave French is going ballistic, but there isn't a lot he can do about it…'

'Let's get out of here,' Amber said, cutting Debbie off mid-sentence.

'Amber, did you hear me?'

Amber stopped outside in the corridor, turning to face Debbie. 'It was Jim, okay? He was the one who leaked the story about Ryan and that betting ring; it was him. I don't know where he got the information from, I'm almost frightened to ask, but… it was him.'

'Okay…' Debbie didn't sound altogether surprised. 'And he told you that, did he?'

Amber nodded. 'When Ryan told me he suspected… I had to,

Debbie. And I hated myself for doubting Jim but – I had to ask him. Ryan left me no choice.'

'So, Ryan *was* right.' It wasn't a question.

Amber said nothing as they made their way down to the Players' Lounge.

'Does Ryan know?' Debbie asked.

Amber shook her head. 'No. It's not really gonna help, is it? Telling him.'

'You don't think he deserves to know the truth?'

Amber stopped walking again, taking her baby's tiny hand in hers as she looked at her friend. 'All that would do is reignite the stupid war between him and Jim, Debbie, and I'm not sure I've got the strength to deal with that any more.'

'You think what Jim did was right?'

'Of course I don't! What he did was wrong, and I've told him so. And I was *that* close to walking away from him, believe me. *That* close. But I can't do it again, Debs. I can't turn my back on that man, no matter what he's done. I can't do it. And I don't care how weak that makes me sound, or how morally wrong some people may think it is, but… I love him. I love him so fucking much. And I feel for Ryan, I do, because I will always care about him. But I can't let this destroy me and Jim. I can't.'

Debbie smiled a small smile, reaching out to gently touch Amber's arm. 'Okay, chick. I kind of understand where you're coming from. But you have to know how Ryan still feels about you…'

Amber vigorously shook her head, picking up the pace again as they headed downstairs. 'I don't want to know, Debbie, do you hear me?' She stopped only briefly to throw Debbie a determined look. 'How he feels doesn't matter. It can't. So, no. I don't have to know how he still feels about me.'

Because she already knew.

*

Ryan stood in the Players' Lounge, leaning back against the wall, his hands in his pockets as he looked out around him. 'I hate fucking losing.'

'It was a close-run thing, mate,' Gary said, handing him a bottle of lager. 'You worked your arse off out there, there wasn't much else you could've done.'

But Ryan's attention was elsewhere now. Amber had just walked into the room, all hot, red hair and incredible smile, Rico balanced on one of her super-sexy hips. Ryan couldn't take his eyes off her. He watched as she walked over to Jim, standing up on tiptoes to kiss him slowly, a smile spreading across her face as she looked up at the man who had everything he wanted. And it tore Ryan apart.

'You're not just talking about the match, though, are you?'

Ryan turned to look at Gary. 'It's not getting any easier.'

Gary leaned back against the wall beside Ryan, sighing heavily. 'I don't know what to say, mate. Except that it's still early days. And maybe you just need to...'

'Find someone else?'

Gary shrugged. 'It wouldn't hurt. Fuck to forget – you've tried it before. It's a good plan to fall back on.'

Ryan looked over at Amber again, their beautiful baby boy snuggling into her as Jim Allen's arm held them both close, and it was the worst pain Ryan had ever felt. 'Fuck to forget... that's all I was to her at times. A fuck, to forget *him*.'

Gary said nothing for a while. 'You coming out with the rest of us tonight? The boss has been good enough to let us have the night here in London, it'd be a shame to waste it. What do you say?'

Ryan stared down at the floor. What else did he have to do? While his ex-girlfriend and their son went back to that ridiculously huge house they now shared with a man Ryan would never understand, what else did *he* have to do?

'Count me in.' Maybe fucking to forget wasn't such a bad idea after all.

'Yeah. We're going out. Never one to say no to a night out in London. You know me.'

She looked at him through slightly narrowed eyes, not entirely convinced by his tone, or his conviction. 'Yeah. I know you. Anyway, come on, baby boy. It's time I got you home. It's way past your bedtime.' She carefully took Rico from Ryan.

'Does that apply to you, too?' Ryan asked, an almost petulant tone to his voice. He couldn't help it.

'Grow up, Ryan.'

'I need to see you alone, Amber.' He wasn't sure where that had come from, maybe he'd just been thinking aloud, but now the words were out, he knew he meant them.

'No. You don't.'

'You have the right to tell me what I want now, have you?'

'If you want to see Rico before you go back up north just give me a call, okay? As long as you're in a fit state.'

'What the hell's *that* supposed to mean? Amber?' But she was walking away before he had a chance to say anything else.

'You're not upsetting my wife, are you?'

Ryan swung around to see Jim Allen standing there. 'She's the mother of my child, Jim. Have you got that? The mother of *my* child.'

Jim let out a small laugh, looking briefly down at the ground before his eyes once more met Ryan's. 'But who gets to touch her, Ryan? Who gets to hold her, to put himself inside that incredible body of hers and hear her moan out loud? Who gets to do all that?'

'Fuck you!' Ryan hissed.

Jim laughed again, rubbing a hand across the back of his neck.

Ryan narrowed his eyes as he stared at his ex-boss. 'It *was* you, wasn't it? It was you who gave that story to the press.'

Jim said nothing, he just fixed Ryan with a look that told him everything he needed to know.

Ryan couldn't help laughing, too. A laugh of utter disbelief, that this man could still do this shit and yet he was the one Amber

Amber's eyes fell upon Ryan the second Jim left the room. He was standing at the back of the Players' Lounge, looking at the floor, one hand in his pocket, the other one clutching a bottle of lager.

'Shall we go see daddy?' Amber whispered into Rico's ear. He was awake now and gaining so much attention from anyone close to him with his gorgeous baby smile and his huge blue eyes. 'Let's go see daddy.'

Ryan looked up as they approached, a smile spreading across his face as he saw Rico's huge baby grin, his arms stretching towards him.

'Hey, kiddo. Come give your daddy a cuddle.'

Amber handed him over to Ryan, her heart melting as she watched Ryan's whole demeanour change the second he had his son in his arms. 'Thanks for looking after him while… while I was busy.'

Ryan looked at her. 'You were busy.' It wasn't a question. 'And it wasn't a chore to look after him, Amber. He's my son.'

Amber said nothing, her eyes staring down at the floor.

'Everything okay?'

'Why wouldn't it be?' she asked, her head shooting up.

Ryan shrugged. 'No reason. Just trying to make polite conversation.' Why the hell were things so strained between them now? He never wanted it to be like this. It was the last thing he'd want. 'You getting used to living down here, then?'

She ignored his question. She wasn't really in the mood for conversation. 'He's tired. It's been a long day for him. We should probably be getting him home.'

When she said 'we' Ryan knew she meant her and Jim, and it only served to make that pain flare up all over again.

'You off out tonight?' Amber asked, her voice jolting Ryan back to reality. 'Debbie says you're all staying over until tomorrow,

'Yeah. We're going out. Never one to say no to a night out in London. You know me.'

She looked at him through slightly narrowed eyes, not entirely convinced by his tone, or his conviction. 'Yeah. I know you. Anyway, come on, baby boy. It's time I got you home. It's way past your bedtime.' She carefully took Rico from Ryan.

'Does that apply to you, too?' Ryan asked, an almost petulant tone to his voice. He couldn't help it.

'Grow up, Ryan.'

'I need to see you alone, Amber.' He wasn't sure where that had come from, maybe he'd just been thinking aloud, but now the words were out, he knew he meant them.

'No. You don't.'

'You have the right to tell me what I want now, have you?'

'If you want to see Rico before you go back up north just give me a call, okay? As long as you're in a fit state.'

'What the hell's *that* supposed to mean? Amber?' But she was walking away before he had a chance to say anything else.

'You're not upsetting my wife, are you?'

Ryan swung around to see Jim Allen standing there. 'She's the mother of my child, Jim. Have you got that? The mother of *my* child.'

Jim let out a small laugh, looking briefly down at the ground before his eyes once more met Ryan's. 'But who gets to touch her, Ryan? Who gets to hold her, to put himself inside that incredible body of hers and hear her moan out loud? Who gets to do all that?'

'Fuck you!' Ryan hissed.

Jim laughed again, rubbing a hand across the back of his neck.

Ryan narrowed his eyes as he stared at his ex-boss. 'It *was* you, wasn't it? It was you who gave that story to the press.'

Jim said nothing, he just fixed Ryan with a look that told him everything he needed to know.

Ryan couldn't help laughing, too. A laugh of utter disbelief, that this man could still do this shit and yet he was the one Amber

Amber's eyes fell upon Ryan the second Jim left the room. He was standing at the back of the Players' Lounge, looking down at the floor, one hand in his pocket, the other one clutching a bottle of lager.

'Shall we go see daddy?' Amber whispered into Rico's ear. He was awake now and gaining so much attention from anyone close to him with his gorgeous baby smile and his huge blue eyes. 'Yeah. Let's go see daddy.'

Ryan looked up as they approached, a smile spreading across his face as he saw Rico's huge baby grin, his arms stretching out towards him.

'Hey, kiddo. Come give your daddy a cuddle.'

Amber handed him over to Ryan, her heart melting as she watched Ryan's whole demeanour change the second he had his son in his arms. 'Thanks for looking after him while... while I was busy.'

Ryan looked at her. 'You were busy.' It wasn't a question. 'And it wasn't a chore to look after him, Amber. He's my son.'

Amber said nothing, her eyes staring down at the floor.

'Everything okay?'

'Why wouldn't it be?' she asked, her head shooting up.

Ryan shrugged. 'No reason. Just trying to make polite conversation.' Why the hell were things so strained between them now? He'd never wanted it to be like this. It was the last thing he'd wanted. 'You getting used to living down here, then?'

She ignored his question. She wasn't really in the mood for a conversation. 'He's tired. It's been a long day for him. We should probably be getting him home.'

When she said 'we' Ryan knew she meant her and Jim, and that only served to make that pain flare up all over again.

'You off out tonight?' Amber asked, her voice jolting Ryan back to reality. 'Debbie says you're all staying over until tomorrow, so...'

wanted to be with.

'Does Amber know that you were the one…?'

'She knows.'

Ryan said nothing for a beat or two. 'Do you hate me so much that you really want to bring me down in that way? Am I that much of a threat?'

Jim fixed him with another look, his eyes boring deep into Ryan's. 'I can deal with threats, Ryan. I can eradicate them, just like that…' He clicked his fingers, and Ryan couldn't help but feel something akin to a cold punch to the stomach. 'If I want to.' And then he just walked away.

Yeah. Tonight Ryan Fisher was going out. And he wasn't coming home until he was well and truly wasted.

*

Jim opened the door and immediately he felt his breath catch in his throat. She was sitting on the edge of the bed, wearing only a short nightdress, her legs crossed as she filed her nails.

'I'm assuming Rico's asleep,' he said, his heart already starting to beat faster as anticipation built.

'You assume correctly.' She didn't look up, she simply continued filing her nails.

He threw his jacket over the back of the couch, rolling his shirtsleeves up to his elbows as he started to walk over to her, but this time she did look up, her eyes meeting his, sending him so many silent messages it was ridiculous.

'You stay exactly where you are, Mr. Allen.'

He watched as she slowly opened her legs so wide, he couldn't help but let out the loudest groan.

'Exactly where you are,' she repeated, sliding a hand down between her legs, running her fingers lightly over herself. 'You only get to watch, remember?'

He swallowed hard, digging his hands into his pockets as he felt his erection spring to life. So quick. Seconds was all it had taken. Shit! Who was he kidding? His hard-on had started while he was driving home and just thinking about this. Thinking about her.

Amber closed her eyes for a second, throwing her head back slightly, her fingers moving back and forth. She could feel that tingling sensation already starting to sweep its way over her body, so she slowed down, opening her eyes as she looked at Jim. It was the most erotic experience, touching herself while he stood there and watched, and she knew it wasn't going to take long before that inevitable climax hit her. But she wasn't ready, not yet. So she pulled her hand away, burying her fingers in her hair as she watched him watch her. His eyes were looking down, of course; she was putting on a show and he had the front row seat.

'Did you speak to Ryan? After the match?'

'Amber, baby…' He lifted his eyes briefly, looking right at her.

She stared back, slowly slipping her hand back down between her legs. 'Did you?'

What the fuck was she doing to him? Talking about Ryan while giving him a hard-on that was killing him. What the hell was she doing? 'Yes, I talked to him.'

She didn't take her eyes off him; her fingers continuing to work against a wetness that was turning her on so badly she could hardly get the words out. 'I hope you were nice to him.'

'Jesus Christ, Amber… do we have to talk about Ryan while you're doing that?'

'Were you nice to him, Jim? Because I wasn't.'

'I can't do this any more,' he said, walking over to the bed, but Amber quickly pulled her hand away, closing her legs.

'I said you could only watch, remember?'

'Are you freakin' serious? Do you know how fucking painful this hard-on is?'

She smiled, shaking her head. 'I don't care. You don't get to touch.'

'Shit!' He backed up against the wall, pushing a hand through his hair, watching as she slowly opened her legs again, even wider this time, and he felt as though he was about to explode, such was the pressure building up inside him. Much more of this and he was going to come right here, right now, without even getting anywhere near her. 'Baby, you have got to let me…'

She shook her head again, and he couldn't help but let out another loud groan as she slipped her fingers inside herself. This was crazy. She was killing him here!

He felt his heart beating wildly now, making him even more breathless as her fingers pushed further inside herself, eliciting tiny moans from her, her head thrown back once more as her other hand picked up a slightly faster rhythm. He wanted to touch her so badly; he wanted to taste her, to dive into that wet heaven and take all of her. It was an ache so painful he could barely deal with it, and watching her like this, watching her touch herself, bring herself to a climax *he* wanted to be a part of – he'd had enough of watching now.

While she had her eyes closed, lost in her own pleasure, he moved towards her with his gaze still fixed firmly on that heaven he was about to visit.

'Oh, no. Get back where you were,' Amber said, her eyes springing open.

'I'm coming over, Amber.'

'You're coming over, are you?'

'Yeah,' he laughed, pushing a hand through his hair. 'I'm coming over.'

'You're not doing as you're told, Mr. Allen.' Her hand was still between her legs and his eyes were still watching her.

'Well, I'm a bit like that, honey. I don't take orders too well.'

A slow smile spread across her face as he crouched down between her legs, his hands on her knees. 'Oh, you want a closer look.'

'You gonna let me touch you yet?' His heart was beating so quickly now, he almost felt faint.

She shook her head. 'No. Not yet.'

He pushed her knees a little further apart, watching as her fingers continued to work against herself, slowly and carefully, but it was too much now. It was too painful, too hard to control. She was driving him crazy and he needed to join in. Observation time was over. 'Amber…'

She shook her head again. 'I'm almost there, Jim. You see? I can do all this shit without you.'

'Okay, that's enough.'

She couldn't help letting out the loudest laugh as he pushed her back onto the bed, replacing her hand with his own, and the relief he felt as he finally touched her was indescribable. It was as if someone had turned a valve somewhere deep inside him and now all that pent-up pressure was slowly being released.

And she wasn't exactly objecting. Those incredible legs of hers had wrapped themselves around him as though it were the most natural thing in the world; her mouth was on his, their kisses urgent and deep, her body telling him how much she needed him. And she was warm and she was wet – Jesus, she was so, so wet he almost slipped straight out of her, and it took her hand guiding him inside for him to make it in there. But once he'd sunk into her, it was as though a blanket of calm had been thrown over him. A feeling so beautiful he could never explain it. He couldn't. He just knew it wasn't something he was willing to give up without a fight.

His fingers intertwined with hers as he pushed deeper, his heart beating so fast it was knocking every ounce of breath right out of him, and he literally had to fight to catch that breath, every gasp painful and raw. But when that climax hit, it hit hard, rushing over him like nothing he'd ever felt before, causing him to cry out so loudly, grip her fingers so tightly and push down into her so deeply it felt as though he was falling right into her.

Her hips bucked and her fingers clung onto him, her head thrown back as she hit her own climax. Every shudder, every convulsion her body made beneath him, he took it all, felt it all, until there was nothing more to give. Nothing more to take. Just this beautiful silence filling the air, punctuated only by their ragged breathing and short, sharp gasps of breath.

'That wasn't watching,' she whispered, her fingers still clinging onto his. 'That definitely wasn't just watching.'

He looked at her, unable to keep the smile off his face. 'Call me weak, but, Jesus, baby, the second you slid those fingers inside yourself I was gone.'

She reached up and touched his cheek, kissing him quickly. 'You just have no willpower, Mr. Allen.'

'Guilty as charged.' He rolled over onto his back, watching as she got up off the bed, watching as that incredible body of hers headed into the bathroom. It gave him a second to get his head together, to try and work out just what the hell was going on here. Because it was so crazy and confusing even *he* couldn't really work it out.

'You okay?'

He opened his eyes and looked at her, sitting cross-legged on the bed wearing nothing but one of his shirts. His beautiful girl. His life. His whole, entire, fucking world. 'I messed up, Amber.'

She cocked her head, frowning slightly.

He sat up, taking her hand as he looked right into her eyes. 'Doing what I did to Ryan… I messed up.'

She stroked his knuckles with her thumb, breaking the stare to watch their every movement. 'It's done now. He'll take his punishment and he'll get over it.' How cold and callous did she sound? This was Rico's dad she was talking about; a man who hadn't deserved anything Jim had done to him. He hadn't deserved to have a past he'd so obviously tried hard to put behind him dredged up all over again. And he didn't deserve the punishment he'd had to take because of her husband's actions. He didn't deserve to be treated the way she was treating him now. But if all that had to happen in order for her to be with this man here, then her conscience would just have to learn to live with that.

'But you blame me, don't you? And that trust I so wanted you to have in me, I've blown it, haven't I?'

Her eyes met his, her fingers clinging onto him. 'I love you, Jim.'

'But you still can't trust me?' He noticed her eyes drop again, once more breaking that stare. 'Amber, baby, look at me. Look at me, honey, please'

She slowly raised her eyes to meet his, letting him pull her astride him because she was weak. She knew this was only going to lead to more sex, and sex was what she wanted right now. Sex was a diversion. A chance to not have to think about anything. 'You're just gonna have to work harder to build that trust back up, aren't you?' she whispered, shrugging the shirt she was wearing back off her shoulders.

'I can work hard,' he murmured. 'I can work *very* hard.'

And that was exactly what he intended to do.

Chapter Twenty-Four

Amber flung open the front door, leaning against the doorpost and folding her arms.

'Morning, sexy.' He grinned at her, that same cocky grin he'd tried to reel her in with just a couple of years ago.

'I thought you'd gone back to Newcastle yesterday.'

'Got the F.A. hearing this afternoon. Not going back 'til this evening. You on your own?'

'If you mean is Jim here, no, he isn't. He's already at the training ground.'

'Can I come in? Or do you want to kick-start the gossip by making me stand out here on the doorstep? One hell of a doorstep, though, I have to admit. How frigging big is this house?'

She pulled him inside by his arm, closing the door behind him. 'Have you come to see Rico before you go?'

'I've come to see *you*, Amber.'

She frowned, heading off into the kitchen. 'Why? You only saw me yesterday.'

'You know Jim was the one who made sure my involvement with that betting ring was made public. You know it was him.'

She stood still, placing her hands on the countertop in front of her, but she didn't turn around to face him. Closing her eyes she swallowed hard, breathing in deep. But she couldn't say anything.

This wasn't going to go away. No matter how hard she tried to pretend it had never happened, it wasn't going to go away. And that was partly because she herself wasn't letting it.

'Amber…'

She swung around to face him, folding her arms across her chest. 'I'm so sorry, Ryan. Really, I am…'

'Is that all you can say? You're *sorry*? Jesus…'

'It wasn't *me* who put it out there, Ryan.'

'But you're defending the bastard who did.'

'That's my husband you're talking about, okay? And you don't get to…'

'What? Out him for what he really is? Are you so fucking blinkered, Amber, that you can't see what he's doing? What he's *still* doing?'

'You really need to go if that's all you've come here to say because you'll upset Rico, do you hear me? We are not getting into this here.'

He moved closer to her, his hands in his pockets, his dark-blue eyes determined as he stared into hers. 'He stood there and he told me himself what he'd done. And believe me, there wasn't one ounce of fucking remorse coming from his direction. He's one cold-hearted bastard and you need to know that.'

'Get out of my house.'

'Is all the great sex blinding you, Amber? Are all those fantastic fucks really worth it?'

'I'm warning you, Ryan…'

'You gonna spout all that crap about how he's changed, huh? Really?'

'I don't need this…'

'And I don't need your fucking husband trying to damage me any more than he already has. I've lost the captaincy at Newcastle Red Star, been overlooked for the international matches at Wembley, been fined so much frigging money even my accountant had to do a double-take, and now it's rumoured the F.A. could be banning me from playing until the end of the season and *you* don't need this?'

'I don't know what you want me to say, Ryan.' And she didn't. What *could* she say? She couldn't make it any better, could she? She couldn't turn back the clock or pretend none of it had happened.

He looked at her, straight into those beautiful pale-blue eyes of hers. 'I want you to tell me you aren't happy, Amber. I want you to tell me you've finally seen through him. I want you to tell me you still love me.'

She shook her head, blinking back stupid tears she really didn't want to cry. 'I can't do that,' she whispered. 'I can't. Because it wouldn't be true.'

Ryan took a couple of steps back, breaking the stare, turning away from her briefly. 'This is so fucking hard…'

'I don't know why he told you, Ryan.'

Ryan swung back around to face her, his expression colder. Tougher. 'He told me because he lives to kick me in the fucking teeth, that's why. You think there was an apology included when he broke the news? Huh?'

'He's changed, Ryan, and I'm…'

'Do you know how fucking deluded you sound, sweetheart? Standing there and telling me that. Because he hasn't changed. He'll never change. Oh, I'm not saying that he doesn't love you, because I'm sure he does. I'm sure he loves you so frigging much but he's insecure, don't you see that? A man who felt confident in his relationship, would he really be trying so fucking hard to make sure another man kept well away? A man he still considers to be one hell of a threat, no matter what he might be telling you. And I can understand his actions, in some weird and warped way. I can. Because I'd probably do the same, in some respects. If you were mine, Amber, I'd fight tooth and nail to make sure I didn't lose you again. But I would never, *ever* try to bring someone down the way he's trying to destroy me.'

'Trying?'

Ryan gave a small, derisive laugh. 'You think this is over?'

She looked at him, hugging herself tighter, trying to get her head around everything Ryan was telling her.

'It's not over, Amber. The game is still on, sweetheart. And there's only gonna be one winner.'

*

'Can I have a word?'

Jim looked up, unable to stop the surprise from registering on his face. 'Ronnie… yes, yes, of course. Come in.' He stood up, walking around the front of his desk and leaning back against it.

Ronnie closed the office door behind him, coming just a couple of steps further into the room. 'I know what you did, giving that story about Ryan to the press.'

Jim just looked at him, his expression stoic.

'You're going to hurt her, Jim. And I'm not gonna stand by and watch that happen. Not any more.'

'Nobody's making you stand by and watch anything, Ronnie. And – not that it's any of your business, but, I am not going to hurt Amber. I can promise you that.'

The cynical laugh escaped before Ronnie had a chance to stop it. 'Yeah, okay. Look, you might have sucked her in with all your charm and a heap of crap about how you've changed, but she's weak, Jim. Where you're concerned she's the weakest person I fucking know, so she'll probably never see through you. But I do. I can see right through you and you'll hurt her.'

It was Jim's turn to laugh, bowing his head and folding his arms. 'You all think you know how my relationship with Amber works…'

'She's fucking obsessed, Jim. That's how it works. You walked back into her life and you took the girl we all know away, and in her place you left this weak woman who is obsessed with you. You should have stayed away from her. She told you to do that; she told you to stay away and yet you ignored her. That's how much

288

you care about her.'

'I love her, you got that?' Jim's expression was hard, angry, even, as he walked over to Ronnie. How dare people assume they knew all there was to know about his and Amber's relationship? They knew nothing.

'You don't love her. You just want to control her. And all it takes is for you to throw her up against a wall and fuck her senseless for all of five minutes and you've got her right where you want her.'

That was it. He'd lit a touchpaper and Jim was having no more of this crap. He'd had enough. Pulling his arm back he threw a punch at Ronnie so quickly the other man hadn't stood a chance. Ronnie was knocked sideways as Jim's punch sent him reeling back against the wall, his body ricocheting so hard, it sent a wave of pain flooding through him.

'Jesus Christ…' Ronnie gasped, clutching his jaw.

'You know *nothing* about me and Amber. Nothing.' Jim hissed, his eyes boring deep into Ronnie's. 'And you don't ever talk about her in that way again, okay? You don't cheapen her name or assume that's the way she acts. You don't fucking do that.'

Ronnie shook his head, his hand still clutching his now-throbbing jaw. 'She needs to be rid of you.'

'She needs to be loved.'

'By you?'

'Get out of my office.'

'She needs you out of her life.'

'Are you jealous, Ronnie? Oh, you want to go back there, is that it? You want to fuck your best friend again? Is that what all this is about?'

'You're fucking unreal. I care about that girl; *that's* what this is about.'

'And so do I. *I* care about her, more than you or anyone else will ever know.'

'They're just words, Jim. They're just empty fucking words…'

'Get out of my office. Before you say something you'll really regret.'

Ronnie reached out to grab the door handle, his eyes never leaving Jim's. 'She deserves better than you.'

Jim said nothing. He just watched as Ronnie slammed the door closed behind him, his stomach dropping so low he felt sick. Amber deserved better than him – and Ronnie was right. She hadn't deserved any of what he'd done to her previously. But she knew why he'd acted that way now; he'd explained it all to her. But had he left everything too late?

Sitting down on the edge of his desk he reached for his phone, quickly scrolling down his contact list until he found the number he was looking for. 'It's Jim Allen… Yeah, I need to speak to him now.' He didn't want to fight any more. He was tired of fighting. But if that was what he had to do to keep Amber in his life, then he was going to have to play this game the only way he knew how.

*

'Ronnie?' Amber frowned as she looked at him, the angry red mark on his jaw evident. 'What are you doing here? What the hell's happened?'

'Why don't you ask your husband, Amber?'

'No, hang on… Ronnie? Jesus!' She almost ran the last few yards to Jim's office. He was sitting on the couch, his head in his hands. 'Jim?'

He slowly looked up, pushing both hands through his hair.

'What was Ronnie doing here?'

Jim sighed, clasping his hands together. 'Coming back down here was never really gonna solve anything, was it?'

'What was Ronnie doing here, Jim?'

'Too many people think they know so much about us, Amber.'

'Did you hit him?'

He looked at her, right into her eyes. 'They don't know the truth. They have absolutely no idea how much I love you.'

'Jim, for Christ's sake, will you just answer a fucking question? What was Ronnie doing here?'

Jim stood up, walking slowly over to her. 'He wants me out of your life, Amber. That's why he was here. To warn me, almost.'

'*Warn* you?' Amber felt as though she was having one of those days where everything was just way too surreal for her to get her head around. First Ryan turning up spouting his speech about how Jim was no good for her and now this. 'Was there some kind of fight?'

'No. Baby, there was no fight. But he said things… he said things. And I lost my temper; I hit out.'

'Jesus, Jim…' Amber turned away, pushing a hand through her hair. 'And that's gonna solve everything, is it?' She swung back around to face him. 'You, lashing out just because someone says something you don't like; *that's* gonna solve all this crap?'

'I love you, Amber.'

'I know you do, but do you know what? I'm beginning to wonder if that's really enough.'

Jim's eyes narrowed as he stared at her. 'What do you mean? Amber…'

'I am crazy about you, and you know that. You've always known that, which is why you knew… you *knew* when you walked back into my life the way you did, that I'd fall. Eventually. You knew that. Same as you know how hard this is for me to stand here and tell you that I'm walking away.'

'Amber, baby…'

'Not forever, Jim. Listen to me, okay? Listen to me. I need to get out of here, away from this… I need some space…'

'No.' He shook his head, reaching out for her hand but she pulled it away. 'Don't do this, Amber. Please.'

'You know, it's strange, but… but I don't regret being with you. I don't regret marrying you or letting you back into my life because if I hadn't… if I hadn't let you back into my life I would have spent the rest of it wondering what would have happened if I had. And now I know, don't I? Exactly what I *knew* would happen.'

'It doesn't have to be this way, baby.'

This time she allowed him to pull her into his arms; she allowed him to hold her, allowed his mouth to close in on hers until she was once more lost in his kiss. And that was a place she wanted to be lost in forever.

'We need that space, Jim.'

'And I think you're wrong. Jesus, you're letting them win.'

'I need to take a step back, that's all. Because… because maybe we rushed into all this. Maybe we should have thought harder before we…'

'You are my whole fucking world, Amber, do you know that? You walk away from me and that world just disintegrates, it's pointless. What I did to you, asking for that divorce, it was the worst mistake of my life, and I regret it every day because I never stopped loving you. Not for one second…'

'Don't use emotional blackmail, Jim, please. Don't do that. I'm going to go back up north for a couple of weeks, that's all. I'm just going to go back home, take some time out, be with my baby… I love you, okay?' She ran her fingertips lightly over his jawline, running them over his slightly open mouth before kissing him slowly, letting the taste of him linger on her lips for as long as she could. 'I love you, so much, but all of this… all these people…'

'You're letting them win.'

She shook her head, her fingers gripping his tighter. 'You know, I don't care, Jim. I'm not thinking about Ryan or Ronnie or anyone else. I'm thinking about *me*. And I know that I need to take a step back, I know that. If you want this to work, baby, then please, please accept that.'

'You want me to just let you go?'

'You're not letting me go, Jim. I'm not going forever, I've told you that. Think of it… think of it as a working holiday.'

He frowned.

'I'm going back to my roots,' Amber said, letting go of him, folding her arms across her chest as she walked over to his desk, leaning back against it. 'I'm going to do a little bit of work for News North East while I'm up in Newcastle. I had a meeting with my bosses at Cloud Sports, told them I needed to go back up north for a couple of weeks, and, along with Kevin, we've worked something out that benefits both of them, and me. If Cloud Sports can get a programme or two out of this then they're not complaining.'

'Oh, well that's okay, then, isn't it? As long as your fucking bosses are alright with it all, then who the hell am I to object? It's just my freakin' marriage that's in trouble.'

She looked at him, taking a deep breath, clutching her arms tighter around herself. 'Our marriage isn't in trouble, Jim.'

'Isn't it? Then why the hell are you walking away from me, huh?'

'To save it.'

He couldn't help the laugh that escaped. 'Do you *want* to save it? Honestly?'

She held his gaze. 'Honestly? I want to save this marriage more than I've ever wanted anything in my life. Because when I told you I wouldn't be able to cope without you, when I told you I wasn't strong enough to do that I meant it. I'm terrified of leaving you behind, Jim. I'm scared of waking up in the morning and you not being there. But I need to do this. I need to be stronger.'

'*He's* up there, Amber. Ryan. He's up there, where you're gonna be.'

'I don't love him, Jim. Do you understand that? I don't love him. I love *you*.'

'And that's why you're walking away from me?'

She still couldn't break the stare. 'That's why I'm walking away.'

'You're breaking my heart here, baby.'

She walked over to him, cupping his cheek in the palm of her hand as she kissed him, long and deep, falling against him as his arm slipped around her waist.

'I can't let you go, Amber. It's too risky, and I…'

She put her fingers to his lips, shaking her head. 'I'll be gone by the time you get home. Okay?'

'Jesus, Amber, please…'

She closed her eyes and let her mouth rest against his one more time, let his arms hold her tightly and felt her heart beat faster as their bodies touched.

'Is this my fault?' he whispered, pushing her hair back off her face, his other hand firmly in the small of her back. 'Is this because of what I did to Ryan?'

'I'm not gonna lie and say it doesn't have something to do with it, because it has *everything* to do with it. I tried to pretend it didn't matter, but it does matter. What you did was wrong. He didn't deserve it, and I'm not saying that because he means anything to me, but he's Rico's dad, and I *have* to care about him, for our son's sake. Does that make sense? You're a father yourself, Jim, so you must understand…'

'He'll make a move, Amber. With you up there and me down here – he'll try.'

'He can try all he likes. But the only relationship Ryan Fisher and I have now is as parents to our baby. That's all.'

'But that's one hell of a fucking bond there and I don't know if I…'

She put her fingers to his lips again, silencing him. 'This is a short and temporary break, Jim. That's all. We aren't separating, we aren't making anything official, and I will be doing my utmost to make sure the media get that. Things have just got all crazy and out of hand and they need to calm down. Everybody needs to calm down. Then maybe we can all get back to normal.'

'And you think you walking away is going to sort all that out?'

She shrugged. 'I don't know. And I don't really care. Like I said, I'm not doing this for anybody – except us. I'm doing this for us because I don't want to lose you, Jim. I don't.'

'I'm finding that so hard to believe, Amber. Baby, I don't know if I can do this.'

'You can. Darling, you can. Remember the Amber Sullivan you

fell in love with? And I'm not talking about that sixteen-year-old kid with an infatuation. I'm talking about the strong-willed, feisty woman you came face to face with a couple of years ago. Remember her?'

He nodded, his fingers gripping her hand so tightly it was beginning to hurt.

'I need her back, Jim. I need to find her again, because she's lost somewhere amongst all these confusing feelings and people trying to tell me what they think is best for me. I lost her. And I need her back.'

'But that Amber didn't love me,' Jim whispered.

'Oh, she did. Believe me, she did.'

He threw his head back, letting out a heavy sigh. 'This is fucking crazy.'

She tried to let go of him, but he pulled her back, his arm circling her waist again, pushing her against him. 'I'm not saying goodbye, you got that? Because you're gonna be back here, before I even know you're gone. You're gonna be back here, in my bed, and I'm gonna be making love to you as though you've never been away. Okay?'

She smiled, reaching up to touch his cheek, rubbing it gently with her thumb. 'Okay.'

'I love you, Amber. And don't ever doubt that. I love you.'

'I love you, too.'

And with every beat of her heart she hoped that love was strong enough. She hoped.

*

'I will *never* be able to keep up with you, kiddo. When the hell did all *this* happen?'

'I don't know, Max.' She zipped up her case and hauled it off the bed, opening another drawer and picking up a pile of stuff that she threw straight into another case. 'I really don't know.'

Max leaned against the doorpost, folding his arms. 'What's happened?'

'Nothing's happened.'

'Yeah, well, call me suspicious, Amber, but you're here throwing clothes into suitcases while telling me you're moving back up to Newcastle for a fortnight. Ryan's in a mood that has nothing to do with the punishment the F.A. has just given him this afternoon, because he got off rather lightly on that score. And Ronnie White is walking around the Cloud Sports complex with a bruise on his chin and a cut lip that he didn't get from bumping into a door in the canteen. Not to mention the fact you're going back to work for News North East...'

'I'm not going back to work for them, Max.'

'What *are* you doing, then? Because, despite the fact I'm your agent – something you appear to forget about on a frequent basis – the first I heard of any of this was the second I walked through your front door twenty minutes ago.'

'I'm doing a programme for Cloud Sports on the state of football in the north-east, that's what I'm doing. And Kevin has kindly allowed me to work from the News North East offices while I'm up in Newcastle. And while I'm there I *might* do one or two pieces for them. For old time's sake. We'll have to see how things go.'

'Thanks for filling me in. A spur-of-the-moment thing, was it?'

She looked at him. 'What do you want me to say?'

He arched an eyebrow, his arms still folded across his chest.

She sat down on the edge of the bed, her shoulders sagging. 'Ever since I had my suspicions about Jim being the one to expose Ryan and his involvement with that betting ring – it's been hard to deal with, Max. And I tried, I did. I tried to believe that what Jim did was a mistake, that he hadn't really meant to hurt Ryan. But I was kidding myself. His only intention in life seems to be to want to hurt Ryan, and I need to step back from it all for a while. I need to lose myself in something that doesn't involve me having to think about all of this for a few days. Even though, in reality, it's all I'm going to think about. But at least I can do it alone, without any of them on my case, trying to fill my head with their own thoughts, their own reasoning…'

'Any of them? Who are we talking about, exactly?'

'You know who, Max. Ryan, Ronnie, Jim… all of them. It's too much, having them all coming at me – having them all going for each other.'

Max sighed, looking down at the floor for a beat or two. 'And Ronnie was involved in a set-to with, who?'

'Jim.'

'Jesus, Amber. You've got enough going on in that complicated life of yours to keep the tabloids going for a year. So, you having second thoughts about being Mrs. Jim Allen?'

She shook her head, standing back up. 'No. Never. I love that man like crazy, I just need some time out, that's all. Because I don't think I've really taken any of that for a long time, Max.' She stopped what she was doing and looked at her agent. 'What *did* happen at Ryan's hearing?'

'He got a three-match ban.'

'Is that all?'

Max shrugged. 'What can I say? We had some very persuasive people on our side.'

'Has he gone back to Newcastle already?'

'Left on the 14.25 flight out of Gatwick. He should be home right about now. And what time are *you* heading for home?'

'I haven't actually booked any flights yet. I thought me and Rico could just head off to the airport, see what flights are available, and if there's nothing today we can spend the night in a hotel. It's not a problem.'

'I'm going back up for a few days. You can come with me. I'll get my assistant to book the seats. I take it Fisher junior just sits with his mum, am I right?'

She nodded. 'Max, are you really going up north for a few days?'

He reached into his pocket for his electronic cigarette. 'I am now.'

Chapter Twenty-Five

'This is freakily like old times,' Kevin said, placing a mug of tea down in front of Amber.

'Except you never made me one cup of tea in all the time I worked at News North East.' Amber smiled, leaning back in her chair, sticking the end of her pen in her mouth.

Kevin perched himself on the edge of her desk. 'Yeah, well, it's like having royalty in the office, having you back. I mean, you're a bit of a celebrity now, aren't you? The face of Cloud Sports football, wife of one of the country's – probably one of the world's – most successful football managers, glamour model…'

She kicked him gently in the shin.

'That hurt!'

'Good. Look, I got my tits out once for *one* photo shoot, can we just forget that now?'

He looked at her, his expression changing slightly. 'You still *are* the wife of one of the country's most successful football managers, aren't you?'

'I explained all of this down in London, Kevin,' Amber sighed, sitting up and logging into her email. 'Yes, I'm still Jim's wife and that's a role I intend to keep. This is nothing but a short break that I really, really need. And you really, really don't want to know the complicated ins and outs of my life right now.'

'Anything to do with Ryan Fisher?'

'It's always to do with Ryan Fisher.'

'Okay,' Kevin said, sliding down from her desk. 'I'll leave you to it. But if there's anything you need…'

She turned and smiled at him. She was so happy to be back in this office – even if it was only a temporary thing. It just felt so – so safe, being back where she'd always felt she'd belonged. A place that reminded her of a time when everything had been so simple, uncomplicated; a time when she'd been alone. 'Thanks, Kevin.'

She turned to look out of the window in front of her, resting her chin in her hand as she stared outside at the view of the city centre just a short way out in the distance. She could see the Tyne Bridge from this window, too; a sight that always made her feel like she was home. And she could just about see Tynebridge Stadium if she squinted slightly. Home of Newcastle Red Star. Ryan's club.

That was enough to make her turn back to her emails, sighing heavily as she saw how many she had to catch up with. Most of them were from the Cloud Sports offices, but there was also one from Ronnie and a handful from Jim. Maybe she should have checked them all earlier on her phone but she just hadn't been in the mood. She'd just wanted to get settled into the house she'd rented for the fortnight, not far from the News North East offices. Rico was spending his days with her Aunty Kim over in Hebburn but she knew, at some point, whether she felt like it or not, she was going to have to face Ryan. He'd want to see Rico, too.

Her phone ringing made her jump slightly. She'd started to lose herself in the kind of thoughts she'd come back home to avoid, and she gave herself a little inner shake before she answered the call. 'Amber Sullivan.' She wasn't using Jim's name on a professional level. Not like the last time. Call her superstitious, but she'd just wanted to keep the name Sullivan this time around. Officially she might be Mrs. Allen, but professionally she was still Amber Sullivan.

'Hey, beautiful.'

Her stomach flipped the second she heard his voice. 'Jim, I… is everything okay?'

He laughed and she felt her heart start to beat faster. 'Everything's fine, baby. I just wanted to hear your voice.'

This really wasn't fair. If he kept calling her, she wasn't even going to get the chance to miss him because all he was doing was clouding her thoughts and making her think everything was all still okay. When it wasn't. Not really.

'I'm kind of busy, Jim.' That was a lie. She wasn't all *that* busy. Not today, anyway.

'Amber, honey, this is killing me, you being up there and me being down here. This wasn't how I envisaged our marriage to be.'

And she hadn't envisaged him trying to play games with people she still cared about, but it had happened. And she was trying to deal with it as best she could, even though she still couldn't quite work out whether what she was doing was actually going to make a difference or not. She just knew that she had to try. And this wasn't helping.

'I know it's hard, Jim. It's hard for me, too, it really is. But…'

'I miss you.'

She closed her eyes for a second. He was doing it again. Even from hundreds of miles away he was reeling her in and filling her mind with nothing but thoughts of him and the things he could do to her that sent her crazy. And she wanted him. She wanted him so much.

'I miss you, too.'

'I should go, huh?'

'I love you, Jim. You know that, don't you?'

'I know, baby. I know.'

She ended the call before she started saying things that were only going to render this whole trip back to Newcastle pointless.

'Everything okay?' Kevin asked, walking past her desk.

'Everything's fine.' She looked at her watch. 'But I think I'm gonna take a break now. Clear my head.' She stood up, grabbing her coat from the back of her chair.

'Amber?'

She looked up at her old boss. 'Yeah?'

'It really is good to see you.'

She smiled. 'It's good to see you, too.' And right now, that was the only thing she was one hundred per cent sure of.

*

Jim sat back in his chair, staring up at the ceiling as though it was about to give him all the answers. But nothing could, not really. He still didn't understand why Amber had felt the need to run back to Newcastle. But the thought that it was because of him terrified him. The thought that she'd run back home because that was where Ryan was terrified him even more.

Leaning forward, he opened his emails, none of which he could be bothered to read. Except one. From Max.

A smile spread across his face as he read it. A feeling of hope swept over him as he shut down his laptop. When it came down to it, Jim had always known this was a game he was never going to lose. It now felt as though, this morning, that certainty had just gotten a little bit closer.

*

It had been the perfect afternoon, just wandering along the streets of her home town. She'd only been away for a matter of weeks but it felt as though she hadn't seen the place for so long. Too long. She'd spent an hour or so looking around Eldon Square, popping into some of her favourite shops, before heading down to the Quayside and a little independent coffee shop she always liked to visit when she was down by the river.

It had been nice, having some time to herself. She'd wished she'd had Rico with her, of course, but it really had been good to just sit and drink coffee and look out at the view of the North Bank, watching the world go by as the backdrop of the Tyne Bridge reminded her she was home. The sun had been shining and all around her people had been enjoying a mild spring day, and she'd wished – just for a brief second – that the past couple of years had been different. She'd never change the fact that Rico was in her life, and she'd never change the fact that her career had taken an upward turn she could never have predicted. But maybe there were other things she could have handled better. Things that, maybe, she would have changed. If she could.

Switching on the TV she turned up the volume. Rico was upstairs asleep and she needed something to take away the silence. She missed Jim with a pain that she really couldn't describe, and even though having time to herself was what she still felt she needed, it didn't mean it was easy. None of this was easy. She was still confused and angry and tired of everything being so complicated, but she missed him. She just wished she could forget what he'd done. She wished she could forget how much he'd hurt Ryan.

A knock at the door almost made her jump. She wasn't expecting anyone. Her dad's team had a home game that night so he was at work. Maybe her Aunty Kim had forgotten something when she'd dropped Rico off earlier. Pulling the robe she was wearing tighter around herself, she walked out into the hall. She hoped it wasn't anything that was going to keep her from that glass of wine and good film she was looking forward to watching now she'd had that much-needed long, hot bath, which had really relaxed her. As much as anything *could* relax her at the minute.

'You honestly think I'm gonna stay down there when my crazily beautiful wife is miles away?'

She felt her heart almost stop in her chest. It had only been a few days ago that she'd last seen him, but it felt like this was the first time she'd laid eyes on him in years. Which in itself was mad.

'You shouldn't be here,' she said, trying to pull herself together. But she was failing.

'Baby, I flew up here as soon as I could get away, and I'm booked on a flight back to London in three hours' time so believe me when I tell you I am desperate. To see you, to be with you… are you gonna let me in?'

She stood aside to let him through, closing the door behind him. 'You flew up here, just for a few hours?'

'That's how much I'm missing you, Amber.'

She looked at him, taking in every inch of this man she was still so much in love with it hurt. He looked tired, but oh so handsome. So heartbreakingly handsome with those dark-green eyes and hair that was slightly longer than he used to wear it, but it only made him look sexier. Her beautiful American man. Oh, Jesus, what was he doing here?

'Is Rico…?'

'He's asleep,' she whispered, her eyes locking onto his as he stood there, his hands in his pockets. 'But you really shouldn't be here. This isn't what we agreed…'

'*We* didn't agree anything, baby. This is all you. I didn't want any of it. And, yes, I may have caused it, I realise that, but I still think we could have sorted all of this out without you running away.'

'I wasn't running away, Jim.'

He moved closer, reaching out to touch her cheek with the back of his hand. 'Yeah. You were. You are.'

She closed her eyes as his mouth touched hers, ever so lightly, but enough to kick-start a chain reaction she knew she wouldn't be able to stop. She was too weak and it was always going to be that way when he was with her. Which is why he shouldn't be here, but now that he was…

'You couldn't just leave me alone, could you?' she breathed, pushing his jacket back off his shoulders until it fell to the floor. 'That's all I asked of you. To leave me alone. Just for a few days.'

'You don't want me to leave you alone,' he said, his voice barely audible, his mouth almost touching hers.

'You know that, do you?'

'I know that.'

'You shouldn't be here.'

'So…' He untied her robe, pulling it open. She was wearing nothing but tiny white knickers and his eyes instantly fell upon her breasts. 'You don't want me to do – this?'

His eyes stared into hers as his fingers stroked her breasts, running over them so lightly, it was all she could do to stop a moan from escaping. Telling him to stay away was never going to work. Was she just being incredibly naïve, again?

'I flew up here because I want to be inside you so badly, I can't even fucking sleep.'

'Oh, Jesus…' she groaned as he gently nudged her knickers down, his hand resting on her hip.

'You're gonna have to work so much harder to get rid of me, baby, because I ain't going anywhere.'

She buried her fingers in his hair as he lowered his head, his mouth covering her breast, so warm against her naked skin and she was way past the point of no return now. She had her handsome husband back with her for a couple of hours, and she was going to make sure she took whatever it was he was going to give her. Even if this wasn't the way she'd planned for things to go.

She kept her fingers in his hair as he sank to his haunches, sliding her knickers right down and she stepped out of them, kicking them away, gasping out loud as his hands ran back up her legs, causing her to open them slightly. And as his mouth touched her down there, just the tiniest of touches brushing over her skin, his tongue sending a thousand and one miniscule electric shocks shooting through her body, she couldn't help but cry out. Just one tiny touch and he'd won. He was always going to win.

'Not here,' she whispered, stroking his cheek with her fingertips as his eyes met hers. 'If I've only got you for a couple of hours I want us to make the most of them.' She slipped her hand into his, leading him upstairs, hoping to God that Rico was having one of his deep sleeps because, as much as she adored that baby beyond anything else imaginable, she loved this man just as much. And she needed this time with him now. Even if he really shouldn't be here.

Closing the bedroom door behind her, she leaned back against it, slipping her robe down off her shoulders, letting it fall to the floor, her eyes locked on his.

'I've fucking missed you,' he said, almost ripping his shirt off, and this time it was Amber's turn to stare. It never ceased to amaze her how incredible he looked for a man of his age. So hard and toned and sexy as hell, to just look at him made her breathless. He had a body men half his age would kill for. And, right now, all she wanted was to feel that body inside her. She wanted that, even though it was probably the last thing she needed.

'You gonna show me how much you've missed me?' She smiled, raising her arms above her head, deliberately pushing her breasts out, arching her back slightly.

'I thought you didn't want me here.'

'I didn't. But you're here now, and it really would be a shame to waste that hard-on, wouldn't it?'

He smiled the most incredible smile that sent her heart racing, her skin tingling with the anticipation. She was too lost in him to care now – about anything. Why she was doing this, why she'd walked away from him, she really didn't care any more. She was lost. And she didn't really want to be found.

He was kissing her before she'd had a chance to get another breath out, his fingers intertwining with hers above her head, their bodies crushed against each other, and it was all she could do to keep it together. For twenty-three years he'd been ruining her life, making her crazy, so maybe it was time to just stop fighting it. Once and for all. Stop fighting it. Whatever he'd done, they'd get over it. Whatever he'd done…

As he lifted her up, she wrapped her legs around his hips, burying her head in his shoulder as he pushed into her with a force that rocked her backwards against the door. The cool wood was rough against her skin, but she didn't care. The pain wasn't registering, all that mattered was that her beautiful American man was back inside her. And it felt so good.

'No,' she whispered, looking into his eyes as he thrust deeper into her. 'It's gonna be over too soon and I don't want that.'

'Okay.' He put her down, slowly pulling out of her, watching as she walked over to the bed, another slow smile creeping across his face.

'Pretend it's the first time we're doing this.'

He pushed a hand through his hair, laughing slightly.

'You don't want to do that?' she asked, sitting down and swinging her legs up onto the bed, hugging her knees to her chest.

'Baby, you could ask me to do anything right now and I wouldn't say no. And I mean, anything.'

She smiled at him, slowly opening her legs. 'Then pretend it's the first time you're seeing me.'

'Jesus Christ,' he groaned, throwing his head back for a brief second before his eyes fell back on her. 'And you really think I'm gonna let you walk away from me?'

She said nothing, just opened her legs wider and waited for him to respond. Which he did, of course he did. His mouth was on her before she'd had time to draw another breath, his tongue soft and warm as it delved into her, his hands keeping her thighs apart so he could work his magic.

Gripping the sheets tight, Amber bit down hard as she felt his tongue run the length of her, his mouth finally covering that one, tiny spot that mattered so much, sending another jolt of electricity shooting through her so fast it caused her body to buck in an almost violent reaction. She was losing it fast. Having him here, doing this, making her crazy all over again; she was losing it.

But she gave in to it, to him; she gave in to every beautiful tingle, every nerve ending in her body screamed out loud as he brought her to a climax that both hurt and yet filled her with the most incredible calm as that familiar blanket of pins and needles flooded through her.

She kept her eyes closed, her arms now thrown up above her head as she felt his body slide up hers, her legs pulling up around him, his fingers intertwining with hers.

He was hard. She could feel him there against her, feel his heart beating fast, his breathing becoming shallow, her own chest rising and falling so quickly it was making her breathless. She was finding it hard to focus, trying to keep one ear out for the baby monitor while the rest of her just wanted to lose herself all over again in this man who was destined to plague her life for the rest of his. But she didn't care. Not if this was how it felt. She really didn't care.

'Are you ready?' he whispered.

She nodded, his eyes almost burning into hers.

He kissed her, and she closed her eyes, her fingers tightening around his as the kiss grew deeper, his tongue dancing around hers, as her skin broke out in a barrage of goosebumps. She'd never felt a desperation like it. The need to feel him inside her was so painful, it almost squeezed the breath from her. So the relief she felt when he finally pushed into her was incredible, as though someone had just opened a door which had been locked for years, allowing her a kind of freedom she'd ached for.

Her fingers gripped his even tighter as he thrust into her, gently, her hips pushing up against his, his mouth now covering the base of her throat with tiny kisses, their bodies moving together in a faster rhythm that was utterly breathtaking. She felt as though the rest of the world had just disappeared, disintegrated around her, leaving only those two, and, once again, she didn't care. She was ceasing to care about much now. She'd vowed this would never happen again, but she was powerless to stop. Absolutely powerless. That's what this man did to her.

Pulling her legs up further, clinging onto his hands as though the world would end if she let him go, she kept her eyes closed as she felt that beautiful wave of intense pleasure return, creeping its way up her body with a wonderfully slow, almost languid, speed, as if it could tell she didn't want this to end. And she didn't. Of course she didn't. In reality, she hadn't wanted to walk away from him, but she'd felt it was something she needed to do. Because there were times when what she felt for him didn't always feel healthy. It took over, *he* took over, until she could see nothing but him. And she couldn't let it be that way, not any more.

Arching her back and raising her hips up once more, she couldn't help but scream out loud as she felt his body stiffen, before the inevitable explosion, that wonderful release that sent her heart into overdrive and her stomach somersaulting a million times over until it was all she could do to catch her breath.

And when it was over, when his body finally went limp and his grip on her hands loosened slightly, she felt the strangest feeling of emptiness. Because, now he was here, she didn't want him to go. But, at the same time, she knew he had to.

'That was worth the plane journey alone,' he breathed, looking at her, a slight smile on his way-too-handsome face.

She couldn't help smiling back. 'I love you, Jim.'

'Hey, I love you, too, baby.' He slowly pulled out of her, rolling over onto his back before turning onto his side, propping himself up on one elbow. 'Which is why I still don't understand why you're doing this. Why you're pushing me away.'

'You call that pushing you away?' she said, still smiling.

'You're making me leave tonight.'

'No, you're leaving tonight because you now manage a football team hundreds of miles away from here and you need to get back there.'

'So, if I *didn't* need to get back there, would you still be making me leave?'

She sat up, pulling her knees to her chest, resting her cheek on them, her eyes meeting his. 'No.'

'Then why the hell don't you just come home, Amber?'

'I can't,' she whispered, her eyes locked on his. She just couldn't break the stare, even though part of her wanted to. Part of her needed to.

'I don't get this,' he sighed, falling onto his back, pushing a hand through his hair.

'It's hard for me to explain, Jim…'

'You're telling me it is.' He got up, walking over to the other side of the room, and still Amber couldn't break her stare; her eyes followed his every move. 'This is fucking crazy, Amber. What the hell are we doing?'

'I'm trying to save our marriage, Jim.'

'Yeah, you see, you keep saying that, honey, but I'm just not getting that vibe. You don't save a marriage by walking away from it.'

'Sometimes you do.'

He leaned against the wall, throwing his head back and letting out a loud, frustrated sigh. 'Jesus!'

Amber got up off the bed, pulling her robe back around her, walking over to him. 'I'm doing this for us, Jim.'

'Are you?' He looked right into her eyes, and she felt a pain she'd never felt before cut right through her. 'Because it sure as hell doesn't feel like it. I can't sleep, Amber. I can't close my eyes and get any rest because it hurts so much, you not being there.'

'I wasn't there for sixteen years, Jim. Remember?'

'That isn't the same fucking thing, baby, and you know that. I didn't have you to lose back then. I didn't know what this shit would feel like, this constant pain, this dull ache that never goes away. There's a constant fear in the back of my mind that you aren't ever coming back and I can't shake it. I can't fucking shake that, and I've tried. I've tried so fucking hard.'

She moved closer to him, reaching up to touch his rough jawline, running her fingers over it, resting them on his slightly open mouth for a matter of seconds before she leaned in to kiss him slowly, his arms falling around her, pulling her closer, pulling her robe away from her body until she was naked and exposed again.

In an instant he'd turned her around so she was facing the wall, his hands in hers, raising them above her head, his mouth covering the back of her neck in those beautiful, tiny kisses and Amber closed her eyes, ready to lose herself in him all over again. And even though she knew that every time she let him do this, she was giving a bigger part of herself away to this man, she knew it was never going to change. Because, deep down inside, she was never going to let it.

He nudged her legs open with his knee, his breath warm on her neck as his fingers tightened around hers, and it was as though some kind of spell had just been cast, making her do what she knew she shouldn't be doing; she'd given him enough tonight. But it was like someone else was taking over every action she made right now. She wasn't responsible for what was happening any more.

She pushed back against him, keeping her eyes closed as he let go of one of her hands, guiding himself back inside her before resting a hand on her hip, keeping her on him. A million and one memories flashed through her mind as she felt him thrust deeply, his breathing and the beating of her heart the only sounds she could hear as she realised just how much of her life this man had invaded. How much he'd taken over. And she didn't want to cry; he was making love to her and she didn't want to cry. But she couldn't stop the tears, and she clung onto his hand, just wanting to see him now, she didn't want it like this any more. She wanted to look at him.

'Jim... please, I don't want...'

He gently kissed the back of her neck, pulling out of her and turning her around. 'Oh, Jesus, baby, I'm sorry.'

She shook her head, taking his hand again. 'No. It's not that. That's not what's making me...' She looked up into his eyes. 'I *want* to miss you, Jim. I want to be away from you so I can miss you.'

'It doesn't make any sense, Amber. Putting ourselves through this. It doesn't make sense. How am I supposed to go back tonight knowing you're this upset?'

'I'm not upset.' She smiled, reaching up to touch his cheek. 'A bit confused, maybe. And you turning up like this hasn't helped, but, I'm not upset. Okay? Maybe those baby hormones haven't left me completely, huh?'

He took her hand, bringing it to his mouth and kissing it. 'I love you *so* much, and what I've done…'

She shook her head again. 'No. Don't. All of that, it's over.'

'Then why are you here, Amber? Why are you *here*, and I'm down in London all on my own?'

'Just know that I love you,' she whispered, her mouth moving closer to his. 'And that is never gonna change.'

'I don't understand this…'

She pushed him down onto the chair beside them, straddling him. 'It's time to say goodbye, handsome.'

He lifted her up slightly, lowering her back down onto him, their eyes locked together as he slid back inside her, and it was the most beautiful feeling. A calming injection. A necessary need. 'I told you, Amber, I'm not saying goodbye.'

'We *are* gonna get through this,' she whispered, her hands either side of his face, their mouths almost touching. 'I promise.'

He held onto her hips, her slow rotations encouraging yet another killer climax out of him. 'I know.' Because he wasn't going to have it any other way.

She continued to rotate her hips, pushing down on him, reaching down to touch herself because she knew he was about to come; she could feel it. And she wanted to share this, to end this journey together, so she closed her eyes and threw back her head, arching her back, pushing her breasts out, and he wasn't going to waste that opportunity. His mouth was on her instantly. Just the touch of his tongue on her skin made her moan quietly as she felt that beautiful warmth start to spread through her. And when it hit her, it hit hard. She tried to keep the noise down, for Rico's sake, but she couldn't stop her cries from filling the room as he flooded her body with the kind of drug only he could give her. And it felt like the most glorious fix; something she'd needed to keep her sane and focus her mind even though, in reality, all this was doing was clouding everything.

'Now you need to go,' she said quietly.

'Amber, baby…'

'You need to go.' She climbed off him, immediately picking up her robe and covering herself up. 'Please, Jim.'

He pushed both hands through his hair. 'This is crazy.' He stood up, pulling his shirt back on.

'Our whole relationship's been crazy,' Amber whispered, her heart breaking, a pain so physical it actually hurt.

'Don't I even get to see Rico?' Jim asked, leaning back against the door, and all Amber wanted to do was pull him back into bed and ensure that he never left her side.

'He's asleep.'

'Can I see him, Amber? Please? Can I just try and act as though all this is normal? Just for a few minutes?'

She folded her arms across her chest, moving a little closer to him. 'Okay. But if he starts crying you're not going anywhere until you've settled him.'

He smiled, reaching out for her, pulling her arms away from her. 'You mean that?'

She couldn't help smiling, too. 'Don't you dare, do you hear me? I need my sleep tonight. You've exhausted me.'

He pulled her against him, and she didn't fight it. If it meant another minute in his arms she was going to take that. 'This is still so fucked up, Amber.'

'I know.'

'I love you.'

'I know that, too.'

'And don't think I won't be back.'

'Jim…'

His mouth on hers stopped her from protesting any more, and she fell against him, her fingers burying themselves in his hair as he kissed her long and deep. He was right, he was so right. This *was* so fucked up. But she just couldn't think of any other way to deal with things right now. Although, she was slowly beginning to forget exactly what those things were.

'I love you.'

She looked up into his eyes. 'Go see Rico.'

She watched him walk across the hall, into Rico's nursery. Watching from the open door as he picked up her tiny boy, holding him to him, kissing his forehead, the pain Amber had felt before intensified as Rico snuggled into Jim. Watching him rock her baby in his arms was something that hurt so much Amber couldn't catch her breath for a second or two. Seeing the two most important men in her life together like that, and knowing that Rico wasn't Jim's, still hit her like a punch to the solar plexus. Because that was something that could never be resolved. It could never change. No matter how many times she prayed or wished or hoped for a miracle, it was never going to change.

'Can you try and let your mommy know how much I love her, kiddo? Huh? Because I think she'll listen to you.'

Amber had to close her eyes as more tears started to stream down her face. What the hell was she doing?

'I love her so much, your mommy. And I really don't think she knows that. I don't think she has any idea just what I would do for her. She's my world, and I know you're hers – I know you come before anybody in her life, and that's the way it should be. You're her little miracle. You're something she never thought she'd have. And that's what she is to me. She's something I never thought I'd have, because I treated her so badly, your mom. I hurt her, so many times… and when you're all grown up, you're probably gonna come gunning for me if you ever find out just how badly I hurt her, because you are gonna love her so much, do you know that? You are gonna love her and you're gonna want to protect her, but that's something we have in common, kiddo. I love her, and all I want to do is protect her. All I want to do is make up for the past and give your mommy so much love…'

He stopped talking, his eyes staring down at Rico, and Amber had to blink away yet more tears.

'I won't lose her,' Jim went on, laying Rico gently down into his cot. 'I won't lose her, not again. So… so you tell your mommy – you tell her I love her, you got that? You tell her.'

Amber moved back inside the bedroom, closing the door quietly behind her, finally letting those tears fall as she sank to the floor. She loved him, too. But, with every inch of her breaking heart, she wished she didn't.

*

Jim bent down to pick up his jacket from the hall floor, slipping it back on as he turned and looked up the stairs. He was walking away from the woman he loved with an obsession that was fast taking over everything. He couldn't sleep, couldn't focus, couldn't get his head together to deal with the kind of things he could usually sort out with his eyes closed. He was walking away from her. He was letting her do whatever crazy thing she thought was right when all he could see was her drifting further and further away from him.

Looking down at the floor he breathed in deeply, exhaling slowly as he turned to open the front door. He was walking away. And it was the last thing he wanted to do.

The cool night air hit him with a wave of reality so brutal he just hadn't seen it coming, and as the door closed behind him, he leaned back against it and cried like he'd never cried before.

314

Chapter Twenty-Six

'You can stop making me cups of tea now, Kevin. Really. I *can* actually make my own, remember? I'm quite capable.'

'Well, I just thought, with you being a big celebrity now, that you'd have people to do that for you. And I want you to feel at home here.'

Amber looked at Kevin, raising an eyebrow. 'I hope you're not being serious, because I'm going to correct you on a couple of things there. One, I'm not some big celebrity, okay? I work for a satellite sports channel and co-host a football-themed game show with Ronnie White, who will always be more famous than I'll ever be. I'm not Angelina Jolie. And two, over at Cloud Sports the tea and coffee is made by anyone who happens to get up from behind their desk at a time when people are gasping for a brew. That's the way it works.'

'So, flashing your legs or wearing a low-cut dress doesn't make you exempt, then?' Kevin winked.

'It's *so* good to see you're still the same old sexist pig you always were, Kevin.'

'It's what I do best, kiddo. You here in the office today?'

'No. I'm going over to Wearside Spartans' training ground this morning. Doing a piece with a couple of their players on their so far, successful F.A. Cup run. Why?'

'No reason.' Kevin shrugged. 'It's just nice having you around again. Even if I've still got no clue as to *why* you're here.'

Amber leaned back against her desk, folding her arms. 'No. And if I'm being honest, Kevin, I'm beginning to wonder myself.'

He looked at her, a genuinely concerned expression on his face. 'Are things really okay with Jim?'

'Things are complicated. I love him so much, yet I've chosen to be apart from him. My relationship with Ryan is in some kind of limbo… I'm being really cold with him and I have no idea why, half the time. I mean, I know he can be a real pain in the arse at times, but all that crap he's had to deal with recently…'

Kevin raised an eyebrow.

'What was *that* look for?'

'Nothing.'

'Now I know how annoying *I* must sound when I say that. Look, having Ryan Fisher's baby has probably complicated my life so much I… but that baby, I wanted him so badly, Kevin. It just all happened the wrong bloody way.'

'What's going on with Ronnie?'

She stared at him, saying nothing for a beat or two. 'I don't know.'

'You two had some kind of falling-out?'

She didn't answer that, she just shrugged.

'He's been on the phone, you know.'

'Has he?'

'He seems pretty down.'

'I haven't spoken to him for a while.'

'Which is why I'm going to repeat my original question – have you two had some kind of falling out?'

Amber pushed a hand though her hair, sighing a touch too heavily. 'He's getting too involved with things that are… things that have got nothing to do with him. We haven't had a fight, as such, it's just that things are a bit strained, I suppose. What he's saying, he has no right to, Kevin.'

'Even if it's only because he cares about you?'

'How much has he told you?'

'He hasn't gone into any detail, but it doesn't take a genius to hazard a guess, does it? Your private life has been anything but over the past couple of years, so – and forgive me if I'm out of line, here, but, maybe Ronnie just doesn't understand how you really feel.'

'About what?'

'About your marriage, Amber. I'm guessing that Ronnie doesn't agree with you marrying Jim Allen. Again. After everything that's happened.'

'Everything?'

'Jesus, sweetheart, I'm not Jeremy Kyle. I'm not going to stand here and help you sort it all out, I'm just saying that, whatever's going on, maybe you should just cut Ronnie a bit of slack. You two, you've been friends for too long to let something – no matter what it is – get between that.'

She looked at Kevin, letting out another, quieter sigh. 'You know we were more than friends, right? And I don't mean back when he was a player. You know about that affair we had last year.'

Kevin looked away briefly before meeting her gaze again. 'Yeah. I knew. Is that still a problem?'

'I think it was just something we both needed to get out of our systems, you know? I'm not saying it was right or that it didn't contribute to all the crazy shit that went on last year, but, it was something that was probably always gonna happen. At some point. But we're over that. That isn't the problem.'

'Well,' Kevin sighed, picking up his mug of tea and making to leave. 'Whatever it is, you should talk to him. He misses you.'

Amber watched her ex-producer's retreating back as he headed towards his office, feeling a headache start to pound behind her eyes.

'Were you ever gonna get round to calling me?'

She swung around at the sound of that familiar Geordie accent, fixing him with a stare. 'I've been busy.'

'Busy complicating your life even more than it already is, huh?'

'What are you doing here, Ryan?'

'I'm on a three-match ban, remember?'

'And that means you can't train, does it?'

'No. Not exactly. But, coincidentally, I've also picked up a slight ankle injury, which means that I can't actually train for a day or two anyway.'

'How lucky,' Amber said, probably a touch too sarcastically.

'So, were you ever gonna call me?'

'Yes, Ryan, I was gonna call you, okay? When I had a spare minute.'

'And you haven't had a spare minute since you got here? What you been doing when you leave work? Partying?'

She threw him a stare that could freeze water.

'Have you left him?' Ryan leaned back against her desk, folding his arms and adopting a stance way too comfortable for Amber's liking. This wasn't like old times. This was so far from old times.

'No, I haven't left him. Not that it's any of your business.'

'You're the mother of my baby…'

'I'm the mother of your baby, Ryan, yes, but that does not give you the right to know every little detail of my life.'

'Why are you here, then? If you haven't left him? Because, and you quite obviously haven't been keeping an eye on the press lately, that's what the papers are saying.'

Amber's head shot up. 'I'm sorry? The papers are saying *what*?'

'That you and Jim have separated.'

'Well, they're wrong.'

'You might want to try telling *them* that.'

'I shouldn't have to. They shouldn't be writing crap like that.'

'Y'know, it amazes me that you *still* haven't quite got the hang of what kind of life you're leading now.'

Amber stared at him.

'You're not Amber Sullivan, local news reporter any more, have you got that yet? You got involved with me, then it all came out about you and Jim Allen; you became one of the most well-known faces in English football … oh, and then you got pregnant. With *my* baby. You've put yourself out there, and whether you like it or not, sweetheart, everybody wants to know your every move now.'

'I'm really not that interesting.'

Ryan just raised an eyebrow.

'I'll ask again, Ryan. What are you doing here?'

'Where's Rico?'

'You know where he is. He's with my Aunty Kim.'

'Can't we go and get him?'

'*We* can't do anything. I'm working.'

He threw her a confused look.

'Oh, I'm sorry. Did you think I was up here for a holiday?'

'I don't know why the frig you're here, Amber. And I'm not sure you do, either.'

'I'm due at Wearside Spartans' training ground in half an hour. I'm recording a piece for Cloud Sports, so if you'll excuse me…'

'Hang on… Amber, wait.'

She swung around to face him. Why the hell did he still have to look so hot? His messed-up dark hair, heavy stubble and those dark-blue eyes always had a habit of pulling her in, even though she had no intention of ever going there again. 'What?'

'Can *I* go and get him?'

'Yes, you can,' she sighed. 'Just give Kim a call and let her know you're on your way. Where are you taking him?'

He looked at her, and for a second Amber remembered just why she'd got into this mess in the first place. Because, once upon a time, he had stood there in front of her, looking just like he did now. And she was never going to be rid of him, because she was always going to remember that.

'I thought we could come and find you. Maybe spend some mum, dad and Rico time together, seeing as we get very little chance to do that.'

Amber rummaged around in her pocket for her car keys, avoiding his gaze. 'That's because mum, dad and Rico time isn't even on the agenda, Ryan.'

'But mum, Rico and Uncle Jim time is, is that it?'

This time she did look at him. 'Do you know how childish you sound at times?'

'I just want us to spend a couple of hours together, Amber. Just you, me and *our* son.'

'I'm not having this conversation here, Ryan.'

He fell into step beside her as she walked towards the lift. 'Is an hour gonna kill you?'

She waited until the lift doors had closed before she spoke again. 'I'm gonna be a couple of hours with the Spartans squad. I'll call you when I'm done, okay? And I'll come meet you. We'll take Rico for a walk on the Quayside. Maybe stop for a drink or something.'

Ryan smiled, a wide and beautiful smile that Amber hoped beyond anything their son would inherit, because, no matter what she felt for him, Ryan Fisher was still one of the hottest men around. She certainly wouldn't be disappointed if Rico turned out to be the same, without his daddy's attitude, of course. 'Okay.'

The lift doors opened at the ground floor, but Amber was going down to the basement car park. 'It's only a walk, Ryan.'

He stepped out into the News North East reception, stuffing his hands in the pockets of his dark-blue jeans. 'Thanks, Amber.'

'Like I said, it's just a walk. And make sure Rico's wrapped up, alright? It's still quite chilly out there.'

As soon as the lift doors shut again, she closed her eyes and wondered if she'd done the right thing. But it was an afternoon out with their baby, that was all. That's all it was.

Tossing her hair back over her shoulder she strode purposefully across the quiet underground car park towards her black Mercedes-Benz. Her beloved pale-blue Fiat 500 was back down in London, safely ensconced in the ridiculously huge garage at her and Jim's new home.

'You still look good in heels, has anyone told you that lately?'

She looked up, rolling her eyes as she saw Ronnie leaning against her car. 'I don't know why I bothered coming up here when everybody just seems to be following me.'

'Everybody?' Ronnie frowned. 'I mean, I knew Ryan was up here, obviously, but… Jim's here?'

She shook her head, pressing the key fob to open the doors. 'Not now he isn't. He has been, though.'

'When?'

She threw him a look that told him it really wasn't any of his business.

Ronnie bowed his head, his arms still folded against him. 'You haven't left him, then?'

'Why does everyone think I've left him?'

'Because that's what it looks like, Amber. Now, I don't know what the hell's going on in your head right now, but whatever *you* think it looks like, to everyone else it looks like you've left him. And that's what the press is saying, too.'

'Yes, thank you, I've already had this off Ryan.'

'Ryan?' Ronnie frowned.

'He was here. Just before. He's picked up an injury or something so he can't train for a couple of days. He's gone to get Rico.'

'Oh, Right.'

She looked at him, cocking her head slightly. 'Something I can do for you?'

'Yeah. You can stop avoiding me.'

'I'm not avoiding you.'

'Oh, really? You're not?'

'Can you move, please? You're in my way. There's somewhere I need to be.'

'Yeah, Spartans' training ground. Kevin told me.'

'Seems you and Kevin have been having a few little chats lately. And he could have told me you were coming up here.'

'I told him not to. Because I knew you'd only try and avoid me.'

Amber threw her head back and let out a frustrated sigh. 'Get in the car.'

'Is that an order?' He threw her a half-smile, but she didn't return it. She wasn't in the mood.

'If you want to talk to me, get in the car. You can come with me. You might even prove to be useful.'

*

Jim leaned back in his chair, swinging his feet up onto the desk as he spoke into the phone. 'How are things going, Max?'

'You're really serious about this, Jim?'

'Never been more serious about anything in my life.'

'Shouldn't you talk to Amber?'

'No. She has to know nothing about this, okay? After what I've just done… it was a mistake. What I did to Ryan, I panicked… I…'

'And you're not panicking now?'

'No.' Jim hadn't even left a beat before answering that. 'This is what I need to do, Max. And, think about it – don't *you* think it's for the best, too?'

Max sighed, rubbing the bridge of his nose. 'Jim, I… I really don't know. I don't know if this is just going to complicate matters even further, and I feel really bad doing this…' He sighed again, a little heavier this time. 'You know, maybe you're right. Let me look into it a bit more, okay? Just, leave it with me.'

'Don't leave it too long, Max. I don't know how much time I've got left before… I just need it to happen, as quickly as it can.'

'Leave it with me,' Max repeated, before ending the call.

Jim put the phone down then leant forward, dropping his head into his hands. He'd never felt so tired. When he'd told Amber he wasn't sleeping that was no word of a lie. He'd go to bed, and he'd try and usher in some form of rest but over the past few nights it hadn't been forthcoming. And now that the press were throwing all sorts of fabricated stories around about their relationship, he

322

didn't think sleep was going to arrive any time soon.

He needed to be with her so badly it was like an ache that wouldn't go away, a reminder of how much he loved this woman. How much he wanted her, every second of every lonely, heart-breaking day he wanted her. And what he was doing was risky, but it was a risk he had to take. He was doing it for her. For their future. Because, if he didn't try to do something, he wasn't sure they were going to have one.

*

'You okay?' Amber asked Brandon as she packed her things away.

'I'm fine.'

'You sure?'

He looked at her, throwing her a half-smile. 'Amber, you really don't need to do the whole concerned step-mum thing. What happened with Ellen is over. It's done. Forget it. I have.'

She walked over to him. 'I'll let you into a little secret – I never really liked her.'

He looked down, laughing slightly. 'Yeah, well, it would seem you had good reason not to like her.' His eyes met hers again. 'She came to see me. Told me she was sorry, that she wanted to try again. She tried to tell me it had all been a big mistake and that she really did still love me.'

'Oh, Brandon, you didn't?'

He shook his head. 'What she did... there are no second chances.' He smiled, a smile so like Jim's. 'I'm gonna give women a rest for a little while, I think. Concentrate on my football. We've got a real chance of winning some silverware this season, and I don't wanna mess that up.'

'You won't mess anything up, Brandon. You're the reason Wearside Spartans are doing so well right now. Look, your dad's worried about you, too. You should go see him the next chance you get.'

'And I could say exactly the same thing to you.'

It was her turn to give a small laugh. 'Yeah. I asked for that really, didn't I?'

'*Have* you separated, Amber? Because, believe me, that concerns me a lot more than any of that crap going on with Ellen.'

'No, sweetheart, we haven't separated. And whatever they're saying in the press, none of it's true. Me and your dad, we just need a bit of time apart, that's all.'

'Really? You're not just telling me that to placate me?'

'Brandon, you're twenty-two not twelve. If there *was* any bad news to tell you I'm sure you'd be able to handle it, at your age.'

He smiled again, leaning back against the dressing-room wall. 'Okay. Well, I'm not gonna ask what's going on, because I doubt I'd understand anyway.'

That would make two of them, Amber thought.

'But, whatever it is, you're working it out, right?'

She returned his smile. 'Yeah. We're working it out. Right, I'd better get out of here. Thanks for making this a very easy morning, by the way.'

'It's good to see you, Amber.'

She pulled him in for a hug. 'Go give your dad a call. Go on.'

Ronnie was outside in the corridor, talking to another Wearside Spartans player. Amber mouthed *"I'll meet you outside"* and made her way out into the bright spring sunshine. The weather was certainly being kind to her on her visit back to the north-east.

She stood by the side of the training pitch, watching as some of the players practised penalties whilst others embarked on some pretty serious stretches and lunges.

'Not sure I could manage that now.'

She turned to look at Ronnie, a small smile on her face. 'Oh, I dunno. You're still quite fit, really.'

Their eyes locked for a brief second, before Amber turned her head away. She didn't want to go back there. That was one complication that really didn't need to be revisited.

'All of this, Amber. Me and you, falling out…'

'We fell out?' Her eyes met his again.

'I hate it. This tension between us? It's wrong.'

'Then stop trying to force your feelings about Jim onto me. You're free to feel whatever you like about him, just know that I don't share that, okay?'

Ronnie sighed, staring out ahead of him. 'It's hard, Amber. Because I don't think he deserves you.'

Amber said nothing. She wasn't going to get into any more arguments over this. It wasn't worth it.

'He might love you, Amber. In fact, I have no doubt he loves you…'

'Then that's all that matters, isn't it?'

'No, baby, it isn't.'

'You know, I remember you telling me, not all that long ago, that I should grab the chance to be with the one person I truly love. You said that to me.'

'That was before I realised he hadn't changed at all, Amber.'

'He has, Ronnie. What happened with Ryan…'

Ronnie threw his head back, letting out a quiet sigh. But it was loaded with frustration. 'Can you hear yourself? You're actually standing there defending a man who is *still* doing the same crap he's been doing for decades. He's lying to you, Amber. And you can't base a marriage on lies.'

'Have you come up here just to irritate me? Because I could have sworn you were supposed to be covering the south London derby tonight, yet here you are in Newcastle, banging on to me about how much you disapprove of Jim.'

'How much I *disapprove*? Jesus, Amber, you make me sound like your dad! I don't disapprove of Jim. I just don't think he's right for you.'

'That's not your decision to make.'

'No.' He sighed again, digging his hands into his pockets. 'It isn't. Anyway, what are you doing now?'

'I'm meeting Ryan. We're taking Rico out.'

'Together?'

She looked at him through slightly narrowed eyes. 'You got a problem with that?'

'I haven't got a problem with anything…'

She couldn't help a slightly derisive laugh from escaping.

'I'll ignore that,' Ronnie said. 'Do you think it's a good idea? You and Ryan? Out together, when all that stuff's in the news about you and Jim separating?'

'We haven't separated!'

'Well, you going out with Ryan Fisher in broad daylight isn't gonna help the rumours.'

'We're spending a bit of time with our son, that's all.'

'In *your* eyes.'

'What the hell is wrong with you?'

He turned to face her. 'What the fuck are you doing here, Amber? If you really love Jim and you want your marriage to survive then what the fuck are you doing *here*?'

'I really don't need this…'

'You have no idea what you're doing, do you? Because you've let him get under your skin…'

'Jesus, Ronnie, he's been under my skin for twenty-three fucking years, this isn't a new feeling for me.'

'And for twenty-three years you've let him control you.'

She glared at him, an anger building up inside her that she'd never felt with this man before. He'd always been the one who was there for her, no matter what. The one she could turn to, talk to; that shoulder to cry on whenever she needed it. But that was disappearing fast. And she hated it. It scared her. But he couldn't stand there and say those things. He couldn't do that.

'You shouldn't have come here, Ronnie. You've wasted your time.'

'Amber!'

She just walked away, before she had a chance to say something she might truly regret.

*

'Do you want to talk about it?' Ryan asked, placing their drinks down on the table in front of them.

Amber looked up at him. 'Sorry?'

'You've quite obviously got a lot on your mind.'

'You don't know the half of it. Look, I know you're probably tired of hearing me say this, Ryan, but, I really am sorry. For what happened.'

'You've got nothing to apologise for, Amber.'

She stared out ahead of her, at the people walking by, at the sun glinting off the River Tyne, anywhere but at him. The guilt was still overwhelming, even though it wasn't her guilt to feel.

'I can't pretend I understand exactly why he did it,' she said quietly. 'But I believe him when he says he's sorry.'

Ryan couldn't help but laugh, picking Rico up out of his push-chair and sitting him on his knee. 'Yeah, well, forgive me if I don't join you in believing anything Jim Allen says. He spoke to me, remember? He told me himself what he'd done, and I told *you* that I saw not one shred of remorse in his eyes.'

Amber hung her head, clasping her hands together. 'He's my soulmate, Ryan.'

'Oh, Jesus, Amber.'

'If this is how it's gonna go I might as well just leave.'

'No, look, *I'm* sorry, okay? I just… I just don't get it. You and him. What the hell is it you see in him?'

She looked up, staring right into his eyes. 'I love him.'

'So much that you *can* actually get past all the shit he throws at people?'

'For Christ's sake'

She sat back in her seat, reaching out for the glass of wine in front of her. 'I'm not even listening any more.'

327

It was a beautiful spring afternoon, the perfect day to sit outside a riverside bar with a drink and take in the view. As a silence fell between her and Ryan, Amber let all the ambient chatter and noise surrounding them wash over her.

'I guess I've got a lot of stuff to be sorry about, too,' Ryan said, breaking that silence. 'I mean, what happened with Ellen…'

'It's not *me* you should be apologising to for that, Ryan.'

'She was trying to get pregnant.'

Amber turned her head sharply to look at him. 'I'm sorry?'

'Deliberately, I mean. Without telling me. She'd told me she didn't want to use condoms any more, and you know me, I'm not one to ignore that request. But I thought she was on the pill. She *told* me she was on the pill…'

'You're really that naïve, huh?'

He looked down at Rico, who was now sleeping in his famous daddy's arms, his blue eyes closed to the world and all the complications going on around him. 'I don't… I found the pills in the bin. She'd just thrown them away.'

'Jesus. The pair of you almost deserve each other. She's just as naïve as you are.'

He leaned forward to kiss Rico's cheek, an action which did something rather strange to Amber's insides. Seeing the two of them together was a beautiful sight. Her gorgeous baby and his handsome daddy. 'It was never a relationship that was going anywhere,' Ryan said quietly, still staring down at Rico.

'Well, maybe you shouldn't have gone back to her every time you needed some kind of escape.'

He looked up, his eyes meeting hers. 'You do realise what you've just said, don't you? I mean, that's exactly how this little guy here was conceived, remember? Because you, me – because we needed some kind of escape. It happens, Amber. People do stupid things under weird circumstances. Mind you…' He threw her a small smile, 'if you ever need another escape – I've told you, haven't I? You come to me.'

She turned away again, almost as though looking at him would burn the retinas in her eyes. 'We're not talking about me.'

There was a brief moment of silence before Ryan spoke. 'Me and Ellen, it was a mistake.'

'It could have been a much bigger one, from what you've just told me.'

'Yeah, well, it's over now.'

'And she knows that for sure, does she?'

Ryan shrugged. 'I haven't heard anything from her. I mean, she's still at the club, obviously. She works there. But I haven't seen her since it all happened.'

'She tried to get back with Brandon.'

'You're kidding? I'm assuming he had more sense than to go there?'

She looked at him. 'You know, we're vilifying this girl, making her out to be the bad guy here, when maybe she just got confused.'

'You're defending her?'

'Of course I'm not defending her. I'm just saying, when we get desperate, sometimes we do things that aren't always in character. Maybe she just loved you so much it was the only thing she could think of to do to try and keep you with her.'

His eyes locked with hers. 'Who are we talking about now, Amber?'

She turned away, saying nothing.

'Amber?'

'Leave it, Ryan.'

'You aren't ever gonna leave him, are you? No matter what he does, you aren't ever gonna leave him.'

She held his gaze, her eyes staring deep into his. 'I don't know.'

Those three words could change everything.

Chapter Twenty-Seven

Jim stared at the newspaper, at the picture staring back at him; Amber and Ryan, out together, with their baby boy. Out together, as a family, and the pain that this caused, it was almost unbearable.

'You're reading way too much into that, Jim,' Max said, leaning back against the sideboard in Jim's Parkfield office.

'The rumours are even more widespread now, Max. Whatever this is, it's what it *looks* like that's important to all those people out there who make a living twisting the truth. But I don't really know what the truth is, do I?'

'Have you called her?'

Jim shook his head. 'As soon as I've finished up here I'm on a flight to Newcastle.'

'Is that wise?'

Jim looked up. 'She's my *wife*, Max. And for some reason I still can't fucking understand, she's up there with him, and I'm down here wondering just what the hell is going on with our marriage. I need to talk to her. Face to face.'

'I thought you were only up there a couple of days ago.'

'There wasn't time to talk.'

'Well, maybe if you concentrated less on the physical side of things…'

Jim's eyes bored into Max's, and Max held his hands up in

surrender, bowing his head. 'Okay. I'm sorry. That was out of line. But… look, just call her, Jim. Before you go up there and accuse her of something you have absolutely no proof of. They've taken the baby out, that's all. In reality there's nothing unusual about that. They're his parents, Amber's back up north for a while, so why wouldn't she?'

'It stops, Max. This ridiculous act she's putting on. She's coming back home, with me. Where she belongs.'

'Well, you go up there with that attitude and you'll be coming home alone. I know Amber. And she won't appreciate that.'

'I've known her a lot longer than anyone, Max. I've known her for twenty-three years…'

'And you fucked up most of those.'

The two men glared at each other, saying nothing for a few, long seconds.

It was Jim who broke the silence. 'I need to see her.'

Max sighed, folding his arms across his chest. 'Don't do anything stupid, Jim. Don't give the press anything more to play with, okay?'

Jim sat down on the arm of the couch, raking both hands through his hair. 'I can't do this. It's fucking killing me, Max.'

'I can only do so much, Jim.'

'Are you any nearer…?'

'I'm looking into it. There isn't a lot we can do just yet anyway. We really need to wait a couple of months.'

Jim picked up the newspaper, taking another look at the photograph. It was a paparazzi photo, of course. And sometimes those photos never did tell the whole truth, but just seeing the three of them together – his beautiful wife, her ex-boyfriend and their baby. *Their* baby.

'I need to see her,' Jim whispered.

And Max knew there wasn't a thing he could do to stop him.

*

Amber opened the door quietly and she couldn't stop a smile from spreading across her face as she saw the sight in front of her. Ryan was lying asleep on his back on the couch, with Rico curled up on his tummy on his daddy's naked chest. Ryan had his hand resting gently on his baby son's back, and the two of them looked so peaceful that Amber felt as though she should just leave them alone. She'd never seen anything quite so gorgeous. Ryan, with all those heavy tattoos and that rock-hard stomach, and their beautiful, beautiful baby boy with his mop of dark hair and those eyes just like his daddy's. And she didn't want to feel that jolt in her stomach, that uninvited somersault, but it was there. It had happened.

Letting Ryan stay the night had been a mistake, even though he'd slept in the spare room. Nothing had gone on. Nothing. But it had been a mistake. And he really needed to go now.

She waited a few more seconds, giving herself a little bit more time to take in daddy and baby together before she walked over to them, crouching down beside them.

'Hey, my handsome pair of sleepyheads. It's time to get up now. Mummy's got work to do.'

Ryan's eyes opened slowly, his smile wide as he looked at her. 'Hey there, gorgeous.' He sat up slowly, a half-asleep Rico still snuggling into him as Ryan swung his legs down. 'He woke up a couple of hours ago so I thought I'd bring him down here, watch a bit of early-morning TV. Leave his beautiful mum to sleep in a bit longer.'

'Well, I can't say I'm not grateful for that, so thank you. Did you sleep alright?'

'Not really. I'd much rather have been next to you, holding that incredible naked body of yours against mine.'

She stood up, walking away into the kitchen. 'Grow up, Ryan.'

'Your mum keeps telling me to do that, kiddo. She keeps telling me to grow up.'

Amber turned to look at him, leaning back against the counter and folding her arms as he followed her into the kitchen, Rico now awake and gurgling away at his daddy. It was almost too cute to watch Ryan smiling, talking to his son and receiving the biggest smile back as Rico tried so hard to talk back. He was growing up so quickly, and sometimes Amber looked at him and still couldn't believe he was here or that he was hers.

'Kim'll be here any minute now to pick him up,' she said, pulling herself swiftly back from her own daydream. 'And *you* shouldn't be here.' The doorbell ringing interrupted any more conversation. 'That'll be Kim.' She walked over to Ryan, reaching out for Rico. 'Time to say bye-bye to daddy, baby.' She let Ryan kiss Rico quickly before she took him from him. 'Stay here, and do *not* let Kim see you.'

'Why? I'm Rico's dad; what's so wrong with me being here?'

'It's half past eight in the morning and you're half-naked, for starters. What kind of message does *that* send out?'

Ryan just grinned, and Amber rolled her eyes, hugging her baby to her. 'Just, stay here. I won't be long.'

He was making coffee when she arrived back in the kitchen ten minutes later.

'Go and put some clothes on, Ryan.'

He turned around, another grin on his handsome face. 'You could do with taking some off.'

'It's like talking to a bloody teenager. Is that coffee made yet?' She walked over to the cupboard, reaching up to take a couple of mugs out, almost dropping them when she felt his hands on her hips, his lips brushing the back of her neck. 'Ryan!' She pushed back with her bottom, nudging him away. 'What the hell are you playing at?'

'Jesus that was actually quite a turn-on. Can you do that naked?'

'For fuck's sake…'

'Come on! You want this just as much as I do, Amber. Otherwise you would have made me go home last night.'

'So, you know what I'm thinking now, do you?'

'Baby, I'm not sure even *you* know what the hell you're thinking half the time. But I *do* think you want this. You just don't realise how much.'

'And I thought Ryan Fisher couldn't get any more arrogant. Go and put some clothes on.'

He walked over to her, reaching out to tuck a strand of hair behind her ear. 'It was nice, last night. Just sitting, talking, watching TV. Like a proper family.'

'I *have* a proper family.'

'Do you? You have a husband you've left behind in London while you come back home to do what, Amber? What *are* you doing here? And if you'd *really* wanted to get away from everybody – from all of us – why did you come back here? Somewhere you knew I'd be. You could have gone anywhere, sweetheart. But you came here.'

'And maybe now I'm just beginning to realise what a mistake that was.'

He shook his head, his thumb gently stroking her cheek. 'It wasn't a mistake.'

'You really need to go now, Ryan.'

He let his fingers trail down over her neck, brushing over her collarbone, and she could feel every touch through the thin material of her shirt. She could feel it all, but she didn't want to.

'Remember the day he arrived, Amber? Our baby. Remember that day?'

'I remember the pain.'

'You were so beautiful. That's what *I* remember. I ran into that room, hoping to God I hadn't missed him coming into the world, and I saw you, so tired… Jesus, you looked tired, but you were so beautiful, Amber. You were my beautiful girl, and at that moment in time I'd never loved you more. What you gave me that day, it was huge. Rico is… he's the most incredible thing to ever happen to me. Him, and you. Because you gave me every reason I ever needed to change the person I was becoming.'

'You don't *have* me, Ryan.'

'I'm still so much in fucking love with you, do you know that?'

She shook her head, desperate to push him away, but it was as though her arms were suddenly made of lead. She couldn't lift them, couldn't make them do what she wanted them to do. 'You have no right to say those things to me, Ryan. No right.'

'I love you. I love that boy of mine and I love his mum. I love you, Amber.'

'No,' she whispered, finally finding the strength to push him away, running out of the room, breathing in deeply as she ran upstairs.

'We need to talk, Amber.' He'd followed her. Of course he'd followed her.

She swung around to face him, trying to stay calm and wishing more than anything that Jim was there. Her handsome American man. Her husband. She wished he was with her, to stop this from happening.

'There is *nothing* to talk about, Ryan. I shouldn't have let you stay here last night…'

'But you did.'

'And you're reading way too much into that.'

'Am I?'

'You need to go.'

'Is that what you want?'

She couldn't help laughing. 'I don't believe you. Go and put some clothes on, and get out, okay? I need to get ready for work.'

He held his hands up in surrender. 'Okay. Okay, I get it. I'm sorry. I'll let myself out, alright?'

She breathed a sigh of relief. But shouldn't she really have been prepared for this? She'd let him stay the night. And she hadn't expected him to read anything into that? And she'd had the nerve to call Ellen naïve.

'I'll call you later, about Rico. Is that okay?'

She nodded. 'Yeah. That's fine.' Closing the door behind her she leaned against it, closing her eyes and breathing in deeply. What the hell was she doing? This had gone far enough now. Was Ryan right? Had she, subconsciously, come back to Newcastle because some things were just a touch *too* familiar? Had she really let that happen? Maybe going further afield was something she needed to do. Maybe that's what she needed to really get her focus back. Because this obviously wasn't working.

She took a quick shower, hoping the blasts of cold water she forced herself to endure would knock some sense back into her and some rational thinking would finally start to take over. But it didn't really help.

Grabbing a towel from the heated rail beside the shower she quickly dried herself, slipping on a pair of knickers before wrapping the towel around herself, taking the clip from her hair and shaking it loose around her shoulders as she stared into the mirror. She looked tired. All of this was supposed to be helping her get her head straight when all it was really doing was confusing her even more.

Running her fingers through her hair, she gave it one more shake before stepping back out into the bedroom.

'You really thought I'd take any notice of you?'

'Jesus, Ryan! What are you still doing here?'

He was leaning against the wall with his arms folded, still half-naked and a cocky smile on his far-too-handsome face.

'You know, you could have any woman you wanted. *Any* woman, Ryan. And yet you still want to waste your time with me.'

He shrugged, his eyes never leaving hers. 'If that's the way I want to spend my time...'

'You're crazy.'

'No, *you're* the crazy one. For staying with a man who's cheated on you, lied to you and treated you like crap for most of your life.'

'Why are you still here?'

'Because I think we've got unfinished business.'

She backed up against the closed bathroom door, clutching the top of the towel that was covering her. 'Ryan, if we're honest with each other, we're probably always going to have unfinished business. So let's just accept that, okay?'

He looked at her from across the other side of the room. It was a weird and slightly erotic Mexican stand-off, both of them standing there in a state of undress, and neither of them willing to move any closer, even though the air was charged with something Amber was choosing to ignore.

'Please, Ryan.'

He said nothing, he just continued to stare at her, and she tried her hardest to break that stare, but he was making it so hard.

'Ryan.'

He didn't move, and she was starting to get angry now. Angry at him for still being here, and angry at herself for giving him the chance to do this in the first place. Her fault. When the hell had she become so weak?

She finally broke the stare, looking down at her fingers as they clutched the towel wrapped around her body.

'You need to go, Ryan.'

'It doesn't matter how many times you keep saying that, Amber, I'm not going anywhere.'

She slowly raised her head, her eyes meeting his again. 'You're not being fair.'

'And neither are you. You're not being fair to me. You're not being fair to Rico. And, most of all, you're not being fair to yourself.'

She shook her head, her fingers gripping the towel even tighter. 'I'm married.'

'Oh, Jesus, Amber, believe me, we're all aware of that fact. We all know you're married.' He started to walk over to her, his hands in the pockets of his jeans. 'But I don't actually care.' He shrugged. 'I don't.'

'But I *do*, Ryan. And I don't want this. This shouldn't be happening.'

'Nothing's happening.' He stopped, just a few inches away from her. 'Nothing.'

She felt a shiver run through her that she didn't welcome. She closed her eyes and tried to think of Jim, but all that did was make her feel guilty. And then she remembered what he'd done to Ryan and the guilt changed. She felt angry, with Jim for lying to her and for doing what he'd done. For making her run – here. Straight to Ryan. Someone she'd vowed never to run back to. Yet here she was. And she hadn't even realised she'd been running.

'I won't let you do this,' she whispered, trying to ignore those dark-blue eyes and the sexy smile and those tattoos that were just so hot. She felt as if she couldn't breathe; it was almost claustrophobic in there now, yet the window was open and the room was full of fresh air.

'I'm not doing anything.' His hands were still in his pockets, but his eyes were staring into hers. 'Unless you want me to.'

'Please, Ryan. Just go. Please.'

He threw his head back, sighing quietly. 'We made a baby, Amber.'

'What's that got to do with anything?'

He took a step closer, reaching out to touch her cheek, stroking it lightly. 'He's that bond that can never be broken. That one thing that will always keep us together, and I think he arrived for a reason.'

'Stop talking, okay? Just, stop talking. I don't love you and I don't want this. I really don't want this.'

'You don't have to love me.'

'This is crazy…'

'Then push me away. Go on. Push me away.'

Once again her arms felt as though they were made of lead, and she tried lifting them but they weighed a ton.

'Push me away, Amber.'

She closed her eyes. Maybe part of her somewhere thought that if she closed her eyes, all of this would just go away. Yeah, that naïve part of her had suddenly come to the forefront.

But she kept them closed, and of course that was an invitation to him. A way of telling him it was okay, and she couldn't see that?

She felt his fingers slide around the back of her neck, burying themselves in her hair, pulling her head back slightly as his lips touched the base of her throat so lightly that she felt another involuntary shiver run the length of her body. He was coaxing the memories she'd tried to forget out of her now, all of them rushing forward like a tidal wave of images playing out all at once inside her head – memories of him touching her, kissing her, making love to her in the most incredible way, because they'd had some great sex. Oh, Jesus, they'd had great sex!

Another shiver flooded through her as his other hand took hold of hers, lifting it up beside her head, their fingers intertwining, locking together as his eyes met hers.

'Push me away,' he whispered, his mouth almost touching hers now, and all Amber could hear was the sound of heart beating so loudly, she was positive he must be able to hear it too.

She couldn't reply; she couldn't get any words out because she was sure that if she spoke she was going to utter something that meant she was saying this was okay, and it wasn't. It was so far from okay. It was wrong. But everything about her life right now was wrong. Would this make that much of a difference? What the hell was she doing?

'Push me away,' he repeated, goading her in an attempt to make her do something she really didn't want to do. Because she didn't want to do this – did she?

'Ryan…'

She closed her eyes again, clinging onto his hand, her body tensing up as his mouth finally rested against hers. And she gave in, oh God, she was giving in to him! She was letting him kiss her in that wonderfully erotic way, with his mouth slightly open and his tongue touching hers. She was letting him do that, and she didn't want him to stop. She wasn't sure she could make him stop, even if she wanted him to. And he tasted so good; he felt warm and hard, his toned and taut body was still not quite touching hers, but almost. She could feel an overwhelming heat.

And once again she felt her chest tightening; he was giving her no room to breathe.

'No,' she whispered, shaking her head as he took hold of the towel covering her. She looked up into his eyes, pleading with him. Where was that strength she needed right now? Where was her handsome husband?

She gave an almost resigned sigh as she pulled her hand away, allowing him to pull off the towel, throwing it aside, his eyes immediately lowering to look at her breasts. And she wished she wasn't breathing quite as heavily, that her chest wasn't heaving quite as hard and fast as it was because that was another sign she was giving him that this was going to happen. And it wasn't. She was going to stop it. Now. She was going to stop it.

'Ryan…' she gasped, taking a sharp intake of breath as his hand cupped her breast, his thumb flicking over her nipple, which was already hard. He didn't need to do any extra work in that department.

'Do you know how many hours I've spent lately looking at those photos you did? Those naked-yet-showing-nothing pictures can give me a hard-on just thinking about them. Because I know what you're hiding. I take those pictures out and I look at them and I remember how fucking hot you really are, and I can come a dozen times from just doing that, Amber. Looking at those pictures, imagining you with those incredible legs wide open; I can come a dozen fucking times.'

Her breathing was becoming more laboured now, listening to him talk, feeling him so close to her. She hadn't let him stand this close since before Rico had been born, but she could still remember it. That night. She'd been almost nine months pregnant but, for some reason, when he'd initiated sex she hadn't pushed him away. She'd let him hold her, his hand on her bump as he'd made love to her, pushing into her from behind with a force so gentle it had almost made her cry. And despite the fact she'd felt big and tired and not in the least bit sexy, he'd made her feel like the most beautiful woman in the world that night. And that was the last time she'd let him get so close because that was the last time she hadn't thought of Jim. Was she thinking of Jim now? As Ryan's fingers continued to stroke her breasts, his mouth on hers, he kissed her so deeply it felt as though she were drowning. Was she thinking of Jim as Ryan's hand dropped lower, skimming over her hip, sliding down her thigh? Was she thinking of Jim now?

He pulled at her knickers, nudging them down just a tiny touch, leaving his thumb hooked into the side as he continued to kiss her. And the fact he was leaving them right where they were was probably the most erotic thing about this whole, wrong scenario. But it was exciting Amber way more than she wanted it to. She wanted it to stop, for him to leave her alone and walk away, yet there was another part of her that wanted him to slide his fingers so deep inside her – an ache he'd caused and one she couldn't control.

Running a hand up over his taut, tattooed arm, she was aware that he was nudging her knickers down a little bit further now, both of his hands concentrating on that task. And that's when it hit her. A cold reality. The realisation that this was wrong. That the only man she wanted to touch her like this was her husband. She wanted to feel *his* hands on her skin, *his* mouth kissing her, it was *his* body she wanted to feel inside her, not Ryan's. Coming here had been a mistake. Letting him into this house had been a mistake. He might be Rico's daddy but he was using that to do this to her, and she was letting him.

'No, Ryan.' She pulled his hands from her hips, pushing him gently away. Yes, he was hot. He was so fucking hot, and yes, he'd pushed her to the point where she'd almost given in to him, and she couldn't deny she was turned on. She could feel that ache between her legs but it wasn't for him, not really. Maybe it had started out that way, with his warm kisses and words that had caused her stomach to flip and her brain to become just a touch confused. But now she only wanted Jim. She wanted her beautiful

American man, with all his flaws and faults; she could forgive them all. She *would* forgive them all. She just wanted him here. She wanted to put all of this crap behind her now and just be his wife. Wasn't that what she'd always dreamed of? Spending her life as Jim Allen's wife?

'Amber, babe, come on!' Ryan groaned, taking a step back, watching as she pulled her knickers back up. 'I've got a hard-on from hell here.'

'You'll have to sort that out yourself. I'm sorry.'

'You're *sorry*? Are you kidding me? You're standing there, practically naked, looking red-fucking-hot with those amazing frigging tits of yours. Since you had Rico, Amber, baby, those tits, they just got sexier, and they were fucking incredible before.'

She looked at him, cocking her head slightly but making no attempt to cover herself up. Was that fair? She didn't really care any more. 'Feel free to do whatever it is you need to do to ease any of that tension, Ryan.' No. She wasn't really playing fair. But since when had life been fair? 'You're just not getting inside me.'

'Jesus Christ, you can't stand there and talk like that, Amber. You can't behave like you just did, sweetheart, and expect me to deal with it… for fuck's sake!' He threw his head back. 'We were almost fucking there!'

'Almost,' she whispered.

He looked at her, those dark-blue eyes of his verging upon sad, something Amber didn't want him to be. He deserved to be happy. 'I love you, Amber.'

She shook her head, her eyes locked on his. 'No, Ryan. You *think* you love me, but you don't. I'm just an infatuation, the older woman who just happened to tick all of your fantasy boxes.'

'We made a baby together, Amber.'

'You keep bringing that up as though it's going to make some kind of difference. It isn't. And as much as I would never, ever change the fact that Rico is here, he wasn't exactly planned, was he?'

'You wanted a baby.'

'I wanted *Jim's* baby.'

Ryan hung his head and pushed his hands back down into his pockets.

'Ryan, I'm sorry. I'm sorry, that was… that was uncalled for. And it wasn't fair, I know that, but…'

He looked back up at her, and once more she felt a pull on her heart she didn't want to feel. 'But it's the truth.'

She shook her head. 'I don't know what the truth is any more, Ryan. But… me and you, we didn't set out to start a family. Rico wasn't a mistake, I could *never* call him that because he is the most incredible thing to have ever happened to me. But me and you…'

He moved a couple of steps closer, reaching out to touch her cheek, but she turned her head slightly, causing him to drop his hand.

'Out of that mixed-up, crazy night came our little boy, Amber. All that pain, all those tears… I held you, because you were almost broken, baby. You were falling apart and I held you, and, yeah, maybe it shouldn't have happened the way it did, but we made him that night. We made our baby. And he is that link forever now. One that can never be broken. He's that link that means we will always be in each other's lives, and we just have to get used to that.'

'This isn't the way to deal with it, Ryan.'

'Maybe there are reasons why it's happening, Amber.'

'I love my husband. Are you listening to what I'm telling you? I love Jim, so, this isn't happening, and I… I don't even know why I'm here any more because every minute without him hurts. And it isn't even a pain I have to endure. I can have him. He's mine. And I don't know why I'm not with him.'

'Even after everything he's done?' Ryan said, making no attempt to move away.

'Even after everything he's done,' Amber whispered. 'I love him *that* much. I know he hurt you, and I'm sorry he did that because, for a while, it got in the way. But I can't do it. I can't walk away from him. I've tried and it just doesn't work. He's walked away from me, and it just doesn't work. Because he's all I can think about.'

'You thought about leaving him?'

She finally pulled on a t-shirt, a sign that this really was over now. 'I thought about it. Because I'm not sure he can stop himself from doing all the crappy things he does. But I'm willing to try hard to learn to trust him. I'm willing to try, because I love him that much.'

Ryan's eyes stared deep into hers. 'I could never really compete with that, could I?'

She said nothing for a second or two, trying to let her own words sink in. Because she'd been talking to herself more than anyone just then. Telling herself what it was she was really feeling. Telling herself what it was she felt she should do. 'Maybe it isn't the best thing for me – maybe *he* isn't the best thing for me, but I can't walk away. If he's out of my life I... I need him, Ryan.'

'You never used to be so weak, Amber.'

She looked down, because looking into his eyes only hurt now. 'I've always been this weak, Ryan. He just wasn't around for a long time so I hid it. I tried to pretend I was a strong, independent woman...'

'That's *exactly* what you are, Amber.'

'No.' She shook her head, blinking back the tears that had started to well up behind her eyes. 'It isn't, Ryan. *This* is the real me – someone who can't function without him. I can't think straight or focus or...'

'I can't do this any more,' Ryan said, grabbing his shirt from the bed before turning to face her. 'You want to throw your life away on him, Amber, then you do that. You do whatever the hell you feel you have to do because I will *never* understand why you feel the need...' He looked down, pushing a hand through his hair, sighing quietly before his eyes met hers one more time. 'I love you. You remember that, okay? I love you.'

She watched as he left the room, closing her eyes and leaning back against the wall, waiting until she heard the sound of the front door slamming shut before she let the tears fall.

Sinking to the floor she hugged her knees to her chest, letting everything flood out of her; the confusion, the anger, the hurt. It all came tumbling out in a mess that she just couldn't get a handle on, and she didn't know how long she'd been sitting there, crying, but it was a knock at the door that roused her out of the well of self-pity she'd seemed to have sunk into.

She blinked a few times, breathing in deeply and exhaling slowly, wiping her eyes with the back of her hand. She wasn't expecting anyone, and she wasn't really in the mood for company. So maybe if she just ignored them, whoever it was would just go away. But another loud rap on the door told her that didn't seem to be the case. So she pulled herself up, wiping her eyes again, running her fingers through her hair as she tried to compose herself.

It wasn't until she got to the bottom of the stairs that she realised she was only wearing her knickers and a t-shirt, but as another sharp knock on the door told her this person wasn't giving up, she figured she didn't really have time to run back upstairs and pull on her jeans.

'Who is it?' she asked, taking another deep breath.

'It's your husband, baby.'

She closed her eyes for a second, her heart suddenly picking up a rhythm that was making her breathless. 'Jim?'

'Open the door, Amber. Come on, honey.'

She slowly opened it, a mixture of emotions forming in her head as she saw him standing there. His dark, slightly-greying hair was pushed back off his face, there was heavier than usual stubble on his jawline and those dark-green eyes of his were staring at her.

'Are you okay?' he asked, his eyes narrowing slightly as he stepped inside, closing the door behind them.

'I'm fine. What are you doing here?' Did it matter? Isn't this what she wanted? Her handsome husband back with her?

'Come here.' He held out his hand and she took it, letting him pull her against him, their bodies almost crashing together as his arm circled her waist, holding her tight, his mouth lowering down onto hers. And in that second she was lost in him, her hand snaking its way around the back of his neck, her fingers sliding into his hair, almost pushing his head down onto her as the kiss grew deeper. He was pushing her knickers down, and she helped him by wriggling out of them and kicking them away. And as he turned her around, almost slamming her back against the wall, she closed her eyes and gave in to it all, wrapping her legs around his hips as he lifted her up, pushing into her with a beautiful pain she'd take every time. Because it was him. Her first love. Her handsome footballer. Her beautiful American man. It was him. So she'd take it. All of it.

His breathing was so heavy, so loud. Amber clung onto him, burying her fingers in his hair as he thrust in and out of her so fast it was making it difficult for her to catch her own breath. Every thrust was pushing her back against the wall, but she didn't care because he was here. They were together, and that was all that mattered.

It took just seconds for the inevitable to happen and as he came in a rush so fast and strong she couldn't help but cry out loud, that cry becoming even louder as her own climax hit just seconds later. And he held her as she shuddered in his arms, burying her face in his hair as that powerful, white-hot jolt shot through her so quickly it literally took her breath away.

She kept her legs wrapped around him as both their bodies jerked to a halt, their breathing still heavy and shallow. 'You've been crying,' he whispered, gently pulling out of her.

She looked up at him as he slowly put her down, zipping himself back up. 'I'm fine.'

He paused for a second before speaking again. 'Has he been here?'

Her eyes stayed locked on his, even though that last question had caused her heart to skip a beat, a mild panic suddenly washing over her.

'Ryan. Has he been here, Amber?'

'I… he's Rico's dad, Jim, so… so of course he's been here.'

'I wasn't talking about him being here as Rico's dad. I meant, has he been here, with you?'

She narrowed her eyes as she continued to stare at him. Why couldn't she say anything? Her silence was speaking volumes.

'You know what they're saying, don't you?' Jim went on, taking the newspaper out of his back pocket and throwing it down onto the hall table; the picture of her and Ryan out with their baby stared up at her. 'They're saying you two are growing closer. That now you and I have separated…'

'We haven't separated,' she said quietly, her eyes not leaving that photograph. They'd managed to catch her at a point when Ryan had made her smile, and maybe it could give off slightly misleading signals. But that really hadn't been the case.

'No. *I* know we haven't separated, Amber, but it would seem everybody else has their own ideas.'

'This is crazy…'

'No, what's crazy, honey, is you doing whatever the fuck it is you're doing up here, feeding all this crap to the paparazzi and journalists who know absolutely nothing about our relationship… *that's* crazy. Now tell me, Amber, has he been here?'

'Yes.' Her voice was steady. Calm, even, which surprised her. 'He's been here.'

'Jesus…' Jim turned away, pushing a hand through his hair.

'Nothing went on, Jim. He was here for Rico, that's all.'

He looked at her, his eyes serious and dark. 'So, you're telling me that he *hasn't* tried to talk you into going back to him? Never? Not once? All through your afternoon together yesterday, all the time he was here, in this house… how long was he in this house, Amber?'

'He came to see Rico.'

'Did he stay the night?'

'Jim…'

'Did he stay the night, Amber?'

'Jim, please, nothing happened…'

He threw his head back and let out the loudest of cynical laughs. 'So, the rumours are true, huh?'

'Nothing happened,' Amber repeated slowly.

'Nothing?' Jim's eyes were back on hers. 'Okay. Then I'll ask again. When he was here, he didn't once try to talk you into going back to him?'

Amber broke the stare, looking down at the ground as another wave of now-familiar guilt washed over her.

'Were you dressed like that? When he was here? All ready to give him exactly what he wanted…'

Her head shot back up. 'Nothing happened.'

'He didn't even try to kiss you?'

Once more that wave of guilt hit her, and it must have registered on her face because Jim's expression changed in an instant, his eyes once more darkening as he looked at her. 'Did he touch you?'

'Jim, please…'

'Did he touch you, Amber?' He reached out, sliding a hand up her t-shirt until his fingers reached her breast, stroking it gently. 'Did he touch you?'

And even though Amber wanted to break the stare now, she couldn't. 'I pushed him away,' she whispered. How could she stand there and lie to him? Because that's what she was doing. She was lying to him.

'You pushed him away,' Jim repeated, his hand still cupping her breast, his eyes still boring into hers. 'So, you didn't fuck him?'

She felt those tears start to well up again and she blinked them away, desperate not to cry, not now. 'No.'

'Did you want to?'

'No.' She hadn't even left a beat there before answering.

'But he wanted to fuck *you*.'

'Please, Jim, don't do this.'

He pulled his hand away, cocking his head slightly as he stared at her. 'Don't *do* this? What? Don't get angry that he touched you? Don't get upset that he got too close to you, that he saw you naked and that he wanted to fuck you? Don't get angry that you let it get that far because, let me tell you, Amber, if you hadn't wanted that – somewhere, deep down inside, if you hadn't wanted that, you would never have let him into this house.'

'He's Rico's dad.'

'You would never have let him into this house… Jesus! I can't believe this is happening all over again.'

'*Nothing* is happening, Jim. I pushed him away.'

'But you let him get so close, Amber.' His voice was a little calmer now, his eyes a little softer as they stared into hers. 'Did he kiss you?'

She stared back at him. The man she loved beyond anything else. 'Yes.'

Jim turned away again, raking both hands through his hair.

'I'm sorry,' she whispered, backing up against the wall, clasping her hands behind her back, twisting her wedding ring round and round her finger. 'I'm so sorry. This is such a mess…'

'All I ever wanted was you.' Jim turned back around, although he couldn't meet her gaze. 'That's all I ever wanted.'

'I love you, Jim.'

'Do you?' This time his eyes did meet hers. 'Do you really love me? Because, I'm just not sure that you do, Amber. Otherwise… otherwise why would you still keep running back to *him*?'

'I didn't run to him…'

'Didn't you?'

'Don't do this, Jim. Please.'

'You shouldn't have let him touch you.'

'I didn't mean it to go that far.' Her voice was quiet, nerves making it slightly shaky.

'His eyes narrowed as they bored into hers. 'I can't believe you let him touch you.'

'I was confused.'

'That excuse isn't gonna work any more, Amber. We're all fucking confused, but the one thing I can't even think of right now is running to anyone else. And the thought of him, touching you… that kills me.'

'I'm sorry.' Her voice was barely a whisper now, so quiet she wasn't even sure of what she'd said herself.

'They're gonna pull us apart, Amber, because of this. They're gonna take all that ammunition you're throwing at them and they're gonna pull us apart, and he'll jump on that…'

'They'll only pull us apart if we let them, Jim.'

He shook his head, taking a step back. 'No. We can stand here and shout from the fucking rooftops that everything is fine and we're still together and anything else that we know to be true; *we* know it's true. But they are gonna pull us apart.'

'That isn't my fault…'

'Of course it's your fucking fault, Amber! *You're* the one who, for some reason I will never understand, ran here because you couldn't get your head around something that was over. It was finished. And no harm was done.'

'No harm was done? You tried to destroy him, Jim.'

'Because he's a fucking threat, Amber.'

She stared at him, not sure he'd meant to say that out loud.

'You're coming back home, with me, do you hear? Right now. Today. You're coming back home.'

'I *am* home,' she said quietly. 'And you don't get to tell me what to do.'

'I'm your husband.' His voice was low, and he'd taken a couple of steps forward, but he wasn't going to do this to her. He wasn't going to control her. 'You're coming home, with me.'

She couldn't help but let out a small laugh. 'I'm not that infatuated teenager any more, Jim.' Wasn't she? 'I love you. Baby, I do. But you don't get to order me around like some downtrodden wife who jumps at your every word.'

'That's not what I'm…'

'You can either let the press destroy us, or we can try and prove them all wrong. But you don't get to do this to me.'

'You're coming home,' he whispered, his face close to hers now, his breath warm on her skin, but she meant what she said. He wasn't doing this to her. Yes, she wanted him, and yes, she wanted to go back home, get their lives back on track. But not this way. Not because he'd *told* her she had to.

'When I'm ready.' Her voice had regained some composure now. It was steady and it was calm, but underneath she was scared. But of what, though? Of this kicking off and turning into something that meant she lost him? Was that really going to happen?'

'This ends, Amber. Right here, right now. It ends.'

She shook her head, laughing that quiet, disbelieving laugh again.

'You're walking away from me?' he said, his voice almost incredulous, which in turn made Amber swing back around to face him.

'While you're talking to me like that, yes. I'm walking away from you.'

'Hey, honey, I'm not the one fucking around – again.'

She'd slapped him before she'd even had a chance to realise what she'd done. Her hand was stinging from the force. 'Maybe it's time you left now.'

He slowly turned his head back to face her, his hand on his cheek as he stared straight at her. 'You want to play that kind of game, Amber, then bring it on, baby.'

'I'm not doing this, Jim.' She turned to walk away again but he grabbed her wrist, swinging her around, pushing her back against the wall.

'Did you like it? When he touched you?'

'I've told you, I'm not doing this.' She pushed him away, walking into the living room, sitting down on the couch, clasping her hands together in her lap. A new confusion had swept over her now. And she had no clue what to do next.

She heard him walk into the room and she stood up, looking

over at him. His jacket was off now, his shirt sleeves were rolled up to his elbows, his dark, grey-flecked hair falling down over his eyes. She hadn't realised how much he'd let it grow over the past few months. How much sexier it made him look.

'Baby, I'm sorry. But my head is so fucked-up right now…'

She couldn't say anything to that. Hers wasn't exactly straight either.

'You let him touch you.'

'I pushed him away.'

'That doesn't matter.'

'Then what exactly are we doing here, Jim?'

He came a little closer. 'I'm not letting you go.'

'Then stop this crap and let's talk about things.'

'Are you sure he didn't fuck you?'

'Oh, Jesus. Enough, Jim! Now either get out, or we talk about this because it's… this, it's scaring me, okay? It's scaring me.'

'Losing you scares me,' he whispered, bending his head to kiss her neck, and despite herself she let him, closing her eyes as his lips ran over her skin, his hand resting on her hip.

'No.' She gently pushed him away.

'No?' He narrowed his eyes as he looked at her, pulling his hand away from her hip.

'No,' she repeated. 'Not like this. It doesn't feel right.'

'Did it feel right when *he* touched you? Huh?'

'Do you see what I mean?' Her voice was barely audible; she could see him straining to hear her. 'You need to go and come back when you've calmed down.'

'I *am* calm, Amber.'

She shook her head. 'Not like this.'

He moved closer again, and even though she tried to summon up every ounce of strength she had left inside she could do nothing to stop him from reaching out to touch her. 'I'm not throwing this away, honey. Not again. Okay, he touched you…' From out of somewhere she found that tiny bit of strength she needed to push him away again, but he was too quick for her, once more grabbing her wrist so she had no option left but to look at him. 'I need to know you love me, Amber.'

'I don't know how many more times I can tell you, Jim.'

'Maybe words aren't always enough.'

Their eyes were locked together in a stare Amber couldn't break, even though every fibre of her being was telling her this didn't feel right. He was her husband, and she loved him, no matter what he thought, she loved him, but this didn't feel right. There were too many crazy emotions flying around, and she just wasn't sure what to feel any more.

'Please, Jim.'

His mouth was back on her neck, his hands playing with the hem of her t-shirt, pushing it up higher, exposing her naked lower half, which in some almost warped way, turned Amber on, despite herself. Despite everything going on around her, she could feel that ache between her legs, that familiar tingle starting up all over again.

'We shouldn't be doing this,' she whispered, but in reality it was the only thing she wanted to do. 'We shouldn't…'

'Do you want me to stop?' His mouth was resting on hers, his breath warm against her skin.

She shook her head. 'No.' She loved him. It was as simple as that. She loved him. And nothing he could do could change that now. That's what it had come down to. All those years of loving him then trying to forget him; all those years of having him back in her life and losing him, only to realise that she couldn't live without him. It had taken over two decades of this crazy, painful cycle but it was never going to end. She could walk away, and it might feel like the right thing to do, but she knew it would never last. He was so far under her skin now, he was always going to be there. He'd stripped her down, weakened her; he'd turned her into something she hadn't wanted to be. But if being all of that meant she could be with him then she would live with that. It was him she couldn't live without.

'Lie down,' he whispered.

They should be talking. They shouldn't be doing this. What was sex going to solve? Nothing. But she still wanted it. She still wanted him.

So she did as he said. She lay down on the couch, closing her eyes as he took her hands, pushing her arms up above her head, pulling off her t-shirt. She was completely naked now, exposed; vulnerable. This man had taken over her entire life. And there was nothing she could do to change that.

She gasped quietly as he took hold of her hips, her back automatically arching in response, her hands still up above her head.

'Keep your eyes closed.' His mouth was close to her ear, his breath felt warm on her neck, his hands holding her so gently it was confusing – given his mood. And it made her slightly nervous. But still she continued to do as he said, because the greater part of her was so turned on it was crazy. How the hell had they got from arguing to this? To his hands on her skin and his mouth on her breasts. To her whole world being turned on its head all over again.

Because she was weak. But she really didn't care.

Keeping her eyes closed, she clasped her hands together above her head, gasping quietly as his mouth moved down, brushing over her hip bone, his hands gently pushing her legs apart. She felt him slide a cushion underneath her, raising her hips up slightly, and she knew what was coming next. Before he'd even touched her she'd breathed in deeply, exhaling slowly, flinching slightly when his mouth finally touched her, his hands on her inner thighs keeping her legs open. Wave after wave of pure, raw pleasure washed over her, her stomach contracting in a constant somersault because he was touching her deeply, right where she needed to be touched, Jesus, he knew exactly what to do and she couldn't help but cry out, an almost despondent groan escaping when he pulled away. And for a few seconds she felt nothing, but she knew he was still there, she could feel him.

'Keep them closed,' he whispered, his fingers intertwining with hers for a few, brief seconds, their mouths almost touching.

She breathed in deeply again, feeling him pull the cushion out from underneath her, his hands on her waist lifting her up and pulling her over so she was straddling him. She automatically wrapped her legs around him, throwing her head back as he pushed into her, and even though she wanted to look at him, she kept her eyes closed. Because he'd told her to? Not any more. She was keeping them closed because it was quickly turning into one of the most incredible experiences of her life. That rush of blood she could feel made her head spin and her heart work faster than it ever had done. What he said to her turned her on so much she didn't want to come out of this.

'Look at me, Amber.'

No. She didn't want to open her eyes. She'd already decided she didn't want to do that.

'Amber, baby, look at me. Please.'

She felt his fingers gently stroke the small of her back, which in turn sent another shiver right through her, but still she kept her eyes closed, leaning back slightly so she could feel him go deeper. She wanted him deeper. She wanted him so far inside her she couldn't even explain.

'Amber, honey, I need to look at you.'

He needed to realise *she* was in control now. He couldn't have it all his own way.

She felt his hand touch her face, his thumb stroking her cheek before he pulled her head down, his mouth resting on hers as he spoke. 'I want to look at you when you come,' he whispered. 'I want to look into your eyes and watch you, Amber. I want to see what I do to you.'

She slowly opened her eyes to look into his. 'You want to know I'm yours?'

'I want to know you're mine.'

She clenched her muscles, gripping him tightly inside her, pushing down onto him, leaning forward just a touch because that helped. It made sure that she had just the right amount of friction needed to give him what he wanted – to give *her* what she needed.

But he shook his head, pushing her back, reaching down to touch her, and the second his fingers were on her she couldn't help but gasp. It felt better to let him touch her.

His eyes were still on hers, boring deep as his fingers pressed against her, his body moving inside her, and Amber felt as though she was going to explode because the tension building up was ridiculous. She could feel it, growing, spreading through her like some erotic kind of wildfire.

His stare intensified as his fingers worked faster, their hard yet gentle motion against her, coupled with the feeling of him deep inside her was building up to a climax Amber knew was going to be a killer. Her breath was quickening, becoming almost painful as it caught in her throat, refusing to escape, her chest heaving with the pressure. So when she finally came, in a rush of something so violent, she couldn't quite get her head around it; it was the most incredible feeling. Because he was coming, too. He was spilling out inside her, flooding her body, his fingers still moving against her even though they'd done their job. But she didn't want him to stop touching her. Not yet. She didn't want this to end because the reality that waited for them, outside of the bubble they'd slipped into, scared her. So she let him take her over, let his fingers touch her and his mouth kiss her so slowly it was painfully beautiful.

She finally closed her eyes again and fell into that kiss, his arms holding her, his body still inside her. Because that's where he belonged. Inside her. He was such a huge part of her now that, without him, she was only half a person. So she didn't want this to end. Because what came afterwards was a truth she was going to have to face. Amber Sullivan was never coming back.

Chapter Twenty-Eight

Max sat forward, pushing both hands through his hair before flinging himself back against his chair, swinging it around so he could look out onto a busy Covent Garden. Everybody was getting on with their lives while he was in the process of changing someone's. And they didn't even know about it.

He pushed his chair back and stood up, sticking his hands in his pockets as he walked over to the other side of his office. The wall housed photographs of many of his famous clients, most of them footballers. Famous footballers. Ridiculously wealthy footballers. Men who lived inside a world very few would ever experience; a world of ridiculous excess and ludicrous pay cheques, which enabled them to have anything they wanted. Anything. Except happiness. Money couldn't buy you that.

And then there was Amber. His slightly left-of-centre client, because she was still the only person on his books who wasn't a footballer. He looked up at a picture of her with her long, dark-red hair hanging loosely over her shoulders, and those pale-blue eyes of hers staring straight into the camera. He knew she had absolutely no idea of how beautiful she really was. How dangerous she'd become.

His eyes moved to the picture beside her. A photograph of Ryan Fisher in his Newcastle Red Star kit, a cocky smile on his handsome face. He was one good-looking kid, that was for sure. But between the two of them, Amber Sullivan and Ryan Fisher had made one hell of a mess of their lives. And not just theirs. Because everything they'd done hadn't just affected them. There'd been a snowball effect even Max had been powerless to stop. But he had the chance to stop it now; to put an end to the damage those two could cause, without even realising it. He just wished it didn't have to be the way it was. But it really was the only option left, no matter how hard he'd tried to fight it. And he had tried. He really had.

Bowing his head for a second he took in a sharp intake of breath. He loved that young man like a son, and to see what he'd been through – to have saved him from crap that could have ended his career; crap that could have ended his life, it was tough to think of what was going on. He was a dad now. That arrogant, self-assured, unpredictable man was a dad now. And just the thought of what might have to happen… But something needed to give, before more people got hurt. That's why Max was doing this. And that's what he had to keep telling himself.

Walking back over to his desk he picked up the phone and punched in a familiar number, waiting just a couple of seconds before it was answered.

'It's all sorted. But now the real work begins.'

*

Amber flung open the shutters and peered outside. It was another beautiful day on the island of Majorca, and from her villa, which was just a five-minute walk from the sea front, she could see the marina and sea so blue she didn't think there was a colour to describe it.

'Maybe we'll go for a walk later, baby, huh?' She turned around and smiled at her eight-and-a-half-month-old son, wondering where the time had gone. He could sit up now; he could crawl so fast she couldn't keep up with him sometimes, and the day he'd said 'mama' Amber had cried for almost half an hour. Her beautiful boy. She loved him so much she couldn't even describe how it felt when she looked at him.

She watched as he looked up at her, smiling a smile so like his daddy's it made her gasp. He was so much like Ryan it was unbelievable. He didn't seem to have a great deal of her in him, although her dad said the dark hair and his perfect little nose was a sign of his slight Mediterranean heritage. Amber just thought he was being nice, because she really couldn't see any of her in Rico at all. He was a mini Ryan; a baby version of the man she'd messed around so much. It hurt to think about what she and Jim done to him because she wanted Ryan to be happy. She just wanted him to stop living in some kind of fantasy world, where he still thought there was a chance she'd go back to him, because she wouldn't. That was never going to happen.

She smiled as she watched Rico fall forward and start to crawl towards her, and she crouched down, holding her arms out to him as he picked up speed, almost racing towards her, gurgling away and smiling his smile.

'Hey, I've got you, little man,' she laughed, scooping him up and spinning him around because that always made him laugh, and his laugh was a sound she never tired of hearing. It was a beautiful sound that rang around the space it filled and made her heart jump with happiness. 'Let's go outside, huh? Shall we go and get some fresh air?'

He looked at her, still smiling his smile, reaching out to gently tug at her hair before he leaned forward to plant a kiss on her mouth.

'I love you so much,' she whispered, hugging him against her, gently rubbing his back as he snuggled into her. 'So, so much. You always remember that, you hear me? Even when you're all grown up and don't want my hugs any more, you always remember how much your mummy loves you.'

She kissed the top of his head, taking his tiny hand in hers as they walked outside onto the terrace, the brilliant sunshine hitting them head-on. It was warm, but not overly hot, as it was still only May. But it was warm enough to sunbathe, and that's exactly what Amber intended to do later on, when Rico had his nap. She was going to lie by the pool and do nothing.

She'd taken Rico to see some of his Spanish relatives yesterday, over in Sant Elm, and even though they'd insisted she and Rico stay with them, she wanted some time alone. It was something she'd tried to find before but that hadn't exactly turned out well. So it was nice to have a second chance to spend a little bit of mummy-and-baby time with her boy.

She walked across the terrace, balancing Rico on her hip, her eyes taking in the beautiful view in front of her – that azure sea, and the almost cloudless blue sky. She'd had so much time to think here, and whilst at first she'd been worried that that time may have made her realise things she didn't want to face up to, it had actually done the opposite. Being away from Jim still hurt. She missed him with a burning pain every day when she woke up and he wasn't there beside her. But he was busy; he couldn't be with her. With just a handful of games left until the end of the football season, Endleigh United needed just one more win to guarantee them the League title, so he had other things to do. But she missed him. Even when he wasn't with her, he took over every inch of her being; invaded every corner of her soul. She was his for the rest of her life. A beautiful prison she could never break free from.

'Dada,' Rico gurgled, looking over Amber's shoulder, resting his chin on it as he clung onto her.

'Daddy's very busy right now, baby.' She rubbed his back again, kissing his cheek. His daddy *was* busy, she hadn't lied there. With Newcastle Red Star not doing as well as they had done when Jim had been in charge, Ryan had become an integral part of their strike force in a bid to win those games needed to keep them out of the bottom half of the league table. He was still stripped of the captaincy, still being punished for what he'd almost got himself into in the past, but he was back on the team now, and they needed him at his best.

'Dada.' Rico repeated, squirming in Amber's arms as he tried to look at her.

'Do you miss your daddy?' she asked, stroking his dark hair, his eyes now concentrating on the toy rabbit he was holding.

'Do you?'

She swung around, her heart almost stopping as she saw Ronnie standing there.

'Jesus, Ronnie! You were supposed to call me when you landed at the airport. I was going to come and pick you up.'

'Well, I thought I'd save you the job, seeing as it's early. You should be careful, though, leaving your door open like that. Anyone could walk in.'

'Anyone just did,' she said, a half-smile on her face. 'And the answer to your question is *no*.'

'What question's that?'

She just looked at him, raising an eyebrow. 'Look who's come to irritate us, baby. Your Uncle Ronnie.'

'Give him here. Come on, kiddo. Come give your old uncle a big hug, because I doubt your mum's got one for me.'

'You thought right. There you go, little man.' She handed Rico over and walked back into the house, leaving the huge French doors open to let the air in.

'We need to talk, Amber,' Ronnie said, following her inside.

'Do we?'

'Why else do you think I'm here?'

'I don't know, Ronnie. I don't know *why* you're here.'

'Your mum is so stubborn, she really is,' Ronnie sighed, smiling at his godson.

Amber ignored that and concentrated on making some fresh coffee.

'Red Star won their match last night,' he went on. 'Ryan scored both goals.'

'Yes, I know. I can get British TV over here.'

'You watched the game?'

'The last half hour.'

'Any reason why?'

She fixed him with a look, because she knew what he was trying to do. 'I work for Cloud Sports, Ronnie. It's my job to watch football.'

'Not when you're on holiday.'

'It's not really a holiday.'

'Isn't it?'

'I wouldn't normally take a holiday this close to the end of the football season, would I?'

'So, what are *you* calling it?'

'I wanted Rico to meet his Mallorcan relatives. My uncle is very ill. They don't know how long he has left, and I wanted him to see the baby. They're very family-orientated here.'

Ronnie just looked at her. 'They must be really confused with *your* situation, then.'

Amber narrowed her eyes. 'And what's that supposed to mean?'

'Well, you're not with Rico's dad – not that I'm aware of, anyway…'

She walked over to him, taking Rico from him. 'If that's all you've come here to do, Ronnie, I'd rather you left.'

'Okay, I'm sorry. I'm sorry.'

'Are you?'

'Yes. Jesus, Amber, I just worry about you, that's all.'

'We've been over this. So many times my brain hurts. I'm with Jim, whether people agree with our relationship or not, I'm staying with Jim.' She looked at her friend, her voice quiet, almost a whisper. 'He's my forever man, Ronnie. My forever man. Deal with it.'

He stuffed his hands in his pockets and leaned back against the counter. 'Things seem to have settled down with you two over the past few weeks anyway.'

'Things are fine, thank you. He's working hard, and he deserves all the praise he's getting for taking Endleigh from mid-table to possible League champions.'

'He's a great manager. Nobody's denying that.'

Amber threw him another look. 'We're going for a walk along the beach. Are you coming with us?'

He smiled at her, pushing a hand through his hair. 'Yeah. Of course I'm coming with you.'

*

Jim leaned back against the huge floor-to-ceiling windows in Max's office, looking around the vast space in front of him.

'This is some place you've got here, Max. I thought my office at Parkfield was big, but this is something else.'

'Sometimes I think it's a little over the top, but…' Max shrugged, sitting down on the edge of his desk. 'This is me.'

Jim smiled, looking down briefly, shoving his hands in his pockets. 'I can't thank you enough, by the way.' He looked up at Max, a genuine expression of gratitude on his face. 'For doing this.'

'Nothing's definite yet, Jim. There are still a number of hurdles to get over.'

'His contract's up at the end of the season. All you have to do is make sure Newcastle Red Star don't offer him a new one. Make sure his choices are limited. That's all we need to do.'

'For a man who's been in this game for as long as you have, Jim, you're coming across as extremely naïve.'

'I'm desperate, Max.'

'You've seen how Red Star's season has panned out since you left. They've gone from a club to be reckoned with, down to mid-table mediocre. Now, I know that isn't *just* due to your leaving – but it was the catalyst for all the unrest and uncertainty, wasn't it? What happened with Ryan…?'

Jim looked down again, scuffing the heel of his shoe on the skirting board in an almost nervous manner. 'I really am sorry for that, Max.'

'Yeah,' Max sighed, clasping his hands together in his lap. 'I know you are. But it didn't help, did it? Getting Ryan banned, all the changes Red Star had to make in his absence. And then look what happens the second he comes back to the first team – they're winning matches again. Convincingly. And I've never been a great believer that one player can make a team but where Ryan Fisher's concerned I'm beginning to think that's true. In his case. Trying to convince Dave French and the Board of Directors not to renew his contract is going to be a tough job. You know their Chief Executive as well as I do, Jim, and he's a tough nut to crack in terms of trying to get him to do something he doesn't agree with. And there's the other thing we have to contend with – the fact that Ryan can just walk at the end of this season. His contract's up, he's under no obligation to anyone, and, quite frankly, if he's still got his heart set on moving back down south, both you and I know there are clubs desperate to sign him. Whatever he's done in the past, however unpredictable he may once have been, Ryan Fisher is still one hell of a player, and he could walk straight into any club he chose. He's that good.'

Jim fixed Max with a look. 'Then you'll just have to make sure he chooses the right club, aren't you?'

'I can only do so much, Jim. I've put the ground work in, put those feelers out and talked to the people who matter, and they want him. They do. They want him. But persuading *him*… Does it really have to be this way?'

'You care about him, right? I mean, you've been with him through so much, and you care about him.'

'I love the kid, if I'm being honest. He's like the son I never had. But I also care about Amber…'

'Let me worry about Amber.'

'If she finds out what you're doing…'

'I said, let me worry about Amber.'

'*She* still cares about him, too, Jim. And you fighting it like this, isn't it only going to make things worse? In the long run?'

Jim said nothing for a beat or two, his eyes back down on the floor. 'You want what's best for him, don't you?'

'Yes,' Max sighed, standing up and walking back over to his wall of photographs. 'Of course I want what's best for him. But this…' He turned around, his eyes fixed on Jim, who was still staring down at the floor. 'This feels wrong. I'm his agent, and I don't think this is in his best interests.'

Jim's head shot up, his eyes burning into Max's. 'I won't lose her to him, Max. Not again. Too much has gone on, and I'm not strong enough to go through it all again.'

'You really need to stop being so paranoid. Amber isn't going anywhere.'

'Maybe not. But the longer he's around, the more chance there is that he can do more damage.'

'He's not the one causing the damage here, Jim.'

'The longer he's around, the more chance there is of him getting back under her skin. He's the father of her baby and I can't compete with that bond.'

Max leaned back against the wall, watching as Jim walked over, his eyes going straight to the photo of Amber.

'I fell in love with her a long time ago, Max. And all those years I tried to deny those feelings I had for her… all those years I wasted. I can't do that again.'

'But you're skating on such thin ice here, Jim. What you're trying to do is immoral, and in a way it's cruel.'

He didn't move his eyes away from the photograph. 'And I'm sorry. But this woman here, I can't risk losing her.'

'This is crazy. I don't even know why I agreed to get involved with this.'

This time Jim directed his gaze straight at Max. 'You know it's for the best, Max. He won't stop, because he's tried… he's tried…'

Max frowned. 'He's tried, what?'

'She nearly gave in to him.' Jim's voice was quiet as his eyes turned back to the photo of Amber. 'She nearly slept with him, and just thinking of him that close to her again…'

'When? Jim, when did this happen?'

'When she spent those few days up in Newcastle a little while ago. And she knew, going back up there – she knew what would happen. And I honestly believe that's *why* she went back there. Because she knew what would happen.' He turned and walked back over to the window, looking out at a crowded Covent Garden. 'And if you let him sign for a London club then it'll happen again, and again. It's not that I don't trust her, Max, it's just…' He turned around, leaning back, his hands back in his pockets. 'I just can't risk it.'

'She won't go back to him, Jim.'

'Well, then we have the other problem, don't we?'

'Other problem?' Max asked, frowning again.

'She rejects him, she tells him *no*, but she lets it all happen first, because that's a possibility. Whether you choose to believe that or not, it's a possibility. Because he gets to her, Max, and of course she still has feelings for him. He's the father of her baby. He is never gonna be out of her life, whether I like it or not…'

'What other problem, Jim?'

'If he won't give up on her; if he continues to pursue her in some vain hope that one day she'll fall completely, who's to say what might happen? And if he chooses to go down that route he's chosen before, the route that enables him to push things aside and forget all the shit that's going on… if he chooses to go back to his old ways when she rejects him, that could destroy him. Really destroy him. And as much as I would once have loved to see that happen, I don't think he deserves that. He's a talent. He's a great player. One of the best of his generation. But if he stays here…'

'You're assuming so much, Jim.'

Jim held Max's gaze. 'Are you saying you don't agree with me?'

'I'm not saying…' Max sighed, closing his eyes for a second, wondering how the hell he'd got himself into this.

'Why did you really get involved when I asked you to help me, Max?'

Max opened his eyes and looked at Jim. 'Because every word you've said, in some warped and surreal way – every word you've said makes sense.'

'Then all that's left for you to do is persuade *him* it makes sense, too.'

*

'So, when are you going back home?' Ronnie asked, gently rocking Rico's pushchair with his foot.

'In a few days. It's nice, being here, away from it all for a little while.'

Ronnie raised an eyebrow. 'Away from it all?'

'You have an ability to read anything into a perfectly innocent comment, do you know that?'

'You don't miss the old man, then? Old being the operative word, too. How old is he now?'

'I'm not getting into this.'

'Fifty years old, and he doesn't look a day over forty… he's such a lucky fucking bastard.'

Amber ignored him, her eyes going to Rico instead, but he was asleep now, shaded from the sunshine, his arms wrapped around his tiny toy rabbit.

'We're thinking of having a big party sometime over the summer. Maybe around my birthday. We never had any kind of wedding celebration after we got back from Vegas, and my dad wants to do something.'

'A wedding reception, huh?'

'If that's what you want to call it. Jim and I are even talking about renewing our vows in church, back up in Newcastle. I think my dad really wants to do the traditional thing, you know? The whole giving-me-away thing, the father-of-the-bride speech, you know how it is.'

'Well, to be fair to Freddie, you have kind of taken all that away from him, haven't you? Twice.'

'And he can have it all if we decide to go ahead with the service and the reception.'

'What's stopping you?'

'Nothing.'

'You sure?'

'You're doing it again.'

'What?'

'Reading something into a perfectly innocent comment.'

'Well, it's just that, if you really love Jim as much as you say you do, why even hesitate at the chance to marry him all over again? I would have thought you'd have been on it so fast you wouldn't stop to take a breath.'

'There's a lot going on right now, that's all.'

'Like what? He's only got to win one more game and he's won another League title, and, let's face it, the bookies have stopped taking bets on Endleigh United becoming champions because it's almost a forgone conclusion. And, I'm guessing here, but I suspect Jim would quite like to get you back up that aisle before the champagne's gone flat from the league-winning celebrations, just to make sure you don't wander off anywhere again. So, that just leaves you, Amber. What's your reason for stalling, huh?'

'You know, I'm really tired of this, Ronnie.'

He leaned forward, folding his arms on the table in front of him. 'Look me in the eye and tell me you don't still feel something for Ryan.'

'Of course I still feel something for him. He's Rico's daddy...'

'Forget all that daddy crap. I'm not talking about the feelings you have for him as that baby's father. That goes without saying.

I'm talking about the feelings you still have for him as a man you once had a relationship with.'

'Past tense. You've just used it. I once *had* a relationship with him. It's over now.'

'Really?' He raised a questioning eyebrow, and Amber looked down, watching her fingers as they fiddled with her wedding ring.

'Really,' she whispered, twisting the ring round and round her finger.

'You might want to stop doing that, then.'

She looked up, her eyes meeting Ronnie's. 'What?'

'Twisting that ring round and round like that. It could give off the wrong signal.'

She pulled her hand away as if it were on fire. 'We should be getting back. Rico needs his nap.'

'He looks like he's napping just fine there to me.'

'I'm tired, Ronnie. I want to go back to the villa and just lie by the pool, listen to some music…'

'Shut out my nagging.'

She looked at him, smiling slightly. 'Yeah. Exactly.'

'Okay,' he sighed, standing up and flicking the brake off Rico's pushchair. 'Sounds like a plan to me. I've got a few hours yet before I have to head back to London.'

'What time's your flight?'

'Not until eight-thirty tonight. I would have stayed another day but they need me to cover *Scoreline* tomorrow, seeing as you're here. I'm kind of guessing they'd prefer to have you back on board, though. You're far prettier, and I'm sure the viewing figures go up when you wear that yellow dress and those pink heels.'

'You need to stop hanging around with Kevin when you're back up north. His sexism is starting to rub off on you.'

He smiled at her, reaching out to take her hand, giving it a quick squeeze. 'I don't want our relationship to be like this, Amber. I want us to be close again. Like we used to be. This tension, I hate it. I want my girl back. I want my best friend.'

'And you know what you have to do, Ronnie. Just deal with the fact me and Jim – we're together. And that isn't going to change. No matter what happens.'

*

'Can I have a word, Ryan?'

'What are *you* doing up here?' Ryan asked, surprised to find his agent standing there, unannounced, on his doorstep.

'I need to talk to you.'

'That sounds ominous. What have I done now?'

'Nothing. Not unless there's something you've omitted to tell me.'

'Jesus, wipe that look off your face, will you? You could try trusting me, for once.'

'Can I come in?'

'Oh, yeah, sorry.' Ryan stood aside to let Max through, closing the door behind him. 'Amber's okay, isn't she?'

'Amber's fine, as far as I know. Would have thought you'd know more about that than me.'

'Haven't spoken to her for a couple of days.' Ryan followed Max into the kitchen, leaning back against the counter, his hands in his pockets. 'She did send me a picture of Rico yesterday, though. With some of his Spanish family. I love that kid so fucking much, Max. And when I see him with her…'

Max watched as Ryan trailed off, his eyes lowering to stare at the floor. 'You okay?'

Ryan looked up. 'I'm fine. You want something to drink?'

'Coffee would be good.'

He turned to grab the jar of coffee from the shelf, spooning some out into the machine, switching it on and turning back to face his agent. 'What's up, Max? It's quite obvious now that you haven't come all the way up here to bollock me, which is good, because I've actually been a very good boy lately. So, you gonna

370

tell me why you are here?'

'There's nothing wrong, Ryan. It's just that, with the end of the season looming, I thought it was time to talk about what happens next.'

'What happens next?'

'Your contract's up at the end of the season, so, we need to start thinking about what's best for you now. What the next step is.'

Ryan frowned, folding his arms as he looked at Max. 'We know what my next step is. We've already talked about this. Now the latest round of crap is behind me, I'm looking for a London club.'

'That's what you want?'

'Yeah, that's what I want, what's the matter with you? You know all this, Max. I owe Newcastle Red Star a hell of a lot, and I'll be forever grateful to them for the help they've given me and the trust they've put in me. I'm sure a lot of clubs would have just washed their hands of me by now. But I want to be near my son. I want to be near Rico. So, if they *do* offer me a new contract, I won't be taking it. You got that?'

Max nodded. This kid really had grown up. Could what Max was about to do set him back, rather than make things better?

'You've been putting feelers out, right?' Ryan asked, his voice breaking into Max's thoughts.

'Sorry, what?'

'London clubs. You've been seeing what's out there, who's interested. Haven't you?'

'Oh, yeah. Yeah. I've been working on something.'

Ryan's frown deepened. 'Working on something? What's *that* mean?'

Max turned his head to look out of the window, taking a brief second to gather his thoughts. 'There's an opportunity, Ryan. For a player like you.' He finally turned back to face Ryan. 'More money than you could ever imagine, a relocation package that is out of this world...'

'A London club?'

Max briefly looked down, taking a deep breath before he faced Ryan again. 'L.A.'

Ryan said nothing for a few seconds. He just stared at his agent as though he were trying to work out whether he was joking or not. 'I'm… sorry. L.A.?'

'The American game is growing bigger every year, Ryan. Some of their teams are attracting world-class players, some real big names – you could be a star over there.'

'I'm a frigging star over here, Max, why the hell would I want to go to fucking L.A.?'

'Okay, listen… just, hear me out. Hear me out.'

Ryan pushed a hand through his hair. 'London clubs, Max. I asked you to look at *London* clubs who were interested in me, so why would you even think about L.A.?'

Max took another deep breath, trying to stay composed. The last thing he needed was for Ryan to think *he* was as unsure of this whole situation as his young player was. 'If you move to London, Ryan, this… this dangerous cycle of you and Amber…'

'Whoa, okay. Hold it right there. You don't think I should move to London because you think I'm just going to spend all my time pursuing my ex-girlfriend?'

'Well, no, that isn't what I was going to say, but…'

'But it's what you mean?'

'You're still in love with her, Ryan. And don't stand there and tell me you aren't, because I can see it. Every time I look at you I see it.'

'It isn't a fucking crime to love somebody, Max. And this has got nothing to do with which club I move to next…'

'It's got *everything* to do with it, Ryan. And you know that.'

'No, hang on. Because you seem to think I'm still hell-bent on getting Amber back, your professional opinion is that I should move halfway across the frigging world?'

'It's not my professional opinion, Ryan. My professional opinion is that you are a world-class player, and staying in the UK isn't going to hurt your career at all.'

Ryan stared at him, his eyes wide and questioning.

'I've been with you for so long, kiddo. I've been with you through some incredible highs and some devastating lows. And I just don't want anything to put your career at risk again.'

'And, you think if I'm too close to Amber that's gonna happen, is that it? You… you can't trust me to just get on with it, to forget all that.'

'*Can* you forget all that, Ryan?' Max stared back, his eyes asking their own set of questions. 'Can you live near her and not want what you once had? Can you honestly stand there and tell me you can cope with seeing her and Jim Allen together all the time? Believe me, Ryan, they are one hot couple right now. Everyone wants to know them, everyone wants to talk to them, and you are gonna be seeing them everywhere. Everywhere, Ryan. Can you honestly cope with that?'

Ryan said nothing for a beat or two. 'I need to be near my son, Max.'

'Can you cut yourself off from his mum?'

Ryan broke the stare, turning his head away, raking a hand through his hair.

'Ryan?'

'I don't know, Max.' His voice was quiet, almost a whisper.

'A "don't know" isn't good enough, son.'

Ryan turned back to face his agent, confusion sweeping over him so fast he felt dizzy. 'It's all I have.' But there was one thing that was clear in his mind now. This game wasn't over. He could still win it. He could. Because, if there was one thing Ryan Fisher didn't do, it was give up without a fight. So this game, it really wasn't over.

Chapter Twenty-Nine

'Where are *you* going?' Debbie asked, shielding her eyes from the sun as she closed her car door and walked over towards Ryan's house.

'Majorca,' Ryan replied, throwing a holdall into the back of a taxi. 'Managed to get a late-afternoon flight.'

'Erm, does Dave French know you're popping off to the Balearics for an impromptu holiday?'

'What's he gonna do, Debbie? Sack me? My contract's up in a couple of weeks. And it isn't a holiday.'

Debbie leaned back against Ryan's black Jaguar, watching as he said something to the taxi driver. 'Does Amber know you're on your way?'

'No.'

'Shouldn't you tell her?'

'She'll find out in a couple of hours, won't she? Have you got her address over there?'

'You don't know where she's staying?'

'I know she's in Palma Nova.'

'Then maybe you should call her. Find out exactly where she's staying.'

'Jesus, Debbie, come on. Just give me her address, okay? I need to get to the airport.'

Debbie's eyes narrowed as she looked at him. 'Why are you going over there, Ryan?'

'My son's over there, Debbie.'

'She's bringing him home in a couple of days.'

'Yeah, and home to her is London now.'

'Newcastle Red Star's next match is in London. At the weekend. You'll be seeing Rico then, surely.'

'Have you got her address, Debbie? Please. This is really important.'

Debbie continued to stare him out for a few more seconds, folding her arms and cocking her head slightly. 'She's married, Ryan.'

'So people keep telling me.'

'Please tell me you're not going over there to mess with her head because she is happy now. She's happy.'

'I'll ask Max,' he said, opening the taxi door. 'He'll know where she's staying.'

'Where's *he* off to?' Gary asked, joining Debbie on Ryan's driveway.

'Majorca,' Debbie replied, taking out her phone.

'Majorca? Ryan, what the fuck are you doing? Does the boss know…?'

Debbie looked at Gary, shaking her head.

'He's gonna go frigging ballistic, mate, you know that, don't you?'

'Yeah, he knows,' Debbie sighed, handing her phone over to Ryan. 'Here. That's where she's staying. A little villa near the marina.'

Ryan took the phone, scribbling down the address on the back of a card he pulled out of his pocket. 'Thanks.'

'I'm not even getting involved…' Gary said, turning and walking back towards his own house.

'You won't tell her, will you?' Ryan asked, his eyes almost pleading with Debbie.

'I should.'

'Debbie, please.'

'What are you playing at, Ryan? I thought this was all over. Can't you just accept that she's made her choice? And that choice is Jim.'

Ryan shook his head, shoving the card back in his pocket. 'I'll see you in a day or so.'

'Ryan!'

But it was too late. He'd already closed the taxi door. His mind was made up. And nobody was going to stop him.

*

'Please tell me you're naked.'

'I can *tell* you I'm naked, but it wouldn't entirely be the truth.'

'Just humour me, Amber, I'm dying here.'

'You haven't had sex for a few days, Jim, it's hardly a matter of life and death. Surely a couple of days' rest wouldn't do a man of your age any harm.'

'Oh, that's right. Make me feel good about myself, go on.'

Amber laughed quietly down the phone, sitting back on the couch that faced the huge French doors in her rented villa; doors that looked out onto that stunning view of the sea and the marina. The sun was just beginning to set and the colours it was giving off were nothing short of beautiful. 'I wish you were here,' she whispered, and she meant it. She wished he were there more than anything. This time away had been welcomed, and she'd enjoyed it. But missing him was becoming too much now. Her ache was becoming a physical pain. All she could think about were his kisses and his arms holding her; all she could think about was the sex they'd have the second she was through their front door.

'I wish I was there, too, baby.'

She smiled, sliding a hand up her dress. 'Do you *want* me to get naked?'

She felt a small wave of excitement wash over her as he groaned down the line. 'Take your panties off.'

She felt that excitement rise as she hooked her fingers into the sides of her knickers, slowly sliding them off. 'Done. Now what?'

'Jesus, Amber… haven't you got Skype over there? Get yourself in front of a computer, honey, and open those legs for your husband because he really is dying here.'

'No Skype, darling. You're just going to have to use your imagination. Now, what do you want me to do next?'

'Touch yourself.'

'Already doing it.'

'I can't do this… baby, I need you so badly right now.'

'You know what you need to do, then, don't you?'

'You're leaving me no choice, beautiful…'

'I'm still touching myself.'

'Are you wet?'

'Soaking.'

Another groan down the line, and Amber smiled to herself.

'Put your fingers inside, Amber.'

She closed her eyes as she slowly slid her fingers inside herself, opening her legs wider. 'I'm putting you on speaker phone,' she said, laying her phone down on the couch beside her. 'I need two hands for this.'

'Amber, honey, I am so close…'

She threw her head back, biting down on her lip as her fingers pushed deeper, her other hand stroking the part of her that was crying out to be touched, and she moaned quietly, for his benefit more than anything, as she felt that all-familiar wave start to wash over her. 'I'm coming, too, baby,' she breathed, rubbing faster, pushing harder, digging deeper, her legs open as wide as they could go, and as that wave finally finished its journey, as her self-inflicted climax hit her like a shock to the system, she cried out his name, pushing down to make sure she felt every second, every tingle.

'Jesus-fucking-Christ,' he groaned, and she could hear how out of breath he was, which sent a shiver right through her, as she pictured what he'd just done. She wished she'd been there to see it. 'What the hell did we just do?'

'Phone sex.' She smiled, pulling her fingers out of herself and closing her legs, enjoying the final few seconds of a lingering tingle. 'And I needed that like you wouldn't believe.'

'I love you so much,' Jim said, his voice finally starting to return to normal. His wonderful, low, deep voice, with that undeniably sexy accent had won her over all those years ago, and it was still doing the same to her now.

'I love you, too,' she whispered, wriggling back into her knickers. 'And I miss you like crazy. I can't wait to come home.'

'Then we get to do what we just did then for real, right?'

'The thought of that happening is the only thing getting me through these last couple of days.'

Another groan, and Amber smiled again, her hand absent-mindedly touching her breasts. Oh, God, she wasn't going to go for this again, was she?

'You hold that thought, honey. You hear me?'

'I hear you, handsome. Good luck for the game tomorrow.'

'You'll be watching?'

'I get to see you if I do, don't I? Goodnight, baby.'

'Goodnight, beautiful.'

She ended the call, looking down at the phone for a few seconds, as though staring at it would suddenly make him materialise.

'I need a drink,' she sighed, hauling herself up from the couch and heading over to the kitchen. She washed her hands, then found the last of the cava she and Ronnie had opened yesterday, pouring herself a glass. She hoped the bubbles would go straight to her head, because she always liked that feeling. That slightly woozy but not-quite-drunk sensation that anything with bubbles caused her to feel.

Taking another quick sip she put her glass down and walked out into the hall, gently pushing open the door of the nursery. Rico was asleep, curled up on his side, his little cuddly rabbit snuggled in beside him. She smiled, walking over to his cot, pulling the blanket he'd obviously kicked off back over him.

'Sweet dreams, baby boy.'

A knock at the door made her jump, and she quickly left the nursery, closing the door behind her. She had no idea who it could be; she didn't know anyone around here. Her family were a good few miles away from Palma Nova, and they'd call her first if something was wrong.

She walked over to the door, putting a hand on it but making no attempt to open it. 'Who is it?'

'Amber, it's Ryan.'

'Ryan?' She flung open the door. There he stood, bold as brass and twice as sexy. His dark hair was pushed back off his face, which carried that heavy stubble he always liked to sport – he'd let it grow back to verging on the point of a beard length again, and she couldn't help but think how hot it made him look, along with those tattoos that she still found incredibly sexy. Despite herself. 'What are you doing here?'

'Can I come in?'

'What are you doing here?'

'Are you gonna keep asking that?'

'Until you give me an answer, yes.'

'I came to see Rico.'

She raised a sceptical eyebrow, folding her arms. 'Does Dave French know you've absconded?'

'I haven't "absconded."'

'Does he know you're here?'

'Well, he probably does by now.'

Amber threw her head back and sighed. 'Ryan! What about Max?'

'What about him? Look, Amber, it's really nice out here and everything, but, can I come in, babe?'

She stood aside, letting him through, closing the door behind her. 'Does Max know you're here?'

'I didn't tell him I was coming, no. But then, I didn't know I was coming myself until last night.'

Amber narrowed her eyes, her arms still folded. 'Why? What happened last night?'

'Amber, baby, can I just see Rico and grab a drink first before we get into anything? I could murder a beer.'

'There's some in the fridge. And Rico's in the nursery, but he's asleep. So don't pick him up, okay? He's slept all through the night since we've been here, and I'd quite like to keep it that way.'

She waited until he'd gone into the nursery before she walked back into the kitchen, grabbing him a beer, and one for herself. She had a feeling she was going to need it.

She took a sip, looking back out at the rapidly darkening view in front of her. The lights of the marina were starting to twinkle in the distance, the sound of crickets becoming louder now that the sun was fast disappearing. It was peaceful. It was beautiful. But she had the wrong man here with her. The man she wanted to share all this with was back home.

'Has he been okay? In the heat, I mean.'

She turned around to see Ryan walk into the room. 'He's been fine. He's been getting loads of attention, everywhere he goes. And not just from his family here. Everybody loves him. And, he's been asking for you.'

Ryan's face broke into a huge grin. 'He said "dada?"'

'He said "dada."' Amber smiled.

'Shit! Who'd have thought a couple of years ago that something like this would make me the happiest frigging man on earth?' He looked at her, their eyes locking together. 'We did good, huh?'

She broke the stare, looking down at the white-tiled floor. 'He's our beautiful little man, so, yeah.' She raised her head to meet his gaze. 'We did good.'

'Amber…'

'I've got you a beer. Come and look at the view from outside, come on.'

He picked up his beer and followed her out onto the terrace. 'My contract with Newcastle Red Star – it's up at the end of the season, you know that, right?' He sat down beside her on a huge wicker couch covered in deep-red cushions.

'It's my job to know these things, Ryan.'

'Max wants me to join L.A. Gamers.'

Amber looked at him, her head turning so fast she'd made herself dizzy. 'L.A. Gamers? I don't… why would he want you to move to Los Angeles?'

'He says it's an amazing opportunity. The Gamers is one of the biggest and best clubs over there; it attracts the biggest names, it gets some of the largest crowds. They average gates of over fifty thousand a match, Amber. That's more than most top-flight clubs over here in the UK attract, even during the biggest, most important games. They… they're offering me this relocation package I can't even begin to get my head around, and the money I could make out there in sponsorship deals alone, before we even start to talk about the wages…'

'Why would he want you to move to Los Angeles, Ryan?'

Her eyes weren't leaving his now, they were staring at him, asking him a question he was going to answer for her. Because he had to.

'He thinks if I… he thinks if I move to a London club, if I stay in the UK – he thinks I'm going to lose my focus.'

'Lose your…?' She frowned, confusion sweeping across her beautiful face.

'I'm in love with you, Amber. I'm head-over-heels, ridiculously in love with you and he's right. Max is right. If I stay in the UK – if I move down to London, I'm not gonna leave you alone. I'm not. Because I can't be around you and not want you. I can't watch you with Jim and not want to *be* him. I can't do that. So Max is right. Maybe a brand-new start, well away from all that – maybe that's exactly what I need.'

'But… Ryan, you've… you've tried that before. You went to CD Adeje…'

'That was on loan, Amber. I always knew I was coming back home, but this time – this time it'd be permanent.'

'I… Jesus! This is a shock, I… what about Rico?'

Ryan bowed his head, closing his eyes for a brief second. 'It's gonna kill me, being away from him for so long. It's gonna fucking kill me, because I love him so frigging much, Amber…' He looked at her, and Amber felt her heart ache as she saw the tears in his eyes. 'I love him. And I love *you*.'

'Ryan, I… Are you going?' she whispered, trying to get her head around everything he was telling her, because she was finding this really hard to understand.

'I don't know.'

'This is crazy…'

'Come with me.'

Her head shot up again, her eyes instantly meeting his. 'Come *with* you?'

'We could have a fucking fantastic life out there, Amber. Me, you, Rico… think about it, babe.'

She shook her head, getting up and going back inside. 'You don't know what you're saying.'

'I know *exactly* what I'm saying, Amber. I love you, and I love that baby of ours, and all I want is a life for the three of us…'

'I *have* a life, Ryan, do you understand that yet?'

'He'll hurt you.'

'Oh, Jesus, we're back on this now, are we?'

'He'll hurt you.'

'And I'll get over it, but I'm not leaving him.'

'Think about it, baby. A whole new life in Los Angeles, with more money than we could ever possibly spend in our whole frigging lifetime…'

'Is that all that matters? Money? Because I *have* money. I have more money than I ever thought I'd have. And Jim, well, he's a multi-millionaire so I doubt we're ever gonna have trouble paying the bills.'

'No, Jesus, of course money isn't all that matters. I'm just trying to say… we'll have no worries, Amber. None. We could even get a house on the beach. How great would that be for Rico, huh? And they'd love you over there…'

'Is this why you've come here? To put all this on me? Because it really isn't fair, Ryan.'

'A whole new start, Amber. Away from someone who is only going to hurt you, and you don't deserve that.'

'But I deserve *you*, huh?'

'We were good together once.'

'Once,' she repeated, turning and walking into the kitchen.

'Why do you keep going back to him, Amber? Why do you keep *marrying* him?'

She swung around, glaring at him. 'He is my world, Ryan. Why does nobody seem to understand that?'

'You keep marrying him because I think you're scared to face up to something else – something you *know* is there. You just don't want to face it.'

'What the hell are you talking about?'

'You're just scared to let go of him because he's been in your life for so long. That's all. He's familiar. He's safe. But it's okay, y'know? To let go of him.'

'I don't *want* to let go of him.' Her voice was quiet, her arms folded back across her chest, putting an almost defensive barrier up between the two of them. 'I love him.'

'You got scared because you fell for a man who was a decade younger than you, and in your world that didn't feel right.'

She shook her head, her eyes staring right at him.

'But it's okay, to feel scared. But marrying a man you *think* you want to spend the rest of your life with, just because he's always been there? Admit it, Amber. You still have feelings for me, and they run so much deeper than you want to believe.'

She threw back her head, letting loose a loud laugh. 'Jesus, you are something else.'

'We're a family, Amber.'

'No, Ryan. Enough! I'm not getting into this.'

'I love you.'

'So you keep saying. But it doesn't make any difference.'

He said nothing, but he didn't take his eyes off her. He held her gaze, determined not to walk away from this until there was no fight left in him. And that was never going to happen. Never.

'I don't want you to go,' she said quietly, leaning back against the counter. Her voice suddenly changed, carrying a tone of something verging upon defeat now. The whole atmosphere had changed, right there, in an instant.

'And I don't want to go without you. But if I stay in the UK, I can't promise things are gonna be easy, Amber. For either of us.'

She felt tears start to prick the back of her eyes, and she quickly wiped them with the back of her hand, finally turning her head away from him, breaking that stare.

'I don't want you to go,' she repeated.

'Then come with me.'

She took a deep breath, throwing her head back, wiping her eyes again as more tears started to fall. 'How's it come to this, Ryan?'

'I don't know, baby. I guess we all made some bad choices along the way, and now we're left with no other option but to go with the only choices left to us.'

'I need to talk to Max…' she said, moving away from the counter to go and look for her phone, but he gently grabbed her wrist, stopping her from going anywhere.

'And what exactly are you gonna say, Amber?'

'This is crazy. You can't go to America. I don't want you to go.'

'But you don't want *me*, right?'

She looked at him, right into those dark-blue eyes of his, her head now a mess of emotions. He had no right to turn up here and lay this on her. He had no right.

Pulling her arm free of his grip she walked back over to the counter, keeping her back to him as she leaned forward, closing her eyes. Her head was spinning now. Yes, she'd known his contract was up at the end of the season, and yes, she'd always known he'd make another attempt to move back down to London, she knew all that. And was that what she'd always secretly hoped for? Really? Deep down, had she actually *wanted* him to move closer?

She kept her eyes closed, breathing in deeply as she became aware of him behind her now. She could feel him standing there, and she was doing nothing to stop him because her head was all over the place when not half an hour ago all she'd been able to think about was rushing back home to be with her husband. The man she loved. The man she wanted to spend the rest of her life with, right? Wasn't that the plan?

So why wasn't she turning around and doing something to prevent whatever this could be from starting? Why wasn't she doing that? Hadn't she learned anything over these messed-up couple of years?

She pulled her stomach in, clenching her muscles as she felt his hand rest on her thigh, his breath warm on the back of her neck. The danger signals were all too obvious, screaming at her so loudly she could hear them ringing in her ears and still she was doing nothing to stop this.

'Ryan…' One half-hearted attempt at making him stop. Yeah, that was going to work. And, anyway, she didn't want him to stop.

His mouth was kissing her neck now, his hands sliding up under her short sundress, slowly pulling her knickers down, and it was then that a brief moment of clarity struck, and she quickly put her hand over his. She stopped him from pushing those knickers down any further. And for a couple of seconds nothing happened. His hand stayed right where it was, and she clung onto it, determined this wasn't going to happen. She was determined, right? So why did she eventually pull her hand away? That action did nothing but give him permission to carry on with what he intended to do.

Those alarm bells couldn't be ringing any louder now as he tugged at her knickers until they fell around her ankles. And still she did nothing. When his hand slid back up her legs to rest on her hips, she moved her feet apart, which gave out completely the wrong message. And letting him pull her knickers down around her ankles had been the right one?

Oh, Jesus, his hands were on her bottom now, his fingers running over it so lightly and sending the most exquisite shivers coursing right through her, and she found herself arching her back slightly, pushing her bottom back at him as she stretched out, and she liked it. What he was doing to her, she liked it. Even though she knew it shouldn't be happening. They shouldn't be doing this.

But still she let him push her dress up over her waist, let his hands continue to run over her bottom, and it was driving her crazy. Every inch of her was screaming at her to push him away, to make him stop this; make him leave. But there was another, tiny part of her that was frozen. A part of her didn't want him to stop, didn't want him to go anywhere. And it was that part that was winning.

His hands had moved up now. They were running over her hips, stroking her waist, and when they reached her breasts, both his hands covering them, she pushed back harder against him, unable to stop the moans of pleasure from escaping, even though she was aware that was the most dangerous thing she could have done. She'd let him know this was okay. She'd let him know she was enjoying him touching her, when this shouldn't be happening. She'd almost let it happen before and that had been wrong, too. But this – this was leading somewhere they hadn't reached last time. And she couldn't stop it. Or should that be, she *wouldn't* stop it?

Stepping out of her knickers she kicked them away, pulling his hands off her as she turned around to face him. 'Is this what you want?' she asked, slipping her sundress down until it fell to the floor, and she kicked that away, too.

He ran a hand along the back of his neck, his eyes scanning her naked body. 'It's what I've always wanted, Amber.' He reached out to touch her cheek, running his fingers over her skin, his eyes locked on hers now. '*You* are all I've ever wanted.'

'Oh, come on now, Ryan. We both know *that* isn't true.'

'It's true now.'

'And the circumstances have changed.' She could feel her breathing start to break up as he moved closer.

'Come with me,' he whispered, cupping her cheek in his hand, his mouth almost touching hers now. 'You, me, and our baby, Amber. We could have a beautiful life out there.'

All she could do was close her eyes and let him kiss her. It was as if all the energy had been sucked right out of her. As though, all of a sudden, someone somewhere had cruelly flicked a switch that was making her do this, making her travel down this road. And if she told herself that enough times she might just start to believe it. Because she obviously wasn't yet ready to take responsibility for her own actions.

'I want you naked, too,' she said quietly, pulling at his belt, sliding it out of his jeans and throwing it down on the floor next to her discarded dress and unnecessary underwear. 'I think that's only fair because I feel at a bit of a disadvantage here. And, besides, if we're gonna do this, I'd quite like to look at that crazy-sexy body of yours.'

He'd whipped off his t-shirt before she'd even finished the sentence, revealing his rock-hard abs and his smooth, naked skin. Her beautiful footballer – that's what he'd once been to her. Her beautiful, beautiful footballer.

And then clarity returned. That nagging voice that was buried somewhere deep inside her. It made itself known, again. 'No, Ryan…' Was this the guilt finally coming to the fore once more? Before she had a chance to do something *really* stupid? 'This is wrong. It's wrong.'

'Does it feel wrong?' He was close to her again, his mouth almost touching her ear, his hand on her hip.

She shook her head, even though she was lying. It felt so, so wrong. But she wanted it. The idea of him leaving, of him being so far away, it had confused her. Scared her. Messed with her head and brought to the forefront thoughts and feelings she hadn't realised she still harboured. And she needed to know. She needed to be sure. So, yes, it was wrong. But she needed to know.

His hand slipped into hers, holding it tightly as their mouths touched; a gentle, slow kiss. A kiss that was making her cry because she knew it shouldn't be happening. But that didn't make it right. She couldn't make it right now; she'd gone too far, crossed that line. She'd let him back in and she shouldn't have done that. But it had happened now. And she couldn't stop it.

Her heart was beating like the loudest of drums, her head spinning as his mouth stayed on hers, his tongue running over the roof of her mouth, leaving her in no doubt it was him who was kissing her. Which only served to set off another wave of guilt.

'I can't do this, Ryan.' That nagging voice inside her head had returned once more, refusing to let her get away with this easily. It had obviously decided she needed to feel the guilt a little more, and it was working. That guilt was washing over her in waves so strong they felt like physical punches to the stomach. 'I can't.'

'No, listen, baby, you can. You can. We keep getting to this point, me and you. We keep getting to this point, so, doesn't that tell you something?'

'It tells me I'm weaker than I ever thought I could be.'

He held onto her hips, keeping her where she was, and she put up no fight. What would be the point? That line she shouldn't have crossed – she was way over it now.

'Look, Amber, whether you stay with him, or see sense and come with me, I'm probably gonna go to L.A. I have to. Because, if you stay with him it's gonna destroy me. I didn't want to face up to it before because I thought I'd get used to it. I thought I'd be able to handle it. I was wrong. I was so fucking wrong. I *can't* handle it. I can't stand by and watch you with him. I can't do that.'

She reached out to touch his face, wiping away his tears with her thumb, that ache in her heart making her breathless. 'You could have any woman you want, Ryan Fisher. Why the hell are you wasting your time on me?'

'I don't want *any* woman, Amber.' He wiped his own tears away with the back of his hand, averting his gaze from hers for just the briefest of seconds before his eyes met hers again. 'I want *you.*'

'This is so messed up,' she whispered, the rush of blood to her head so sudden she felt slightly faint, and she had to quickly grab onto him to steady herself.

His arm circled her waist, pulling her against him, and she closed her eyes as his mouth lowered down onto hers again, sending her spiralling down into that vortex of confusion she was falling deeper into. She'd thought she knew what she wanted. She'd thought everything was so clear in her mind, but she'd only been kidding herself. All the fighting against him and all the pretence that she didn't want him around – she'd just been kidding herself. Because all it had taken was for him to tell her he was leaving, going somewhere so far away – that's all it had taken for her to realise she didn't want him to leave. But did she want to go with him?

'I can't,' she whispered, finally finding the strength to gently push him away, crouching down to pick up her discarded dress.

'You're right, Amber. This is one really messed-up situation.' Ryan watched as she stepped back into her sundress, covering that body he craved like a drug. 'But don't we owe it to that baby in there to give us a chance?'

'Oh no. Don't you dare start bringing our son into this. Don't play the emotional card, Ryan, because that really isn't fair. Don't you think I would love for Rico to have his mum and dad together? Don't you think that's what I would have wanted for him?'

'Then make it happen. It's right there, Amber. Just waiting for you to reach out and take it.'

'I'm not doing this,' she said, walking away, back out onto the terrace. It was dark outside now, the terrace lit up by wall lights and fairy lights that hung from the trees around the pool. Out in the distance she could see the lights of Palma Nova, the resort coming to life once more as the bars and restaurants got ready for another night on this beautiful island. And for a few seconds she felt a wave of – was that peace? It was something she could only really describe as calm as she looked out ahead of her. All she could hear were the crickets and the faint sound of music coming from a nearby bar; it was almost perfect.

'It's right here, Amber. *I'm* right here.'

She turned around, her heart picking up that ridiculous rhythm again as she looked at him, his hands in the pockets of his jeans, his dark hair slightly dishevelled. He looked like the man she'd spent the past year trying to deny she'd ever been in love with. But of course she'd been in love with him. Of course she had.

'I'm right here.'

She walked slowly over to him, reaching out to touch his face with her fingertips, letting them run lightly over his jawline, his stubble rough beneath her fingers, but she didn't care. She loved the way he looked with that beard and his sexy-as-hell tattoos. 'I don't know what to do, Ryan.'

'You don't have to do anything yet,' he whispered, pushing her back against the whitewashed wall. 'Just let me love you. Even if it's just for a few hours, Amber, please. Just let me love you.'

'It's dangerous.'

'So what?' He was pushing her dress down, and she was helping him, whether she realised she was doing it or not, she was helping him.

'This is gonna hurt people.'

'They won't find out.'

Her dress was down around her ankles now, and she kicked it away. What else could she do? 'He'll find out, Ryan. Jim. He'll know, and I can't do this to him…' Ryan kissed her, so hard and so deep she had no other option but to give in to him. That switch had been flicked again, and there was no turning back now.

Before she even had a chance to realise what was happening, her arms were around his neck, his hands firm against the wall behind her as he leaned into her, their mouths still together. It was wrong, but it was so, so hot. She could feel herself burning up, so she was grateful for the feel of that cool wall behind her; grateful for the slight breeze that was blowing across the terrace because having him so near was almost too much to bear.

'Do you want this?' he asked, his mouth resting on hers as he spoke, her hand on the back of his neck keeping him close. He reached into his back pocket, pulling out the foil-wrapped packet. 'We'll be careful, okay?'

Her eyes met his for what felt like the longest minute, and she nodded, her stomach flipping over, pushing aside all the guilt. For now. Because as he ripped open the condom packet with his teeth, somehow, he made that one of the sexiest things she'd ever seen.

'Come here,' she whispered, a sharp jolt of something almost electric shooting through her as their fingers touched. 'Let me do that.' He was so hard it was easy, his mouth closing in on hers as her fingers ran over him. There was no turning back now. That chance had gone.

So, when he lifted her up she had no choice but to wrap her legs around him, holding onto him so tightly, and then she felt him – something she hadn't felt in so long, because she'd stopped it from happening. She felt him push into her, and she couldn't stop the cry from escaping. A cry of pleasure, a cry of pain and confusion, a cry of guilt; it didn't really matter. He was there, she'd let him back in and it was wrong, but it was happening. She could feel him pushing deep, each thrust sending wave after wave of that guilt crashing over her, but she could push it aside. For now. Because it felt like the release she'd needed.

She buried her face in his hair as he pushed harder, her legs crushing him against her, her hands clinging onto his shoulders as she felt those tingles start to build, her body responding faster as his thrusts got quicker. And then it hit her: that blanket of pins and needles, that rush of white-hot pain spreading through her so fast she couldn't breathe.

'Jesus, Amber…' he groaned, his body stiffening for a second or two as his own release took hold, and she clung on even tighter as he gave that one, final thrust. 'Jesus!'

She kept her eyes closed as she felt him withdraw, unwrapping her legs from around him, and she hoped those legs of hers would hold her up because they felt so weak.

'You okay?' he asked, his hand cupping her cheek, his forehead resting against hers.

She nodded, running her hand up and down his arm, her whole body still tingling. 'What do we do now, Ryan?'

'The ball's in your court, Amber.'

She looked down, her hand gripping his wrist. 'Just an hour ago I was talking to my husband,' she whispered. 'I was so sure. And now…' Her eyes met his. 'Now I don't know what to do. Because you've walked in here and you've fucked all that up, Ryan. All of it. I thought I was so much in love with him that nothing could ever get in the way of that. But now…' She trailed off, because she wasn't entirely sure of what she was saying. She didn't know whether what they'd just done had affected her thinking temporarily or permanently, and the confusion was just overwhelming. It was too much.

'Let me stay the night, Amber. Please.'

'I shouldn't…'

'Please.'

She looked right into his eyes, and she felt the most beautiful pain cut across her. A pain she didn't know how to ease. And she didn't even know if she wanted to.

Chapter Thirty

'What the fuck is he doing over there, Max?' Jim had never felt an anger like it; a burning emotion so strong it was the hardest of pains to control.

'Believe me, Jim, I had no idea, not until Dave French called me to see why he hadn't turned up for training.'

'Jesus!' Jim threw himself back against his office wall. He had to try and compose himself. Tonight was a big match for Endleigh United. If they won this, then the League title was theirs. They'd be champions. Another trophy to add to his growing list. Another accolade to chalk up. Jim Allen had walked back into this club and returned it to its former glory in the space of just a few months. So why, right now, did none of that matter? Because Ryan Fisher was still messing with his wife. And he could tell by the look on Max's face that this worried him, too.

'Maybe telling him why L.A. is such a good move for him was a bad idea,' Max said, sitting down on the arm of the couch.

'I said that, didn't I?' Jim sighed, pushing a hand through his hair.

'Well, I hate to tell you this, Jim, but there was no other way that kid was gonna buy into this. He needed to know the truth. He needed to know what was at stake here.'

Jim looked at Max, his anger showing no signs of subsiding,

even though he was trying his hardest to get it under control. 'What's at stake, Max, is my fucking marriage.'

'We didn't think this through, not properly.'

'He's over there, trying to persuade her to leave me…'

'You know that, do you? For sure? Because the only evidence we have is one photograph of him at Newcastle airport.'

Jim threw his head back and laughed. 'Come on, Max! Don't treat me like a ten-year-old. You *know* he's in Majorca. And you know as well as I do why he's over there.'

Max sighed, standing up and walking over to the sideboard. 'Do you want a drink?'

'No, I don't want a fucking drink. I've got to go out there in a minute and act as though everything's fine when I don't know what the fuck is going on.'

'It's one tiny picture, hidden away…'

'He's over there, Max. And so is she; so is their baby. And I have never felt so freakin' helpless.'

'You have to trust her, Jim.'

He closed his eyes, pulling in a sharp intake of breath before he exhaled slowly. 'I can't do anything. I can't go to her or try and stop this, and I know I've got to try and get some kind of grip on it all, but… but it's so fucking hard, Max.'

'He's going, Jim. You know that, don't you? I told you. He's going to L.A. I'm talking to the Gamers this afternoon, sorting out his contract, making sure everything's just as we discussed. So, he's going.'

Jim's eyes met Max's again, panic now taking over from the anger. Because Max was right. They hadn't thought this through, not really. Otherwise they'd have known this would happen. 'But what if he takes her with him?'

*

Amber leaned against the archway, watching as Ryan lay on his stomach on the huge rug in the centre of the living room, Rico sitting up in front of him. Daddy and son were playing – Rico's laugh echoing around the room, and just the sound of it made Amber's heart sing, because he was such a happy baby. And he loved his daddy, that was so obvious. His daddy had made sure that he'd been a huge part of that baby's life, even when she'd decided to end their relationship. To go back to Jim. To give Rico another man in his life. What was going to happen when Ryan couldn't be there as often as he was now? How was that going to affect Rico? How was it going to affect Ryan? How was it going to affect her?

She closed her eyes for a second, trying not to think about this curveball that had just been thrown at them. When she and Jim had decided to get married again and decided to start their new life down south, she'd panicked that Ryan would follow them and he'd find that London club he was so desperate to find; that he'd invade her life way more than she wanted him to. Back then, wouldn't the idea of him moving to America have been one she'd welcomed? Having him so far away so she could finally get on with her life would have been the perfect scenario. But now it was happening and now it was real. She was so scared of him not being around any more. Of not being able to watch as their son smiled and laughed with a man who'd done nothing but be an incredible dad to their child, despite anything else he might have done. Anything else he might have been. Ryan was an incredible dad and Rico adored him.

She opened her eyes as the sound of her little boy's laughter rang around the room again, merging with Ryan's, the two of them completely engrossed in each other. Amber felt her stomach contract, and she hugged herself; that confusion washed back over her in waves. It hadn't stopped doing that since yesterday. Since Ryan had walked in here and told her he was leaving. Since he'd made love to her and confused her even more. Since he'd held her in his arms in bed last night and told her a million reasons why going to L.A. with him would be the best decision she'd ever made.

Rico was banging his cuddly rabbit on the floor now, making gurgling noises as he did so, showing off in front of his daddy, and Amber watched as Ryan said something to him, something which made him stop flinging his rabbit up and down. Instead, he tossed it aside, falling forward, crawling towards his daddy, who knelt up and scooped his son into his arms, holding him up in the air, which set off another barrage of baby giggles.

Amber backed away, walking outside onto the front terrace, leaning back against the wall as she looked out at nothing in particular. The sun was shining and it was another warm, early-May day on this beautiful island. But she felt as though she were trapped inside some kind of painful, confusing prison. And even though she was the only one who held the key that could free her from that prison, she couldn't use it yet. Because she didn't know what to do with it.

'I've settled him in his cot. Said goodbye.'

Amber turned to see Ryan standing in the doorway, so handsome and hot in black jeans, heavy black boots and a white shirt, the sleeves rolled up to the elbows. He looked unbelievably handsome, and she couldn't stop her stomach from turning those somersaults he'd been making it do ever since he'd got here. 'What time's your taxi coming?'

'In about half an hour. Believe it or not the boss wants to see me as soon as I land back in Newcastle. A bollocking at midnight, huh? He must be desperate to reprimand me.'

Amber couldn't help but smile. 'Well, you will do these disappearing acts, Ryan.'

He looked down at the ground, running a hand along the back of his neck. 'I bring it all on myself, huh?'

'Something like that.'

'Amber?'

His eyes were on hers again and she couldn't look away. She didn't want to.

'Last night… thank you.'

She couldn't say anything. Because she wasn't entirely sure that last night should have happened.

'And I'm sorry. If my coming here has…'

'Rico's had the time of his life, Ryan. Whatever else you came here to do, you made that little boy incredibly happy.'

'Did I make his mum happy, too?'

She didn't move as he stood in front of her, his hand resting on the wall beside her head, those dark-blue eyes of his staring deep into hers.

'Did I make *her* happy?'

She still couldn't seem to get the words out, her breath catching in her throat as he inched closer. So she said nothing, just closed her eyes and let his mouth touch hers; let his kiss wipe away anything else she was thinking about, just for a few seconds. Because she wasn't sure she was ready to let him go yet. She didn't know what was going to happen when she got back home, and that alone scared her. But the thought that this was the last time she might be so close to him, scared her more than anything.

So she slipped a hand around the back of his neck, the other one sliding into the back pocket of his jeans as he kissed her longer, deeper. She wanted to have one more taste of him in case she never got another chance.

'Come with me, Amber.'

'Don't push me, Ryan. Please. Neither of us knows what's gonna happen when we get back home, I just know that – I know that you, coming here, it's changed things. Whether I want that or not. And I can't forget that.'

'There's a chance?'

She stared up at him again, her fingers playing with the hair at the back of his neck. 'I don't know.'

He closed his eyes for a beat or two, his head bowed. 'What do I do, Amber?'

She put a hand to his cheek, making him look at her. 'I can't answer that for you, Ryan.'

'How am I gonna cope without you and Rico?'

There were tears in his eyes as he spoke, and Amber felt her heart break for all the chances they'd missed, and the mess they'd all made. 'Oh, baby… you'll do okay. You're Ryan Fisher! You can cope with anything.'

He smiled, but those tears were still spilling down his face. 'Just tell me there's still a chance, Amber. Even if it's just the tiniest one. Even if it's so remote… Just tell me there's still a chance.'

She leaned forward to kiss away his tears, stroking his hair back off his face. 'There's still a chance.' She wasn't entirely sure she'd meant to say that out loud, but maybe doing that had been the best thing to do. It made her realise what was happening here – that she *did* have a choice. If she wanted one.

He let out a sigh, throwing back his head, his arm falling around her waist, pulling her closer. 'Jesus, this is so fucking hard!'

She snuggled in against him, clinging onto his shirt, allowing his arms to hold her tightly as a million and one thoughts and memories flashed through her mind.

'Half an hour still leaves us time,' he whispered, kissing the top of her head.

'Time?' She pulled away slightly, frowning as she looked at him.

'For me to get between those incredible legs of yours and love you one last time.'

His mouth was so close to hers as he spoke, his voice so low and sexy it made Amber's head spin. What choice was he leaving her with here?

'Rico's asleep, so, that gives daddy time to make mummy love him. Doesn't it?'

'Ryan…'

'It gives us time, Amber.'

But she wasn't altogether sure that was something they had the luxury of any more.

*

'What the hell are you playing at?'

Ryan held the phone away from his ear as he handed the taxi driver a handful of Euros, smiling his thanks.

'You've had your phone switched off for over a day now. Do you know how many people have been trying to get in touch with you?'

'That's exactly why I've had it switched off, Max.'

'Where are you?'

'About to go into the airport. And, for your information, I've already spoken to the boss.'

'Yes, I know you have. And he'll be waiting for you when you land in Newcastle, and believe me, Ryan, if I was up there *I'd* be waiting for you, too. Jesus! I thought you were over all this selfish, childish behaviour.'

'Hey, hang on there. You suddenly tell me that moving to Los Angeles is the best thing for my career, for my life – you drop that fucking bombshell on me and you expect me to just take it? Especially after you reel off every reason why you think I should be making that move. It doesn't work like that, Max.'

'I take it you've been to see Amber.'

'Yes, I've been to see Amber.'

'Have you any idea how pissed off Jim Allen is right now?'

'He knows?'

'There was a picture of you in the paper at the airport. It didn't exactly take a genius to put two and two together after that. And I tried to calm him down, but he is gunning for you, Ryan. He's beyond fucking angry.'

'Jesus, Max, like I frigging care.'

'He's her fucking husband! He has every right to be angry. For Christ's sake, what fucking fantasy world are you living in?'

'I want her to come with me. To L.A.'

There was a pause down the line as Max took in what he'd just been told. 'And you've said this to her, have you? You've actually told her you want her to come with you?'

'I've told her.'

'And?'

'And, nothing. She doesn't know.'

'She doesn't *know*? What the hell's gone on over there, Ryan?'

'I love her, Max. And last night I held her and I made love to her and...'

'Jesus-fucking-Christ! I don't fucking believe this... Do you know what you've just done?'

Ryan leaned back against the wall outside the airport, watching as people walked in and out in an almost constant stream, most of them wheeling cases behind them. Did any of them have lives as complicated as his was right now?

'I'm sorting my life out, Max. That's what I'm doing.'

*

Amber crossed her legs underneath her, clutching tightly onto the bottle of lager she was holding, watching as the final whistle blew and Parkfield erupted into a cacophony of noise so loud it drowned out the TV commentators, one of whom was Ronnie.

Endleigh United were League champions. Her wonderful husband had done the job they'd employed him to do, and she felt a wave of sadness wash over her because she wasn't there to share this with him. She wasn't by his side.

She turned away from the TV for a second, breathing in deeply as the events of the past couple of days flooded her brain, and when she turned back she saw him there on the screen. Dressed in his trademark dark suit, his head bowed down slightly, he stood on the touchline with his hands in his pockets, watching his team celebrate. He was the most beautiful man she'd ever seen. He wasn't smiling, but he wasn't known for his outward displays of emotion on the football pitch; that wasn't him. But he knew. Amber could tell that he knew. He knew Ryan had been over here. And her heart broke all over again at what she was doing to people who didn't deserve it. This had gone way past stupid games people had played in the past. This was the rest of their lives.

The noise in the stadium wasn't showing any signs of subsiding as the Endleigh players ran around the pitch, thanking all their fans, enjoying the achievement, and once more, Amber felt her heart ache because she wasn't there with Jim. She should be there, instead of sitting here, thinking about things she shouldn't even be considering.

She took a swig of beer, her eyes still glued to the screen, her heart suddenly giving a little judder as they cut to an interview pitchside – with Jim. And even though he was smiling now, Amber could see a sadness there, and it tore her apart.

'I'm so, so proud of you, baby,' she whispered, feeling tears start to stream down her face, but she didn't wipe them away. She deserved to feel pain. She deserved to feel this guilt. Just the sound of his voice cut her deeply, but when she heard him say her name those tears fell faster, that pain cutting deeper.

She hugged her knees to her chest, watching as he spoke to one of her Cloud Sports colleagues. She couldn't take her eyes off him, this man who'd walked into her life all those years ago and taken everything she'd ever had. He'd taken it all. He'd invaded her life and stolen her heart; he'd stirred up every emotion it was ever possible to feel and she knew she would gladly do it all again, because she loved him. No matter what had gone on here, or anything she might still feel for Ryan, she loved that man there on her TV. She loved him.

'I know she isn't here tonight…'

Amber's heart seemed to miss another beat as Jim turned to face the camera, and she couldn't stop the loud, uncontrollable sobs from escaping, those tears streaming from her eyes so fast now she could barely see.

'… But, baby, if you're watching, and you said you would be… if you're watching, I wanna say thank you. And just know that I love you, okay? I love you so much, honey.'

She had to put a hand over her mouth to stop those sobs from waking Rico. Because what he'd just said there had sounded like a message. Oh, God, how could she ever have thought she could leave this man?

The pain she felt now was indescribable. It was like a knife being ripped right through her; it was physical, and it hurt like nothing she'd ever felt before.

'I love you, too,' she whispered, that pain intensifying as the picture cut back to the studio. 'And I'm sorry, baby. I am so, so sorry.'

Chapter Thirty-One

'You do not just take it upon yourself to wander off. You are still under contract until the end of this season, do you hear me, Ryan? This is isn't fucking high school, you don't get to slack off just because there are only a couple of weeks left and you can't really be bothered to concentrate any more.'

'You finished?' Ryan asked, folding his arms as Max paced up and down his Covent Garden office.

'I haven't even fucking started, son.'

'Give it a rest, okay? I've heard it all from Dave French, and I've been suitably fined.'

Max stood still and looked at him, raising his eyebrows. 'Oh, so, you think that's the end of it, then, do you? You should think yourself lucky Red Star need you otherwise you'd probably have found your playing career at that club already over.'

'That wouldn't have been such a bad thing.'

Max raised his eyebrows even higher. 'What? Because then you could keep your arse down here and do a bit more marriage wrecking?'

'I'm not wrecking anybody's marriage, Max…'

'Have you heard yourself? No, seriously, have you? Because you're standing there actually saying words that are totally untrue.'

'They haven't got a frigging marriage. Jesus…'

'Oh, so, all of a sudden you're the expert on relationships, are you?'

'I know she still has feelings for me.'

'Really? You know that, do you? One night in the Balearics and you've managed to turn her head, is that what you're saying?'

'I felt it. I could see it in her eyes, I could feel it when we…'

Max held up his hands, stopping him from talking. 'I don't want to hear it, Ryan. I don't want to know what you did or what kind of a mess you've caused, but you need to know one thing. Whatever you *think* she might still feel for you, it isn't going to happen.'

'And how do you know that, huh? How do *you* know that?'

'I don't,' Max sighed, holding his hands up for another reason now – defeat. He couldn't do this any more. He couldn't make the kid see sense, no matter what he said. 'I don't know anything. But what I *do* know is that you need to calm down, get your head straight, and just accept that she's probably made her choice. I mean, have you seen or spoken to her since she got back from Majorca?'

Ryan shook his head, his eyes back down on the floor. 'I've tried calling her, but it goes straight to answer phone.'

'And that doesn't tell you anything?'

Ryan looked up, shoving his hands in his pockets as he stared at his agent. 'Not really.'

'Stop being so naïve, Ryan. Get your head out of the sand and start thinking about the next couple of weeks. Two more games for Newcastle Red Star then you've got a whole new future to look forward to.'

'She said there was still a chance, Max.'

'I'm sorry?' Max frowned, watching as Ryan slowly lifted his head.

'She said there was still a chance. That she and Rico would come with me to L.A. And I'm gonna cling onto that chance until the very last second, you got that? The very last second.'

*

'Are you coming with me?' Amber asked, leaning back against the door of Jim's Parkfield office. 'To this photo shoot.'

'I thought Ronnie was with you,' Jim said, not looking up from his laptop.

'He's doing the photo shoot with me, yes.'

'You don't need me, then, do you?'

'Is something wrong?'

'Nothing's wrong, Amber.'

'You could have fooled me. I just wondered if you were going to pop in, that was all.'

'Where is it?' he asked, his eyes still focused on his laptop screen.

'They've set up something in one of the function rooms upstairs. And I think they want to do one or two pictures outside on the pitch, I'm not sure…'

'I thought you weren't doing this kind of thing any more?'

Amber's eyes met his as he finally looked up. 'Have you got a problem with it?'

'No, Amber. I don't have a problem with anything.'

'Yeah. Sounds like it. Look, I'll see you later. You might be in a better mood by then.'

'Amber, honey, wait.' He got up and walked over to her, and she leaned back against the door, folding her arms across herself. 'Baby, I'm sorry. I'm sorry, okay? It's just… the idea of you putting yourself out there…'

'My clothes are staying on, Jim. It isn't that kind of photo shoot. They're publicity photos for Cloud Sports and promotion shots for *Back of the Net*. That's all.'

He threw his head back, letting out a loud sigh. 'Jesus, Amber, I'm having so much trouble dealing with this.'

'Dealing with what? They're just publicity shots, Jim. I'm not running off to the Playboy mansion.'

He slid an arm around her waist, pulling her closer. 'Yeah, but, if they could see how hot you were they'd want you over there ASAP.'

'Oh, you're such a flatterer, Jim Allen.' She smiled, playing with the collar of his shirt and wrinkling up her nose. 'But I think the Playboy boat has sailed.'

'Not in my eyes,' he whispered, his mouth lowering down onto hers, and she let herself fall into that kiss. Because she needed to feel him this close to her; she needed him to kiss her and touch her and make love to her over and over again until she was absolutely sure she was making the right decision.

'So, are you coming with me?' she asked, not really in the mood to let him go now.

'I'll be over as soon as I can. I promise.'

'Okay.' She stood up on tiptoes, still holding onto his shirt collar, kissing him again, a little longer this time. A little slower. 'I'll see you later.'

He watched her turn to leave, that crazy red hair of hers falling loose down her back, her killer figure poured into a dress that was practically giving him a hard-on.

'Amber?'

She turned around, smiling that smile and breaking his heart. 'Yeah?'

'I don't want to know what happened, over in Majorca. Okay? I told you I didn't want to know…' He looked down at the floor, his hands dug deep into his pockets. 'I just…' He raised his head, his eyes once more meeting hers. 'I love you, okay? Don't ever forget that.'

She walked over to him, gently touching his cheek with the palm of her hand, kissing him again. She could kiss him forever. 'I am so in love with you, Jim Allen, I can't even tell you.'

He rested his hand over hers, smiling a smile that made her heart leap. 'Then that's all I need to know.'

One more kiss and she'd disappeared outside, on her way to do what she did best – look beautiful, and make men fall in love with her. And she didn't even know she was doing it. His wife.

His world.

He walked back over to his desk, leaning against it, pushing both hands through his hair as he let loose another loud, frustrated sigh.

That threat he'd always feared was still very much there. And he had to put a stop to it.

*

'Everything okay?' Max asked.

Amber looked up as she slipped on a pair of heels so high she doubted whether she'd be able to walk in them. 'I didn't know you were coming down here today.'

'Well, I've got a few hours spare before my next meeting, so, I thought I'd come and see how you were doing.'

Amber eyed him slightly warily. 'Well, I'm fine, thank you. Everything's fine. Why wouldn't it be?'

'You know Ryan's down here, don't you?'

Amber didn't miss the look Ronnie gave her, but she ignored it. 'I'm assuming he's got permission this time.'

'I needed to talk to him regarding some details concerning his new contract with L.A. Gamers.'

Amber felt her stomach dip at the mention of Ryan's impending move to America. It was just a couple of weeks away now, but she was trying to pretend it wasn't coming. 'Is it all sorted, then?' She asked that without looking up, mainly because she knew Ronnie was still watching her.

'We're getting there. Just one or two personal terms to iron out and he's all ready to go. Their season's already up and running so they want him there as soon as.'

Amber's stomach dipped even lower as Max talked. All he was doing was describing a reality she didn't want to face, when she'd been quite happy pretending it wasn't happening at all.

'Is Jim here?'

'He's in his office. Said he might pop in later. Where's Ryan now?' Did she really want to know?

Max shrugged. 'No idea. Hasn't he arranged to come and see Rico while he's here?'

'I haven't been answering his calls,' she said quietly, feeling a little guilty, because that was selfish. It wasn't that she'd been keeping Rico away from him – he'd spent a few days up in Newcastle with her dad after she'd come back from Majorca, and she knew Ryan had seen him then. But she hadn't spoken to him for a while now. And that was selfish.

'Yeah. He told me.'

Amber stood up, shaking out her hair and wishing she hadn't done that as these heels really were too high for her, and now she felt a little unsteady on her feet. 'I know these things are supposed to make your legs look better but they're a bitch to walk in.'

Max smiled, watching as she steadied herself.

'Do you know? What went on in Majorca?' Amber asked, looking straight at Max and still ignoring Ronnie, although he was out of earshot now, talking to the photographer.

Max's expression changed, turning serious again. 'I didn't *want* to know, but Ryan offered up the information before I'd had a chance to shut him up. Look, Amber – he said you'd told him… he said there was still a chance. A chance that you might go with him. To L.A.'

She looked down at her feet, pulling the hem of the dress she was wearing down so it covered just a touch more thigh. 'I did say that, yes.' Now she was really glad Ronnie was out of earshot because if he had any idea…

'And? Are you serious about that? I mean…'

'I don't know, Max.' Her eyes met his, holding his gaze for a good few seconds.

He was in no hurry to break that stare. 'You don't know?'

'I don't know.'

'But…'

'Everything's so complicated now. Ryan coming over there, to

Majorca – it changed things. It… it threw up stuff I didn't even know I was feeling and I just don't know.'

'And what about Jim? Does *he* know what went on over there?'

'He says he doesn't want to know. But I think he has every idea what really went on. He's not stupid.'

'Jesus, Amber…'

'I panicked. When Ryan told me he was leaving for America, I panicked. I got scared. The thought of him not being there terrified me and I panicked.'

'This is one hell of a mess.'

'But it's going to be sorted soon.' She looked at Max, right into his eyes, her expression almost pleading. 'Isn't it?'

'Yeah,' he sighed, holding her gaze, not breaking the stare. 'I really hope so.'

*

'What was all that about?' Ronnie asked, wandering back over to Amber.

'Nothing.'

'Here we go again,' he sighed, leaning back against the wall beside Amber, who was still trying to get used to the heels. 'You know, every time Ryan's name is mentioned there's something in your eyes that scares the hell out of me,' Ronnie went on, shoving his hands into his pockets.

Amber turned her head to look at him, but she said nothing.

'I'm going to assume that what happened in Majorca – I'm going to assume it was…'

'I don't want to talk about it, Ronnie.'

'You used to be able to talk to me about anything, Amber.'

She looked down at the floor, her fingers fiddling with her wedding ring.

'And you're doing that weird thing with your wedding ring again.'

Amber quickly pulled her hand away. 'It's not "weird," as you put it. It's a nervous habit.'

'You got something to be nervous about?'

'I didn't say that.'

'You're not saying much.'

'Do we have to do this here?'

'We don't have to do it at all.'

'Good.'

'You really want to carry on living this way, Amber?'

She looked at him again, saying nothing for a beat or two. 'It would have been so much simpler if me and you had worked out, wouldn't it?'

His eyes locked onto hers, and it was his turn to say nothing for a few seconds. 'Yeah. It would. It really would.'

*

'Close the door,' Jim said, leaning back against his desk, his arms folded. 'I'm surprised to see you here, if the truth be told. I didn't think you'd come.'

'I didn't know if I was going to. But then I remembered what's at stake.'

Jim glared at Ryan as he stood by the door, handsome, young and cocky with his hands in his pockets and a look on his face that, for some reason, made Jim feel uncharacteristically nervous. 'I've told Amber this, and I'm telling you – I don't want to know what you did. What happened over there, it doesn't matter…'

'It does to me.'

Jim's expression darkened. 'I don't want to know, Ryan. So don't push me, okay?'

'She told me there was a chance, Jim.' Ryan moved further into the room, but Jim stayed exactly where he was, his eyes boring into Ryan's. 'That her and Rico – she told me there was a chance they'd come with me. To America.'

'She won't go,' Jim said, his expression stoic now, his arms still folded.

Ryan let out a quiet chuckle, bowing his head for a second before raising it back up to look straight at his ex-boss. 'And, you know that for sure, do you?'

'She won't go. Because I won't let her.'

'You won't *let* her? You see, this is what I told her…'

Jim stood up, that calm exterior fading now as the anger took over. 'And what *did* you tell her, Ryan? Did you tell her I was no good for her? That I'd hurt her again? That I'd never change and the worst thing she could do would be to stay with me?'

'And you don't think that's true?'

'You have no idea – no idea at all. I love her. I've always loved her. For over twenty years I have wanted her. I have fucking ached for her, and now that I finally have her I won't lose her again. I won't. Not to you. Not to anyone, but especially not to you. Do you hear me? So you step away and you leave her alone. You back off. And I'm not asking you to do this, I'm warning you. You get on that plane and you go to L.A. and I wish you all the luck in the world over there, I really do, because, despite the fact I can't even bear to look at you, you're a talent this game needs. But Amber *doesn't* need you. So you back off, and you leave her alone.'

'Well, that's gonna be hard, Jim. Because she has my baby.'

'You leave *her* alone. You show no interest, don't make her think you want her…'

'But I *do* want her. And I can't hide that any more. I leave for L.A. in a couple of weeks, and I don't want to go without her. So I can't pretend she doesn't matter to me, when she does.'

'I'm warning you, Ryan. You take a fucking step back from this or, so help me, I will kill you.'

Ryan's eyes widened, another laugh escaping as he stared at Jim. 'Is that a fucking threat?'

'It's whatever you want it to be.'

'She didn't put up much of a fight, y'know. Over in Spain.'

Ryan continued to stare at Jim as he spoke, knowing that he was fuelling the fire, making the whole situation worse, but he couldn't help himself. 'And the second she let that dress drop to the floor I knew I wasn't leaving until I'd been back inside her, and let me tell you, she felt just as good as she always did.'

'I'm warning you, Ryan, you really don't want to push me…'

'Or what? You're all talk, Jim. You're not gonna do anything, because you're all out of ideas; you've tried them all. You've tried every way you can to bring me down and push me further away from Amber but none of them worked, did they? You can't stop it because she feels something for me that will *never* go away. It'll never die. It's always gonna be there, whether you like it or not.'

Jim shook his head, his hands in his pockets, but his fists were clenched tightly it was verging on painful. 'I am so fucking angry that you did what you did.'

'It was always gonna happen.'

'But that's it. It's over now. You took her and you got it out of your system…'

'Out of my system? Do you think you're the only one here who has the monopoly on feelings, Jim? You say I have no idea how much you love her, but what about me, huh? *You* have no idea how much *I* love her.'

'You don't love her. You just want her because she's out of reach.'

'She isn't out of reach.'

'Oh, she is, Ryan. She's so far out of your reach you'll never touch her again.'

Ryan said nothing for a few seconds, he just stared Jim out, determined to stand his ground. He was serious now. The time for playing games was over. 'Shouldn't that be up to Amber to decide?' And with that Ryan turned and walked out of the office, almost slamming the door shut behind him.

Jim leaned back against his desk, throwing his head back and closing his eyes. Had that actually made things worse? But he'd had to face him. He'd had to know how serious Ryan really was about taking his wife away from him. And now that he knew, it terrified him.

*

'What the hell are you doing here?' Max hissed as Ryan walked into the room where Amber's photo shoot was taking place, leaning back against the wall as though he had every right to be there.

'Jim wanted a word.'

'Are you *serious*?' Max could feel his blood pressure rising by the second. What the hell had he done to deserve this today?

'He wanted to "warn me off."'

'Jesus Christ… and you think being in here, when his wife is over there… You think this is going to diffuse the situation?'

'Look, Max, I really don't care any more, okay? I'm sick of pretending, sick of avoiding the subject. I'm leaving the country in a matter of weeks and I want her to come with me. I want Amber, and I want our baby, and what Jim Allen wants just doesn't fucking matter to me. He isn't important.'

'Have you banged your fucking head or something? Actually, maybe that would knock some sense into you… You are gonna kill me, Ryan.'

Ryan ignored him, his eyes on Amber now. She was laughing as she leaned over the photographer's shoulder, looking at the pictures he'd just taken, her smile lighting up the room, and he'd never felt a pain like it. He couldn't let her go. He just couldn't do it. 'I love her, Max.'

'Look, Ryan…' Max trailed off as he noticed Amber's gaze wander over to them, her smile fading the second her eyes met Ryan's. 'This is not going to end well,' Max sighed, backing away as Amber walked over.

'What are you doing here?' she asked, stopping a little way in front of him.

'Can I see Rico?'

'He isn't here. What are you doing at Parkfield, Ryan?'

'Your husband wanted a word.'

Amber frowned. 'I'm sorry? Why would Jim want a word with you?'

'Because he doesn't want to lose you, Amber. So he's warning me off. Telling me to back away, to leave you alone…'

'I don't believe this.'

'Can I see Rico?'

'He's at home.'

'On his own?'

'Don't start, Ryan. He's with his new childminder. If you want to go and see him I'll call her, tell her you're coming over. Her name's Allie, and she won't take any of your crap, so be nice to her. Rico adores her.'

'Your husband gonna be alright with that, is he? Me going over to your place?'

Amber's eyes met his again, and Ryan wished with all his heart that they were back in Majorca. Because he'd felt as though he'd got through to her there. But here – here she was back to being the cold, distant Amber she'd started to become with him over the past few months. And he hated that. He didn't want that.

'Did you tell him?'

'He fucking knows, Amber. Before I told him he already knew we'd had sex over there, I could tell. It was written all over his face. And you know that, too. He isn't stupid.'

'You're making one hell of a mess even worse, do you know that?'

'I don't care. Because I'm desperate here, Amber. It's killing me, watching the days go by and not knowing what you're thinking… it's fucking killing me.'

'I can't do this here.'

'We need to talk.'

'There's nothing to talk about.'

'Really? That's what you think?'

'They need you, Amber,' Max said, and Amber almost breathed

the biggest sigh of relief.

'I'm coming.' She looked at Ryan, and she cursed the fact that seeing him like this had just reopened those floodgates and let those waves of confusion and guilt surge forward all over again. 'We'll talk, Ryan. Just, not now.'

Ryan watched her walk back over to Ronnie and the photographer, his eyes focused on those super-sexy hips of hers. Hips he'd held onto not that long ago as he'd pushed inside her and remembered just why he couldn't let her go.

'I'd raise your eye level if I were you.'

He turned around to see Jim standing there, a stoic expression on his face and his stance one of a man who wasn't about to be messed with.

'She doesn't deserve you,' Ryan said, deliberately returning his gaze to Amber.

'She doesn't need a boy, Ryan. She needs a man.'

Ryan couldn't help but let out a laugh. 'Are you kidding me?'

'I don't kid. I never kid.'

'Yeah. Okay.'

'Shouldn't you be packing?'

'Do you know how childish you sound? We're not kids in a playground fighting over the prettiest girl in school.'

'Corey Reynolds, the owner of your new club, is not someone to be messed about with either. But I'm sure he knows what he's letting himself in for.'

Ryan narrowed his eyes slightly. 'What the hell are you talking about? Do you *know* Corey Reynolds?'

'We go way back, Corey and I. He wanted me to come over and manage the team at one point, but it's not for me. I've got no desire to go back to the States just yet. I'm happy here.'

Ryan said nothing for a second or two. 'I don't understand…'

'Just giving you a heads-up, that's all. When Max told me what side you'd signed for, well – I think you're gonna fit in just fine over there.'

'That's enough, Jim,' Max said, walking over. 'I think your wife wants a word.'

'Just remember what I said, okay?' Jim fixed Ryan with one last look before he walked over to Amber.

'What the hell was he talking about, Max? Did you know he knew Corey Reynolds? Did he…?'

'Jim Allen has a lot of connections over in the States as well as over here, Ryan. That's what makes him a bloody good man to be on the right side of. And not a particularly pleasant man to make an enemy of.'

'Did he have anything to do with…?'

'Stop being so paranoid. Go see that little man of yours. Go on.'

Ryan didn't move for a second or two. He was too busy watching Amber, a stabbing pain piercing his heart as she stood up on tiptoes to kiss Jim's mouth, her hand resting on his waist. Even after everything he'd told her, the first thing she did was kiss him.

'Go and see Rico,' Max said, his voice quiet, his hand giving Ryan's shoulder an almost protective squeeze. 'Go on.'

'This isn't over,' he whispered, finally pulling himself away from the wall. 'This isn't fucking over.'

*

'Was talking to Ryan just now really a good idea?' Amber asked, absentmindedly playing with the collar of Jim's shirt.

'I'm scared, Amber.'

'Of what?' She looked around, making sure they were out of anyone else's earshot.

'Do I have to spell it out? Can't you see what he's trying to do?'

'Confronting him isn't the way to deal with it.'

'So, what do you want me to do, Amber? Just let him get on with it? Stand by and watch as he lures you back into his bed…'

'He isn't "luring" me anywhere, Jim. And you're starting to sound as childish as he is now.'

'Are you finished here?'

'In a bit. Why?'

Jim slipped an arm around her waist, pulling her against him, his mouth close to her ear as he spoke. 'I want to fuck you.'

'Here?'

He laughed quietly, letting his hand drop slightly so it rested on her hip. 'Oh, believe me, baby, I don't care where we do it. I just want to fuck you.'

'Because telling Ryan how things stand has turned you on, is that it?'

'Is that such a bad thing?'

'Yes, actually.'

'Then that isn't the reason.'

She wriggled free of his grip. 'This isn't really the place for this conversation, Jim.'

He dug his hands into his pockets, lowering his gaze.

'Are you doing this because Ryan's still in the room?' Amber said, stepping back slightly.

Jim just raised an eyebrow.

'Because the time for playing games is over.'

'I'm not playing games, Amber.'

It was her turn to raise an eyebrow. 'It's just that, as far as you and public displays of affection are concerned, they're usually few and far between.'

He moved closer to her, sliding his hand down onto her bottom, his mouth close to hers as he spoke. 'If I want to put my hand on my wife's ass, it doesn't matter where we are, baby, I'll put my hand on my wife's ass.'

'Not if I don't want it there you won't. Move it. Now.'

He pulled it away, smiling. 'Do you know how hot you are when you're angry?'

'Can you go now? Please?'

He slowly backed away, his hands in his pockets, that smile still on his face as he mouthed *"I still want to fuck you."*

And, despite herself, Amber couldn't help smiling too, shaking her head as he walked away.

'You ever gonna grow out of this teenage phase?'

She turned to look at Ronnie. 'And you and Hayley are, what? Already at the "married twenty years so we never kiss in public any more" stage?'

'You've known *him* over twenty years,' Ronnie said, looking in Jim's direction as he stopped by the door to say something to Max. 'I would have thought you'd be well past that stage yourself by now.'

'I'll never even reach that stage with him, Ronnie.' Amber's eyes stayed on Jim until he finally left the room.

'So where does that leave Ryan?'

Her head shot around to stare at him. 'What's any of this got to do with Ryan?'

'I don't know. You tell me.'

'I thought we'd agreed to drop this subject.'

'Funny how everything seems to come back to him, though, isn't it?'

She continued to stare at her best friend, wondering if shutting him out of everything as much as she had done had been such a good idea. Could he, maybe, have helped her make some kind of sense of all this? If she'd just let him in.

'What happened to you just wanting me to be happy, Ronnie?'

'I still want that more than anything, Amber, believe me. To see you finally happy is all I want for you. But, right now, as far as you being happy is concerned, I don't think you're anywhere near it.'

Chapter Thirty-Two

Jim stood by the French doors, looking out onto the play area they'd created in part of their beautiful back garden. With swings and a sand pit, a climbing frame and a huge winding slide, it was full of things Rico was way too young to play with just yet, but they'd wanted to create a family garden from the start. Somewhere they could all enjoy and a place where memories would be made. But now there was a fear bubbling away inside of him; a fear that those memories would never be created. Rico might never get the chance to sit on that swing or play in that sand pit because he wouldn't ever be here, because his mum wouldn't be here.

It was a fear that wouldn't go away now, and it scared him even more because Ryan was right. Jim had used all his ammunition. There was nothing left to fire, no winning shot that would make sure Amber stayed here. He was all out of ideas. But that didn't mean Ryan had won.

Turning away from the window, Jim set his empty coffee mug down on the counter and headed back upstairs. It was still early, but he hadn't been able to sleep and he hadn't wanted to wake Amber or Rico. He could hear her voice now as he climbed the stairs. He could hear her talking to her baby son, and he had to stop on the landing for a second, just to breathe in deeply and say another silent prayer that this wouldn't be the thing that finally swayed her. That beautiful baby wasn't his, but he would love him as though he were and she knew that. He just had to hope that was enough and the pull of Rico's real father being around twenty-four-seven wouldn't be the winning argument in this situation.

Walking further along the landing, he stopped at the doorway to the nursery and leaned against the doorpost, watching as she stood at the window, talking to Rico, pointing outside and smiling at him as she held him close. His whole world stood just there; everything he'd ever wanted, even though he knew he'd probably realised this far too late. But she loved him, he knew she loved him. He just had to hope that, in the end, it was enough. Because he really wasn't sure he was strong enough to cope with losing her; another woman he didn't want to live without.

He let his mind wander back to last night. They'd been out together at a charity function organised by Cloud Sports. All eyes had been on them, every camera in that press line followed their every move. And she'd just oozed professionalism, even when the questions fired at her had been way too personal. She'd kept her arm tightly around his waist, holding onto him as though the world would end if she let him go, and he'd never felt more proud of her. More in love. She'd looked beautiful in a green jumpsuit and heels, that dark-red hair of hers loose and tousled, and he'd wanted the whole fucking world to know she was his. She was *his*. And nobody was taking her away from him. Nobody. Least of all Ryan Fisher.

Before that fear started rising again and before that anger returned, he walked back into their bedroom, opened the wardrobe and pulled out a small carry-on case. They needed to pack a few things for their visit to the north-east. It was the final weekend of the English football season, and Endleigh's last match was, ironi-cally, against Newcastle Red Star at Tynebridge. They were due to fly up there later that morning, giving them all a bit of time to relax before tomorrow's match, although relaxing was the last thing on Jim's mind. When Ryan Fisher was going to be so close to Amber – she was covering the match for Cloud Sports – how could Jim possibly relax? He knew what Ryan was trying to do; Ryan was making no secret of the fact he wanted her back. Jim knew Ryan was willing to fight just as hard as he was. How could he possibly relax?

'Do you have to do that right now?'

He turned around to see her standing there, dressed in nothing but the shortest of nightdresses, that incredible body of hers almost all on show.

'No. I don't have to do it right now. Where's Rico?'

'He's still a bit sleepy, so I've laid him down for a little while longer. He'll let us know when he wants to wake up properly. I'm just grateful I've got a baby who likes his sleep.'

'Let's hope that doesn't carry on into his teenage years, huh?'

Amber smiled, and Jim tried desperately to see if it had reached her eyes, to grab any kind of confirmation that she would actually still be here when Rico was a teenager. That they'd both still be here, with him. Living the life he wanted so badly.

'Are you still flying up to Newcastle with me and the squad? Or…'

'Both me and Ronnie are coming with all of you.'

'Good. That's good.'

'What's wrong, Jim?'

'Nothing's wrong.'

'I keep asking the same question and you keep giving me the same answer.'

He looked at her, watching as she slowly pushed the straps of her nightdress down over her shoulders, her eyes never leaving his.

'Maybe, if we make love first, you'll feel more like talking to me?'

He swallowed hard as her nightdress fell to the floor, revealing that beautiful body of hers in all its naked glory. 'There's nothing to talk about,' he whispered, his eyes focusing on her breasts as her breathing became a little heavier, his stomach turning those somersaults that made him feel like the teenager in love with the girl every guy in school wanted to date.

'I love you, Jim. Have you got that yet?'

He raised his eyes to meet hers, holding her gaze for what felt like an eternity. 'I know you love me, Amber. And I love you, too. Baby, I love you so much…'

'Come here.'

He walked over to her, sliding an arm around her waist, pulling her naked body close to his, and he couldn't stop the tears. He couldn't stop them. He hadn't even felt them coming until he'd touched her, but now they were streaming from his eyes and he couldn't stop them.

'We're gonna be fine,' she whispered, gently kissing those tears away, her fingers brushing his damp skin as her mouth touched his, briefly at first, but enough to make his stomach flip again, and that fear of losing her hit harder. 'We're gonna be okay.'

'Are we? Amber, I really need to know… I want you to tell me…'

She shook her head, laying her fingers lightly over his lips. 'No.'

'Baby…'

'I want you to make love to me, Jim. Right now, that's all I want. I want to feel you touch me,' She kissed him again, her mouth opening, her lips soft against his. 'I want to feel you inside me.'

And there was no place he wanted to be more than inside her, touching her deeply, feeling those muscles of hers hold him tightly the way they always did, coaxing another killer climax right out of him. He wanted that, too. Oh, Jesus, did he want that!

'I want to be your forever man, Amber. You know that, don't you?'

She looked up at him with eyes that were wide and trusting; eyes that were screaming out how much she loved him, he could see that. And if he'd had any idea that she'd already called him her 'forever man' he would know how much hearing those words from him meant to her. But he didn't know that. He just knew that he had to tell her everything he was feeling; he had to go against everything he'd ever been or tried to be. He had to lay himself bare and expose every fear because he wasn't going to lose her. He wasn't.

'Make love to me, Jim.'

She was in his arms, her legs wrapped tightly around him before their mouths had even touched, the kiss growing deeper and harder as he carried her over to the bed, laying her gently down as he threw off his clothes. Everything felt different all of a sudden, as if Ryan Fisher had thrown down some kind of gauntlet and now he had no option left but to fight this battle to the end. And he would, if that's what it was going to take. He'd fight so fucking hard.

Her skin was soft beneath his fingers as he ran his hands up over her legs, stroking those incredible hips of hers. He needed her like an addict craved their next fix. He would never tire of this. Never tire of touching her, of pushing inside her and feeling her taking him so deep he felt as though he was falling; he would never tire of that. And as she pulled her legs up around him, his stomach flipped once more as he felt her push against him, all beautiful and wet and ready for him.

Slipping his fingers between hers, he raised her arms up above her head, gasping quietly as she arched her back, pushing those breasts out towards him, her hips bucking up to meet his. And he was inside her before he'd even had a chance to realise it was happening; their bodies joined together as one, the way it was always meant to be. Amber Sullivan and Jim Allen were always meant to happen. There was no other script, no second draft or brand-new edit of this life they should be living. Because they were always meant to happen.

So why was he still crying? As he pushed deeper into her, her fingers gripped his as he thrust slowly in and out of her, but why was he still crying? Why was this so emotionally painful it hurt so badly, like nothing he'd ever felt before? It hurt. So badly.

Her hips bucked up again, harder this time, taking him as deep as he could go, and his fingers tightened around hers as those muscles inside her gripped him like the strongest of vices. But she came first, crying out loud as she pushed herself against him, and he took it all, preparing for his own release, which happened just seconds later, a mixture of beautiful pain and heartbreaking sadness flooding through him as their bodies moved together, taking every last second they could from the moment.

His baby girl. His beautiful wife. His whole fucking world. And he'd never been so scared.

*

'I didn't know you were gonna be here,' Ryan said, opening his front door to see Max standing there.

'You really think I'm gonna stay away when your last game is against Endleigh United?'

'It's just another club, Max.'

'Don't do it, Ryan.'

Ryan closed the door and leaned back against it, staring at Max. 'Don't do what?'

'If I was the begging type, then that's what I would do. I would beg you not to do this. But I'm not the begging type. So I'm asking you. As a friend, Ryan. I'm asking you this as a friend now. As someone who cares about you. As someone who cares about Amber. Please, don't do this. Just let her live her life. Let yourself live yours.'

'I don't know what you're talking about.' He headed off into the living room and Max followed him.

'You have no guarantee that she'll even talk to you. Her and Jim, they were out last night, did you know that? They were out, together, and there wasn't a photographer or a journalist out there that didn't want a piece of them. But some of the questions those reporters were throwing her way, they were past the point of personal. And that was because of you. You saw to that the second you stepped off that plane in Majorca. But she fended off

424

all those questions about you as she walked that press line like the true professional she is. She fended them off and she told it how it was. And I think she meant every word, Ryan. When she stood there, with her arms wrapped around her husband, telling everyone how much in love with him she was, I think she meant that.'

Ryan ignored everything Max was saying, instead choosing to pace the floor of his living room, checking his watch every few seconds.

'Are you listening to a word I'm saying?' Max asked, sitting down on the arm of a nearby couch. 'And why the hell are you obsessively checking your watch like that?'

'She's bringing Rico over as soon as she gets up here.'

'*She's* bringing him over? She said that, did she? She actually said *she* was bringing him over? After everything Jim said to you?'

'She's bringing him over. And I don't think Amber cares too much about what Jim says'

'That wasn't the impression I got last night.'

'I don't want to know, Max.'

'Well I think you *should* know. You should know that putting those thoughts into her head, whatever you're telling her, it isn't fair.'

'And it's fair that I should have to move so fucking far away just because I can't handle… Jesus, Max, I'm not forcing her, okay? I'm not coercing her into coming with me or making her do anything she doesn't want to do. I'm just trying to make her realise what's best for her.'

Max just looked at him. 'You do realise what you're saying, don't you?'

Ryan leaned back against the wall, pushing a hand through his hair, bowing his head as he let out the loudest sigh. 'I'm really not forcing her into anything, Max.'

'But you're not making it easy for her.'

Ryan looked up. 'And this is easy for me, is it? I'm the one who could be leaving my baby behind. I'm the one who could be leaving behind the woman I'm crazy about, and you have no idea how much that hurts. It's fucking killing me, Max.'

'Look, son, I know this isn't easy. I know it isn't; I can see that. But she's with Jim. She married him, they're making a life together…'

'With *my* baby, Max.'

'I know, Ryan. I know. But you've got to be strong, kiddo. Don't let this destroy you, because it nearly did, remember? And you really don't want to go back there.'

'I can't do it without her.'

'Yes, you can. Do you hear me? You can. This could be the making of you, Ryan, I truly believe that. A whole new start without any distractions…'

'Amber and Rico aren't *distractions*. Jesus, Max…'

'Okay, I'm sorry, I didn't mean it like that. I just meant that you need this, Ryan. You need to get away. And I wasn't sure when he…' Max stopped talking, realising he was saying way too much now.

'When, who, Max?' Ryan's eyes narrowed as he looked at his agent. 'You just said you weren't sure when he – who's *he*?'

'It doesn't matter. You just need to concentrate on the future now.'

'No, it *does* matter. Are you telling me it wasn't you who came up with the idea of me signing for a club in America?'

'No, it was, it's just that… It was a friend of mine, okay? Another football agent.'

'Who?'

'Does it matter who?'

'Yes. Who?'

'I'm not talking to you when you're in this mood.' Max stood up, straightening his jacket as he made for the door. 'You sort your head out, you hear me? Because I'm calling Amber and I'm telling her to get Freddie to drop Rico round here because she shouldn't be anywhere near you right now.'

'Who the hell do you think you are, Max? You're not my fucking father. You can't tell her to stay away from me.'

'No, you're right. You're right. I can't tell her to do anything. But what I *can* do is make sure neither of you do anything that either of you might regret. Now, you get that head of yours straight, and start thinking like an adult. A few more days and you're out of here. And as far as I'm concerned, the sooner the better.'

*

'You look like you've got the weight of the world on your shoulders,' Ronnie said, sitting down beside Amber on the step outside the back door in Freddie's kitchen.

'I'm fine. Just got a lot on my mind.'

'A big decision to make, huh?'

She looked at him. And it felt as though something had suddenly just broken inside her. 'I don't know what to do, Ronnie. I really don't know what to do. And I'm so fucking scared.'

He reached for her hand, squeezing it gently. 'Okay. I'm gonna stop telling you what I think now, because all that's done is push us further apart and I hate that. I hate it.'

'You were only saying those things because you cared about me.'

'Oh, so *now* you see what I was doing.'

She smiled, giving his hand a quick squeeze back. 'I've been so stupid.'

'It hasn't been the easiest of times, Amber.'

'Sleeping with Ryan… I shouldn't have done that. I shouldn't have let him wear me down, or get to me so much. I was weak, Ronnie. I was so fucking weak.'

Ronnie sighed, his hand still holding onto hers. 'Amber, sweetheart… Jesus, it's so hard not to wade in here with what I really want to say to you, but I promised, didn't I?'

She smiled again, looking down at their joined hands. 'You wouldn't be saying anything I don't already know. I've messed up so much, and now I'm left not knowing what to do.'

427

'You're seriously thinking about *going* with Ryan?'

She shook her head, pulling her hand free of his as she resumed her habit of fiddling with her wedding ring. 'No… I don't know. I mean, there isn't just me to think about any more, is there? What *I* want – well, should that really come first now? Shouldn't I be putting Rico's needs before mine?'

'Rico needs a mum who's happy, Amber.'

'It makes me so happy when I see him and Ryan together.'

'And what about Jim?'

'I would have thought the most wonderful words in the world you could hear right now would be ones that told you I was leaving Jim behind.'

'Despite everything I've ever said about that man, Amber, if leaving him is going to make you unhappy then don't do it. Just *be* happy. That's all I want for you, babe.'

She sat back against the door, stretching her legs out in front of her, clasping her hands together in her lap. 'I love him so much I can't really explain, because sometimes I find it hard to understand myself. But after everything we've been through…' She turned her head to look at Ronnie. 'But there's still something there, still some feelings buried deep inside me for Ryan. And maybe they're feelings I've tried to ignore or tried to deny, I don't know. And I can't say I love him, because I love Jim. That's one thing I'm sure of. But Ryan, he's… he's Rico's daddy, Ronnie. And that means a hell of a lot.'

'Is it a good enough – a *big* enough reason to leave Jim, Amber? To move away from everything you know just because you think it's the best thing to do for Rico? It doesn't really make sense, kiddo.'

'I know,' she sighed, pushing both hands through her hair. 'I know it doesn't. But constantly making sure I avoid Ryan, I can't do that for much longer, can I? Not when I might have to interview him tomorrow and then we have all those arrangements to make regarding Rico. Maybe if I just spoke to him face to face…' She looked at Ronnie again. 'If I speak to him, maybe things will seem clearer.'

'And what about Jim?'

She looked down at her clasped hands, at her nails digging into her skin, and she hadn't even realised she'd been doing that until she felt a sharp, stabbing pain below her knuckles. 'When we made love this morning, he cried, Ronnie. My beautiful, strong American man cried. And it broke my heart, because this time – this time none of this was his fault. *I* caused all this pain; I made this mess we're in. And I don't want to sound as though I'm wallowing in self-pity because I hate that. But I know I've been selfish. And I know that whatever happens one of those men is going to be hurt, and I caused that.'

'They had their fair share of input, Amber, so don't be too hard on yourself, okay? There's blame to be laid all over the place here. Some of it even lies with me because my outbursts over my personal feelings towards Jim Allen haven't really helped. But, and I do believe I've been telling you to do this for a while now, you need to make a decision, kiddo. And you really, really need to make sure it's the right one. Because this time, there might be no going back.'

*

'You're here, then.'

'Why wouldn't I be?' Amber frowned, closing the front door behind her. 'I said I was bringing Rico over, didn't I?'

'It's just that Max told me he was going to tell you not to come here today,' Ryan said, taking Rico from her.

'Well, he did say something about it probably being a better idea to get my dad to drop Rico off, but Max can't tell me what to do, Ryan. I'm an adult.'

Ryan smiled at Rico as he carried him into the living room. Amber followed him, throwing her bag down onto the chair near the door. 'Yeah. He kind of said that, too. But he certainly seemed

429

adamant he was gonna try to make sure you didn't come here.'

'I had to come.'

Ryan looked at her. 'You did?'

She nodded. 'I'm not a child who's easily led, Ryan.' Really? She might not be now, but she had been – once. And wasn't that how she'd got into this mess that had now spanned over two decades? Because she'd been easily led by a handsome American footballer with a beautiful smile and a way with words that had drawn her in and never let her go.

'Do you – do you want a drink?'

She shook her head, walking over to the window, looking out at Debbie who was crouched down by the flower beds out on her front lawn. 'Is she *gardening*?' Amber asked, unable to stop a surprised laugh from escaping. 'Have they cut the wages over at Red Star? Only, the Debbie I know would never do her own gardening. I can't believe she's pulling out weeds with those nails. I have to go and see this…'

'Amber, hang on…'

She swung around to look at him. Was she just using Debbie as an excuse to get out of there? Before she did something she might really regret? Before she made a decision she wasn't sure of, but one she might make anyway, because she still thought it was for the best.

'We need to talk. Please.'

She looked briefly back out of the window. 'I shouldn't have come here. Max was right.'

'Time's running out, Amber.'

Her eyes met his, and all the memories of being with this man flooded her brain, taking over her head completely for a few, painful seconds, ending with the visit he'd made to Majorca just a couple of weeks ago. Everything he'd said, every touch of his fingers on her skin; she could hear it all as though it were happening right now. But then all that was quickly pushed aside as the memory of her husband crying in her arms just a few short hours ago replaced those images of Ryan. The pull on her heart was so strong, so forceful.

'I don't think I can walk away from him, Ryan. We've been through too much. And I married him for a reason, didn't I? I married him because I'm in love with him.'

Ryan shook his head, gently laying Rico down in his carry-seat before he faced Amber again. 'Just think about it, Amber, please. Think about what he's done.'

'And he's sorry for everything. He's sorry.'

'And you believe him?'

'He's my husband.'

'That doesn't answer my question.'

'I believe him,' she said, her voice so quiet even she had trouble hearing herself.

'All he's ever wanted was to drive a wedge between us, Amber.'

'I think you managed to do a good job of that all by yourself at times, Ryan.'

He walked over to her, stopping just in front of her. 'And I regret every mindless, stupid second. Because I had you, Amber. Right there. You were wearing my engagement ring, I'd asked you to marry me and you'd said yes. And we were that close… we were almost there.'

'It was you who threw all that away,' she whispered, aware that he'd moved a step closer now.

'I know. And for what? A cheap thrill that was over in seconds? I threw my whole life away because I was an idiot, I admit that. And I regret it. With every beat of my heart I regret it.'

'It's too late.'

'Is it?'

She nodded, leaning back against the wall, her heart starting to pick up a speedy rhythm now. But she wished it would calm down, return to normal. Because she didn't want this. 'It's too late. Our time? It's passed. And it didn't work; we just have to accept that.'

'And what if I can't, Amber? What if I don't *want* to accept it?

What happens then?'

'I don't know, Ryan. How can I possibly answer that?'

'He doesn't deserve you.'

'You have no idea… He needs me. And I need him. We just don't work without each other.'

'And what about *me*, Amber? *I* need you, too. I need you so much…'

'You're going to L.A., Ryan. And you really want to take me with you?'

'I want to take you with me and I want to make sure we have the best life, Amber. I want to be a proper dad to Rico, I want…'

'You *are* a proper dad to Rico.'

'How can I be, when I'm thousands of miles away?'

'He'll see you as much as he can, Ryan, I promise you that. I'll make sure of that.'

'This is all wrong, Amber. This isn't how I wanted this to play out.'

'We don't always get what we want, Ryan.'

'But we can fight as hard as we fucking can to make sure we try.' She looked up into those deep, dark-blue eyes of his, her gaze not wavering for a good few seconds. 'I'm tired of fighting. Aren't you?'

He shook his head, reaching out to gently nudge her shirt open a bit more, letting his fingers run down over her collar bone, onto her cleavage. And she wasn't pushing him away. Not yet, anyway. 'Why did you really come here, Amber?'

Her eyes were still on his, but just as it had been over in Majorca, her arms felt like lead, and she couldn't seem to stop him from touching her in ways he really shouldn't have been touching her. 'I guess I just needed to know,' she whispered, her eyes focused on his mouth now. She'd always loved his mouth. She'd always loved that dark, heavy stubble of his and those sexy-as-hell sleeve tattoos. She'd loved all of that. But had she ever really loved *him*? Or was it just the idea that this man, eleven years younger than her, actually wanted to be with her. Had this little thing flattered her so much that she'd let herself think she'd loved him?

'You needed to know what?' he asked, his mouth moving closer to hers, his hand resting on her hip now.

'I love my husband.'

'Do you?'

'You really aren't being fair.'

'The time for being fair is over, Amber. It's every man for himself now, and I refuse to go down without a fight.'

She narrowed her eyes slightly, before she gently pushed him away. 'This isn't right. I've made my decision, Ryan. And I think, if I'm being completely honest with myself, it was a decision I'd already made a long time ago.'

'You're staying with him?'

She looked down at the floor briefly before raising her eyes, staring into his as she nodded. 'I'm staying with him.'

Ryan felt his whole world come crashing down around him. 'Baby, you can't. You can't stay with him. You can't do it.'

She felt tears start to build up behind her eyes, and she wished they'd go away, because crying here, in front of him, was only giving him a reason to think she wasn't sure of the decision she'd just made. And she was sure. Wasn't she? She was sure.

'I have to do this. Ryan, you are so young, so beautiful – you're going to have your pick of women over there in L.A. and they are gonna fall at your feet so fast it'll take your breath away...'

'I've told you, Amber, I don't want *any* woman. I want *you*.'

'I can't... It isn't going to happen, Ryan.'

'Because you won't let it?'

She waited a couple of beats before answering. 'Because I won't let it.'

He watched as she pushed past him, crouching down to quickly kiss Rico's now-sleeping face. 'I'm leaving you with daddy for an hour or so, little man. You be a good boy, now, you hear? And look after daddy for me, you got that?' She stood back up, turning to face Ryan.

He shook his head. 'I don't need looking after, Amber.'

'I'll get my dad or Kim to come and collect him later. And I'll see you at Tynebridge tomorrow.'

'Amber!'

He followed her out into the hall, quickly grabbing her hand before she had a chance to leave, swinging her back around to face him. And his mouth was on hers before she had a chance to even think about what was happening. The second his lips touched hers, she tried to push him away, but his grip stayed firm, his fingers slipping into hers and holding onto her so tightly she really couldn't break free. And she really wanted to leave, to get out of there, before something happened that she was too weak to control, but the more he kissed her, the more she gave in. The more his grip on her relaxed, the less she struggled to leave his arms, until he had her backed up against the wall, their bodies touching, that heat once more turned up and she knew she had to find that strength again; the strength to walk away from this.

'Ryan, no. No!'

He let go of her, pulling away slightly, his hands now in his pockets, his head down. 'I'm sorry.'

'So am I,' she whispered, taking one more look at him before she turned to open the door. 'So am I.'

Chapter Thirty-Three

'I can't believe this is your last match for Newcastle Red Star,' Gary said, sitting down next to Ryan in the dressing room as they prepared for their final game of the season, against Endleigh United.

'No. Neither can I,' Ryan sighed, leaning forward, clasping his hands between his knees. 'It all feels a little surreal, if I'm honest.'

'I'm really gonna miss you.'

Ryan turned to face Gary, a smile slowly spreading across his face. 'Yeah. I guess I'm gonna miss you, too.'

'Still, I'll be coming over to visit. You can bet your life on that.'

'You mean *we'll* be coming over to visit, surely. You *and* Debbie?'

'I'm not bringing Debbie. Jesus, mate, we're talking L.A. here! I'm not gonna bring the wife.'

'Then you might want to tell *her* that.'

They both looked up as Amber walked into the dressing room, Ryan's heart immediately stopping dead in his chest. She looked as hot as hell in a cobalt-blue dress that clung to her every curve, and bright-red, wedge-heeled ankle boots. She'd certainly made sure she had the colours of both teams playing this afternoon covered, that was for sure – red for Newcastle Red Star and blue for the colours of Endleigh United. Had she done that on purpose? Yeah. She probably had. She still looked as hot as hell, though, and he felt the first stirrings of an inappropriate hard-on start to make itself felt. Him and every other player in the room right now, he thought, watching their reactions as she leaned back against the wall, propping one foot up behind her, which only served to raise that dress a little higher up her thigh. Something that, once again, didn't fail to get a reaction.

'Jesus!' she sighed, looking around the dressing room. 'Most of you have seen me naked, for Christ's sake. I'm sure you can all handle a bit of leg.'

'She means that *Ice* photo shoot,' Ryan said, noticing Gary's expression change.

'Oh. Yeah, of course.'

'She's already planning her shopping trip along Rodeo Drive,' Amber went on, fixing Gary with a look. 'Debbie, that is. You know, your wife. The one you don't want to take with you when you visit *him* over in the States.' She jerked her head at Ryan.

'She might get bored.'

Amber just raised an eyebrow. 'You think?'

Ryan couldn't say anything. He'd known she was working this afternoon. He'd known she was going to be everywhere around this ground, but he guessed he hadn't quite been prepared for just how beautiful she was going to look. How much she'd changed over these past couple of years, from the cold but still beautiful ice-queen bitch he'd first met, to this incredible, red-hot woman in front of him. And she could have been his. She could have been.

'Anyway, I just came in to see how you were all doing. Dave said I should make sure you were all decent before I walked in here but, hell. Come on. It's nothing I haven't seen before, huh?' She threw them all a wink, and with a smile thrown over her shoulder she left just as quickly as she'd arrived. But Ryan couldn't let her go. Not yet.

'Amber, hang on. Wait!'

'Shouldn't you be back in there getting ready?' she asked, looking at the dressing room door he'd just burst through.

'It's my last game, Amber. The rule book's just been thrown out. Is Rico here?'

'My dad's got him up in his box.'

'Can I go see him?'

'Of course you can. Look, I've got to go, Ryan. Jim and the Endleigh squad are about to arrive, and…'

'You still sure?'

She looked at him, cocking her head slightly. 'Still sure about what?'

'About staying with him. You've still got time to change your mind, I don't leave for L.A. for another few days, so…'

'I'm sure, Ryan. So, please, let's just leave this, okay? Because it isn't fair on either of us now.'

'I love you, Amber. That hasn't changed, and I doubt it ever will.'

She smiled, and all that did was make his heart shatter into more tiny pieces. 'It'll change. And you'll find someone who can love you back the way you deserve to be loved.'

'I wanted that person to be you.'

She kept her eyes on him, taking in his handsome face with that heavy stubble and those dark, dark-blue eyes. Her handsome Geordie boy. 'There was a time when I wanted that person to be me, too, Ryan. But things have changed.'

He looked down at the ground at his black boots, his hands in the pockets of his match-day suit pants. He had one chance left. And he wasn't even sure it would work, because he had no proof. None. And it was something that could backfire spectacularly if he was wrong. But he had a hunch, and it was the only card he had left to play now.

'Ask Jim something for me, Amber.'

She frowned as she looked at him. 'Ask him what?'

'How much involvement he really had in making sure I signed for an American club.'

She felt as though someone had punched her hard in the stomach. 'I… what are you talking about?'

'Just something Max said. Or didn't say would be more accurate. Something he let slip. It wasn't his idea to make me go to the States. He all but said that.'

'And what's Jim got to do with it?'

'The idea was all his.'

*

She walked outside, onto the steps of the Tynebridge main entrance, the warm May sunshine hitting her face as she looked up at the clear blue sky. It was a beautiful day for a game of football. A pretty pointless game, if the truth be told, because Endleigh were already League champions and Newcastle Red Star could finish no higher than eighth place this season, even if they won all three points this afternoon. But Ryan had just thrown a little black cloud up into that perfect sky; something that had made her think twice and question everything.

She turned to look down the steps as the Endleigh United team bus drew up outside the stadium and she watched the players, dressed in their matching suits, some of them wearing headphones, others chatting away to each other as they stepped down from the bus and made their way up the steps and into the stadium.

She didn't take her eyes off that bus until she saw him. The Endleigh United manager. A man who was so good at his job clubs from all over the world wanted him to take charge of their teams. Her husband. Was he the man who really had tried to make sure Ryan Fisher left this country?

Those trademark aviator shades of his covered his eyes as he walked up the steps, his head slightly down, but as soon as he reached the top, it was almost as if he'd sensed she was there. He looked up, took his shades off and slid them into the top pocket of his jacket.

He smiled at her and she couldn't help but smile back. He looked so handsome. So heartbreakingly handsome, and when he came over to her, uncharacteristically breaking his match-day focus to do something so unlike him, she had to take a deep breath. But maybe that focus wasn't so necessary today, seeing as his team had nothing to play for. They'd already won it.

'You look incredible,' he whispered, sliding an arm around her waist and surprising her even more by kissing her, something which didn't go unnoticed by the members of the press, who were hanging around outside. 'Meet me back out here in five minutes.'

'Jim?'

'Five minutes, Amber.' And with a quick squeeze of her waist he left her standing there while he followed the last of his squad inside.

Amber leaned back against the wall, closing her eyes briefly as she tried to get her head around what Ryan had said. Was it just another hunch? Was he just trying to stick the boot in one last time in the hope that she'd finally give in?

'Here you are. I was wondering where you'd got to.'

Her eyes sprung open to see Ronnie standing there. 'Oh, sorry. Yeah, I just… I just needed a bit of fresh air.'

'They've arrived, then,' Ronnie went on, nudging his head in the direction of the Endleigh team bus, which was currently being parked in a space directly opposite the Tynebridge Stadium entrance.

'Yeah. Just now.'

Ronnie frowned. 'You alright?'

'I'm fine. Just feel a bit light-headed, that's all.'

'You're not…?'

'No. I'm not. If only it were that easy.'

He leaned back against the wall beside her. 'Come on. What's he said?'

'Who?'

'I dunno. Either of them. But one of them's obviously said something.'

'It's nothing,' she sighed, pulling herself away from the wall. 'It's just a bit of an emotional day, you know? What with it being

Ryan's last match for Red Star. His last match for a British club.'

'You having second thoughts?'

She didn't answer straight away, her eyes focused on the dispersing crowd, who were now all making their way to the various entrances around the stadium that led inside. 'Jim has a lot of contacts in the USA.' She turned to look at Ronnie. 'Doesn't he?'

Ronnie shrugged. 'He's got a few.'

'And some of those contacts are connected to L.A. Gamers, right?'

'I don't know, Amber. They might be. Where's all this leading?'

'Would he really have done that?' She'd turned her head away again, staring back down at the car park below.

'Done what? Amber, sweetheart, you're making no sense again.'

'I need to see Max.'

'Why?'

'After everything we've been through…'

'Amber!'

But she'd ran back inside before he had a chance to ask anything else.

'Whoa, where are *you* running off to?'

She looked up as Jim caught her arm.

'You okay?' He frowned, his grip on her wrist loosening.

'I'm fine,' she replied, taking a step back. 'Look… what did you want to meet me for?'

He smiled, that wonderful smile that made his eyes crinkle up and her heart miss that proverbial beat. 'I would have thought that was obvious.'

It was her turn to frown. This wasn't like Jim at all. His behaviour was different; his whole match-day routine had apparently been thrown out of the window, and it was all slightly unsettling. Was this really just because it was the last day of the season and his team had nothing to play for today? 'Shouldn't you be in the dressing room?'

'Colin's taking care of all that. It's not like the guys need a lot of direction for this game, is it?'

'I'm supposed to be working, Jim.'

He moved closer and she let him. Despite what was happening inside her head she let him circle her waist and pull her closer, right there where everyone could see them. But that didn't matter. He was her husband. He was the man she'd chosen to spend the rest of her life with, right? 'It won't take long, believe me. With you looking like that, it really won't take long.'

'Not here,' she said, gently pushing him away, her hand sliding into his. 'Come on. I know a little room just off the corridor downstairs that…' She stopped talking. He really didn't need to know it was a place she and Ryan had used many a time when they'd needed a quick fix. 'It's quiet. And nobody ever comes down there. Not on a match day, anyway. They're far too busy up here.'

He didn't argue, he simply clung onto her hand as she led him out of the reception area and down some stairs that led away from the main part of the stadium. All of a sudden she really needed this. She *wanted* this. Yes, she was confused and she didn't know what to think any more, but she wanted this. She wanted to fuck him; to feel him and know that he was there for her. She needed to know he was real. She needed to know if he was a liar.

Pushing the door open with her bottom she pulled him inside, kicking the door shut behind her and leaning back against it. It had no lock, so that was the only safe way to do this.

'Amber?'

She kept her eyes on his as she reached up under her dress, slipping off her knickers. 'Is this what you wanted?' she asked, sliding her dress up over her thighs, just high enough to give him a tiny glimpse of what he could have. Of what he was going to get.

'You know it's what I want.'

She reached out and pulled him closer by his tie, sliding his suit jacket back off his shoulders until it fell to the floor. 'Then you can have it,' she breathed, taking his hand and placing it between her legs, watching as his eyes closed and his head dropped, a low, quiet groan escaping from him as he pushed his hand up against her. 'You can have it all.' Before she took everything away? That all depended.

'I love you so much,' he gasped, burying his face in her hair as he pushed her dress a little further up over her hips, holding onto her tightly as he kissed her, their tongues touching as he lifted her up, pushing her back against the door. She wrapped her legs around him, her fingers in his hair as their kiss deepened, and she couldn't help but cry out a little as he pushed into her. It felt so good. It felt right, when he was inside her. It felt right. He was her husband and she loved him. She still loved him so much. But if he'd done this – if he'd done what Ryan had insinuated…

'Oh, baby, you are so good to me,' he groaned, pushing just that little bit harder, that little bit faster, until they both came in a flood of cries, her fingers grabbing his hair as she felt him take her over, filling her up with everything he had to give her. Her beautiful American man. The love of her life. A manipulative control freak? Or someone who just got scared? This was what she needed to know.

She held onto him tightly as their breathing slowed down, their bodies still joined together and she wasn't really ready to let him go just yet. So she stayed where she was, holding onto him, because she was frightened of what she was going to hear when this was over.

She kept her eyes closed as he slowly pulled out of her, putting her back down.

'Jesus, Amber… you have no idea how much I needed that.' He pushed a hand through his hair, watching as she slipped back into her knickers, pulling her dress down over her thighs with a wiggle of her hips that almost brought his hard-on back to life.

'I kind of needed that, too,' she said, reaching out to touch his cheek, kissing him again, letting the taste of him linger on her lips for as long as she possibly could. 'But I really should be getting back to work. And you've got a team to run.'

'They can look after themselves,' he said quietly, his fingers intertwining with hers, his breath warm on her cheek as he stayed close.

She could feel her heart still hammering hard, her stomach turning for reasons that weren't all good. Why had Ryan said that? Why had he, once again, tried to make her think twice about what she was doing? But hadn't he been right the first time? When he'd accused Jim just a few months ago, he'd been right. So there was every chance he was going to be right again. And that's what scared Amber more than anything.

'Kiss me again,' she breathed, looking up into his eyes, a pain cutting right across her chest that made her flinch slightly. 'I want you to kiss me forever,' she whispered. She just had no idea how long their 'forever' was going to be any more.

'I think I can do that.' He smiled, cupping her cheek in the palm of his hand, his thumb gently stroking her skin as his mouth rested on hers and she just fell against him. He was kissing her deep and slow, his fingers clinging onto hers, their bodies touching, the heat surrounding them almost unbearable. And Amber took in every wonderful second of his lips on hers, his fingers holding onto her hand so tightly – she took it all in. She let her head spin and her stomach flip; she let the confusion fade away for a few, glorious seconds as she enjoyed nothing but her husband kissing her. Her husband. A man she'd really thought she couldn't live without.

'Did you have any input in making sure Ryan signed for an American club?'

The question had come out before she'd even had time to think about asking it. The words had just slipped out of her mouth, and she couldn't take them back now, even though a part of her wished she could.

Jim took a step back, but his hand was still holding hers, his head cocked slightly to one side, those beautiful green eyes of his narrowed as he stared at her. 'Where the hell has this come from?'

'Ryan,' she whispered, letting her fingers slip away from his.

'Ryan?' he laughed, pushing a hand through his hair. 'He said it was *me* who made sure he signed for an American club?'

She nodded, trying to read his face. Trying to see if he was lying to her. 'He said it was all your idea. Or that you had something to do with it, at least. What's he talking about, Jim?'

'Baby, I don't know…'

'What is he talking about?'

'Amber, you know what he's trying to do. He won't be happy until he's driven us apart…'

'Did you?'

He looked at her, and she felt her heart shatter into a million tiny pieces. 'Did I what?'

'Have anything to do with it?'

'Amber, I…'

She shook her head, tears starting to prick the back of her eyes as she looked at him. She couldn't say anything. No words would come out. But what *could* she say? She just wanted to get out of there. She *had* to get out of there. Even though he was calling her back, shouting her name, she still walked away. She had to get back to work; she didn't have time for this now.

By the time she got back to the main reception area she'd composed herself. Just about. She'd paid a visit to the ladies' room, redone her make-up, made sure she looked as calm as she needed to feel, because she had a lot to get through before she could concentrate on what she'd found out. But there was one thing she needed to do first, and her eyes searched him out before she walked over to him.

'I need to speak with you,' she said to Max, who was talking to a couple of the Red Star board members.

'Now?' he asked, frowning slightly as he looked at her.

She pulled him aside. 'When this game is over you are going to answer some questions for me, and I'm warning you, Max, you'd better tell me the truth.' She turned on her heels and started to walk away, leaving Max more than a little confused.

'Huh? Amber? Hang on, sweetheart…'

She swung back around to face him, suddenly feeling a strength she didn't know she had well up inside her. 'You're going to tell me the fucking truth, Max, because this isn't a game any more. You got that?'

'Amber?'

She was stopping for nobody as she strode through the main atrium, making her way up to her dad's executive box. She wanted to see her baby. Five minutes with Rico would get her head sorted; he could always ground her. Until she could finally work out just what the hell was going on here.

But she hadn't expected to see Ryan there. Why not, though? She'd told him he could come and see Rico. She just hadn't expected him to do it before the match, and seeing him kind of startled her.

'Everything okay, sweetheart?' Freddie asked, looking up as Amber walked into the room.

'Can I have a word with Ryan, Dad? Please?' It wasn't what she'd planned to do, but he was there. And she needed to say something.

Freddie looked from Amber to Ryan, but all Ryan could do was shrug. He looked as surprised as Freddie did, although Amber suspected he knew exactly what she was going to say.

'Yeah. Of course you can. Do you want me to make sure this place stays quiet for a little while?'

She just nodded, her eyes fixed firmly on Ryan. 'Can you take Rico with you, please?'

Freddie frowned. 'Okay. Are you sure you're alright?'

'I'm fine. I just need a private word with Ryan.'

Freddie took Rico from Ryan, his gaze fixed on Amber for a few seconds more, but she was still looking at Ryan. 'I'll be over in the main bar if you need me.'

Amber said nothing, she just waited for her dad to close the door behind him before she spoke. 'What is it exactly that you think he's done, Ryan?'

'I don't know, Amber. All I know is Max said something about it not being *his* idea, and he started to talk about someone else, but then stopped. But he had a look on his face that told me he was hiding something. I swear to God, Amber, I'm not just trying…'

She held up her hand. She didn't really want to hear any more. 'You are, Ryan. You'll try anything you can to make me change my mind you said as much yourself. You said you won't give up without a fight, that it's every man for himself, and you know – you *know* that if I find out Jim has anything to do with this…' She had to stop talking because the tears were threatening to fall and she didn't want that. She didn't want to cry or be weak at a time when she needed to be strong.

'I wouldn't do anything to deliberately hurt you, Amber.'

'Are you… are you only assuming he's involved with this because of what happened with the betting ring story?'

'Of course I am, Jesus! If he can do that, don't you think he's capable of this, too?'

'I don't know what he's capable of any more, Ryan.' Her voice was quiet, almost defeated.

She leaned back against the table in the corner of the room, looking up as he walked over to her, still dressed in his match-day suit, his white shirtsleeves rolled up, showing his tattooed forearms, that familiar dark, heavy stubble covering his jawline.

'Have you spoken to him?' Ryan asked, digging his hands into his pockets.

She nodded, looking back down for a second before her eyes met his. 'Just now. But this is how fucking twisted everything's got. I had to fuck him first. I *wanted* to fuck him first. I wanted to hold him and kiss him and feel him inside me before I… before I knew…'

Ryan bowed his head, and she could see him breathe in deeply, his body exerting itself with the weight of that breath.

'How wrong is that?' Amber whispered, looking outside at the still almost-empty stadium. Only a few people were already in their seats, the rest of the crowd making the most of the pre-match time to grab a drink and something to eat. But the atmosphere was still palpable; that wonderful feeling of anticipation that Amber loved. Even at a match that carried no importance for either team, the atmosphere was still there. And wasn't that what this game was built on? Wasn't that what had made Ryan want to be a part of all this? Would it feel the same over in the States? 'It's going to be so different over there, Ryan. And he… he's taken you away from all of this, hasn't he?'

Ryan looked at her, his eyes locking onto hers. 'It's probably for the best, when all's said and done.'

She shook her head, trying desperately to keep those tears at bay. She needed to stay calm – focused. She still had a job to do. 'Can't you change your mind?'

'I've signed a contract, Amber.'

'For how long?'

'A year. To begin with. But there are options…'

She looked away again. She didn't know what to do. She truly had no idea what to do next. 'I think he really did have something to do with it.' Her voice was still quiet. Because it wasn't Ryan she was angry with. He was an innocent victim caught up in the middle of some twisted power game that she couldn't understand.

'Amber, look, I have no proof, but…'

She turned back to face him. 'Once this match is over I'm going to talk to Max. And he's going to tell me the truth, Ryan. He's going to tell me just how the hell we got to this point because I am lost here. I'm lost.'

Ryan pulled her up and into his arms, and he held her close – that was all. He just held her, neither of them saying anything for a few seconds. But they were the most heartbreaking, confusing few seconds of her life.

'I've got to go,' she whispered, pulling away from him, but he didn't let her go straight away. He kept a loose grip of her waist, his mouth gently lowering down onto hers, and she didn't fight it. She didn't want to. It didn't help matters, but she didn't want to fight it. She didn't want to fight anything any more. She was tired of it all. 'I've really got to go.' She pulled free of him, turning to walk away.

'Amber?'

She turned around, her eyes meeting his.

'Does this change anything?'

She held his gaze for a few seconds more. 'I don't know, Ryan. I really don't know.'

Closing the door behind her, she took another deep breath before heading quickly downstairs. She should be mic'd up by now, preparing for her pitch-side interviews. She'd let herself get far too distracted.

'Amber!'

She stopped walking, closing her eyes briefly, taking in another deep breath. 'I'm late, Jim.'

'I need to talk to you.'

She swung around. 'I'm late.'

'You believe him?'

'I don't know what to believe.'

'We need to talk.'

'I'm supposed to be working. So this really is going to have to wait.' She turned away again, resuming her brisk pace along the corridor.

'I'm sorry, okay?'

Once more his voice caused her to stop in her tracks, and she slowly turned back around. 'You're sorry?'

'I love you, Amber. What I did, I did because I love you so much…'

'I can't do this now, Jim. I really can't. So, just leave it. Please. Because doing this now isn't fair. It really isn't fair.'

She didn't look back as she finally pushed through the double doors that took her back out into the main atrium, which was quieter now as more and more people drifted off to the bars or their hospitality suites.

'Where the hell do you keep disappearing to?' Ronnie said. 'I've been looking everywhere for you. They're going spare upstairs. You should have been mic'd up half an hour ago… What's wrong? And if you say "nothing" I swear I'll do something that will really draw attention to us.'

'I don't want to do this here, Ronnie.'

'So something *is* wrong, then?'

'Yes, something's wrong.'

'Is it serious?'

She looked at her best friend. And at that moment in time she wished with every fibre of her being that they could go back to the time when they'd been together. He'd been a player in Manchester and she'd been an up-and-coming local sports reporter, and she knew, right at that very second, that if she could go back to that time she would hang onto him so tightly and never let him go and it would change all this. She'd change it all. Because this was just too exhausting now.

'I don't know, Ronnie. Right now, I really don't know.'

Chapter Thirty-Four

Jim stood at the edge of the technical area, checking his watch as the referee dragged out the last few seconds of time added on for as long as he could. But even when that final whistle was blown, he had to stand and watch as Ryan Fisher was given a standing ovation from the home crowd. He watched as a player who was, undoubtedly, going to be missed by the English league, ran around to every corner of the ground, saluting the supporters, making sure they knew how grateful he was for the support they'd all shown him during a turbulent couple of years at Newcastle Red Star. He watched as Ryan ran back to the touchline, over to Amber, who was waiting with microphone in hand to grab an all-important few words with him before he left this club for good. And it tore Jim apart to see her smile at him. Because he didn't know how much she was putting on for the camera and how much of it was real. He didn't know if what he'd done had changed her mind, and sent her running back to Ryan when this was supposed to have made sure that didn't happen.

He watched as Ryan's eyes stayed fixed upon her, and, even from where he was standing, Jim could almost see the chemistry between them. And though he wanted to turn away, he couldn't. Because if he was losing her then he wanted to make sure he took in every last detail of a woman he would never stop loving. She was his world, and she'd continue to be just that, no matter where she was or who she was with. She was his world. A world that was quickly starting to crash down around him.

*

Autopilot got her through the afternoon. She'd been running on empty, stumbling through everything with a blurred mind and a focus she had to pull out of nowhere and she had no idea how she'd done it. But she'd managed to keep that front up, the professional image she'd needed to portray so that this mess they were all in didn't become public knowledge. And interviewing Ryan had been the hardest thing of all to do, to stand there and look at him; to treat him like any other player when he was so much more than that. Even though everyone knew their history, knew their relationship was so far past professional, she'd still had to make it look like any other interview. The hardest thing she'd ever had to do. Under the circumstances.

And now, as she said her thanks and they cut back to the studio, he was still there in no hurry to run back up that tunnel one more time to join in the celebrations with his soon-to-be ex-teammates.

'Are you okay?' he asked.

She nodded, still trying to keep up her professional exterior until she could take her mic off. Not that any of her life was that private any more. 'I'm fine.'

'You sure?'

'Ryan, please, I'm fine. Go and enjoy yourself, okay?' She threw him a look that told him this wasn't the time or the place for this conversation, and turned away from him. It was all she could do. But, as she unclipped her mic pack and handed it over, finally free to say and do what she wanted, she felt a sadness wash over her that seemed to overtake the confusion. She just needed to dig up that strength she'd found earlier and start dealing with this. One way or another.

451

Jim's eyes stayed on Ryan as he watched him lean in closer to Amber, and whatever she'd said to him had made him step away, but that meant nothing. She was still mic'd up, so whatever conversation they were having post-interview, it couldn't be anything too personal. She wouldn't want any of this to be out there in the open just yet, just as he was in no hurry to make anything public. Unless it involved her commitment to him. Unless it involved them making those plans to renew their vows and showing the world just how much they loved each other, and he could only hope that was still a possibility. Because the thought that everything could now be taken away from him was the fear he'd tried to push aside. The fear that wouldn't lie low. The fear that was well and truly making itself known now.

He watched as Ryan ran back towards the tunnel, his arms high above his head as he clapped more thanks to the fans who were still inside the stadium, making sure they got one last glimpse of one of the best players this club had seen in a long time. Could he have become even better if Jim hadn't have come back here and messed with his head, pushed him into doing things and taking paths he may never normally have taken. Or was Ryan Fisher one of those people who was always going to go down a certain path, with or without provocation?

It wasn't until he reached the mouth of the tunnel that Ryan turned around, coming face to face with Jim, who'd been determined to go nowhere until he'd seen him. And although they were surrounded by club officials and other players who still hadn't retreated to the dressing rooms, he still needed to let him know. He still needed to make him aware of what was at stake here.

'That was one hell of a final game. Because you're one hell of a player,' Jim said, his eyes locking onto Ryan's. 'Young, talented – an asset any club would be proud to have.' He moved a step closer, gently holding onto Ryan's arm, although his grip was far tighter than it might have looked to anyone watching. 'But what you've done today, putting those thoughts into Amber's head – you had no right to do that.'

'I had every right,' Ryan hissed, tugging his arm free of Jim's grip. 'She needs to know what you are. She needs to know what you're capable of.'

'If she comes running to you, you tell her it's over. You hear me? All of this, it's over.'

'You must be so desperate, Jim. And I'm not doing this here. So you back off, okay?' And with that he just walked away, leaving Jim more alone than he'd ever felt in his life. A man who had once been famous for his controlled and calm exterior was now helpless. And that was a feeling that scared him to the core.

*

'He's avoiding me,' Amber said, impatiently tapping her fingers on the bar in the Players' Lounge.

'Who? And what the hell is going on with you this afternoon?' Ronnie asked, pushing a gin and tonic towards her.

'He's got some fucking nerve,' Ryan said, joining them at the bar, showered and changed, his dark, damp hair pushed back off his face.

'Again, *who*?' Ronnie asked, his voice slightly more agitated now. 'I feel like I'm in the middle of the frigging Twilight Zone here. Is someone going to explain what's going on?'

'Has he said something to you?' Amber looked at Ryan, taking a sip of her gin. The alcohol hit was greatly appreciated.

'He cornered me in the tunnel. Said if you came running to me, to tell you it was over.'

'Something can't be over if it never really started.'

'Is anyone gonna tell me what the fuck is going on?' Ronnie asked, raising his voice slightly, if only to get some sort of reaction. Because being nice obviously wasn't getting him anywhere.

453

Both Amber and Ryan looked at him. But neither of them seemed in any hurry to offer an explanation. 'I'll talk to you later,' Amber said, not really making it clear whether she was aiming that at Ryan or Ronnie, but she'd spotted Max, and she was determined he wasn't going to avoid her any longer. 'Max! Jesus, if he walks away from me one more time…' She followed him out of the Players' Lounge. 'Max!'

He turned to face her just as Jim appeared from around the corner. She looked from one to the other, not missing the glance that passed between the two of them.

'Okay. Now I *know* you both had something to do with this.'

'Amber, baby…'

'No, Jim!' She stared at him. Her beautiful husband. Her strong American man. How could she still love him so much, yet resent everything he'd tried to do? How could she still love him – so fucking much? 'Not now. I want to hear what Max has to say.'

'We need to talk. Have you any idea how this is making me feel?'

'Making *you* feel?' She couldn't help but laugh. 'Maybe if you didn't stir up so much shit then none of this crap would be happening.'

'He was taking you away from me.'

'He was doing nothing, Jim. Because I have a mind of my own, and no matter what he tried to do it would have been *me* who'd ultimately made whatever decision needed to be made.'

'And what *is* that decision?'

'You honestly think it's that easy? Huh? After all of this… you think it's that easy? You think I can just stand here and tell you what's gonna happen next? Because I haven't got a fucking clue, Jim.'

'Okay, okay… let's all just calm down a bit here,' Max said, and even he had to flinch at the look Amber threw him.

'I told you before, Max, I'm going to ask you questions and you're going to tell me the truth.'

'Amber, come on…'

She swung around to look at Jim, stopping him from saying any more. 'I don't need you around right now, Jim. Okay? I want to talk to Max. Alone.'

'This isn't happening…' Jim sighed, leaning back against the wall, pushing a hand through his hair.

'Oh, it's happening. It's really happening.' She turned her attention back to Max. 'Follow me. We're going somewhere more private.'

'Amber!' Jim shouted after her, but she wasn't listening any more. She was on a mission to find out the truth. To find out exactly what had been going on. The reasons *why* it had happened could wait. For now.

Arriving back downstairs, at the room she and Jim had been in earlier, Amber opened the door to let Max through, closing it quietly behind her.

'Why did you let him persuade you?'

Max looked at her, his expression one that said he didn't quite know how to deal with this.

'Jesus, come on, Max! You can tell I know what's going on, so don't even bother trying to look surprised. He asked you to look for a foreign club for Ryan. Is that true?'

Max sighed, bowing his head as he dug his hands deep into his pockets. 'Yes, Amber. It's true. But it wasn't that simple…'

'You actually let him talk you into doing that?'

'I didn't *let* him talk me into anything.'

'Has he got something against you? Is there some big secret you're hiding that only he knows about, and if you didn't do what he wanted…?'

'You're blowing this all out of proportion, Amber.'

'I'm *sorry*? Did you just say I was blowing this all out of proportion? The father of my baby is about to leave the country to live thousands of miles away…'

'And is that all he really is?'

She looked at him, frowning. 'Again, I'm *sorry*?'

'Is that all Ryan really is? The father of your baby?'

'I don't want him to be all those miles away, Max. I never wanted that.'

'But you didn't want him living just around the corner, either. Did you? Because neither of you can trust yourselves. You keep going round and round in these fucking circles, sleeping with each other then pretending you hate each other, before something happens and you're back fucking each other like a couple of out-of-control teenagers instead of two adults who should know better. And that isn't good for anybody, Amber. But it's especially dangerous for Ryan. Because you know the kind of person he is. You know how vulnerable he can be; how much he can let things get to him. And what you two do to each other, it isn't healthy. He needs stability. And, okay, when Jim first asked me to look into clubs further afield than Europe, I didn't want to get involved, because his motives – they were different.'

'How?'

'You know how. He wants Ryan out of the way, out of arm's reach. He wants him to no longer be a threat to your marriage because that's all he sees Ryan as now. A threat.'

'So why did you do it? If you didn't agree with…'

'Because I care about that kid. Yes, he's been an idiot in the past, and it beggars belief how he's still in one piece when I think about what could have happened to him. But I love him, Amber. I love him like a fucking son, and I knew – I *knew*, given everything that's happened over the past couple of years, I knew that if you two were still around each other, it'd eventually destroy him. If he was around you all the time, but he couldn't have you, it *would* destroy him.'

'He's stronger than that,' Amber whispered, wiping her eyes with the back of her hand as those tears finally started to fall.

Max shook his head. 'No, Amber. He isn't. Sweetheart, he isn't strong. And I can't risk him throwing his life away. Not again. He hasn't got that many chances left.'

She backed up against the wall, covering her mouth with her hand as those sobs started to escape.

'Oh, Jesus, come on, kiddo…' Max moved towards her, but she held up her other hand, shaking her head, stopping him from coming any closer. She didn't want to be hugged or made to feel as though this was alright. Because it wasn't. It was so far from alright. 'Amber…'

'We could have worked something out, Max.'

He shrugged, his hands still in his pockets. 'Maybe. I don't know. But I wasn't prepared to risk it. What Jim told me, I knew it was for his own – I don't know, call them slightly selfish reasons, but after I thought about it, after I sat down and actually thought about it, I realised it was probably the best thing for Ryan. In the long run. That's why I agreed to contact L.A. Gamers after Jim told me Corey Reynolds was on the look-out for a big-name British player. Everyone wants their own David Beckham, huh?'

Amber looked down at the floor, at her bright-red boots, at the dark tiled floor; anywhere but at Max.

'But we didn't think it through one hundred percent,' Max went on, his voice a little calmer now, a little more controlled. 'Otherwise we would have seen this coming. And we were naïve to think nobody would find out.'

She finally looked back up. 'I don't know what to do, Max. I'm angry and upset and so fucking confused I can't even get my head straight. I mean, is this – is this all *my* fault? Because… because I don't know…'

'Listen, kiddo, it isn't all your fault, okay? This is a mess that was caused by so many different people and actions that have had knock-on effects we can't even begin to think about. It's just one of those things. And maybe we should have seen it coming a long time ago.'

'You should have told me,' she whispered, twisting her wedding ring round and round her finger as she stared down at her left hand. 'That this was happening. You should have told me.'

'Jim, he… he really does love you, Amber. In his own, sometimes misguided way, he loves you. And what he did here, it was because he was scared. He was desperate. He loves you, and Ryan was a threat, someone who could take you away from him, so…'

'You should have told me.'

'He loves you, Amber. And maybe you should hear him out.'

Her head shot up, her eyes boring into Max's. 'It's because of him that Ryan is moving thousands of miles away from his son. I'm not sure I *want* to hear him out.'

Max threw his head back, letting out another heavy sigh. 'You need to think about this, Amber.'

A loud rap at the door made Amber jump, and she stepped away, flinging it open to find Ronnie standing there, a look on his face that suddenly made her feel nothing but panic.

'You really need to stop disappearing, Amber. Or at least tell someone where the hell you're going.'

She could hear the wail of sirens in the distance, noise coming from upstairs that didn't sound like any form of celebrating, and all of a sudden she felt sick to her stomach. Whatever was happening, she knew it wasn't good. Ronnie's face was telling her that much. 'Ronnie? What's wrong? What's happened…? Oh, Jesus, is it Rico? Oh God, no, not Rico…'

'Rico's fine. Sweetheart, he's fine. He's with your dad… It's Jim.'

'Jim?'

She felt that panic rise, along with another wave of nausea she had to try and batter down.

'He collapsed, in the Players' Lounge. There were paramedics already in the stadium so they got to him pretty quickly, but… Amber, are you listening to me? Can you look at me, babe? Please. Look at me.'

He put his hand to her face, making her look at him. But all she could hear was the sound of blood rushing to her head, and all she could feel was that rapidly rising panic washing over her.

'They think he might have had a heart attack…'

'No,' Amber whispered, shaking her head. 'No.' She pushed past him, running so fast along the corridor her chest hurt, but she didn't care. She just needed to run.

'Amber, hang on… Max, do you want to meet us at the hospital?'

'Is he…?'

'I don't know. Look, I'll make sure she's alright, go on.'

Amber could hear faint voices in the background as she continued to run, a new-found energy coming up from somewhere that she just hadn't had before. But it was there, and she was using it. But then, almost as though someone had just flicked a switch, it seemed to drain out of her, and she could do nothing but lean back against the wall, watching as Ronnie ran up to her.

'Come on. I'll take you to the hospital.'

She looked at him, her eyes full of so many tears, but they didn't seem to want to fall. 'Is he…?'

'He was awake when they put him in the ambulance, that's all I know, Amber.' He held out his hand, and she took it. Why couldn't she cry? She'd just been told her husband might have had a heart attack and she couldn't cry. She felt nothing but a numbness wash over her. This whole day felt somewhat surreal, and she closed her eyes for a second, hoping that when she opened them this would all have been a dream. But it was real. The noise and Ronnie's hand holding hers, his voice trying to explain things to her that she could never take in right now, it was all real.

'Do you…?'

'I know what's going on, yes. Ryan explained everything to me…'

'Oh, God… Brandon. Ronnie, someone needs to tell Brandon. He's in… he's in Manchester… Ronnie, he needs to be told…'

'Hey, it's okay. It's okay. They're telling him, alright? They're trying to get in touch and they're gonna try and get him back here as soon as they can. He'll be here, don't worry.'

'I…I need to be with Jim.' She started walking again, her pace quickening as she almost dragged Ronnie behind her, but he gripped her hand tight, slowing her down. 'I need to be with him, Ronnie. What if he...?' She closed her eyes as those tears finally started to fall. 'I've got to get to him. I've got to... I've got to get to him.'

He pulled her into his arms, holding her tight, stroking her hair as she clung onto him. 'Come on,' he whispered, kissing the top of her head. 'Let's get out of here.'

Chapter Thirty-Five

She was out of the car before Ronnie had a chance to stop her, pushing past the waiting press and crowds who had gathered outside the hospital, all of them desperate to find out what had happened. And even though people were shouting things at her, questions she couldn't make any sense of, she ignored them all. What could she tell them when she knew nothing herself?

They knew who she was the second she entered the hospital, voices telling her from every angle which ward Jim had been taken to, and how she remembered the information she'd been given she had no idea. Someone had offered to take her up there themselves but she was hanging around for nobody, not even Ronnie. She just kept on running, crashing through the double doors that led onto the ward she'd been told to go straight up to. It was full of people, an overwhelming noise filling the air – a sound of panic and fear and she felt her stomach twist itself up into the tightest of knots as she stood still for just one second. One second to get her bearings, to try and work out what was happening.

And then she saw it – a side room to her left. The door was wide open, the bed was surrounded by a mass of people shouting as someone pressed down on the chest of the person lying in that bed, and all Amber could do was let out the loudest of wails, a sound not unlike that of a wounded animal as she sank to the floor.

'It's okay, I've got you. Come on, babe, I've got you.'

Ronnie had managed to catch her before she hit the ground, but her eyes wouldn't leave that room. She watched as someone shouted "clear," and Jim's body jerked upwards, a nurse beside him shaking her head as she began another set of compressions.

'No!' Amber howled as she tried to break free of Ronnie's grip but he held her back, stopped her from running in there, because what good would that do? 'No! That isn't him, it can't be him.'

'What the…?' Freddie came running around the corner, following Amber's gaze before he looked straight at Ronnie, taking a sharp intake of breath as Ronnie shook his head.

'No.' Amber's voice was almost a whisper now as she watched them shock Jim one more time, watched his body jerk up and fall back onto the bed, and in that split second her whole world came together then fell apart, shattering into a million tiny pieces, memories scattering around her brain like confetti. And then it was almost as if a strange kind of calm had taken over. As though all emotion had just been wiped clean out of her, she turned to her father, an almost stoic expression on her face. 'Where's Rico?'

'He's with Ryan, sweetheart. He's taken him home, he's fine.'

'Good.' Her voice was barely a whisper as she turned her attention back to Jim's room, and all of a sudden there seemed to be a kind of calm taking over in there, too. She could hear the faint beeping of a machine, and the number of people gathered around his bedside had diminished somewhat.

She cocked her head as she watched a nurse lean over Jim, checking the machine beside his bed, and again she felt a strange sense of calm wash over her. But then the fear came back as the shock wore off and she looked at Ronnie. 'What's happening?'

'I don't know, babe.'

'I want to see him.' She turned to see a tall, kind-looking man talking to her father, and she cocked her head again as she tried to read his expression, but she couldn't. She couldn't see anything there that was telling her that this was okay.

'Mrs. Allen?'

She squeezed Ronnie's hand tightly as the doctor turned to face her.

'Your husband, he experienced a heart attack – a pretty mild one – at the stadium. His collapse, however, was an extra concern, which is why he was brought straight up to the ward instead of being taken to A&E. He was awake, alert and responsive when he got here – he was asking for you…'

Amber felt her heart break, a pain so physical it cut to the core, and she couldn't stop more tears from streaming down her face.

'Would you prefer to go to my office?' the doctor asked quietly, his expression one of concern now.

'No,' Amber replied, shaking her head. 'No. Thank you. I'm not… I'm not leaving him.' Her eyes were back on Jim, his body still, but those machines were beeping, and that had to mean something, didn't it?

'He went into cardiac arrest, Mrs. Allen…'

'Amber. Please, call me Amber.' She finally took her eyes off Jim, looking straight at the doctor. 'I… is he… is he okay?'

'The next few hours are critical, Amber. But, in the context of what's happened to him, your husband's been very lucky. He wasn't down for long, just a couple of minutes, and he's breathing on his own. Which is good. That's really good. But we need to keep a very close eye on him.'

'Is he going to live?'

'Amber, sweetheart, the doctor's telling you everything he knows…'

Amber ignored her dad, her eyes still fixed on the doctor. 'Is he going to live?'

'He's stable. That's all I can tell you right now. But the signs are good.'

She squeezed Ronnie's hand again, her eyes back on Jim now. 'Can I… can I see him?'

'Of course. We've given him something to make him sleep,

so he won't be responsive, I'm afraid, but you can sit with him.'

'Do you want me or your dad to come in with you?' Ronnie asked.

She shook her head, her eyes not leaving Jim. 'No, I… I want to be on my own.' She let go of his hand without looking at him, or her dad, and followed the doctor into Jim's room.

'Oh, Jesus…' she whispered, her hand covering her mouth again as she breathed in deeply, blinking back more tears. She needed to be stronger than she'd ever been now. She needed to be really strong. For both of them. 'Will he… will he wake up himself?'

The doctor nodded. 'He's probably going to sleep for a while now, because we've given him a pretty strong sedative, but, yes. He'll wake up, when he's ready.'

'Can I touch him?'

'Of course you can.' The doctor smiled. 'He won't break, I promise.'

Amber tried to smile back but she just couldn't do it.

'Look, I know this must all seem very scary right now, Amber, but, like I said before, Jim's been very lucky, considering. His early signs are good, and the fact he's breathing on his own is extremely promising. We just need to try and find out if there's some underlying condition that might have caused this to happen. And, if there is, then hopefully we can deal with it.'

'Could stress have brought this on?' she asked, her eyes focused on Jim's chest as it slowly rose and fell.

'Stress can play a part, yes. Has he been under any extreme stress lately?'

She felt those tears threaten again but she blinked them back, quickly wiping her eyes with the back of her hand. 'He's a football manager. Aren't they always stressed?'

Her own weak attempt at humour made the doctor smile again. 'He isn't the first person in that profession to suffer something like this. Has work been particularly stressful for him recently?'

She shook her head. 'No. But we… there've been a few things…'

She couldn't get the words out, and she closed her eyes for a second as she felt the doctor's hand on her shoulder giving it a friendly, gentle squeeze.

'Stress *can* be a factor, Amber. But it isn't always the main cause. Okay?'

She nodded, finally managing a smile. 'Okay. And, thank you.'

'You stay here as long as you like, and if you need anything, the nurses' station is just outside. We'll be checking him at regular intervals, so try not to worry, alright?'

She nodded again, watching as he left her alone. She sat with the man she'd thought she'd lost. And that's what made the tears fall hard and fast, almost blinding her as she sat down beside Jim, reaching out for his hand.

She gasped quietly as she touched him, because he was warm, and even though she hadn't really known what to expect, she hadn't expected him to feel so warm. But just the feel of his hand in hers made her cry again, slow, silent tears falling down her cheek that she let slide, watching as they fell onto their joined hands.

She leaned over and gently kissed his forehead, stroking his dark, grey-flecked hair from his eyes. 'You know, if you really wanted to get my attention, all you had to do was shout a bit louder. Because this – this is kind of extreme.'

She sat back down, bringing his hand up to her mouth and kissing his fingers, squeezing them tight.

'It shouldn't have come to this, Jim,' she whispered, the sound of his breathing just audible over the beeping of the machines. 'And I'm sorry, baby, if what I did caused this, because the last thing I ever wanted to do was hurt you. I love you so much, and I… I just love you, so much…' She rested her forehead on their joined hands as more tears streamed from her eyes, falling onto his skin, but she swallowed them down, breathing in deeply again to try and control her emotions. But there were so many clashing for space inside her head right now it was hard to control anything. 'I love you, Jim Allen. You walked into my life all those years ago and you never left. You never left me. And you are not leaving me now, do you hear me? You aren't leaving me now.'

*

'Is he okay?' Ryan asked, sitting down beside Max, clasping his hands between his knees as he leaned forward.

'As he can be. He's still sedated, as far as I know. They haven't told us all that much, and I haven't seen Amber since I got here. But Ronnie's spoken to her, and from what I can gather, Jim's a very lucky man.' Max looked at Ryan. 'I thought you were supposed to be looking after Rico.'

'Freddie's taken over for a couple of hours. He said there wasn't much anyone could do here, so, he thought I might like a breather.'

'Amber doesn't know you're here?'

Ryan shook his head, staring down at the floor. 'This really does change everything.' He looked up, right into Max's eyes. 'Doesn't it?'

Max sat back, pushing both hands through his hair. 'Ryan, I really don't know. But, if you want me to give you an honest answer – yes. I think this changes everything.'

'You spoke to her, didn't you? Just before all this happened.'

'Well, it was more like *her* speaking to *me*, actually, but, yeah. I talked to her.'

'And, did she give you any idea? Did she... did it sound as though she might have made a decision...?'

Max sat forward, matching Ryan's stance, his hands also now clasped between his knees. 'She was confused, Ryan. She was... she didn't really know what she was going to do. She was angry and upset and...' Max bowed his head, closing his eyes for a second or two. 'I wouldn't get your hopes up, son. Because I don't think she's going anywhere now.'

Ryan sighed, throwing himself back into his chair, and letting out a heavy, frustrated sigh. 'I mean... Jesus! I never wanted anything bad to happen to the guy, but... this doesn't change what he did, Max.'

'Maybe not. But you have to realise that that isn't going to be the most important thing on Amber's mind right now. Her husband could have died, Ryan. Okay, he was lucky, under the circumstances, but he *could* have died. So whatever he's done in the past, I doubt that's even going to bother her now.'

Ryan sat forward again, his eyes once more down on the floor. 'I want to postpone my flight to the States, Max. I want to stay here a little while longer, help Amber look after Rico. I think that's only fair, don't you? She's gonna have enough to cope with, so the least I can do is help out with our son.'

Max looked at Ryan. 'This time I really *am* begging you, Ryan. If you only want to do this because you still think…'

'I'm doing this because I don't want Amber to have to cope with a sick husband and a baby all on her own.'

'She has family, Ryan.'

'And Rico has a daddy who wants to stay and look after him for a little while longer. And that's all I'm doing this for, Max. That's all I'm doing this for. It gives me a little bit more time with my baby boy and it takes the pressure off Amber.'

Max held Ryan's stare for a little while longer. 'Okay. I understand, and I'm sure Corey Reynolds will understand, too. I'll go give him a call. Let him know what's happened.'

'Thanks, Max.'

Ryan sat back, another sigh – one of relief this time – escaping as he watched Max head off to make the call to L.A.

'I thought you were looking after Rico.'

He turned his head to see Amber standing there, her arms folded, her face stained with tears. She'd changed out of that figure-hugging blue dress and killer red boots now, into jeans, baseball boots and an oversized white shirt, her dark-red hair piled up on top of her head. She looked tired. And Ryan felt his heart pull apart. Because he really had to let go now. He had to let go. Even though it was still the last thing he wanted to do. 'Your dad's taken over for a little while. I… I didn't know whether you wanted me to bring him here…'

Amber shook her head as she sat down in the chair Max had just vacated, her arms still folded across her chest. 'No. Not yet. This isn't really the place for him.' She looked straight at Ryan, her eyes meeting his and staying there, and he felt that pull on his heart again. 'Is Rico okay?'

'He's fine.' Ryan smiled, and she tried to return it, but smiling still wasn't something she felt like doing. 'How about you? How are *you* doing?'

She turned away, staring straight ahead of her. 'It doesn't matter how I'm doing.'

'It does to me.'

She turned to face him again. 'Thanks. For coming, I mean.'

'I care about you, Amber.'

'This isn't about me, Ryan. None of this is about me. All I care about now is that Jim wakes up and he's okay and we can…' She trailed off, looking down at her left hand, her fingers fiddling with her wedding ring.

'How is he?' Ryan asked, watching as she continued to twist that ring round and round her finger.

She shrugged. 'He's still asleep, and he probably will be for a good few hours yet, but… I don't know. Nobody really knows anything until he wakes up.'

'You're not staying here all night, are you? Only, it's getting late now. You should really go home and get some rest.'

'I don't want to sleep, Ryan. How can I sleep when Jim's lying there? I don't want to leave. I'm not leaving until he wakes up. Ronnie brought me a change of clothes and he's staying with me, you know – supplying me with coffee and bringing me food I don't want to eat, but it's good to have him here. I don't know if I could do this on my own.'

'You're not on your own.'

She looked back up at him. 'Why do you care what happens

to him?'

'Because I'm not a monster, Amber. Jesus, come on! Whatever he might have done, I wouldn't wish this on anyone.'

She sat back, finally unfolding her arms, sighing quietly. 'I know. I'm sorry. I didn't mean to say that, I'm just...' She sighed again, briefly closing her eyes. 'I'm sorry.'

He wanted to reach out and take her hand, but he wasn't sure what her reaction would be, so he kept his hands clasped together. But he really wanted to touch her. To let her know he was there for her. If she needed him. 'You know Freddie's only gonna come back here later and nag you into getting some sleep.'

'I can sleep here.'

He wasn't going to argue with her. But he didn't know what else to say now. Everything had changed. Everything.

'If you want me to bring Rico to see you, just let me know. Okay?'

She looked at him again, and this time there was the faint trace of a smile there on her tired but still oh-so-pretty face. 'Thank you. It means a lot to have you here. To have you taking care of Rico. It's a huge help.'

'I've put my flight to L.A. back. I want to stay here for a little while longer, help out with Rico. If that's... if that's what you want.'

She leaned over and hugged him. A totally unexpected reaction, but after a split second of wondering what he should do, he let his arms fall around her, holding her tight as she held onto him. 'It's what I want,' she whispered, staying in his arms. And he didn't let her go, not until she pulled away and stood back up, folding her arms again. Those barriers were back up now. 'I'm really grateful, Ryan.'

'I'm his dad, Amber. I want to spend as much time as I can with him.'

Another weak smile before she turned and walked away. And at that second, Ryan knew she was walking away forever.

*

'Amber?'

She swung around to see Brandon standing there, a look of fear and confusion all over his young and handsome face. 'Oh, baby…' She walked over to him, pulling him into her arms, holding him tight as every emotion the poor kid must have been bottling up for hours came tumbling out.

'I was so scared, Amber. I didn't… I didn't know what to do, and nobody could really tell me anything…'

'I know… Sshh, it's okay. Sweetheart, it's okay.' She wiped his tears away, gently stroking his hair as she looked into his eyes – eyes that were so much like his dad's.

'Is he… is he alright?'

'He's asleep. They've given him a sedative to help him get the rest he needs, but, he's holding his own. I'll get Mr Whelan – that's your dad's consultant – to come and talk to you as soon as he gets here. He can explain more because I'm not sure how much I've really taken in.'

Brandon looked at her, his hand holding tightly onto hers. 'I was so scared, Amber. I was so fucking scared.'

'I know, baby. We all were.' She pulled him in for another hug, her eyes going straight to someone standing at the far end of the ward. And Brandon must have felt her tense up because he turned his head to see what she was looking at.

'I didn't know who else to call, Amber. And… and she was there. When it happened. She was there, and she offered to pick me up from the airport and bring me here…'

Amber smiled, squeezing his hand tight. 'Brandon, it's okay. Do you want to see your dad now? He's asleep, but you can sit with him for a while.'

He nodded, and Amber couldn't help but notice how young he looked. How frightened he was. It was strange, how fear could suddenly make someone who was usually so strong seem so vulnerable.

'He's just in there. You go tell him how much you love him,

okay? I'll be there in a second.' She waited until he was by Jim's side before she walked over to Ellen, her eyes never leaving the young woman's. 'Thank you for bringing him here.'

'It was the least I could do, Amber. I still care about him, and I know… I know what I did to him, it was wrong. And I regret…'

'It doesn't matter, Ellen. Right now, it really doesn't matter.'

'I do still care about him.'

'I know. But he really doesn't need any more complications in his life, okay? I know I'm not his mum, and he probably wouldn't thank me for saying this to you, but I really would appreciate it if you'd leave him alone now.'

Ellen looked down and Amber felt a little sorry for her. Had she herself not acted irrationally because she was confused about what it was she really wanted? So how could she blame this young woman for doing the same?

'Is Jim alright?' Ellen asked, her voice quiet as she looked back up at Amber.

'We'll know more when he wakes up.'

'I'm sorry, Amber. For everything.'

Amber shook her head, once more folding her arms against herself. 'Don't be. I'm wiping a lot of slates clean tonight, Ellen. Yours is just one of them.'

Ellen managed a small smile. 'Thank you.'

'You've got nothing to thank me for, Ellen.' And with that, she turned and walked away.

*

'What are *you* doing here?' Ryan asked, looking up as Ellen walked past him in the corridor.

She stopped and turned to face him. 'I brought Brandon here.'

'Oh. Okay.'

'And now I'm going home. I've still got work in the morning and I could do with some sleep.'

471

'Ellen, hang on… wait!'

She stopped walking and turned to face him again. 'What, Ryan? I thought we had nothing left to talk about?'

'We haven't. Not really, it's just that, well – with everything that's happened today, can we just wipe the slate clean?'

'Yeah. That's kind of what Amber said,' Ellen sighed, leaning back against the wall.

'You've spoken to her?'

Ellen nodded, rooting around in her bag for her purse. 'Why do I never have a pound coin handy when I need one? I could really do with a coffee…'

'Here. Have this one,' Ryan said, handing her his cup. 'I haven't touched it yet, I promise.'

She looked up at him, smiling slightly. 'Thanks.'

'So, are you… are you doing okay?'

'I'm doing fine. My world didn't stop just because you dumped me.'

He leaned against the wall beside her, shoving his hands in his pockets. 'That's not what I meant.'

She took a sip of coffee. 'Sorry. I'm just a bit tired. It's been a strange day.'

'Yeah,' Ryan sighed, throwing his head back. 'Tell me about it.'

She turned to look at him. 'When are you leaving for the States?'

'Well, it was supposed to be in a couple of days' time, but, given what's just happened, I'm delaying it for a while. I want to stay here, help Amber out with Rico.'

Ellen looked down into her coffee. 'You wanted her to go with you, didn't you? To America.'

'Yeah. I wanted her to come with me. I still do, but I've kind of accepted that it's not gonna happen now.'

'Are you going to spend the rest of your life loving a woman you'll probably never have?'

Ryan looked down at the floor, his hands still buried deep in his pockets. 'I don't know, Ellen. And, believe me, this isn't how

I want to feel because it hurts, y'know? Every day I wake up and it hurts, so I don't *want* to feel this way. But sometimes life gives you no fucking choice.'

*

'Don't start, Ronnie.'

'You might call it nagging, Amber, but what use are you gonna be if you can't keep your bloody eyes open. Is that fair on Jim? Huh? To wake up and find you're a wreck because you refuse to close your eyes for half an hour.'

'I'm not going home.'

'Nobody's making you go home, kiddo. Christ, we've all tried that and look where it got us. Just go get your head down some-where quiet. The nurses have said you can use one of the on-call rooms.'

'I'm fine where I am. I'm not leaving him, Ronnie, so you might as well save your breath.'

'Stubborn as ever,' Ronnie sighed. 'But, it's ten past four in the morning and, quite frankly, I can't argue with you any more. I haven't got the energy. You might be able to function on no sleep, but I need some shut-eye. Otherwise who's gonna look after you, huh?'

She smiled, giving him a hug. 'Thank you. For everything. And I mean that, Ronnie. I really need you right now.'

'Yeah, I know you do.' He smiled, too, gently rubbing her back as he held her. 'But you're not frigging easy to cope with, let me tell you.'

'No. She never is.'

Amber pulled away from Ronnie as though he were on fire, turning around so quickly she felt dizzy. 'Jim! Jesus, don't try and sit up…' She ran over to the bed, sitting down beside him, taking his hand in hers. A new, fresh batch of tears started to fall slowly down her cheeks. 'Ronnie, go get someone, go!'

'What the hell happened?' Jim whispered, his voice slightly hoarse. 'Last thing I remember was lying here, asking for you…' He looked at her, his eyes tired and slightly red, but there was colour back in his face. And all Amber could see was her beautiful American man. Awake, and alive.

'The doctor's will explain everything, but… I thought I'd lost you.' She wiped her eyes with her forearm, desperately trying to stop crying now. 'I really thought I'd lost you.'

He reached out to touch her cheek, slowly brushing away tears with his fingers. 'Hey, come on. It's gonna take something way bigger than this for you to get rid of me.'

'I love you so much, Jim.'

'I love you, too, Amber. Jesus, baby, I love you, too.'

'And Brandon's here. I think he may have gone to get something to eat…'

All of a sudden the room was full of people again, and she had to take a step back while they checked Jim out. She had to leave the room when all she really wanted to do was stay there and make sure he wasn't going anywhere because she was still scared. He was awake, and he seemed okay, he seemed fine. But she was still scared.

'It's a good sign, Amber. If he can wake up and recognise that you're still the stubborn, hard-to-deal-with woman we're all so familiar with, then I'm sure he's gonna be fine.'

She couldn't help smiling, her hand slipping into Ronnie's as they sat down by the nurses' station. 'Where's Brandon?'

'Someone's gone to find him. I think he went to get a coffee.'

'Would you like a cup of tea?'

Amber looked up as one of the nurses arrived back at the large, semi-circular desk. They'd all been so friendly to her these past few hours, and that just made Amber start crying again.

'That'd be great, thanks.' Ronnie smiled at the nurse, squeezing Amber's hand gently.

'Okay. Coming right up.'

'What if something's wrong, Ronnie? I mean, what if this happened because he's ill or there's something wrong with his heart? What if there's every chance I could lose him again?'

'Hey, come on, listen. Amber, listen to me. He's only just woken up, okay? So nobody knows anything yet. They're gonna do tests and he's probably gonna be here for a while, so let's start getting used to that first, alright? But, if there *is* something wrong, then I'm sure they'll find out what that is. And they'll deal with it. But you need to stop thinking the worst when the poor guy's only just woken up. He needs to see you strong, okay? You might not feel it, but that's what you need to be.'

She clung tightly onto his hand, her eyes going back to Jim's room. She could hear his voice; she couldn't make out what he or the doctors were saying, but she could hear his voice. 'This has been such a wake-up call, Ronnie.'

He slipped an arm around her shoulders, pulling her in for another hug. 'Yeah. I kind of get that, kiddo.'

As soon as she saw Mr. Whelan approaching, she was up and out of her seat. He was still the same, kind-looking doctor she'd seen yesterday, and even though he had a smile on his face, and she wanted to smile too, she really did, she didn't feel as though she could do that just yet. Not yet. 'I didn't think you'd still be here,' she said, folding her arms against herself. It was becoming a bit of a security blanket, that arm-folding thing.

'I have actually been home, if I'm being honest.' He was still smiling. 'But I came into work early because I had a feeling Jim would wake up at some point this morning. Have you been here all night?'

She nodded.

'You really should get some rest.'

'That's what we've all been telling her,' Ronnie sighed, standing up beside Amber, his hand resting lightly in the small of her back. 'Is everything alright?'

'Well, from what I can gather by talking to him just now, he seems remarkably fine. He's tired, of course. But, outwardly, he seems to have suffered no lasting damage.'

Amber breathed an audible sigh of relief, determined not to cry any more. It was just too exhausting.

'We will, however, have to run quite a few tests, to see if there's any obvious reason why this happened, and we'll be doing that over the course of the next few days. We'll also be keeping him in hospital for a little while yet, so, you really should think about going home and getting some rest, Amber.'

'Did you hear that? Are you gonna listen to him?'

'Yes, thank you, Ronnie. I'm not five.' She turned her attention back to Mr. Whelan. 'Can I go back in and see him?'

He nodded, smiling again. He had the most comforting smile, which was probably good, given his profession. It certainly had the knack of calming *her* down. 'Of course you can. We'll keep checking in on him, and we'll get started on those tests in a little while. You think about what I said now, okay?'

She gave a brief nod before leaving Ronnie's side, walking back into Jim's room. He was sitting up slightly now, his chest still wired up to that machine, and there was a drip in his arm too. But he looked okay. He looked like the man she loved.

'Are you alright?' he asked as she sat down on the edge of the bed.

'Shouldn't I be asking *you* that? And I'm fine. Just tired of people nagging me to get some sleep – and don't *you* start, okay? I've had enough from him out there.' She jerked her head in the direction of Ronnie, who was leaning over the desk at the nurses' station, obviously keeping them all amused because they were laughing at whatever he'd just said. And one or two of them seemed to be looking at him with more than a hint of lust. She'd almost forgotten what an attractive man Ronnie White actually was.

'He just cares about you, Amber.'

'I know,' she sighed. 'And I'm grateful, to all of them, for being here. Because I was so scared, Jim.'

'Can I let you into a little secret?' he asked, taking her hand, his thumb gently stroking her wedding ring. 'So was I.'

'Oh, baby,' she leaned forward, her lips gently brushing over his.

'I won't snap in two, Amber.'

She looked at him, and he smiled – that all-encompassing, full-on smile that got to her every time. Every, single, time.

'I nearly died. I think the least I deserve is a proper kiss, don't you?'

She smiled, too, leaning forward again, resting her mouth against his a little harder this time. And it was like she was kissing him for the very first time all over again. She had the same butter-flies in her tummy; the same feeling of light-headedness; the same overwhelming feeling of complete love for this complicated, hard-to-understand man.

'You're really going to have to start taking things a bit easier now, you know that, don't you?' she whispered, snuggling in against him, his arm sliding around her shoulders.

'I'm not gonna be some invalid, Amber. I mean, I feel kinda rough right now, but hopefully that won't last.'

'Look, I know how crap it is when people start nagging you to do things you don't feel much like doing, but this is important, Jim. This is your life we're talking about here. And I really don't want to lose you. So, please. Just – just start taking things a bit easier.'

He kissed her forehead, his hand rubbing her shoulder. 'You're cold.'

'I'm fine. And stop changing the subject.'

He took her hand in his, his fingers once more rubbing her wedding ring, his eyes looking down. 'What happened, Amber? With Ryan…'

'No. It's over, okay? All of that, forget it. I've spoken to Ryan, and it's over.'

'Is it?'

She felt those tears start falling again – tears of relief, this time – and she closed her eyes as his mouth once more covered hers, his kiss calming her. And just to feel him there and know that he was real, that he was okay; that was enough. It was enough to make her realise what she had to do. 'It's over.'

Chapter Thirty-Six

'Debbie! There's a case of pink champagne just lying here in the kitchen. Where's it come from? Because I'm absolutely positive I didn't order it.'

'Oh, sorry, hon. That was me. I got Gary to drop it off before he…' She stopped talking, and Amber looked at her, a slightly wary expression on her face.

'You can say it, Debbie. Gary dropped it off before he went over to Ryan's. I'm well aware he leaves for L.A. today so you can all stop trying so hard not to mention it.'

'Pretty rough timing, though, don't you think?' Debbie said, pulling a bottle of champagne out of the crate. 'I mean, I know you probably wouldn't have wanted him here today anyway. Where do you keep your champagne flutes, chick?'

'Cupboard behind you. And I'm not sure Ryan would have wanted to come to mine and Jim's vow renewal even if I'd asked him. But, yeah. You're right. The timing is a bit off.'

'You're not gonna let it ruin your day, are you?' Debbie asked, pulling the cork out of the bottle with a pop so loud it made Amber jump.

'No, of course I'm not gonna let it ruin my day. Debbie, I care a lot about Ryan. But his leaving… I'm kind of used to it now. Well, more than I was before, anyway. I mean, Rico's had him around for an extra couple of months, and that was more than I could have wished for. He was the biggest help to me while Jim was in hospital. But, I always knew he was going to have to leave at some point.' She shrugged. 'And today's the day.'

'Have you said goodbye?' Debbie handed Amber a glass of pink champagne, and Amber took it, taking a long sip.

'Rico and I went to see him last night.' Amber stared down at the floor. 'Seeing him with our little boy, Debbie… it broke my heart.'

'Oh, chick… come here.' Debbie pulled her in for a hug, and Amber held onto her, glad of that hug. But she was determined not to cry or even get upset at the thought of Ryan leaving. It was the way things were meant to be. She knew that now. 'He's gonna miss Rico's first birthday, Debbie. That's what hurts the most.'

'We'll have a huge party for him, chick, and we'll video it and make sure Ryan gets to see it all. He won't miss a thing.'

'At least he saw him take his first steps. That's something.'

'They grow up so fast, don't they?'

Amber nodded, taking another sip of champagne. 'It doesn't feel like five minutes since I was sitting there, panicking that Ryan was going to miss the birth altogether. And now we're just a couple of weeks away from Rico's first birthday. Another year gone, just like that.'

'And what a year, huh?'

Amber looked at her friend, smiling slightly. 'What a year.'

Debbie gave her another quick hug. 'I'm so glad you spent the summer back up north.'

'Well, with Jim being ill, and everything else that's been going on, I wanted family and friends around us. It just made sense to rent this place and stay here. Endleigh United have put Colin in temporary charge of the team until Jim's fit enough to return to work, which he thinks he is but I'm not so sure about. And I think the rest has done him the world of good. Although, I know for a fact he's still been in constant contact with Colin. He thinks I don't know what he's been doing, but I know.'

Debbie smiled, topping up their glasses. 'He's one of those men you can only keep down for so long, hon.'

'Tell me about it.'

'What about the pre-season tour?'

'Oh, he thinks he'll be back in charge by then. And I doubt I'll be able to stop him, if I'm honest. But, at least it's only a tour of Germany, so it's not like he's having to fly halfway across the world, because then I *would* have been putting my foot down… Jesus, listen to me! I sound like the kind of nag I hate.'

'You love him, chick. And after what he went through, of course you're worried. Anyway, can't you go with him? On this tour?'

'I've got to get back to work myself, Debs. So, we'll be going back home, to London, next week. Try and get everything back to normal as soon as possible.'

Debbie raised her glass, and Amber did the same. 'To resuming normality.' Debbie smiled.

'I'll second that,' Amber sighed, taking another long drink, just as her phone started ringing. She leaned over to see who it was, picking it up and answering it the second she saw it was Jim. 'Are you okay?'

'Jesus, Amber, baby, can you please stop asking me that every time I call you?'

'You want to stop me from worrying? Then try doing as you're told.'

'I love you.'

'I love you, too. And I'm sorry. I'm nagging again, aren't I?'

'Yeah, but I'll live with it. Sometimes it's actually quite a turn-on.'

'You shouldn't even be thinking about that just yet.'

'Amber, honey, Mr. Whelan said if I can climb a flight of stairs without anything feeling wrong, then I can have sex. And that was a month ago. You're killing me here.'

'Have you called me because you want sex?'

Debbie couldn't help but look up as Amber said that.

'Yes, actually. Baby, you have no idea… the stress of *not* having sex is actually worse than having it. And I'm sure Mr. Whelan…'

'I don't believe you… You're seriously gonna lay medical guilt on me?'

'What're you wearing?'

She threw her head back and sighed, but she couldn't help smiling. Almost two months without sex wasn't just frustrating for him, it had pretty much been a killer for her, too. 'I'm not sure I should be doing this right now. I want you fit and well when I walk up that aisle.'

'I'm assuming it's way too early for you to have your dress on?'

'Of course it's too early. I've only just got up. We've got hours yet. I've only just stepped out of the shower.'

'So… you'll not be wearing all that much, then?'

She couldn't help smiling again. 'I'm not naked, Jim. And I'm not even gonna pretend that I am.'

'I'm outta here,' Debbie said, heading out of the kitchen. 'I'm going to see if my mum and your dad are managing alright with the kids.'

Amber leaned back against the counter, playing with the belt of her bathrobe. 'Are you really okay, Jim?'

'Baby, I'm fine. Really. Brandon's looking after me, so quit worrying.'

'I love you.'

'I love you, too… Look, I can't do this any more. It's been two months, and I swear, honey, I am about to freakin' explode. I can't get married feeling like this… I'm coming over.'

'Jim!'

'I'm only around the corner, so, give me ten minutes and I'll be right there.'

He'd hung up before she could say anything. She just stared at her phone, a slow smile starting to creep across her face, that familiar tingle building up in her thighs. Yes, the house was full of people, but she didn't care. She was going to make love to her beautiful American man after way too long, and she couldn't wait.

'What's got you looking so happy?' Debbie asked, eyeing Amber slightly warily.

'Are the kids alright?'

'The kids are fine. Your dad's pretty much done in, but I'm sure he'll find his second wind by the time we leave for the church. So, I take it Jim's okay, then?'

'Jim's good, yeah. What time's make-up and hair getting here?'

Debbie checked the clock on the wall. 'Another couple of hours yet. Why?'

'No reason. Just trying to make sure we've got time to fit everything in.'

Debbie narrowed her eyes. 'You're acting weirdly now. Maybe you should lay off the champagne until later.'

Amber picked up her glass and downed the last of her drink. 'I'm fine. Anyway, I love that feeling a glass or two of bubbly gives me. It just takes the edge off.'

'The edge off what? And where are you going?'

'Upstairs. I've got a busy day ahead, so, a little lie-down before it all gets going won't hurt, will it?'

'I worry about you sometimes… here.' She handed Amber the half-empty bottle of champagne. 'Take this. And drink it slowly.'

Amber smiled, clutching the bottle in her hand as she ran out of the room and back upstairs. All of a sudden she felt like an excited kid on Christmas morning as nothing but the thought of being close to Jim took over.

'Amber!'

Debbie yelling up the stairs interrupted her daydreaming, and she ran back downstairs, raking her fingers through her hair as she almost bounded back into the hallway.

'I think this belongs to you,' Debbie said, jerking her head in Jim's direction as he stood beside her, looking tall and handsome in jeans and a dark shirt, his face carrying a few days' worth of stubble, his hair pushed back off his face. Amber felt her stomach flip over and she had to bite down on her lip to stop herself from groaning out loud. Oh, God, she loved this man so much. How the hell had she managed to keep her hands off him for all this time?

'Do you two not know it's bad luck to see each other before the wedding?'

'We're already married, Debbie,' Amber pointed out, her eyes not leaving Jim's. And he was giving her the kind of smile that was making her thighs ache for him. God, he was hot! 'So I'm not sure all that stuff applies, really.'

Freddie came out of the living room, Rico in his arms, his eyes going straight to Jim. 'Something wrong?'

'No. Nothing's wrong,' Jim replied, still not taking his eyes off Amber. 'I just came to see Amber.'

'Why? I thought you'd both decided not to see each other today until you got to the church.'

'That's what I thought, too,' Debbie said. 'But it would seem these two have got other ideas.'

'Okay, well, you've seen her now, so....'

'No, he hasn't, actually, Dad.' Amber smiled at Jim, holding out her hand, which he took, letting her pull him up the stairs. 'We won't be long. I promise.'

Freddie looked at Debbie, both of them exchanging a surprised look. 'Are they...?'

Debbie shrugged, then nodded. 'Amber Allen, I'm ashamed of you, chick! In front of your dad, too...'

'We're not doing anything in front of anybody, Debbie,' Amber shouted down the stairs. 'We're keeping it all strictly private.' She pulled Jim inside the bedroom, kicking the door shut behind her, leaning back against it. 'Or as private as it can be. In a house full of people.'

He smiled, digging his hands in his pockets as he moved closer to her. 'You're *almost* naked,' he whispered. 'You could have told me *that* much.'

'You don't know what I've got on under this robe, though. Do you?'

He smiled again, reaching out to gently touch her cheek. 'I'm hoping, very little.'

'Oh, I can go one better than that,' she whispered, her breathing already starting to quicken as his mouth moved closer to hers.

'I have waited too long for this,' he breathed, his mouth brushing across hers so lightly she couldn't help but gasp loudly, pulling him even closer by his shirt. 'Way too freaking' long.'

She was lost in his kiss within seconds, his body pressed against hers, his erection strong and hard against her thigh. 'Baby, are you sure…?'

'Amber, honey, I'm fine, okay? I'm not ill any more, and I won't break if you touch me. I just want to make love to you and feel human again. I just want to feel like your husband, because I love you. I love you so, so much.'

'And you have to realise how terrified I was, Jim. How scared I've been these past few weeks. Because, if I'd lost you…' She felt totally unexpected tears start to fall down her face, and he kissed them away, which just made her cry even more.

'This isn't how I envisaged this.' He smiled, and she couldn't help but smile back.

'I'm sorry…' She looked up into his eyes. 'I can't even pretend to understand what you went through when Carrie died, but… but I know that if I'd lost you, I'm not sure I could have carried on. So… so some of what you must have felt back then, I can almost feel that same pain you must have felt. Because, for a few terrifying minutes, I felt it, too.'

'Oh, baby…' He pulled her in against him, holding her tight. 'Baby, believe me, I'm not going anywhere. You won't get rid of me that easily, I promise you that.' He looked at her, stroking her tears away with his thumb. 'I *promise* you.'

She smiled, because, after everything they'd been through, only now could she really believe him when he promised her something. His stay in hospital had given them both time to think about everything that had happened, how close they'd come to losing each other all over again. It had given them both time to realise what was really important – and what needed to be pushed aside for the sake of their future. It had put a lot of things into perspective. And now she knew he would never let her down, never hurt her. He wouldn't do that now. He wouldn't. 'None of this should have happened, Jim.'

'We're gonna stop dwelling on the past now, okay? And I know we've tried to do that before, and all kinds of crap happened, but, things are different now. They're different.'

She nodded slowly, closing her eyes as his mouth lowered onto hers, and once more she lost herself in his kiss, sliding her hand around the back of his neck, winding her fingers in his hair.

'No, not here,' she whispered, taking his hand and pulling him towards the bed.

'Amber…'

She just smiled at him, dropping her robe. 'You want this?'

He pushed a hand through his hair, his eyes scanning her naked body. 'Jesus, you really don't play fair. You know I want it.'

'Then we do this my way.'

She sat down on the bed, swinging her legs up, hugging them to her, resting her chin on her knees.

'Okay?'

He smiled, unfastening his shirt, sliding it off to reveal the body that Amber had fallen in love with over two decades ago. He might be older now, but he was just as sexy, just as beautiful, and just as hot as he had been back then. 'I don't care which way we do it, honey. I just want to do it.'

'And who said romance was dead?' She lay back, slowly opening her legs, smiling as she saw his expression change, his eyes only looking in one place now. 'Come on, then, handsome. What you waiting for?'

She pulled him down between her legs, drawing them up around him, her arms up above her head as their fingers intertwined, their bodies touching. And it took just the tiniest of seconds for her skin to break out in those familiar goosebumps, every inch of her tingling as his lips started to brush over her breasts, sending a million, beautiful shivers coursing right through her.

She gasped again as his hips pressed down on hers, and her fingers tightened around his as she prepared for something she hadn't felt in so long, too long. And even though it still felt strange, and the worry that this was hurting him in some way was probably never going to disappear completely, she still wanted it more than she'd ever wanted anything.

'Look at me, Amber,' he whispered, his grip on her fingers tightening as she slowly opened her eyes, gazing up into his. 'I love you. So much.'

'I love you, too.'

And then she felt it, that wonderful hit of something only he could give her; that beautiful, slow hit of intense pleasure mixed with white-hot pain as he pushed into her. And she took him, all of him, lifting up her hips so he fell deeper, his grip on her fingers tightening even more as he thrust harder, and she tried to slow him down. Tried to make sure he didn't overdo it. But all she could do was let it happen; close her eyes and let every move he made inside her wash over her, until she could feel nothing but those crazy pins and needles, those tingles she welcomed start to creep up her body.

She pulled her knees up slightly, taking him as deeply as he could go, and the brief shot of pain she felt was worth it as her whole body rocked with a climax she just hadn't been prepared for. She hadn't wanted to cry out loud, given where they were, but she couldn't help it as he gave that last, beautiful thrust before he too came in a barrage of cries and moans, their bodies moving together until that last wave subsided, their fingers still entwined, his face buried in her shoulder.

'Are you okay?' she whispered, letting go of his hand and stroking his hair.

'Baby, you have no idea how okay I am feeling right now.' He rolled over onto his back, the biggest grin on his face as he flung one hand behind his head. 'I needed that, so fucking much.'

She turned onto her side, propping herself up on one elbow. 'I can feel your heart beating from here,' she said, running her fingers lightly over his chest.

'Yeah, and a beating heart means I'm alive.'

'Not if beats so hard it wears itself out.'

He turned his head to look at her, taking her hand. 'You've really got to stop this, Amber. I'm fine, okay? There is nothing wrong with me, no underlying heart condition, no reason why what happened to me happened. And I have no idea how that can be, but I'm taking it, alright? I'm not worrying about the fact it may or may not happen again, because it just ain't worth it, honey. To be always stressing out, isn't that the worst thing we could do?'

She looked down at their joined hands, smiling slightly. 'Yeah. I suppose you're right.'

'Oh, I'm always right.'

'Really?' she laughed, straddling him, taking hold of both his hands. 'You're always right?'

'When it comes to most things, yeah.'

She leaned forward, kissing him slowly. 'Well, I beg to differ, Mr. Allen, but, seeing as it's our wedding day – sort of – I'll let that one slide.'

He smiled at her, and once more she felt her heart jump about and those stomach flips return with a vengeance.

'Because I love you,' she whispered, letting him push her over onto her back, closing her eyes again as he kissed her slowly, her arms falling around him. And she never wanted to let him go. She wanted to hold on tight and never let him go. He was her world, her life; he was everything she lived for. Her forever man.

*

'You *are* kidding me, aren't you?' Ronnie said, raising an eyebrow as

Jim followed Amber down the stairs, not looking quite as groomed as he had done an hour ago, although Amber had thrown on jeans and a t-shirt now.

'What?' Amber asked, standing on the last stair as she straightened Jim's shirt collar, kissing him quickly. 'There you go, handsome.'

Jim slid a hand round to cup her bottom, giving it a tiny squeeze, and she giggled, like the infatuated teenager she'd once been with this man. If only she'd realised back then that fighting her love for him was the worst thing she could possibly do, would everything have been different? No. She had to stop thinking of 'what ifs,' and dwelling upon the past. They were looking forward now. All of them.

'You are so fucking beautiful,' Jim whispered, his mouth close to hers as he spoke, his hand squeezing her bottom again as he kissed her. 'And I'm never gonna get tired of telling you that.'

'I love you, so much,' Amber groaned, letting him pull her against him, his hand slipping up under her t-shirt, just a touch, until she quickly pulled it back down. She wasn't putting on a free show here. 'But you'd better go now. I've got to get ready.'

'It's such a shame to put clothes on that incredible body.'

'I could say the same about you.'

'Well, that's just put me off that bacon sandwich,' Ronnie sighed, leaning back against the wall.

Amber ignored him, continuing to stroke the back of Jim's neck, leaning in for another kiss before she, reluctantly, had to let him go.

'I'll see you later.' He smiled, his hands in his pockets as he backed slowly out of the front door.

'Yeah, you will.' She smiled back, mouthing *"I love you"* one last time before she closed the door behind her.

'Subtle,' Ronnie said, shoving the last of his sandwich into his mouth.

'I thought you weren't eating that.'

'Why? Did you want it?'

'Yeah. I'm starving! It's amazing how much of an appetite sex can give you.'

'I didn't need to hear that, kiddo,' Freddie said, walking past on his way back into the living room.

'None of us needed to hear that.' But Ronnie had a smile on his face as he looked at Amber. 'Everything okay in that department, I take it?'

'It's fine.' She looked at him. 'You didn't hear...?'

'I turned the radio up.'

'Thanks.'

'Don't mention it.'

'Make me one of those, will you?'

'Make one yourself. You're perfectly capable.'

'Please.' She stood up on tiptoes, kissing his nose. 'It's my wedding day.'

'It's about the fourth one you've had, isn't it?'

'You're funny.'

'I'm hilarious. Just wait 'til you hear my speech.'

'It had better be clean.'

'Yeah, 'cause you're as pure as the driven snow.'

She smiled, playing with his shirt collar. 'Oh, I'm a dirty, dirty girl, I know that...'

'Jesus, Amber, do you have to?'

'... But, there'll be relatives of mine there that really don't need to be subjected to filth.'

'So you'll be keeping your hands off your husband all day, then?'

'Can't promise that.' She let go of him, almost skipping into the kitchen. 'Now, where's that frying pan?'

'You can't eat bacon!' Debbie gasped, lifting Rico up onto the countertop and handing him a beaker of juice.

'Erm, why not?' Amber asked, smiling at her baby boy, who threw her the most gorgeous smile back.

'You want to eat fried food before you get into that dress?'

'Again, why not?'

'Because it clings to every curve, chick.'

'I hardly think one bacon sandwich is going to make me gain two stone in an hour.'

'In white bread? Do you know how much that stuff bloats you?'

'Do you know what, I've gone right off the idea now. I'll just have a cup of tea.'

'A much more sensible idea. I'll stick the kettle on.'

Amber turned her attention back to her baby, watching as he concentrated so hard on his beaker, lifting it slowly to his mouth. She couldn't believe how much he'd grown; how quickly time had passed. She couldn't believe how like his dad he was – that same dark hair, those same blue eyes. That same smile. And she felt a pull on her heart that made her breathless as she remembered Ryan's last few hours with him last night; how he'd held Rico's hands as he'd walked him around the living room, how he'd played with him and cuddled him and cried when they'd said goodbye. And suddenly everything came flooding forward like an unexpected, violent tidal wave. And she couldn't stop the tears from falling.

*

'Ryan! I...' Brandon stood in the doorway, a more-than-surprised look on his face. 'I thought you were heading off to L.A. this morning?'

'I am. I just... I wanted a word with your dad. Is he around?'

'Erm, yeah... hang on.'

Ryan took a step back as Brandon pushed the door to, staring down at the ground with his hands in his pockets. The sun was shining and it was a glorious summer day in the north-east of England. The perfect day for a wedding. He just wished with all his heart that it was his. That she was walking up that aisle to be with him, not the man he'd come to see. Before he left this place for somewhere so far away.

He looked up as the front door opened again, and Jim stood

there. Their eyes met and a look passed between them that Ryan couldn't quite read.

'You look… you look well,' Ryan said, keeping a small distance between them.

'Thank you. I feel well.'

Ryan broke the stare, looking back down at the ground.

'I'm really sorry it had to come to this, Ryan,' Jim went on, and Ryan's eyes once more met his.

'Yeah. So am I.'

'In the end… you could've said no, you do know that, don't you? Given everything that's happened, you could have refused the move. Max is one of the best agents out there…'

'Maybe it's for the best.'

Jim said nothing for a couple of beats, his eyes staring deep into Ryan's. 'Is that how you really feel?'

'I… I need to be some place that gives me a little bit of space. I can't be around…' He looked back down, scuffing his trainer off the front step. 'Look after them, okay?' He raised his head slowly, meeting Jim's gaze one more time. 'And love them. Please. Just… just love them. He's my little boy, Jim, and I… I'm gonna miss him like you wouldn't believe.'

'I'll take care of them both, Ryan. You know I will.'

'Do I?'

'Things have changed. Everything's changed.'

'Yeah. Everything has. Just – just look after them. Because… even though I want that to be *my* job, it can't be. And that breaks my fucking heart, so, I need you to do that for me. Okay? I need you to look after them and love them.'

Jim stared at him, his eyes were warm and kind. But all that did was add to Ryan's confusion. His mind filled with dashed hopes and a life he wanted so badly, but could never have.

'I love her so much, Ryan. And I know you probably don't want to hear me say that, but, it's true. I love Amber so, so much. And I love that boy of yours, too. They're my world now, okay? They're my whole world. Both of them.'

Ryan had to break that stare now because those words were cutting through him like the sharpest of blades, causing a pain so raw to hit him he almost couldn't breathe. The world he wanted belonged to somebody else, and this was the hardest thing he'd ever had to face up to.

'I'll look after them. I promise you that, Ryan. I promise you.'

And all Ryan could do now was hope that this promise was one Jim Allen could actually keep.

*

'Amber! Max is here!' Debbie shouted through from the hall. 'Make him a cup of tea, will you? I'm going to call the hotel and make sure everything's going to plan with the reception.'

Amber looked up as Max walked into the kitchen, his expression changing immediately the second he saw her. 'That doesn't look like the face of a woman who's about to marry the man of her dreams.'

'We're already married. It's a vow renewal.'

Max came closer, leaning back against the counter, smiling at Rico as he continued to bang his beaker on the marble work surface.

'Rico, baby, no. Don't do that,' Amber sighed, turning around to switch the kettle on.

'It's okay, kiddo. I've had enough cups of tea this morning to last me a lifetime.'

She turned back to face Max, picking up Rico and taking his beaker from him, which, thankfully, didn't seem to bother him. 'He's too young to realise he won't be seeing his daddy again for a while yet,' she said, kissing her baby boy's forehead.

'Ryan will be over as much as he can, Amber. You know that.'

'Yeah,' she whispered, smiling at Rico as he gurgled away at her, waving his arms up and down. 'I know he will. But it isn't the same, is it?'

'It won't be forever.'

'Won't it? He could go over there and love it. He could realise it's what he's always wanted, I mean, we're talking about Ryan Fisher here.'

'And he's a very different Ryan Fisher to the one who arrived here a couple of years ago.'

She looked at Rico, stroking his dark hair off his face as he lay his head against her shoulder, clinging onto her t-shirt, his eyes slowly closing. 'Yeah. A lot of things are different, Max.'

'It's his decision, Amber. You do know that, don't you?'

Her eyes met his. 'It wasn't to begin with, though. Was it?'

'Maybe not.' Max looked briefly out of the window, at the sun shining down from a perfect blue sky. 'But, in the end, he chose to go.'

'Because he had no choice,' Amber whispered, kissing Rico's forehead again, cuddling him closer to her. He was a part of Ryan she would have forever, and that was something she was truly grateful for; to have a part of Ryan with her. Always.

Max turned to face her again, his expression concerned now; caring. 'You deserve to be happy, Amber, and Ryan knows that. It's all he really wants for you.'

'And I want *him* to be happy, Max.' She lay Rico down on the couch, watching for a second as his eyes closed properly, his hands clinging onto the toy rabbit she'd just given him. 'And I don't know whether he is.'

'He will be. This change of scenery he's about to have thrust upon him really will be good for him. He's got a lot to get his head around when he gets over there – it's a different game in a lot of respects. And then there's a whole new lifestyle to get used to. It's what he needs, Amber. Things to take his mind off it all.'

She couldn't say anything. There was nothing *to* say, because Max was right. Everything he was saying was right. But there was a part of Amber that still wished it could all be different.

'Now, I just popped in here to make sure my most beautiful client was all set for her big day…' He moved closer, pulling her in for a hug, and she clung onto him. This man who'd suddenly become such a big part of her life. The only man she could trust to make sure Ryan was okay. 'So, you enjoy yourself, do you hear me? You go out there and you renew those vows to a man who is so in love with you, it's sickening.'

She couldn't help but smile.

'And when I get back from L.A., we'll talk about some of those offers of work that keep landing on my desk, alright?'

She nodded, hugging him again. 'Tell him… tell him I…' She pulled away, folding her arms as she turned to look at a now-sleeping Rico, his little body curled up, his tiny fingers clinging onto that rabbit he loved so much. 'Tell him we're thinking about him – me and Rico. Tell him. Please. Tell him we… we love him.'

Max smiled, squeezing her hand gently. 'I'll tell him. I promise.' He checked his watch. 'Right, well, I'd better get going. I said I'd meet him at the airport in half an hour.' He looked at her one more time. 'You take care, kiddo. And you have the best day today, okay? I'll see you when I get back to London.'

She leaned back against the counter as he left the kitchen, looking over at Rico again. He was still curled up, still asleep, his mop of dark hair all messed up. He was making little snuffling noises, and she couldn't help but smile. Ryan Fisher had given her the most incredible little boy. He'd given her something she'd never thought she'd have. And it was something they were always going to share. Something which meant he would always be a part of her life, and that was a comfort. Because, all of a sudden, she was finding it really hard to let go.

Closing her eyes for a second, she took a deep breath, before crouching down beside Rico and gently stroking his hair, kissing his warm and tiny cheek. 'I love you so much, baby boy. And I'm sorry, okay? For the way things have worked out. I'm so sorry.'

Standing back up she pushed a hand through her hair and

checked the clock on the wall.

'What's up with you?' Ronnie asked, walking into the kitchen.

She looked at him. 'I need you to take me to the airport.'

He stared at her. 'I'm sorry? What did you just ask me?'

'I need you to take me to the airport.'

He was still staring at her. 'I'm confused now.'

'Yeah, well, welcome to my world.' She was busy throwing some of Rico's things into his baby bag.

'Amber… what the hell are you doing?'

'Can you take me to the airport or not, Ronnie?'

'Well, yes, but… why?'

She scooped Rico up into her arms, hugging him as he snuggled in against her, still holding on for dear life to that rabbit. 'Just get there as fast as you can, okay?' She threw Rico's baby bag at him, which he caught, even though he was still staring at her.

'And on the way there are you gonna explain what's going on?'

'Yes. And we're going out the back way. I really can't be bothered to explain to everyone where I'm going.'

'And you don't think they'll miss you?'

'I'll text Debbie from the car. Now, come on. Let's get going.'

'Amber…'

She swung around to look at him, her eyes telling him she was serious. She was doing this. She had to. She thought she'd be able to get through today as though this wasn't happening, as though Ryan's leaving didn't bother her, and she'd tried. She'd really tried. And she'd almost succeeded. Almost. 'I really need to do this, Ronnie. So, please. Can we just go?'

'No, hang on. Come here, will you? Just for a minute. Please.'

She sighed, but she did as he asked. 'We really need to go.'

'Are you sure about this? Whatever it is you're going over there to do, are you sure?'

'I can't say I'll ever be one hundred percent sure of anything any more, Ronnie.' She looked up into his eyes. 'Except that… I need you, okay? As my friend, I need you. And I'm sorry…'

'There's nothing to be sorry for, Amber. I just want you to listen to your heart and do whatever it is you need to do. No matter how crazy it is.'

She couldn't help smiling, standing up on tiptoes to kiss him quickly, his arm catching her by the waist to keep her there just a little while longer.

'I do love you, Ronnie White. You know that, don't you?'

'Yeah. And I love you, too. Even though you can be the most infuriating woman ever to have walked this earth.'

'I can be a real pain in the arse sometimes, can't I?'

Ronnie arched an eyebrow. 'Sometimes?'

She smiled, kissing him again, hugging him close with her free arm. 'I need you, okay? To stop me from doing *really* stupid things.'

'You think I can *stop* you?'

She smiled again, pulling away from him slightly.

'Look, Amber, I'm gonna ask you this again, because it's what I do. I nag you into submission. That's my job, apparently, so, whatever you're about to do, are you sure?'

She looked at him, nodding slowly, cuddling Rico closer to her, kissing the top of his head.'

'Okay then,' Ronnie sighed, fishing his car keys out of his pocket. 'Let's get out of here.'

*

Ryan hauled his case out of the back of Gary's car, dumping it down on the ground outside Departures.

'They're sending the rest of your stuff over in the next couple of days, right?' Gary asked, shutting the car door and leaning back against it.

'Yeah. I'll just pick it up from LAX as soon as it arrives.'

'I can't believe you're really going, mate. I guess I always thought you might change your mind, y'know? After everything that happened with Jim.'

'That was the one thing that made me realise I had to go,' Ryan said, sticking his hands in his pockets as he looked around him, taking in one of his last glimpses of his beloved north-east England, for a while, at least. And even though he fully intended to be making regular trips back here, it still felt like he was leaving this place forever. 'She's never gonna let him go, Gary.' Ryan's voice was quiet, the resigned tone almost permanent now. 'Not after this.'

'Come here,' Gary stood up and enveloped his best friend in a huge hug. 'I'm gonna frigging miss you. It's gonna be so fucking boring without you around.'

Ryan smiled, hugging Gary back. 'I'm sure you'll find yourself another partner-in-crime. Maybe one that doesn't give you quite so much grief, huh?'

'Yeah. The grief I can do without. Seriously, though, I really am gonna miss you.'

Ryan stuck his hands back in his pockets, once more looking out around him. 'I'm gonna miss you, too.' He turned to face his friend. 'And thanks, Gary. For everything. I really mean that. If it hadn't been for you and Debbie…'

'Forget all that. Come on! You're going to fucking L.A., man! How big is that? You're gonna make David Beckham look like an amateur.'

Ryan couldn't help but laugh. 'Well, I'm not sure about that.' He stared down at his trainers, a sudden sadness washing over him that didn't escape Gary's notice.

'You okay?'

'When she was there, last night, I… I just wanted to hold her and tell her to come with me - *beg* her to come with me, and I could have done. I could have done that, but… it would have been pointless. And yet, I still wanted to try. Because leaving here is killing me, Gary. Leaving her, leaving Rico… I thought they were my future, y'know? I thought we were gonna be a family, and when I think…' He stopped talking, throwing back his head and blinking away tears he'd promised himself he wouldn't cry. 'I still love her, so fucking much.'

'Jesus, mate, I really had no idea things were so bad.'

'He won,' Ryan whispered. 'And I'm not gonna stand here and say it was a fair game, because it wasn't. He played dirty, and he broke the rules. But, ultimately, it doesn't really matter how you play the game, does it? It's the end result that counts. And I can't change that final score.'

Gary scuffed his heels against the tyres of his Mercedes, shoving his hands in his pockets as he looked at Ryan. 'You're gonna be okay, mate. You know that, don't you? You're gonna be better than okay.'

Ryan nodded, wiping his eyes with his forearm, throwing his head back again as he took a deep breath. 'Yeah. I know. I know.'

Gary reached out and gently squeezed Ryan's arm. 'You take care of yourself, okay? And call me the second you get there. You lucky bastard.'

Ryan smiled, giving Gary one more hug. 'Keep an eye on her, please.'

Gary nodded.

'Okay, I'd… I'd better get in there. Max'll be waiting.'

'As soon as you get there,' Gary shouted as he climbed back into his car.

Ryan watched as he drove off, taking one more look around. It seemed fairly quiet, but that was good. If there was one thing Ryan didn't want today it was any attention being drawn to what was happening. They'd deliberately chosen today for his departure to the States because Max had told him everyone – and by that he meant the media – would be far more concerned with Amber and Jim's "wedding." So they'd tried to keep all of this as much of a secret as it could be. And so far it seemed to be working.

But just the thought of Amber with Jim caused another wave of pain to wash over him and he had to close his eyes again to stop more tears from escaping.

'Ryan?'

His eyes shot open and he swung around at the sound of that

voice, his heart feeling as though it had stopped dead, before it struck up a rhythm so fast he couldn't catch his breath. She stood there, tanned and pretty, his beautiful baby boy balanced on one of those incredible hips. And he couldn't stop the smile from spreading across his face as Rico stretched out his arms and reached out for him, shouting *"dada, dada!"* over and over again until Ryan took him.

'Hey there, little man. I didn't think I'd be seeing you again for a while.' He kissed Rico quickly, before looking over at Amber. She had her arms folded, her eyes locked onto his. 'I… I didn't think…'

'I had to see you, Ryan. I mean, I know I saw you last night, but… I had to see you.'

Ryan felt a wave of hope flood his body as she moved closer. 'Tell me you've changed your mind,' he whispered. 'Please, Amber. Please tell me you've changed your mind.'

Amber felt tears start to fall silently and slowly down her cheeks and she immediately wiped them away with her fist. 'I just need you to know I love you, Ryan. I need you to know that.'

Ryan couldn't stop his voice from shaking, tears of his own starting to fall from his eyes, but at the same time he couldn't stop smiling as Rico wiped them away with his tiny hand.

'But it's not the same. I… it isn't the same. The way I love you, it isn't the same way I love him, Ryan.'

'Oh, Jesus…' Ryan felt that wave of hope being washed away by a painful despair so strong that breath was catching in his throat again. It hurt like never before, and he'd certainly felt pain over the past few years. 'Amber, baby, please…'

She shook her head, folding her arms against herself, her eyes still looking deep into his. 'Maybe this is selfish, you know? Maybe this is the most selfish thing I have ever done, but, when I asked Ronnie to bring me here… when I asked him to do that, I didn't know what I would do when I saw you. And that's the truth, Ryan. I didn't know if I was suddenly going to want to come with you because something happened this morning… something I can't explain, but it happened, and for a few, brief seconds I honestly didn't know what I was going to do.'

'Come with me. I love you both so much, Amber, you know that…'

'I can't,' she whispered. 'Ryan, I can't. Now that I'm here… Jesus. I'm sorry. I shouldn't have come.'

'No. No, I'm glad you're here.' He threw his head back quickly, hoping those tears would fall away, but more kept on coming and all he could do was hold his little boy close and make the most of what were obviously his last few minutes with the two people he loved most in the world. And, for once in his life, one of them wasn't himself. 'I'm glad, Amber.'

Their eyes locked together one more time, and she moved a little closer, not stopping him when he reached out for her hand, his fingers wrapping around hers.

'I love you, Amber.'

She could hardly see through the tears now, and watching him cry was breaking her heart, but she'd had to do this. It was the only way she was going to know for sure that she was making the right decision.

'I love you, too, Ryan.'

'Just not the same way you love him, huh?'

She stared deep into those dark, dark-blue eyes of his, trying desperately to get a handle on this pain now. She'd made her decision. Right there, in that very second, she'd made her decision. She shook her head.

'So he really did win, in the end,' Ryan whispered.

Amber looked down briefly, pulling her hand out of Ryan's, closing her eyes for a second, opening them to see tears hit the concrete below. 'He's my forever man, Ryan. And I just can't change that. I can't.'

Ryan kissed Rico again, stroking his hair as he snuggled in tighter against him. 'This really is it, then.'

She nodded, her eyes back on his. 'I guess it is.' She took another step closer. And as her eyes closed again she felt his mouth touch hers, a kiss so beautiful and so special it broke her heart a million times over, when she'd doubted there was anything left there to break. It was a kiss goodbye that said so much more, and before she knew it she was in his arms, and he was holding her and their baby so tightly it was leaving her breathless. But it was the most beautiful kiss. And a part of her didn't want it to end. A part of her wanted to stay there forever as all the memories of her time with this man played out in her head, all merging together, making her realise she would never be able to truly let him go. And what that meant for the future, she really couldn't say. All she knew was that right now she had to say goodbye.

'Make sure he looks after you. Both of you,' Ryan whispered, his forehead resting against hers.

'He will. I promise you, he will.'

His mouth touched hers again, another kiss that sent a shot of pain cutting across her chest.

'I'll speak to you soon, okay?'

He nodded, finally pulling away from her. 'Yeah. Yeah, you will.' He looked at Rico, who had a slightly confused expression on his little face. 'Okay, my beautiful little man. Daddy's got to go now. But, you take care of your mum, you hear me? And be good for your Uncle Jim.'

Amber had to close her eyes again as he said that, biting down on her lip because she was tired of crying. She was tired of it. But when she opened her eyes, she was just in time to see Ryan give Rico the biggest hug, kissing him gently before he handed him back to her.

'Shouldn't you be somewhere else?' he asked, trying to lighten the mood.

'Yeah... yeah, I probably should... I'd better go, huh? I don't want you to be late.'

'Amber, I... Have a good day, okay? And when you walk up that aisle to him you be beautiful and you be strong and you know...

you know that if you *ever* need me… if you ever need me, baby, then you just come running. You come running. And I promise you, I'll be there. I promise you.'

She looked at him, trying to smile, but those tears that wouldn't stop falling seemed to be putting up a barrier to any other emotion right now. And the only thing she could do before she broke down completely was walk away and not look back.

'You come running,' he whispered, watching as she headed back to Ronnie. Watching as his world walked away.

But, this was it now. The result was in. The final score was settled. And as he looked up at the sky, shielding his eyes from the bright sunshine, he watched a plane take off into the air, heading somewhere far away. He knew that's where his future was now. Away from here. So, yes, this result may have been decided; this score may have been settled. But nothing was ever really final. He just needed to move onto the next game.